SLOTH

How we love the luxury of doing nothing!
Stay in bed all day. Just let the time
pass. But if work must be done—the solution is very simple. Find *someone else*
to do it....

ANGER

The rage that shakes us can have its
uses. Immune to reason, we are forced
into action. And great deeds have been
accomplished in that crimson rage. And
sometimes, nothing can *ever* undo
them....

GLUTTONY

Surely there's *something* you don't think
you'll ever get enough of. Chocolate ice
cream? Very dry martinis? Diamonds
and furs? Love? And what would possibly be wrong if *all* your dreams came
true?...

AVARICE

"Millions for defense, but not one cent
for tribute!" What? Count pennies when
principle is at stake? Never! Just count
the coins—and the wars *will* take care
of themselves....

THE
SEVEN DEADLY SINS
OF
SCIENCE FICTION

Edited by
Isaac Asimov, Charles G. Waugh, and Martin H. Greenberg

Headnotes by Isaac Asimov

Central Department Store Ltd.
306 Silom Road Bangkok
Sole Distributor In Thailand

FAWCETT CREST • NEW YORK

THE SEVEN DEADLY SINS OF SCIENCE FICTION

Published by Fawcett Crest Books, a unit of CBS Publications, the Consumer Publishing Division of CBS Inc.

Copyright © 1980 by Isaac Asimov, Charles G. Waugh and Martin H. Greenberg

All Rights Reserved

ISBN: 0-449-24349-4

Printed in the United States of America

First Fawcett Crest printing: November 1980

10   9   8   7   6   5   4   3   2   1

"Sail 25" by Jack Vance. Copyright © 1962 by Ultimate Publishing Company. Reprinted by permission of the author and his agent, Kirby MacCauley.

"Peeping Tom" by Judith Merril. Copyright © 1954 by Standard Magazines. Copyright © 1973 by Judith Merril. Reprinted by permission of the author and her agent, Virginia Kidd.

"The Invisible Man Murder Case" by Henry Slesar. Copyright © 1958 by the Ziff-Davis Publishing Company. Reprinted by permission of the author.

"Galley Slave" by Isaac Asimov. Copyright © 1957 by the Galaxy Publishing Corporation. Reprinted by permission of the author.

"Divine Madness" by Roger Zelazny. Copyright © 1966 by Health Knowledge, Inc. Reprinted by permission of the author.

"The Midas Plague" by Frederik Pohl. Copyright © 1954 by the Galaxy Publishing Corporation. Reprinted by permission of the author.

"The Man Who Ate the World" by Frederik Pohl. Copyright © 1956 by the Galaxy Publishing Corporation. Reprinted by permission of the author.

"Margin of Profit" by Poul Anderson. Copyright © 1956 by Street & Smith Publications, Inc. Reprinted by permission of the author and his agents, the Scott Meredith Literary Agency, Inc., 845 Third Avenue, New York, NY 10022.

"The Hook, the Eye and the Whip" by Michael G. Coney. Copyright © 1974 by UPD Publishing Corporation under International, Universal and Pan-American Copyright Conventions. Reprinted by permission of the author.

CONTENTS

INTRODUCTION

by MARTIN H. GREENBERG

Modern science went into high gear with the work of the great Italian scientist, Galileo Galilei, in the 1590s. Modern science fiction can be traced back to a posthumously published story, "Somnium," by Galileo's contemporary and sometime friend, Johannes Kepler, an equally great scientist. The two are intertwined from the beginning.

The now standard quartet of the scientific method—observation, classification, hypothesis, and testing—can be applied to almost any field of scholarly endeavor, even if it is not very scientific. They can be applied, for instance, to the study of science fiction. (Why else anthologies?)

Of the four items, *classification* would seem to be the least creative, the most uninteresting, and, indeed, the most subjective. Those who spend their time inventing categories and trying to place nearly round Objects into only slightly elliptical Holes are not as highly regarded in the scientific world as those who produce and test theories, or who make shrewd observations, or produce a subtle collection of data. And yet classification has its fascinations, too.

Few subjects or objects have escaped the drive to classify all things, and this includes Sin, which has a long and distinguished intellectual history and is not a subject to take lightly. The concept of sin developed from the idea of *evil*, which, for many thinkers, has been considered to be weakness inherent in human nature itself. The ancient Greeks considered evil to be a necessary component of human beings and hence we speak of "a necessary evil," which is not to be confused with moral correctness or failure. This rather resembles the Christian idea of "original sin," by which Adam's sin of disobedience is indelibly inherited by all his descendants—a kind of moral inheritance of acquired characteristics.

Sin was not always classified. The early stoics did not distinguish between different kinds of sin—they thought them all bad, with none any worse than any other.

It was in the Egyptian desert that the first attempt to classify sin took place. The classification was the product of a monastic order, which made sense, for the monks fled the world to escape the sins with which it was saturated and then spent much of their time desperately fighting the sins within themselves.

Concentrating, as they did, almost exclusively on the various aspects of sin, it was natural for them to attempt to enumerate the different aspects of human existence that would severely test man and tempt him away from a life of purity and goodness.

Inevitably, perhaps, the major sins were listed as seven in number. Seven was a number that preoccupied the ancients, perhaps because there were seven planets in the heavens. It was probably from this that we gained seven days to the week (explained in theological terms by the Jews, who picked up the notion in Babylonia). There were also the seven wonders of the world, the seven liberal arts, and, in modern times, *Seven Brides for Seven Brothers* and, of course, *The Magnificent Seven*.

The Catholic Church, concerned with the problem of identifying those sins which were direct threats to the souls of its members, distinguished the "deadly sins" from the lesser "venial sins" for which pardon could be sought. Saint Augustine developed three general categories of sinning—of thought, of word, and of deed (sometimes listed as those deriving from infirmity, ignorance, and viciousness).

It was Thomas Aquinas, though, who really got specific and listed Seven (what else?) Deadly Sins. These were (1) Sloth, (2) Pride, (3) Lust, (4) Envy, (5) Anger, (6) Gluttony, and (7) Covetousness. Sometimes Avarice is listed in place of Covetousness, and they may, perhaps, be considered (7a) and (7b).

The Seven Deadly Sins were contrasted with the Seven

(of course!) Cardinal Virtues: (1) Humility, (2) Liberality, (3) Chastity, (4) Meekness, (5) Temperance, (6) Brotherly Love, and (7) Diligence.

The reader will note that there are many important sins that are not included in the Seven: lying, watching soap operas, admiring Idi Amin, remaining only half-safe, not going for it, and indulging in literary criticism. There are also virtues not included in the Seven, of which the chief are reading and enjoying science fiction.

Well, we, the editors, do read and enjoy science fiction, and, activated by Brotherly Love, we would bring the joy to others. Possessing Meekness and Temperance, we do not claim to have achieved perfection; possessing Chastity, we know our results to be pure; and possessing Diligence, we know we have done the best we can.

For we have labored beyond measure to observe and classify; we hypothesize you will enjoy the results, and it is for you to test it. Here we have stories which, in the science-fiction mode, exemplify and illustrate each of the Seven Deadly Sins, and give each a dimension perhaps not thought of by Saint Thomas Aquinas. So we hope you will enjoy and learn from the stories we have selected, and it is with considerable Humility that we hope you will appreciate the years of field work and the variety of sin that we engaged in to make this book a reality.

SLOTH

How we love our ease! How we long for retirement, when we can settle back and drowse in the sun! When we can sleep as late as we like and let the time pass! But what if work *must* be done? The answer is simple—stick someone else with it! So here we have a study of magnificent laziness, of a man who goes through a long trip doing nothing at all. Well, not quite nothing at all. He did do a few little things— very little things—scarcely enough to disturb his splendid record of SLOTH.

SAIL 25

JACK VANCE

Henry Belt came limping into the conference room, mounted the dais, settled himself at the desk. He looked once around the room: a swift bright glance which, focusing nowhere, treated the eight young men who faced him to an almost insulting disinterest. He reached in his pocket, brought forth a pencil and a flat red book, which he placed on the desk. The eight young men watched in absolute silence. They were much alike: healthy, clean, smart, their expressions identically alert and wary. Each had heard legends of Henry Belt, each had formed his private plans and private determinations.

Henry Belt seemed a man of a different species. His face was broad, flat, roped with cartilage and muscle, with skin the color and texture of bacon rind. Coarse white grizzle covered his scalp, his eyes were crafty slits, his nose a misshapen lump. His shoulders were massive, his legs short and gnarled.

"First of all," said Henry Belt, with a gap-toothed grin, "I'll make it clear that I don't expect you to like me. If you do I'll be surprised and displeased. It will mean that I haven't pushed you hard enough."

He leaned back in his chair, surveyed the silent group. "You've heard stories about me. Why haven't they kicked me out of the service? Incorrigible, arrogant, dangerous Henry Belt. Drunken Henry Belt. (This last of course is slander. Henry Belt has never been drunk in his life.) Why do they tolerate me? For one simple reason: out of necessity. No one wants to take on this kind of job. Only a man like Henry Belt can stand up to it: year after year in space, with nothing to look at but a half-dozen round-faced young scrubs. He takes

them out, he brings them back. Not all of them, and not all
of those who come back are space-men today. But they'll all
cross the street when they see him coming. Henry Belt? you
say. They'll turn pale or go red. None of them will smile.
Some of them are high-placed now. They could kick me loose
if they chose. Ask them why they don't. Henry Belt is a terror,
they'll tell you. He's wicked, he's a tyrant. Cruel as an axe,
fickle as a woman. But a voyage with Henry Belt blows the
foam off the beer. He's ruined many a man, he's killed a few,
but those that come out of it are proud to say, 'I trained with
Henry Belt!'

"Another thing you may hear: Henry Belt has luck. But
don't pay any heed. Luck runs out. You'll be my thirteenth
class, and that's unlucky. I've taken out seventy-two young
sprats, no different from yourselves; I've come back twelve
times: which is partly Henry Belt and partly luck. The voyages average about two years long: how can a man stand it?
There's only one who could: Henry Belt. I've got more space-
time than any man alive, and now I'll tell you a secret: this
is my last time out. I'm starting to wake up at night to strange
visions. After this class I'll quit. I hope you lads aren't su-
perstitious. A white-eyed woman told me that I'd die in space.
She told me other things and they've all come true.

"We'll get to know each other well. And you'll be wondering on what basis I make my recommendations. Am I
objective and fair? Do I put aside personal animosity? Naturally there won't be any friendship. Well, here's my system.
I keep a red book. Here it is. I'll put your names down right
now. You, sir?"

"I'm Cadet Lewis Lynch, sir."

"You?"

"Edward Culpepper, sir."

"Marcus Verona, sir."

"Vidal Weske, sir."

"Marvin McGrath, sir."

"Barry Ostrander, sir."

"Clyde von Gluck, sir."

"Joseph Sutton, sir."

Henry Belt wrote the names in the red book. "This is the

system. When you do something to annoy me, I mark you down demerits. At the end of the voyage I total these demerits, add a few here and there for luck, and am so guided. I'm sure nothing could be clearer than this. What annoys me? Ah, that's a question which is hard to answer. If you talk too much: demerits. If you're surly and taciturn: demerits. If you slouch and laze and dog the dirty work: demerits. If you're overzealous and forever scuttling about: demerits. Obsequiousness: demerits. Truculence: demerits. If you sing and whistle: demerits. If you're a stolid bloody bore: demerits. You can see that the line is hard to draw. Here's a hint which can save you many marks. I don't like gossip, especially when it concerns myself. I'm a sensitive man, and I open my red book fast when I think I'm being insulted." Henry Belt once more leaned back in his chair. "Any questions?"

No one spoke.

Henry Belt nodded. "Wise. Best not to flaunt your ignorance so early in the game. In response to the thought passing through each of your skulls, I do not think of myself as God. But you may do so, if you choose. And this"—he held up the red book—"you may regard as the Syncretic Compendium. Very well. Any questions?"

"Yes sir," said Culpepper.

"Speak, sir."

"Any objection to alcoholic beverages aboard ship, sir?"

"For the cadets, yes, indeed. I concede that the water must be carried in any event, that the organic compounds present may be reconstituted, but unluckily the bottles weigh far too much."

"I understand, sir."

Henry Belt rose to his feet. "One last word. Have I mentioned that I run a tight ship? When I say jump, I expect every one of you to jump. This is dangerous work, of course. I don't guarantee your safety. Far from it, especially since we are assigned to old 25, which should have been broken up long ago. There are eight of you present. Only six cadets will make the voyage. Before the week is over I will make the appropriate notifications. Any more questions?...Very well, then. Cheerio." Limping on his thin legs as if his feet hurt, Henry Belt departed into the back passage.

For a moment or two there was silence. Then von Gluck said in a soft voice, "My gracious."

"He's a tyrannical lunatic," grumbled Weske. "I've never heard anything like it! Megalomania!"

"Easy," said Culpepper. "Remember, no gossiping."

"Bah!" muttered McGrath. "This is a free country. I'll damn well say what I like."

Weske rose to his feet. "A wonder somebody hasn't killed him."

"I wouldn't want to try it," said Culpepper. "He looks tough." He made a gesture, stood up, brow furrowed in thought. Then he went to look along the passageway into which Henry Belt had made his departure. There, pressed to the wall, stood Henry Belt. "Yes, sir," said Culpepper suavely. "I forgot to inquire when you wanted us to convene again."

Henry Belt returned to the rostrum. "Now is as good a time as any." He took his seat, opened his red book. "You, Mr. von Gluck, made the remark, 'My gracious,' in an offensive tone of voice. One demerit. You, Mr. Weske, employed the terms 'tyrannical lunatic' and 'megalomania,' in reference to myself. Three demerits. Mr. McGrath, you observed that freedom of speech is the official doctrine of this country. It is a theory which presently we have no time to explore, but I believe that the statement in its present context carries an overtone of insurbordination. One demerit. Mr. Culpepper, your imperturbable complacence irritates me. I prefer that you display more uncertainty, or even uneasiness."

"Sorry, sir."

"However, you took occasion to remind your colleagues of my rule, and so I will not mark you down."

"Thank you, sir."

Henry Belt leaned back in the chair, stared at the ceiling. "Listen closely, as I do not care to repeat myself. Take notes if you wish. Topic: Solar Sails, Theory and Practice Thereof. Material with which you should already be familiar, but which I will repeat in order to avoid ambiguity.

"First, why bother with the sail, when nuclear jet-ships are faster, more dependable, more direct, safer and easier to navigate? The answer is threefold. First, a sail is not a bad way to move heavy cargo slowly but cheaply through space. Secondly, the range of the sail is unlimited, since we employ the mechanical pressure of light for thrust, and therefore need carry neither propulsive machinery, material to be ejected, nor energy source. The solar sail is much lighter than its nuclear-powered counterpart, and may carry a larger complement of men in a larger hull. Thirdly, to train a man for space there is no better instrument than the handling of a sail. The computer naturally calculates sail cant and plots the course; in fact, without the computer we'd be dead ducks. Nevertheless the control of a sail provides working familiarity with the cosmic elementals: light, gravity, mass, space.

"There are two types of sail: pure and composite. The first relies on solar energy exclusively, the second carries a secondary power source. We have been assigned Number 25, which is the first sort. It consists of a hull, a large parabolic reflector which serves as radar and radio antenna, as well as reflector for the power generator, and the sail itself. The pressure of radiation, of course, is extremely slight—on the order of an ounce per acre at this distance from the sun. Necessarily the sail must be extremely large and extremely light. We use a fluoro-siliconic film a tenth of a mil in gauge, fogged with lithium to the state of opacity. I believe the layer of lithium is about a thousand two hundred molecules thick. Such a foil weighs about four tons to the square mile. It is fitted to a hoop of thin-walled tubing, from which mono-crystalline iron cords lead to the hull.

"We try to achieve a weight factor of six tons to the square mile, which produces an acceleration of between g/100 and g/1000 depending on proximity to the sun, angle of cant, circumsolar orbital speed, reflectivity of surface. These accelerations seem minute, but calculation shows them to be cumulatively enormous. G/100 yields a velocity increment of 800 miles per hour every hour, 18,000 miles per hour each day, or five miles per second each day. At this rate interplanetary distances are readily negotiable—with proper manipulation of the sail, I need hardly say.

"The virtues of the sail I've mentioned. It is cheap to build and cheap to operate. It requires neither fuel nor ejectant. As it travels through space, the great area captures various ions, which may be expelled in the plasma jet powered by the parabolic reflector, which adds another increment to the acceleration.

"The disadvantages of the sail are those of the glider or sailing ship, in that we must use natural forces with great precision and delicacy.

"There is no particular limit to the size of the sail. On 25 we use about four square miles of sail. For the present voyage we will install a new sail, as the old is well-worn and eroded.

"That will be all for today." Once more Henry Belt limped down from the dais and out the passage. On this occasion there were no comments.

II

The eight cadets shared a dormitory, attended classes together, ate at the same table in the mess-hall. In various shops and laboratories they assembled, disassembled and reassembled computers, pumps, generators, gyro-platforms, star-trackers, communication gear. "It's not enough to be clever with your hands," said Henry Belt. "Dexterity is not enough. Resourcefulness, creativity, the ability to make successful improvisations—these are more important. We'll test you out." And presently each of the cadets was introduced into a room on the floor of which lay a great heap of mingled housings, wires, flexes, gears, components of a dozen varieties of mechanism. "This is a twenty-six-hour test," said Henry Belt. "Each of you has an identical set of components and supplies. There shall be no exchange of parts or information between you. Those whom I suspect of this fault will be dropped from the class, without recommendation. What I want you to build is, first, one standard Aminex Mark 9

Computer. Second, a servo-mechanism to orient a mass ten kilograms toward Mu Hercules. Why Mu Hercules?"

"Because, sir, the solar system moves in the direction of Mu Hercules, and we thereby avoid parallax error. Negligible though it may be, sir."

"The final comment smacks of frivolity, Mr. McGrath, which serves only to distract the attention of those who are trying to take careful note of my instructions. One demerit."

"Sorry, sir. I merely intended to express my awareness that for many practical purposes such a degree of accuracy is unnecessary."

"That idea, cadet, is sufficiently elemental that it need not be labored. I appreciate brevity and precision."

"Yes, sir."

"Thirdly, from these materials, assemble a communication system, operating on one hundred watts, which will permit two-way conversation between Tycho Base and Phobos, at whatever frequency you deem suitable."

The cadets started in identical fashion by sorting the material into various piles, then calibrating and checking the test instruments. Achievement thereafter was disparate. Culpepper and von Gluck, diagnosing the test as partly one of mechanical ingenuity and partly ordeal by frustration, failed to become excited when several indispensable components proved either to be missing or inoperative, and carried each project as far as immediately feasible. McGrath and Weske, beginning with the computer, were reduced to rage and random action. Lynch and Sutton worked doggedly at the computer, Verona at the communication system.

Culpepper alone managed to complete one of the instruments, by the process of sawing, polishing and cementing together sections of two broken crystals into a crude, inefficient, but operative maser unit.

The day after this test McGrath and Weske disappeared from the dormitory, whether by their own volition or notification from Henry Belt no one ever knew.

The test was followed by weekend leave. Cadet Lynch, attending a cocktail party, found himself in conversation with a Lieutenant-Colonel Trenchard, who shook his head pityingly to hear that Lynch was training with Henry Belt.

"I was up with Old Horrors myself. I tell you it's a miracle we ever got back. Belt was drunk two-thirds of the voyage."

"How does he escape court-martial?" asked Lynch.

"Very simple. All the top men seem to have trained under Henry Belt. Naturally they hate his guts but they all take a perverse pride in the fact. And maybe they hope that someday a cadet will take him apart."

"Have any ever tried?"

"Oh yes. I took a swing at Henry once. I was lucky to escape with a broken collarbone and two sprained ankles. If you come back alive, you'll stand a good chance of reaching the top."

The next evening Henry Belt passed the word. "Next Tuesday morning we go up. We'll be gone several months."

On Tuesday morning the cadets took their places in the angel-wagon. Henry Belt presently appeared. The pilot readied for take-off.

"Hold your hats. On the count..." The projectile thrust against the earth, strained, rose, went streaking up into the sky. An hour later the pilot pointed. "There's your boat. Old 25. And 39 right beside it, just in from space."

Henry Belt stared aghast from the port. "What's been done to the ship? The decoration? The red? the white? the yellow? The checkerboard."

"Thank some idiot of a landlubber," said the pilot. "The word came to pretty the old boats for a junket of congressmen."

Henry Belt turned to the cadets. "Observe this foolishness. It is the result of vanity and ignorance. We will be occupied several days removing the paint."

They drifted close below the two sails: No. 39 just down from space, spare and polished beside the bedizened structure of No. 25. In 39's exit port a group of men waited, their gear floating at the end of cords.

"Observe those men," said Henry Belt. "They are jaunty. They have been on a pleasant outing around the planet Mars.

They are poorly trained. When you gentlemen return you will be haggard and desperate and well trained. Now, gentlemen, clamp your helmets, and we will proceed."

The helmets were secured. Henry Belt's voice came by radio. "Lynch, Ostrander will remain here to discharge cargo. Verona, Culpepper, von Gluck, Sutton, leap with cords to the ship; ferry across the cargo, stow it in the proper hatches."

Henry Belt took charge of his personal cargo, which consisted of several large cases. He eased them out into space, clipped on lines, thrust them toward 25, leapt after. Pulling himself and the cases to the entrance port, he disappeared within.

Discharge of cargo was effected. The crew from 39 transferred to the carrier, which thereupon swung down and away, thrust itself dwindling back toward earth.

When the cargo had been stowed, the cadets gathered in the wardroom. Henry Belt appeared from the master's cubicle. "Gentlemen, how do you like the surroundings? Eh, Mr. Culpepper?"

"The hull is commodious, sir. The view is superb."

Henry Belt nodded. "Mr. Lynch? Your impressions?"

"I'm afraid I haven't sorted them out yet, sir."

"I see. You, Mr. Sutton?"

"Space is larger than I imagined it, sir."

"True. Space is unimaginable. A good space-man must either be larger than space, or he must ignore it. Both difficult. Well, gentlemen, I will make a few comments, then I will retire and enjoy the voyage. Since this is my last time out, I intend to do nothing whatever. The operation of the ship will be completely in your hands. I will merely appear from time to time to beam benevolently about or, alas! to make marks in my red book. Nominally I shall be in command, but you six will enjoy complete control over the ship. If you return us safely to Earth I will make an approving entry in my red book. If you wreck us or fling us into the sun, you will be more unhappy than I, since it is my destiny to die in space. Mr. von Gluck, do I perceive a smirk on your face?"

"No, sir, it is a thoughtful half-smile."

"What is humorous in the concept of my demise, may I ask?"

"It will be a great tragedy, sir. I merely was reflecting upon the contemporary persistence of, well, not exactly superstition, but, let us say, the conviction of a subjective cosmos."

Henry Belt made a notation in the red book. "Whatever is meant by this barbaric jargon I'm sure I don't know, Mr. von Gluck. It is clear that you fancy yourself a philosopher and dialectician. I will not fault this, so long as your remarks conceal no overtones of malice and insolence, to which I am extremely sensitive. Now as to the persistence of superstition, only an impoverished mind considers itself the repository of absolute knowledge. Hamlet spoke on this subject to Horatio, as I recall, in the well-known work by William Shakespeare. I myself have seen strange and terrifying sights. Were they hallucinations? Were they the manipulations of the cosmos by my mind or the mind of someone—or something—other than myself? I do not know. I therefore counsel a flexible attitude toward matters where the truth is still unknown. For this reason: The impact of an inexplicable experience may well destroy a mind which is too brittle. Do I make myself clear?"

"Perfectly, sir."

"Very good. To return, then. We shall set a system of watches whereby each man works in turn with each of the other five. I thereby hope to discourage the formation of special friendships, or cliques.

"You have inspected the ship. The hull is a sandwich of lithium-beryllium, insulating foam, fiber, and an interior skin. Very light, held rigid by air pressure rather than by any innate strength of the material. We can therefore afford enough space to stretch our legs and provide all of us with privacy.

"The master's cubicle is to the left; under no circumstances is anyone permitted in my quarters. If you wish to speak to me, knock on my door. If I appear, good. If I do not appear, go away. To the right are six cubicles which you may now distribute among yourselves by lot.

"Your schedule will be two hours study, four hours on watch, six hours off. I will require no specific rate of study progress, but I recommend that you make good use of your time.

"Our destination is Mars. We will presently construct a new sail, then, while orbital velocity builds up, you will carefully test and check all equipment aboard. Each of you will compute sail cant and course and work out among yourselves any discrepancies which may appear. I shall take no hand in navigation. I prefer that you involve me in no disaster. If any such occur I shall severely mark down the persons responsible.

"Singing, whistling, humming, are forbidden. I disapprove of fear and hysteria, and mark accordingly. No one dies more than once; we are well aware of the risks of this, our chosen occupation. There will be no practical jokes. You may fight, so long as you do not disturb me or break any instruments; however I counsel against it, as it leads to resentment, and I have known cadets to kill each other. I suggest coolness and detachment in your personal relations. Use of the microfilm projector is of course at your own option. You may not use the radio either to dispatch or receive messages. In fact I have put the radio out of commission, as is my practice. I do this to emphasize the fact that, sink or swim, we must make do with our own resources. Are there any questions?... Very good. You will find that if you all behave with scrupulous correctness and accuracy, we shall in due course return safe and sound, with a minimum of demerits and no casualties. I am bound to say, however, that in twelve previous voyages this has failed to occur. Now you select your cubicles, stow your gear. The carrier will bring up the new sail tomorrow, and you will go to work."

III

The carrier discharged a great bundle of three-inch tubing: paper-thin lithium hardened with beryllium, reinforced with filaments of mono-crystalline iron—a total length of eight miles. The cadets fitted the tubes end to end, cementing the joints. When the tube extended a quarter-mile it was bent bow-shaped by a cord stretched between two ends, and further sections added. As the process continued, the free end curved far out and around, and presently began to veer back in toward the hull. When the last tube was in place the loose end was hauled down, socketed home, to form a great hoop two miles and a half in diameter.

Henry Belt came out occasionally in his space suit to look on, and occasionally spoke a few words of sardonic comment, to which the cadets paid little heed. Their mood had changed; this was exhilaration, to be weightlessly afloat above the bright cloud-marked globe, with continent and ocean wheeling massively below. Anything seemed possible, even the training voyage with Henry Belt! When he came out to inspect their work, they grinned at each other with indulgent amusement. Henry Belt suddenly seemed a rather pitiful creature, a poor vagabond suited only for drunken bluster. Fortunate indeed that they were less naïve than Henry Belt's previous classes! *They* had taken Belt seriously; he had cowed them, reduced them to nervous pulp. Not this crew, not by a long shot! They saw through Henry Belt! Just keep your nose clean, do your work, keep cheerful. The training voyage won't last but a few months, and then real life begins. Gut it out, ignore Henry Belt as much as possible. This is the sensible attitude; the best way to keep on top of the situation.

Already the group had made a composite assessment of its members, arriving at a set of convenient labels. Culpepper: smooth, suave, easy-going. Lynch: excitable, argumentative, hot-tempered. Von Gluck: the artistic temperament, delicate with hands and sensibilities. Ostrander: prissy, finicky, over-tidy. Sutton: moody, suspicious, competitive. Verona: the plugger, rough at the edges, but persistent and reliable.

Around the hull swung the gleaming hoop, and now the carrier brought up the sail, a great roll of darkly shining stuff. When unfolded and unrolled, and unfolded many times more, it became a tough gleaming film, flimsy as gold leaf. Unfolded to its fullest extent it was a shimmering disk, already rippling and bulging to the light of the sun. The cadets fitted the film to the hoop, stretched it taut as a drum-head, cemented it in place. Now the sail must carefully be held edge on to the sun, or it would quickly move away, under a thrust of about a hundred pounds.

From the rim braided-iron threads were led to a ring at the back of the parabolic reflector, dwarfing this as the reflector dwarfed the hull, and now the sail was ready to move.

The carrier brought up a final cargo: water, food, spare parts, a new magazine for the microfilm viewer, mail. Then Henry Belt said, "Make sail."

This was the process of turning the sail to catch the sunlight while the hull moved around Earth away from the sun, canting it parallel to the sun-rays when the ship moved on the sunward leg of its orbit: in short, building up an orbital velocity which in due course would stretch loose the bonds of terrestrial gravity and send Sail 25 kiting out toward Mars.

During this period the cadets checked every item of equipment aboard the vessel. They grimaced with disgust and dismay at some of the instruments: 25 was an old ship, with antiquated gear. Henry Belt seemed to enjoy their grumbling. "This is a training voyage, not a pleasure cruise. If you wanted your noses wiped, you should have taken a post on the ground. And I have no sympathy for fault-finders. If you wish a model by which to form your own conduct, observe me."

The moody introspective Sutton, usually the most diffident and laconic of individuals, ventured an ill-advised witticism. "If we modeled ourselves after you, sir, there'd be no room to move for the whiskey."

Out came the red book. "Extraordinary impudence, Mr. Sutton. How can you yield so easily to malice?"

Sutton flushed pink; his eyes glistened, he opened his mouth to speak, then closed it firmly. Henry Belt, waiting politely expectant, turned away. "You gentlemen will perceive that I rigorously obey my own rules of conduct. I am regular as a clock. There is no better, more genial shipmate than Henry Belt. There is not a fairer man alive. Mr. Culpepper, you have a remark to make?"

"Nothing of consequence, sir."

Henry Belt went to the port, glared out at the sail. He swung around instantly. "Who is on watch?"

"Sutton and Ostrander, sir."

"Gentlemen, have you noticed the sail? It has swung about and is canting to show its back to the sun. In another ten minutes we shall be tangled in a hundred miles of guy-wires."

Sutton and Ostrander sprang to repair the situation. Henry Belt shook his head disparagingly. "This is precisely what is meant by the words 'negligence' and 'inattentiveness.' You two have committed a serious error. This is poor spacemanship. The sail must always be in such a position as to hold the wires taut."

"There seems to be something wrong with the sensor, sir," Sutton blurted. "It should notify us when the sail swings behind us."

"I fear I must charge you an additional demerit for making excuses, Mr. Sutton. It is your duty to assure yourself that all the warning devices are functioning properly, at all times. Machinery must never be used as a substitute for vigilance."

Ostrander looked up from the control console. "Someone has turned off the switch, sir. I do not offer this as an excuse, but as an explanation."

"The line of distinction is often hard to define, Mr. Ostrander. Please bear in mind my remarks on the subject of vigilance."

"Yes, sir, but—who turned off the switch?"

"Both you and Mr. Sutton are theoretically hard at work watching for any such accident or occurrence. Did you not observe it?"

"No, sir."

"I might almost accuse you of further inattention and neglect, in this case."

Ostrander gave Henry Belt a long dubious side-glance. "The only person I recall going near the console is yourself, sir. I'm sure you wouldn't do such a thing."

Henry Belt shook his head sadly. "In space you must never rely on anyone for rational conduct. A few moments ago Mr. Sutton unfairly imputed to me an unusual thirst for whiskey.

Suppose this were the case? Suppose, as an example of pure irony, that I had indeed been drinking whiskey, that I was in fact drunk?"

"I will agree, sir, that anything is possible."

Henry Belt shook his head again. "That is the type of remark, Mr. Ostrander, that I have come to associate with Mr. Culpepper. A better response would have been, 'In the future, I will try to be ready for any conceivable contingency.' Mr. Sutton, did you make a hissing sound between your teeth?"

"I was breathing, sir."

"Please breathe with less vehemence."

Henry Belt turned away and wandered back and forth about the wardroom, scrutinizing cases, frowning at smudges on polished metal. Ostrander muttered something to Sutton, and both watched Henry Belt closely as he moved here and there. Presently Henry Belt lurched toward them. "You show great interest in my movements, gentlemen."

"We were on the watch for another unlikely contingency, sir."

"Very good, Mr. Ostrander. Stick with it. In space nothing is impossible. I'll vouch for this personally."

IV

Henry Belt sent all hands out to remove the paint from the surface of the parabolic reflector. When this had been accomplished, incident sunlight was now focused upon an expanse of photoelectric cells. The power so generated was used to operate plasma jets, expelling ions collected by the vast expanse of sail, further accelerating the ship, thrusting it ever out into an orbit of escape. And finally one day, at an exact instant dictated by the computer, the ship departed from Earth and floated tangentially out into space, off at an angle for the orbit of Mars. At an acceleration of g/100 velocity built up rapidly. Earth dwindled behind; the ship was isolated in space. The cadets' exhilaration vanished, to be replaced by an almost funereal solemnity. The vision of Earth

dwindling and retreating is an awesome symbol, equivalent
to eternal loss, to the act of dying itself. The more impres-
sionable cadets—Sutton, von Gluck, Ostrander—could not
look astern without finding their eyes swimming with tears.
Even the suave Culpepper was awed by the magnificence of
the spectacle, the sun an aching pit not to be tolerated, Earth
a plump pearl rolling on black velvet among a myriad glittering diamonds. And away from Earth, away from the sun,
opened an exalted magnificence of another order entirely.
For the first time the cadets became dimly aware that Henry
Belt had spoken truly of strange visions. Here was death,
here was peace, solitude, star-blazing beauty which promised
not oblivion in death, but eternity.... Streams and spatters
of stars... The familiar constellation, the stars with their
prideful names presenting themselves like heroes: Achernar,
Fomalhaut, Sadal, Suud, Canopus...

Sutton could not bear to look into the sky. "It's not that
I feel fear," he told von Gluck, "or, yes, perhaps it is fear. It
sucks at me, draws me out there....I suppose in due course
I'll become accustomed to it."

"I'm not so sure," said von Gluck. "I wouldn't be surprised
if space could become a psychological addiction, a need—so
that whenever you walked on Earth you felt hot and breathless."

Life settled into a routine. Henry Belt no longer seemed
a man, but a capricious aspect of nature, like storm or lightning; and like some natural cataclysm, Henry Belt showed
no favoritism, nor forgave one jot or tittle of offense. Apart
from the private cubicles, no place on the ship escaped his
attention. Always he reeked of whiskey, and it became a
matter of covert speculation as to exactly how much whiskey
he had brought aboard. But no matter how he reeked or how
he swayed on his feet, his eyes remained clever and steady,
and he spoke without slurring in his paradoxically clear
sweet voice.

One day he seemed slightly drunker than usual, and ordered all hands into space-suits and out to inspect the sail
for meteoric puncture. The order seemed sufficiently odd that

the cadets stared at him in disbelief. "Gentlemen, you hesitate, you fail to exert yourselves, you luxuriate in sloth. Do you fancy yourselves at the Riviera? Into the space-suits, on the double, and everybody into space. Check hoop, sail, reflector, struts and sensor. You will be adrift for two hours. When you return I want a comprehensive report. Mr. Lynch, I believe you are in charge of this watch. You will present the report."

"Yes, sir."

"One more matter. You will notice that the sail is slightly bellied by the continual radiation pressure. It therefore acts as a focusing device, the focal point presumably occurring behind the cab. But this is not a matter to be taken for granted. I have seen a man burnt to death in such a freak accident. Bear this in mind."

For two hours the cadets drifted through space, propelled by tanks of gas and thrust tubes. All enjoyed the experience except Sutton, who found himself appalled by the immensity of his emotions. Probably least affected was the practical Verona, who inspected the sail with a care exacting enough even to satisfy Henry Belt.

The next day the computer went wrong. Ostrander was in charge of the watch and knocked on Henry Belt's door to make the report.

Henry Belt appeared in the doorway. He apparently had been asleep. "What is the difficulty, Mr. Ostrander?"

"We're in trouble, sir. The computer has gone out."

Henry Belt rubbed his grizzled pate. "This is not an unusual circumstance. We prepare for this contingency by schooling all cadets thoroughly in computer design and repair. Have you identified the difficulty?"

"The bearings which suspend the data-separation disks have broken. The shaft has several millimeters play and as a result there is total confusion in the data presented to the analyzer."

"An interesting problem. Why do you present it to me?"

"I thought you should be notified, sir. I don't believe we carry spares for this particular bearing."

Henry Belt shook his head sadly. "Mr. Ostrander, do you

recall my statement at the beginning of this voyage, that you six gentlemen are totally responsible for the navigation of the ship?"

"Yes, sir. But—"

"This is an applicable situation. You must either repair the computer, or perform the calculations yourself."

"Very well, sir. I will do my best."

V

Lynch, Verona, Ostrander and Sutton disassembled the mechanism, removed the worn bearing. "Confounded antique!" said Lynch. "Why can't they give us decent equipment? Or if they want to kill us, why not shoot us and save us all trouble."

"We're not dead yet," said Verona. "You've looked for a spare?"

"Naturally. There's nothing remotely like this."

Verona looked at the bearing dubiously. "I suppose we could cast a babbitt sleeve and machine it to fit. That's what we'll have to do—unless you fellows are awfully fast with your math."

Sutton glanced out the port, quickly turned away his eyes. "I wonder if we should cut sail."

"Why?" asked Ostrander.

"We don't want to build up too much velocity. We're already going thirty miles a second."

"Mars is a long way off."

"And if we miss, we go shooting past. Then where are we?"

"Sutton, you're a pessimist. A shame to find morbid tendencies in one so young." This from von Gluck.

"I'd rather be a live pessimist than a dead comedian."

The new sleeve was duly cast, machined, and fitted. Anxiously the alignment of the data disks was checked. "Well," said Verona dubiously, "there's wobble. How much that affects the functioning remains to be seen. We can take some of it out by shimming the mount...."

Shims of tissue paper were inserted and the wobble seemed

to be reduced. "Now—feed in the data," said Sutton. "Let's see how we stand."

Coordinates were fed into the system; the indicator swung. "Enlarge sail cant four degrees," said von Gluck, "we're making too much left concentric. Projected course..." He tapped buttons, watched the bright line extend across the screen, swing around a dot representing the center of gravity of Mars. "I make it an elliptical pass, about twenty thousand miles out. That's at present acceleration, and it should toss us right back at Earth."

"Great. Simply great. Let's go, 25!" This was Lynch. "I've heard of guys dropping flat on their faces and kissing Earth when they put down. Me, I'm going to live in a cave the rest of my life."

Sutton went to look at the data disks. The wobble was slight but perceptible. "Good Lord," he said huskily. "The other end of the shaft is loose too."

Lynch started to spit curses; Verona's shoulders slumped. "Let's get to work and fix it."

Another bearing was cast, machined, polished, mounted. The disks wobbled, scraped. Mars, an ocher disk, shouldered ever closer in from the side. With the computer unreliable, the cadets calculated and plotted the course manually. The results were at slight but significant variance with those of the computer. The cadets looked dourly at each other. "Well," growled Ostrander, "There's error. Is it the instruments? The calculation? The plotting? Or the computer?"

Culpepper said in a subdued voice, "Well, we're not about to crash head-on at any rate."

Verona went back to study the computer. "I can't imagine why the bearings don't work better.... The mounting brackets—could they have shifted?" He removed the side housing, studied the frame, then went to the case for tools.

"What are you going to do?" demanded Sutton.

"Try to ease the mounting brackets around. I think that's our trouble."

"Leave me alone! You'll bugger the machine so it'll never work."

Verona paused, looked questioningly around the group. "Well? What's the verdict?"

"Maybe we'd better check with the old man," said Ostrander nervously.

"All well and good—but you know what he'll say."

"Let's deal cards. Ace of spades goes to ask him."

Culpepper received the ace. He knocked on Henry Belt's door. There was no response. He started to knock again, but restrained himself.

He returned to the group. "Wait till he shows himself. I'd rather crash into Mars than bring forth Henry Belt and his red book."

The ship crossed the orbit of Mars well ahead of the looming red planet. It came toppling at them with a peculiar clumsy grandeur, a mass obviously bulky and globular, but so fine and clear was the detail, so absent the perspective, that the distance and size might have been anything. Instead of swinging in a sharp elliptical curve back toward Earth, the ship swerved aside in a blunt hyperbola and proceeded outward, now at a velocity of close to fifty miles a second. Mars receded astern and to the side. A new part of space lay ahead. The sun was noticeably smaller. Earth could no longer be differentiated from the stars. Mars departed quickly and politely, and space seemed lonely and forlorn.

Henry Belt had not appeared for two days. At last Culpepper went to knock on the door—once, twice, three times: a strange face looked out. It was Henry Belt, face haggard, skin like pulled taffy. His eyes were red and glared, his hair seemed matted and more unkempt than hair a quarter-inch long should be.

But he spoke in his quiet clear voice. "Mr. Culpepper, your merciless din has disturbed me. I am quite put out with you."

"Sorry, sir. We feared that you were ill."

Henry Belt made no response. He looked past Culpepper, around the circle of faces. "You gentlemen are unwontedly serious. Has this presumptive illness of mine caused you all distress?"

Sutton spoke in a rush, "The computer is out of order."

"Why then, you must repair it."

"It's a matter of altering the housing. If we do it incorrectly—"

"Mr. Sutton, please do not harass me with the hour-by-hour minutiae of running the ship."

"But, sir, the matter has become serious; we need your advice. We missed the Mars turnaround—"

"Well, I suppose there's always Jupiter. Must I explain the basic elements of astrogation to you?"

"But the computer's out of order—definitely."

"Then, if you wish to return to Earth, you must perform the calculations with pencil and paper. Why is it necessary to explain the obvious?"

"Jupiter is a long way out," said Sutton in a shrill voice. "Why can't we just turn around and go home?" This last was almost a whisper.

"I see I've been too easy on you cads," said Henry Belt. "You stand around idly; you chatter nonsense while the machinery goes to pieces and the ship flies at random. Everybody into space-suits for sail inspection. Come now. Let's have some snap. What are you all? Walking corpses? You, Mr. Culpepper, why the delay?"

"It occurred to me, sir, that we are approaching the asteroid belt. As I am chief of the watch I consider it my duty to cant sail to swing us around the area."

"You may do this; then join the rest in hull and sail inspection."

"Yes, sir."

The cadets donned space-suits, Sutton with the utmost reluctance. Out into the dark void they went, and now here was loneliness indeed.

When they returned, Henry Belt had returned to his compartment.

"As Mr. Belt points out, we have no great choice," said Ostrander. "We missed Mars, so let's hit Jupiter. Luckily it's in good position—otherwise we'd have to swing out to Saturn or Uranus—"

"They're off behind the sun," said Lynch. "Jupiter's our last chance."

"Let's do it right, then. I say, let's make one last attempt to set those confounded bearings...."

But now it seemed as if the wobble and twist had been eliminated. The disks tracked perfectly, the accuracy monitor glowed green.

"Great!" yelled Lynch. "Feed it the dope. Let's get going! All sail for Jupiter. Good Lord, but we're having a trip!"

"Wait till it's over," said Sutton. Since his return from sail inspection, he had stood to one side, cheeks pinched, eyes staring. "It's not over yet. And maybe it's not meant to be."

The other five pretended not to have heard him. The computer spat out figures and angles. There was a billion miles to travel. Acceleration was less, due to the diminution in the intensity of sunlight. At least a month must pass before Jupiter came close.

VI

The ship, great sail spread to the fading sunlight, fled like a ghost—out, always out. Each of the cadets had quietly performed the same calculation, and arrived at the same result. If the swing around Jupiter were not performed with exactitude, if the ship were not slung back like a stone on a string, there was nothing beyond. Saturn, Uranus, Neptune, Pluto were far around the sun; the ship, speeding at a hundred miles a second, could not be halted by the waning gravity of the sun, nor yet sufficiently accelerated in a concentric direction by sail and jet into a true orbit. The very nature of the sail made it useless as a brake, always the thrust was outward.

Within the hull seven men lived and thought, and the psychic relationship worked and stirred like yeast in a vat of decaying fruit. The fundamental similarity, the human identity of the seven men, was utterly canceled; apparent only were the disparities. Each cadet appeared to others only as a walking characteristic, and Henry Belt was an incomprehensible Thing, who appeared from his compartment at unpredictable times, to move quietly here and there with the blind blank grin of an archaic Attic hero.

Jupiter loomed and bulked. The ship, at last within reach of the Jovian gravity, sidled over to meet it. The cadets gave ever more careful attention to the computer, checking and counterchecking the instructions. Verona was the most assiduous at this, Sutton the most harassed and ineffectual. Lynch growled and cursed and sweat; Ostrander complained in a thin peevish voice. Von Gluck worked with the calm of pessimistic fatalism; Culpepper seemed unconcerned, almost debonair, a blandness which bewildered Ostrander, infuriated Lynch, awoke a malignant hate in Sutton. Verona and von Gluck on the other hand seemed to derive strength and refreshment from Culpepper's placid acceptance of the situation. Henry Belt said nothing. Occasionally he emerged from his compartment, to survey the wardroom and the cadets with the detached interest of a visitor to an asylum.

It was Lynch who made the discovery. He signaled it with an odd growl of sheer dismay, which brought a resonant questioning sound from Sutton. "My God, my God," muttered Lynch.

Verona was at his side. "What's the trouble?"

"Look. This gear. When we replaced the disks we dephased the whole apparatus one notch. This white dot and this other white dot should synchronize. They're one sprocket apart. All the results would check and be consistent because they'd all be off by the same factor."

Verona sprang into action.

Off came the housing, off came various components. Gently he lifted the gear, set it back into correct alignment. The other cadets leaned over him as he worked, except Culpepper who was chief of the watch.

Henry Belt appeared. "You gentlemen are certainly diligent in your navigation," he said presently. "Perfectionists almost."

"We do our best," greeted Lynch between set teeth. "It's a damn shame sending us out with a machine like this."

The red book appeared. "Mr. Lynch, I mark you down not for your private sentiments, which are of course yours to entertain, but for voicing them and thereby contributing to an unhealthy atmosphere of despairing and hysterical pessimism."

A tide of red crept up from Lynch's neck. He bent over the computer, made no comment. But Sutton suddenly cried out, "What else do you expect from us? We came out here to learn, not to suffer, or to fly on forever!" He gave a ghastly laugh. Henry Belt listened patiently. "Think of it!" cried Sutton. "The seven of us. In this capsule, forever!"

"I am afraid that I must charge you two demerits for your outburst, Mr. Sutton. A good space-man maintains his dignity at all costs."

Lynch looked up from the computer. "Well, now we've got a corrected reading. Do you know what it says?"

Henry Belt turned him a look of polite inquiry.

"We're going to miss," said Lynch. "We're going to pass by just as we passed Mars. Jupiter is pulling us around and sending us out toward Gemini."

The silence was thick in the room. Henry Belt turned to look at Culpepper, who was standing by the porthole, photographing Jupiter with his personal camera.

"Mr. Culpepper?"

"Yes, sir."

"You seem unconcerned by the prospect which Mr. Sutton has set forth."

"I hope it's not imminent."

"How do you propose to avoid it?"

"I imagine that we will radio for help, sir."

"You forget that I have destroyed the radio."

"I remember noting a crate marked 'Radio Parts' stored in the starboard jet-pod."

"I am sorry to disillusion you, Mr. Culpepper. That case is mislabeled."

Ostrander jumped to his feet, left the wardroom. There was the sound of moving crates. A moment of silence. Then he returned. He glared at Henry Belt. "Whiskey. Bottles of whiskey."

Henry Belt nodded. "I told you as much."

"But now we have no radio," said Lynch in an ugly voice.

"We never have had a radio, Mr. Lynch. You were warned that you would have to depend on your own resources to bring us home. You have failed, and in the process doomed me as well as yourself. Incidentally, I must mark you all down ten demerits for a faulty cargo check."

"Demerits," said Ostrander in a bleak voice.

"Now, Mr. Culpepper," said Henry Belt. "What is your next proposal?"

"I don't know, sir."

Verona spoke in a placatory voice. "What would you do, sir, if you were in our position?"

Henry Belt shook his head. "I am an imaginative man, Mr. Verona, but there are certain leaps of the mind which are beyond my powers." He returned to his compartment.

Von Gluck looked curiously at Culpepper. "It is a fact. You're not at all concerned."

"Oh, I'm concerned. But I believe that Mr. Belt wants to get home too. He's too good a space-man not to know exactly what he's doing."

The door from Henry Belt's compartment slid back. Henry Belt stood in the opening. "Mr. Culpepper, I chanced to overhear your remark, and I now note down ten demerits against you. This attitude expresses a complacence as dangerous as Mr. Sutton's utter funk." He looked about the room. "Pay no heed to Mr. Culpepper. He is wrong. Even if I could repair this disaster, I would not raise a hand. For I expect to die in space."

VII

The sail was canted vectorless, edgewise to the sun. Jupiter was a smudge astern. There were five cadets in the wardroom. Culpepper, Verona, and von Gluck sat talking in low voices. Ostrander and Lynch lay crouched, arms to knees, faces to the wall. Sutton had gone two days before. Quietly donning his space-suit, he had stepped into the exit chamber and thrust himself headlong into space. A propulsion unit gave him added speed, and before any of the cadets could intervene he was gone.

Shortly thereafter Lynch and Ostrander succumbed to inanition, a kind of despondent helplessness: manic-depression in its most stupefying phase. Culpepper the suave, Verona the pragmatic, and von Gluck the sensitive remained.

They spoke quietly to themselves, out of earshot of Henry Belt's room. "I still believe," said Culpepper, "that somehow there is a means to get ourselves out of this mess, and that Henry Belt knows it."

Verona said, "I wish I could think so.... We've been over it a hundred times. If we set sail for Saturn or Neptune or Uranus, the outward vector of thrust plus the outward vector of our momentum will take us far beyond Pluto before we're anywhere near. The plasma jets could stop us if we had enough energy, but the shield can't supply it and we don't have another power source...."

Von Gluck hit his fist into his hand. "Gentlemen," he said in a soft delighted voice, "I believe we have sufficient energy at hand. We will use the sail. Remember? It is bellied. It can function as a mirror. It spreads five square miles of surface. Sunlight out here is thin—but so long as we collect enough of it—"

"I understand!" said Culpepper. "We back off the hull till the reactor is at the focus of the sail and turn on the jets!"

Verona said dubiously, "We'll still be receiving radiation pressure. And what's worse, the jets will impinge back on the sail. Effect—cancellation. We'll be nowhere."

"If we cut the center out of the sail—just enough to allow the plasma through—we'd beat that objection. And as for the radiation pressure—we'll surely do better with the plasma drive."

"What do we use to make plasma? We don't have the stock."

"Anything that can be ionized. The radio, the computer, your shoes, my shirt, Culpepper's camera, Henry Belt's whiskey..."

VIII

The angel-wagon came up to meet Sail 25, in orbit beside Sail 40, which was just making ready to take out a new crew.

The cargo carrier drifted near, eased into position. Three men sprang across space to Sail 40, a few hundred yards behind 25, tossed lines back to the carrier, pulled bales of cargo and equipment across the gap.

The five cadets and Henry Belt, clad in space-suits, stepped out into the sunlight. Earth spread below, green and blue, white and brown, the contours so precious and dear to bring tears to the eyes. The cadets transferring cargo to Sail 40 gazed at them curiously as they worked. At last they were finished, and the six men of Sail 25 boarded the carrier.

"Back safe and sound, eh, Henry?" said the pilot. "Well, I'm always surprised."

Henry Belt made no answer. The cadets stowed their cargo, and standing by the port, took a final look at Sail 25. The carrier retro-jetted; the two sails seemed to rise above them.

The lighter nosed in and out of the atmosphere, braking, extended its wings, glided to an easy landing on the Mojave Desert.

The cadets, their legs suddenly loose and weak to the unaccustomed gravity, limped after Henry Belt to the carry-all, seated themselves, and were conveyed to the administration complex. They alighted from the carry-all, and now Henry Belt motioned the five to the side.

"Here, gentlemen, is where I leave you. Tonight I will check my red book and prepare my official report. But I believe I can present you an unofficial résumé of my impressions. Mr. Lynch and Mr. Ostrander, I feel that you are ill-suited either for command or for any situation which might inflict prolonged emotional pressure upon you. I cannot recommend you for space duty.

"Mr. von Gluck, Mr. Culpepper, and Mr. Verona, all of you meet my minimum requirements for a recommendation, although I shall write the words 'Especially Recommended' only beside the names 'Clyde von Gluck' and 'Marcus Verona.'

You brought the sail back to Earth by essentially faultless navigation.

"So now our association ends. I trust you have profited by it." Henry Belt nodded briefly to each of the five and limped off around the building.

The cadets looked after him. Culpepper reached in his pocket and brought forth a pair of small metal objects which he displayed in his palm. "Recognize these?"

"Hmf," said Lynch in a flat voice. "Bearings for the computer disks. The original ones."

"I found them in the little spare-parts tray. They weren't there before."

Von Gluck nodded. "The machinery always seemed to fail immediately after sail check, as I recall."

Lynch drew in his breath with a sharp hiss. He turned, strode away. Ostrander followed him. Culpepper shrugged. To Verona he gave one of the bearings, to von Gluck the other. "For souvenirs—or medals. You fellows deserve them."

"Thanks, Ed," said von Gluck.

"Thanks," muttered Verona. "I'll make a stick-pin of this thing."

The three, not able to look at each other, glanced up into the sky where the first stars of twilight were appearing, then continued on into the building where family and friends and sweethearts awaited them.

LUST

How we, all of us who happen to be of the male persuasion, love and admire the purity of womanhood. How soft and delicate and fragrant they all are from the very young ("Thank heaven—for little girls") to the very old ("Put them all together—they spell M-O-T-H-E-R"). It's wonderful to have half the human race so much superior to the other—except that that is sexist nonsense, isn't it? All you need is a special sense and you'll discover that what the two sexes have in common is LUST.

PEEPING TOM

JUDITH MERRIL

You take a boy like Tommy Bender—a nice American boy,
well-brought-up in a nice, average, middle-class family;
chock-full of vitamins, manners, and baseball statistics;
clean-shaven, soft-spoken, and respectful to women and his
elders. You take a boy like that, fit him out with a uniform,
teach him to operate the most modern means of manslaugh-
ter, reward him with a bright gold bar, and send him out to
an exotic eastern land to prove his manhood and his patriotism.

You take a kid like that. Send him into combat in a steam-
ing jungle inferno; teach him to sweat and swear with conviction; then wait till he makes just one wrong move, pick
him out of the pool of drying blood, beat off the flies, and
settle him safely on a hospital cot in an ill-equipped base
behind the lines, cut off from everyone and everywhere, except the little native village nearby. Let him rest and rot
there for a while. Then bring him home, and pin a medal on
him, and give him his civvies and a pension to go with his
limp. You take a boy like Tommy Bender, and do all that to
him, you won't expect him to be quite the same nice, apple-
cheeked youngster afterwards.

He wasn't.

When Tommy Bender came home, he was firmly disillusioned and grimly determined. He knew what he wanted out
of life, had practically no hope of getting it, and didn't much
care how he went about getting the next-best things. And in
a remarkably short time, he made it clear to his erstwhile
friends and neighbors that he was almost certain to get anything he went after. He made money; he made love; he made

enemies. Eventually, he made enough of a success so that the enemies could be as thoroughly ignored as yesterday's woman. The money, and the things it bought for him, he took good care of.

For almost five years after he came home, Tommy Bender continued to build a career and ruin reputations. People tried to understand what had happened to him; but they didn't really.

Then, abruptly, something happened to change Tommy. His business associates noticed it first; his family afterwards. The girls he was seeing at the time were the last to know, because he'd always been undependable with them, and not hearing from him for two or three weeks wasn't unusual.

What happened was a girl. Her name was Candace, and when she was married to Tommy, seven weeks after her arrival, the papers carried the whole romantic story. It was she who had nursed him back to health in that remote village on the edge of the jungle years ago. He'd been in love with her then, but she'd turned him down.

That last part wasn't in the news story, of course, but it got around town just as fast as the paper did. Tommy's bitterness, it seemed, was due to his long-frustrated love. And anyone could see how he'd changed since Candace came back to him. His employees, his debtors, his old friends and discarded women, his nervous mother and his angry brother all sighed with relief and decided everything was going to be all right now. At last they really understood.

But they didn't. They didn't, for instance, understand what happened to Tommy Bender in that God-forsaken little town where he'd spent two months on crutches, waiting for his leg to heal enough to travel home.

It was hot and sticky in the shack. The mattress was lumpy. His leg itched to the very fringes of madness, and the man on his right had an erratically syncopated snore that took him past the raveled edge straight to insanity. All he needed to make the torture complete was the guy on his left— and the nurse.

The nurse was young and round and lithe, and she wore

battle fatigues: slacks, and a khaki shirt that was always draped against her high, full breasts in the damp heat. Her hair, dark blonde or light brown, was just long enough to be pinned back in a tiny bun, and just short enough so wisps of it were always escaping to curl around her ears or over her forehead.

When she bent over him to do any of the small humiliating services he needed done for him, he could see tiny beads of sweat on her upper lip, and that somehow was always the one little touch too much.

So that after she moved on to the next bed, and beyond it, it would be torture to have Dake, the guy on the left, turn toward him and start describing, graphically, what he would do if he could just get his remaining arm out of the cast for fifteen minutes some day.

You see Tommy Bender was still a nice young man then— after the combat, and the wound, and the flies, and the rough hospitalization.

Dake was nothing of the sort. He'd been around, and he knew exactly what value he placed on a woman. And he enjoyed talking about it.

Tommy listened because there was no way not to, and he wriggled and sweated and suffered, and the itch in his leg got worse, and the stench from the garbage pile outside became unbearable. It went on that way, hour after hour and day after day, punctuated only by the morning visit from the medic, who would stop and look him over, and shake a weary, discouraged head, and then go on to the next man.

The leg was a long time healing. It was better after Dake left and was replaced with a quietly dying man who'd got it in the belly. After him, there was a nice young Negro soldier, somewhat embarrassed about being in sick bay with nothing more dramatic than appendicitis. But at least, now, Tommy could keep his thoughts and dreams about Candace to himself, untarnished.

Then one day, when it had begun to seem as if nothing would ever change again in his life, except the occupants of the beds on either side of him, something happened to break the monotony of discomfort and despair. The medic stopped a little longer than usual in front of Tommy's cot, studied the neat chart Candy was always filling in, and furrowed his brow with concern. Then he muttered something to Candace, and she looked worried too. After that, they both turned and looked at Tommy as if they were seeing him for the first time, and Candy smiled, and the doctor frowned a little deeper.

"Well, young man," he said, "We're going to let you get up."

"Thanks, doc," Tommy said, talking like a GI was supposed to. "What should I do with the leg? Leave it in bed?"

"Ha, ha," the doctor laughed. Just like that. "Good to see you haven't lost your spirit." Then he moved on to the next bed, and Tommy lay there wondering. What would he do with the leg?

That afternoon, they came for him with a stretcher, and took him to the surgery shack, and cut off the cast. They all stood around, five or six of them, looking at it and shaking their heads and agreeing it was pretty bad. Then they put a new cast on, a little less bulky than the first one, and handed him a pair of crutches, and said: "Okay, boy, you're on your own."

An orderly showed him how to use them, and helped him get back to his own bed. The next day he practiced up a little, and by the day after that, he could really get around.

It made a difference.

Tommy Bender was a nice normal American boy, with all the usual impulses. He had been weeks on end in the jungle, and further weeks on his back in the cot. It was not strange that he should show a distinct tendency to follow Candy about from place to place, now he was on his feet again.

The pursuit was not so much hopeful as it was instinctive. He never, quite, made any direct advance to her. He ran little errands, and helped in every way he could, as soon as he was sufficiently adept in the handling of his crutches. She was certainly not ill-pleased by his devotion, but neither, he knew, was she inclined to any sort of romantic attachment to him.

Once or twice, acting on private advice from the more

experienced ambulant patients, he made tentative approaches to some of the other nurses, but met always the same kindly advice that they felt chasing nurses would not be good for his leg. He accepted his rebuffs in good part, as a nice boy will, and continued to trail around after Candy.

It was she, quite inadvertently, who led him to a piece of good fortune. He saw her leave the base one early evening, laden with packages, and traveling on foot. Alone. For a GI, these phenomena might not have been unusual. For a nurse to depart in this manner was extraordinary, and Candace slipped out so quietly that Tommy felt certain no one but himself was aware of it.

He hesitated about following at first; then he started worrying about her, threw social caution to the winds, and went swinging down the narrow road behind her, till she heard him coming and turned to look, then to wait.

She was irritated at first; then, abruptly, she seemed to change her mind.

"All right, come along," she said. "It's just a visit I'm going to pay. You can't come in with me, but you can wait if you want to, and walk me back again."

He couldn't have been more pleased. Or curious.

Their walk took them directly into the native village, where Candace seemed to become confused. She led Tommy and his crutches up and down a number of dirty streets and evil-looking alleys before she located the small earthen hut she was looking for, with a wide stripe of blue clay over its door.

While they searched for the place, she explained nervously to Tommy that she was fulfilling a mission for a dead soldier, who had, in a period of false recovery just before the end, made friends with an old man of this village. The dying GI had entrusted her with messages and gifts for his friend— most notably a sealed envelope and his last month's cigarette ration. That had been three weeks ago, and she'd spent the time since working up her courage to make the trip. Now, she confessed, she was more than glad Tommy had come along.

When they found the hut at last, they found a compara-

tively clean old man sitting cross-legged by the doorway,
completely enveloped in a long gray robe with a hood thrown
back off his shaven head. There was a begging bowl at his
side, and Tommy suggested that Candace might do best just
to leave her offerings in the bowl. But when she bent down
to do so, the old man raised his head and smiled at her.

"You are a friend of my friend, Karl?" he asked in astonishingly good English.

"Why...yes," she fumbled. "Yes. Karl Larsen. He said to
bring you these...."

"I thank you. You were most kind to come so soon." He
stood up, and added, just to her, ignoring Tommy. "Will you
come inside and drink tea with me, and speak with me of his
death?"

"Why, I—" Suddenly she too smiled, apparently quite at
ease once more. "Yes, I'd be glad to. Thank you. Tommy," she
added, "would you mind waiting for me? I...I'd appreciate
having someone to walk back with. It won't be long. Maybe—" She looked at the old man who was smiling, waiting.
"Maybe half an hour," she finished.

"A little more or less perhaps," he said, in his startlingly
clear American diction. "Perhaps your friend would enjoy
looking about our small village meanwhile, and you two can
meet again here in front of my door?"

"Why, sure," Tommy said, but he wasn't sure at all. Because as he started to say it, he had no intention of moving
away from that door at all while Candy was inside. He'd stay
right there, within earshot. But by the time the second word
was forming in his mouth, he had a sudden clear image of
what he'd be doing during that time.

And he was right.

No sooner had Candy passed under the blue-topped doorway than a small boy appeared at Tommy's other elbow. The
youngster's English was in no way comparable to that of the
old man. He knew just two words, but they were sufficient.
The first was: "Youguhcigarreh?" The second: "Iguhsisseh."

Tommy dug in his pockets, came out with a half-full pack,
registered the boy's look of approval, and swung his crutches
into action. He followed his young friend up and down several

of the twisty village alleys, and out along a footpath into the forest. Just about the time he was beginning to get worried, they came out into a small clearing, and a moment later "Sisseh" emerged from behind a tree at the far edge.

She was disconcertingly young, but also unexpectedly attractive: smooth-skinned, graceful, and roundly shaped....

Somewhat later when he found his way back to the blue-topped door in the village, Candy was already waiting for him, looking thoughtful and a little sad. She seemed to be no more in the mood for conversation than was Tommy himself, and they walked back to the base in almost complete silence. Though he noted once or twice that her quiet mood was dictated by less-happy considerations than his own, Tommy's ease of mind and body was too great at that moment to encourage much concern for even so desirable a symbol of American womanhood as the beautiful nurse, Candace.

Not that his devotion to her lessened. He dreamed of her still, but the dreams were more pleasantly romantic, and less distressingly carnal. And on those occasions when he found his thoughts of her verging once more toward the improper, he would wander off to the little village and regain what he felt was a more natural and suitable attitude toward life and love in general.

Then, inevitably, there came one such day when his young procurer was nowhere to be found. Tommy went out to the clearing where Sisseh usually met them, but it was quiet, empty and deserted. Back in the village again, he wandered aimlessly up and down narrow twisting streets, till he found himself passing the blue-topped doorway of the old man whose friendship with a dead GI had started the whole chain of events in motion.

"Good morning, sir," the old man said, and Tommy stopped politely to return the greeting.

"You are looking for your young friend?"

Tommy nodded, and hoped the warmth he could feel on his face didn't show. Small-town gossip, apparently, was much the same in one part of the world as in another.

"I think he will be busy for some time yet," the old man

volunteered. "Perhaps another hour.... His mother required his services for an errand to another village."

"Well, thanks," Tommy said. "Guess I'll come back this afternoon or something. Thanks a lot."

"You may wait here with me if you like. You are most welcome," the old man said hastily. "Perhaps you would care to come into my home and drink tea with me?"

Tommy's manners were good. He had been taught to be respectful to his elders, even to the old colored man who came to clip the hedges. And he knew that an invitation to tea can never be refused without excellent good reason. He had no such reason, and he did have a warm interest in seeing his dusky beauty just as soon as possible. He therefore overcame a natural reluctance to become a visitor in one of the (doubtless) vermin-infested native huts, thanked the old man politely, and accepted the invitation.

Those few steps, passing under the blue-topped doorway for the first time, into the earthen shack, were beyond doubt the most momentous of his young life. When he came out again, a full two hours later, there was nothing on the surface to show what had happened to him ... except perhaps a more-than-usually-thoughtful look on his face. But when Sisseh's little brother pursued him down the village street, Tommy only shook his head. And when the boy persisted, the soldier said briefly: "No got cigarettes."

The statement did not in any way express the empty-handed regret one might have expected. It was rather an impatient dismissal by a man too deeply immersed in weighty affairs to regard either the cigarettes or their value in trade as having much importance.

Not that Tommy had lost any of his vigorous interest in the pleasures of the flesh. He had simply acquired a more far-sighted point of view. He had plans for the future now, and they did not concern a native girl whose affection was exchangeable for half a pack of Camels.

Swinging along the jungle path on his crutches, Tommy was approaching a dazzling new vista of hope and ambition. The goals he had once considered quite out of reach now seemed to be just barely beyond his grasp, and he had already embarked on a course of action calculated to remedy that situation. Tommy was apprenticed to telepath.

The way it happened, the whole incredible notion seemed like a perfectly natural idea. Inside the one-room hut, the old man had introduced himself as Armod Something-or-other. (The last name was a confusion of clashing consonants and strangely inflected vowels that Tommy never quite got straight.) He then invited his young guest to make himself comfortable, and began the preparation of the tea by pouring water from a swan-necked glass bottle into a burnished copper kettle suspended by graceful chains from a wrought-iron tripod over a standard-brand hardware-store Sterno stove.

The arrangement was typical of everything in the room. East met West at every point with a surprising minimum of friction, once the first impact was absorbed and the psychological dislocation adjusted.

Tommy settled down at first on a low couch, really no more than a native mat covering some woven webbing, stretched across a frame that stood a few inches off the floor on carved ivory claws. But he discovered quickly enough that it did not provide much in the way of comfort for a long-legged young man equipped with a bulky cast. An awful lot of him seemed to be stretched out over the red-and-white-tile-pattern linoleum that covered the center of the dirt floor ... and he noticed, too, that his crutches had left a trail of round dust-prints on the otherwise spotless surface.

He wiped off the padded bottoms of the crutches with his clean handkerchief, and struggled rather painfully back to his feet.

The whole place was astonishingly clean. Tommy wandered around, considerably relieved at the absence of any very noticeable insect life, examining the curious contents of the room, and politely refraining from asking the many questions that came to mind.

The furnishing consisted primarily of low stools and tables, with a few shelves somehow set into the clay wall. There was one large, magnificently carved mahogany chest, which might have contained Ali Baba's fortune; and on a teakwood table in the corner, with a pad on the floor for a seat, stood a large and shiny late-model American standard typewriter.

A bookshelf near the table caught Tommy's eye, and the old man, without turning around, invited his guest to inspect it. Here again was the curious mixture of East and West: new books on philosophy, psychology, semantics, cybernetics published in England and America. Several others, though fewer, on spiritualism, psychic phenomena, and radio-esthesia. And mixed in with them, apparently at random, short squat volumes and long thin ones, lettered in unfamiliar scripts and ideographs.

On the wall over the bookshelf hung two strips of parchment, such as may be seen in many Eastern homes, covered with ideograph characters brilliantly illuminated. Between them was a glass-faced black frame containing the certification of Armod's license to practice medicine in the state of Idaho, U.S.A.

It did not seem in any way unnatural that Armod should come over and answer explicitly the obvious questions that this collection of anomalies brought to mind. In fact, it took half an hour or more of conversation before Tommy began to realize that his host was consistently replying to his thoughts rather than to his words. It took even longer for him to agree to the simple experiment that started him on his course of study.

But not *much* longer. An hour after he first entered the hut, Tommy Bender sat staring at eight slips of white paper on which were written, one word to each, the names of eight different objects in the room. The handwriting was careful, precise and clear. Not so the thoughts in Tommy's mind. He had "guessed," accurately, five of the eight objects, holding the faded piece of paper in his hand. He tried to tell himself it was coincidence; that some form of trickery might be involved. *The hand is quicker than the eye....* But it was his *own* hand that held the paper; he himself unfolded it after making his guess. And Armod's calm certainty was no help in the direction of skepticism.

"Well," Tommy asked uncertainly, "what made you think I could do it?"

"Anyone can do it," Armod said quietly. "For some it is easier than for others. To bring it under control, to learn to do it accurately, every time, is another matter altogether. But the sense is there, in all of us."

Tommy was a bit crestfallen; whether he *believed* in it or not, he preferred to think there was something a bit special about it.

Armod smiled, and answered his disappointment. "For you, it is easier I think than for many others. You are—ah, I despise your psychiatric jargon, but there is no other way to say it so you will understand—you are at ease with yourself. Relaxed. You have few basic conflicts in your personality, so you can reach more easily into the—no, it is *not* the 'subconscious.' It is a part of your mind you have simply not used before. You can use it. You can train it. You need only the awareness of it, and—practice."

Tommy thought that over, slowly, and one by one the implications of it dawned on him.

"You mean I can be a mind reader? Like the acts they do on the stage? I could do it professionally?"

"If you wished to. Few of those who pretend to read minds for the entertainment of others can really do so. Few who have the ability and training would use it in that way. You— ah, you are beginning to grasp some of the possibilities," the old man said, smiling.

"Go on," Tommy grinned. "Tell me what I'm thinking now."

"It would be most…indelicate. And…I *will* tell you; I do not believe you will have much chance of success, with *her*. She is an unusual young woman. Others…you will be startled, I think, to find how often a forbidding young lady is more hopeful even than willing."

"You're on," Tommy told him. "When do the lessons start, and how much?"

The price was easy; the practice was harder. Tommy gave up smoking entirely, suffered a bit, got over it, and turned his full attention to the procedures involved in gaining "awareness." He lay for hours on his cot, or sat by himself on a lonely hillside in the afternoon sun, learning to sense the presence of every part of himself as fully as that of the world around him.

He learned a dozen different ways of breathing, and discovered how each of them changed, to some slight degree, the way the rest of his body "felt" about things. He found out how to be completely receptive to impressions and sensations from outside himself; and after that, how to exclude them and be aware only of his own functioning organism. He discovered he could *feel* his heart beating and his food digesting, and later imagined he could feel the wound in his leg healing, and thought he was actually helping it along.

This last piece of news he took excitedly to Armod—along with his full ration of cigarettes—and was disappointed to have his mentor receive his excited outpourings with indifference.

"If you waste your substance on such side issues," Armod finally answered his insistence with downright disapproval, "you will be much longer in coming to the true understanding."

Tommy thought that over, swinging back along the jungle path on his crutches, and came to the conclusion that he could do without telepathy a little longer, if he could just walk on his own two feet again. Not that he really believed the progress was anything but illusory—until he heard the medics' exclamations of surprise the next time they changed the cast.

After that, he was convinced. The whole rigamarole was producing *some* kind of result; maybe it would even, incredibly, do what Armod said it would.

Two weeks later, Tommy got his first flash of *certainty*. He was, by then, readily proficient in picking thoughts out of Armod's mind; but he knew, too, that the old man was "helping" him...maintaining no barriers at all against invasion. Other people had habitual defenses that they didn't even know how to let down. Getting through the walls of verbalization, habitual reaction, hurt, fear and anger, to find out what was really happening inside the mind of a telepathically "inert" person took skill and determination.

That first flash could not in any way be described as "mind reading." Tommy did not *hear* or *read* or *see* any words or images. All he got was a wave of feeling; he was sure it was not his own feeling only because he was just then on his way back from a solitary hillside session in which he had, with considerable thoroughness, identified all the sensations his body then contained.

He was crossing what was laughably referred to as the "lawn"—an area of barren ground decorated with unrootable clumps of tropical weeds, extending from the mess hall to the surgery shack and surrounded by the barracks buildings—when the overwhelming wave of emotion hit him.

It contained elements of affection, interest, and—he checked again to be certain—desire. Desire for a *man*. He was quite sure now that the feeling was not his, but somebody else's.

He looked about, with sudden dismay, aware for the first time of a difficulty he had not anticipated. That he was "receiving" someone else's emotions he was certain; *whose,* he did not know.

In front of the surgery shack, a group of nurses stood together, talking. No one else was in sight. Tommy realized, unhappily, that the lady who was currently feeling amorous did not necessarily have to be in his line of vision. He had learned enough about the nature of telepathy by then to understand that it could penetrate physical barriers with relative ease. But he had a hunch....

He had learned enough, too, to understand some part of the meaning of that word, "hunch." He deliberately stopped *thinking,* insofar as he could, and followed his hunch across the lawn to the group of nurses. As he approached them, he let instinct take over entirely. Instead of speaking to them, he made as if to walk by, into the shack.

"Hey there, Lieutenant," one of them called out, and Tommy strained his muscles not to smile with delight. He turned around, innocently, inquiring.

"Surgery's closed now," the little red-headed one said sharply. That wasn't the one who'd called to him. It was the big blonde; he was *almost* sure.

"Oh?" he said. "I was out back of the base, on the hill there, and some damn bug bit me. Thought I ought to get

some junk put on it. You never know what's hit you with the
kind of skeeters they grow out here." He addressed the remark to the group in general, and threw in a grin that he
had been told made him look most appealing like a little boy,
meanwhile pulling up the trouser on his good leg to show a
fortuitously placed two-day-old swelling. "One leg out of commission is enough for me," he added. "Thought maybe I ought
to kind of keep a special eye on the one that still works." He
looked up, and smiled straight at the big blonde.

She regarded the area of exposed skin with apparent lack
of interest, hesitated, jangled a key in her pocket, and said
abruptly, "All right, big boy."

Inside the shack, she locked the door behind them, without
appearing to do anything the least bit unusual. Then she got
a tube of something out of a cabinet on the wall, and told him
to put his leg up on the table.

Right then, Tommy began to understand the real value
of what he'd learned, and how to use it. There was nothing
in her words or her brisk movements to show him how she
felt. While she was smoothing the gooey disinfectant paste
on his bite, and covering it with a bandage, she kept up a
stream of light talk and banter that gave no clue at all to
the way she was appraising him covertly. Tommy had nothing to do but make the proper responses—two sets of them.

Out loud, he described with appropriate humor the mon-
strous size and appearance of the bug that they both knew
hadn't bitten him. But all the time he kept talking and kid-
ding just as if he was still a nice American boy, he could feel
her *wanting* him, until he began to get confused between
what she wanted and what he did; and his eyes kept meeting
hers, unrelated to the words either of them were saying, to
let her know he knew.

Each time her hand touched his leg, it was a little more
difficult to banter. When it got too difficult, he didn't.

Later, stretched out on his cot in the barracks, he reviewed
the entire incident with approval, and made a mental note
of one important item. The only overt act the girl made—
locking the door—had been accompanied by a strong isolated
thought surge of "Don't touch me!" Conversely, the more

eager she felt, the more professional she acted. Without the aid of his special one-way window into her mind, he knew he would have made his play at precisely the wrong moment—assuming he'd had the courage to make it at all. As it was, he'd waited till there was no longer any reason for her to believe that he'd even noticed the locking of the door.

That was Lesson Number One about women: *Wait!* Wait till you're sure she's sure. Tommy repeated it happily to himself as he fell asleep that night; and only one small regret marred his contentment. It wasn't Candace....

Lesson Number Two came more slowly, but Tommy was an apt pupil, and he learned it equally well: *Don't wait too long!* The same simple forthright maneuver, he found, that would sweep a normally cooperative young lady literally off her feet if the timing was right would, ten minutes later, earn him nothing more than an indignant slap in the face. By that time, the girl had already decided either that he wasn't interested (insulted); or that he wasn't experienced enough to do anything about it (contemptuous); or that he was entirely lacking in sensitivity, and couldn't possibly understand her at all (both).

These two lessons Tommy studied assiduously. Between them, they defined the limits of that most remarkable point in time, *the Precise Moment.* And the greatest practical value of his new skill, so far as Tommy could see, was in being able to locate that point with increasing accuracy. The most noticeable property of the human mind is its constant activity; it is a rare man—and notoriously an even rarer woman—who has only one point of view on a given subject, and can stick to it. Tommy discovered soon enough that whatever he was after, whether it was five bucks to get into a poker game, or a date with one of the nurses, the best way to get it was to wait for that particular moment when the other person really *wanted* to give it to him.

It should be noted that Tommy Bender retained some ethics during this period. After the first two games, he stopped playing poker. Possibly, he was affected by the fact that suspicious rumors about his "luck" were circulating too freely; but it is more likely that the game had lost its punch. He didn't really need the money out there anyhow. And the process of his embitterment was really just beginning.

Three weeks after the incident in the surgery shack, Tommy got his orders for transfer to a stateside hospital. During that short time, though still impeded by cast and crutches, he acquired a quantity and quality of experience with women that more than equaled the total of his previous successes. And along with it, he suffered a few shocks.

That Tommy had both manners and ethics has already been established. He also had morals. He thought he ought to go to church more often than he did; he took it for granted that all unmarried women were virgins till proved otherwise; he never (or hardly ever) used foul language in mixed company. That kind of thing.

It was, actually, one of the smaller shocks, discovering the kind of language some of those girls knew. Most of them were nurses, after all, he reminded himself; they heard a lot of guys talking when they were delirious or in pain, but—but that didn't explain how clearly they seemed to *understand* the words. Or that the ones who talked the most refined were almost always the worst offenders in their minds.

The men's faults he could take in stride; it was the women who dismayed him. Not that he didn't find some "pure" girls; he did, to his horror. But the kind of feminine innocence he'd grown up believing in just didn't seem to exist. The few remaining virgins fell into two categories: those who were so convinced of their own unattractiveness that they didn't even know it when a pass was being made at them; and those who were completely preoccupied with a sick kind of fear-and-loathing that Tommy couldn't even stand to peep at for very long.

Generally speaking, the girls who weren't actually *looking* for men (which they did with a gratifying but immoral enthusiasm), were either filled with terror and disgust, or were calculating wenches who made their choice for or against the primrose path entirely in terms of the possible profit involved, be it in fast cash or future wedded bliss.

Tommy did find one exception to this generally unpleasant picture. To his determined dismay, and secret pleasure, he discovered that Candace really lived up to his ideal of the American girl. Her mind was a lovely, orderly place, full of softness and a sort of generalized liking for almost everybody. Her thoughts on the subject of most interest to him were also in order: She was apparently well-informed in an impersonal sort of way, ignorant of any personal experience, and rather hazily, pleasurably, anticipating the acquisition of that experience in some dim future when she pictured herself as happily in love and married.

As soon as he was quite sure of this state of affairs, Tommy proposed. Candace as promptly declined, and that, for the time being, terminated their relationship. The nurse went about her duties, and whatever personal matters occupied her in her free time. The soldier returned to his pursuit of parapsychology, women, and disillusion.

Tommy had no intention of taking these troubles to his teacher. But neither did Armod have to wait for the young man to speak before he knew. This time he was neither stern nor impatient. He spoke once again of the necessity for continuing study till one arrived at the "true understanding," but now he was alternately pleading and encouraging. At one point he was even apologetic.

"I did not know that you would learn so quickly," he said. "If I had foreseen this—doubtless I would have done precisely what I did. One cannot withhold knowledge, and..."

He paused, smiling gently and with great sadness. "And the truth of the matter is, you did not *ask* for knowledge. I offered it. I *sold* it! Because I could not deny myself the petty pleasure of your cigarettes!"

"Well," Tommy put in uncomfortably, "You made good on it, didn't you? Seems to me you did what you said you would."

"Yes—no," he corrected himself. "I did nothing but show the way. What has been done you did for yourself, as all men must. I cannot see or smell or taste for you; no more could I open the way into men's hearts for you. I gave you a key, let us say, and with it you unlocked the door. Now you look on the other side, but you do not; you cannot, understand what you see. It is as though one were to show an infant, just learning to use his eyes, a vision of violent death and bloody birth. He sees, but he does not *know*...."

Tommy stirred on the low couch, where he could now sit, as the old man did, cross-legged and at ease. But he was uneasy now. He picked up the cane that had replaced the crutches, toying with it, thinking hopefully of departure. Armod understood, and said quickly, "Listen now: I am an old man, and weak in my way. But I have shown you that I have knowledge of a sort. There is much you have yet to learn. If you are to perceive so clearly the depths of the human soul, then it is essential that you learn also to *understand*...."

The old man spoke on; the young one barely listened. He knew he was going home in another week. There was no sense talking about continuing his studies with Armod. And there was no need to continue; certainly no wish to. What he had already learned, Tommy felt, was very likely more than enough. He sat as quietly as he could, being patient till the old man was done talking. Then he stood up, and muttered something about getting back in time for lunch.

Armod shook his head and smiled, still sadly. "You will not hear me. Perhaps you are right. How can I speak to you of the true understanding, when I am still the willing victim of my own body's cravings? I am not fit. I am not fit...."

Tommy Bender was a very disturbed young man. He was getting what he'd wanted, and he didn't like it. He was grateful to Armod, and also angry at him. His whole life seemed to be a string of contradictions.

He drifted along in this unsettled state for the remaining week of his foreign service. Then, in a sudden flurry of affection and making amends, the day he got his orders, he decided to see the old man just once more. Most of the morning he spent racing around the base rounding up all the cigarettes he could get with what cash he had on hand, plus a liberal use of the new skills Armod had taught him. Then he got his gear together quickly. He was due at the air strip at 1400 hours, and at 1130 he left the base for a last walk to the village, the cane in one hand, two full cartons of butts in the other.

He found Armod waiting for him in a state of some agitation, apparently expecting him. There ensued a brief formal presentation of Tommy's gift, and acceptance of it; then for the last time, the old man invited him to drink tea, and ceremoniously set the water to simmer in the copper pot.

They both made an effort, and managed to get through the tea-drinking with no more than light polite talk. But when Tommy stood up to leave, Armod broke down.

"Come back," he begged. "When you are free of your service, and have funds to travel, come back to study again."

"Why, sure, Armod," Tommy said. "Just as soon as I can manage it."

"Yes, I see. This is what they call a social lie. It is meant not to convince me, but to terminate the discussion. But listen, I beg you, one moment more. You can see and hear in the mind now; but you cannot talk, nor can you keep silence. Your own mind is open to all who come and know how to look—"

"Armod, please, I—"

"You can learn to project thought as I do. To build a barrier against intrusion. You can—"

"Listen, Armod," Tommy broke in determinedly again. "I don't *have* to know any of that stuff. In my home town, there isn't anybody else who can do this stuff. And there's no reason for me to ever come back here. Look, I'll tell you what I can do. When I get back home, I can send you all the cigarettes you want—"

"No!"

The old man jumped up from his mat on the floor, and took two rapid strides to the shelf where Tommy's present lay. He picked up the two cartons, and tossed them contemptuously across the room, to land on the couch next to the soldier.

"No!" he said again, just a little less shrilly. "I do not want your cigarettes! I want nothing, do you understand? Nothing for myself! Only to regain the peace of mind I have lost through my weakness! Go to another teacher, then," he was struggling for calm. "There are many others. In India. In China. Perhaps even in your own country. Go to one who is better fitted than I. But do not stop now! You can learn more, much more!"

He was trembling with emotion as he spoke, his skinny frame shaking, his black eyes popping as though they would burst out of his head. "As for your cigarettes," he concluded, "I want none of them. I vow now, until the day I die, I shall never again give way to this weakness!"

He was a silly, excitable old man, who was going to regret these words. Tommy stood up feeling the foolish apologetic grin on his face and unable to erase it. He did not pick up the cigarettes.

"Good-bye, Armod," he said, and walked out for the last time through the blue-topped door.

But whatever either of them expected, and regardless of Tommy's own wishes, his education did not stop there. It had already gone too far to stop. The perception-awareness process seemed to be self-perpetuating, and though he practiced his exercises no more, his senses continued to become more acute—both the physical and the psychological.

At the stateside hospital, where his leg rapidly improved, Tommy had some opportunity to get out and investigate the situation with the nice old-fashioned girls who'd stayed at home and didn't go to war. By that time, he could "see" and "hear" pretty clearly.

He didn't like what he found.

That did it, really. All along, out at the base hospital, he'd clung to the notion that the women at home would be different—that girls so far from civilization were exposed to all sorts of indecencies a nice girl never had to face, and *shouldn't* have to. Small wonder they turned cynical and evil-minded.

The girls at home, he discovered, were less of the first, and far more of the second.

When Tommy Bender got home again, he was grimly determined and firmly disillusioned. He knew what he wanted out of life, saw no hope at all of ever getting it, and had very few scruples about the methods he used to get the next-best things.

In a remarkably short time, he made it clear to his erstwhile friends and neighbors that he was almost certain to get anything he went after. He made money; he made love; and of course he made enemies. All the while, his friends and neighbors tried to understand. Indeed, they thought they did. A lot of things can happen to a man when he's been through hell in combat, and then had to spend months rotting and recuperating in a lonely Far Eastern field hospital.

But of course they couldn't even begin to understand what had happened to Tommy. They didn't know what it was like to live on a steadily plunging spiral of anger and disillusionment, all the time liking people less, and always aware of how little they liked you.

To sign a contract with a man, knowing he would defraud you if he could; he couldn't, of course, because you got there first. But when you met him afterward, you rocked with the blast of hate and envy he threw at you.

To make love to a woman, and know she was the wrong woman for you or you the wrong man for her. And then to meet *her* afterward...

Tommy had, in the worst possible sense, got out of bed on the wrong side. When he first awoke to the knowledge of other people's minds, he had seen ugliness and fear wherever he looked, and that first impress of bitterness on his own mind had colored everything he had seen since.

For almost five years after he came home, Tommy Bender continued to build a career, and ruin reputations. People tried to understand what had happened to him...but how *could* they?

Then something happened. It started with an envelope in his morning mail. The envelope was marked "Personal," so it was unopened by his secretary and left on the side of his desk along with three or four other thin, squarish, obviously non-business, envelopes. As a result, Tommy didn't read it till late that afternoon, when he was trying to decide which girl to see that night.

The return address said "C. Harper, Hotel Albemarle, Topeka, Kansas." He didn't know anyone in Topeka, but the name Harper was vaguely reminiscent. He was intrigued

enough to open that one first, and the others never were
opened at all.

"Dear Tommy," it read. "First of all, I hope you still remember me. It's been quite a long time, hasn't it? I just heard,
from Lee Potter (the little, dark girl who came just before
you left...remember her?)"—Tommy did, with some pleasure—"that you were living in Hartsdale, and had some real-
estate connections there. Now I'd like to ask a favor....

"I've just had word that I've been accepted as Assistant
Superintendent of the Public Health Service there—in Hartsdale—and I'm supposed to start work on the 22nd. The only
thing is, I can't leave my job here till just the day before. So
I wondered if you could help me find a place to stay beforehand? Sort of mail-order real-estate service?

"I feel I'm being a little presumptuous, asking this, when
perhaps you don't even remember me—but I do hope you
won't mind. And please don't go to any special trouble. From
what Lee said, I got the idea this might be right in your line
of business. If it's not, don't worry. I'm sure I can find something when I get there.

"And thanks, ahead of time, for anything you can do.

"Cordially," it concluded, "Candace Harper."

Tommy answered the letter the same day, including a
varied list of places and prices hurriedly worked up by his
real-estate agent. That he owned real estate was true; that
he dealt in it, not at all. His letter to Candy did not go into
these details. Just told her how vividly he remembered her,
and how good it would be to see her again, with some questions about the kind of furnishings and décor she'd prefer.
"If you're going to get in early enough on the 21st," he wound
up, "how about having dinner with me? Let me know when
you're coming, anyhow. I'd like to meet you, and help you get
settled."

For the next eleven days, Tommy lived in an almost happy
whirl of preparation, memory, and anticipation. In all the
years since he had proposed to Candace, he had never met
another girl who filled so perfectly the mental image of the
ideal woman with which he had first left home. He kept
telling himself she wouldn't, couldn't, still be the same per-

son. Even a non-telepath would get bitter and disillusioned in five years of the Wonderful Post-War World. She *couldn't* be the same....

And she wasn't. She was older, more understanding, more tolerant, and, if possible, warmer and pleasanter than before. Tommy met her at the station, bought her some dinner, took her to the perfect small apartment where she was, unknown to herself, paying only half the rent. He stayed an hour, went down to run some errands for her, stayed another half-hour, and knew by then that in the most important respects she hadn't changed at all.

There wasn't going to be any "Precise Moment" with Candy; not that side of a wedding ceremony.

Tommy couldn't have been more pleased. Still, he was cautious. He didn't propose again till three weeks later, when he'd missed seeing her two days in a row due to business-social affairs. If they were married, he could have taken her along.

When he did propose, she lived up to all his qualifications again. She said she wanted to think it over. What she *thought* was: *Oh, yes! Oh, yes, he's the one I want! But it's too quick! How do I know for sure? He never even thought of me all this time...all the time I was waiting and hoping to hear from him...How can he be sure so soon? He might be sorry....*

"Let me think about it a few days, will you, Tommy?" she said, and he was afraid to take her in his arms for fear he'd crush her with his hunger.

Four weeks later they were married. And when Candy told him her answer, she also confessed what he already knew: that she'd regretted turning him down ever since he left the field hospital; that she'd been thinking of him, loving him, all the long years in between.

Candy was a perfect wife, just as she had been a perfect nurse, and an all-too-perfect dream girl. The Benders' wedding was talked about for years afterwards; it was one of those rare occasions when everything turned out just right. And the bride was so beautiful....

The honeymoon was the same way. They took six weeks to complete a tour of the Caribbean, by plane, ship and car.

They stayed where they liked as long as they liked, and did what they liked, all the time. And not once in those six weeks was there any serious difference in *what* they liked. Candy's greatest wish at every point was to please Tommy, and that made things very easy for both of them.

And all the while, Tommy was gently, ardently, instructing his lovely bride in the arts of matrimony. He was tender, patient, and understanding, as he had known beforehand he would have to be. A girl who gets to the age of twenty-six with her innocence intact is bound to require a little time for readjustment.

Still, by the time they came back, Tommy was beginning to feel a sense of failure. He knew that Candace had yet to experience the fulfillment she had hoped for, and that he had planned to give her.

Watching her across the breakfast table on the dining terrace of their new home, he was enthralled as ever. She was lovely in negligee, her soft hair falling around her face, her eyes shining with true love as they met his.

It was a warm day, and he saw, as he watched her, the tiny beads of sweat form on her upper lip. It took him back...way back...and from the vividness of the hospital scene, he skipped to an equally clear memory of that last visit to Armod, the teacher.

He smiled, and reached for his wife's hand, wondering if ever he would be able to tell her what had come of that walk they took to the village together. And he pressed her hand tighter, smiling again, as he realized that now, for the first time, he had a use for the further talents the old man had promised him.

That would be one way to show Candace the true pleasure she did not yet know. If he could project his own thoughts and emotions...

He let go of her hand, and sat back, sipping his coffee, happy and content, with just the one small problem to think about. *Maybe I should have gone back for a while, after all,* he thought idly.

"Perhaps you should have, dear," said innocent Candace. "I did."

ENVY

There's nothing wrong with wanting to be the best. And if you are the best, there's nothing wrong with wanting to stay the best. That's a noble aspiration— the drive for excellence. Of course, while you're trying to make it, there's sure to be some rotten old fossil squatting on the accolade and refusing to vacate. And if you happen to be on top, there's invariably some rotten young punk trying to push you aside. It's no wonder you can be driven to any deed by ENVY.

THE
INVISIBLE MAN
MURDER CASE

HENRY SLESAR

When you come right down to it, I'm a pretty nice guy. I'm not so homely that you couldn't face me across a luncheon table, and not so handsome that you wouldn't mind bringing your girl along. I make pleasant small talk, and know how to listen sympathetically. I'm relatively modest about my accomplishments, even if I am a sort of celebrity (my last book sold one million four hundred thousand copies in the paperback edition). So, being fully aware of the general niceness of me, Jeff Oswald, it came as a rude shock to realize that there was somebody in this world who hated my guts. Someone who despised me.

I got my first hint of this alarming fact when the Mystery Authors Association extended me an invitation to take their podium for half an hour. It was a big moment for me, being asked to speak before such an auspicious gathering. I had just published my first novel (*Kill Me Quietly,* Wharton Publishers, $2.95) and the ink hadn't dried on my second contract. As you might know, the book became something of an instantaneous best-seller, and there was a public clamor for further adventures of my private-eye hero, Rufe Armlock. Always alert to public demand, I've since responded with nine more novels, each slightly gorier (and more successful) than the last.

Anyway, the MAA slipped me a nice note, asking me to lecture, and I willingly obliged. I don't believe my speech

71

made any great impression, but I think the membership was amused to get a look at me. After reading about Rufe Armlock, they must have expected something different. *(His face was like a granite slab, chiseled on by a bad sculptor. His shoulders were too wide for most doorways. When he smiled, he could chill a hood's blood or boil a woman's.)* Actually, my face is more the kind you see in graduation-class photos, the big-eared kid in the back row with the pink cheeks and silly grin. I guess I didn't look like the author of *Kill Me Quietly* at all.

It was after the lecture that I met the man who hated me. I didn't realize the enmity at first; I was too flattered just to be introduced to Kirk Evander. Evander had been a kind of hero of my childhood, when I discovered his intricate detective novels after exhausting the output of Conan Doyle, S. S. Van Dine, John Dickson Carr, Ellery Queen, and the rest. Once I had thought that an Evander novel was the epitome of the classic mystery yarn, but his most recent efforts hadn't held the old magic. He was past sixty now; he was beginning to plagiarize himself.

"Gee, Mr. Evander," I said, in a voice that sounded boyish to my own ears, "this is a great pleasure for me."

He was a small, wispy man with mournful features, but there was a lot of incandescence in his eyes and he shook hands as if we were trading fish.

"Thank you," he said dryly. "This book of yours, Mr. Oswald. Did you say it was called *Kill Me Quickly?*"

"Quietly," I corrected. "I'm afraid it's one of these hardboiled novels, Mr. Evander. Nothing like the things you write."

"I imagine not." He pursed his lips. "And do you seriously classify this work as a mystery?"

"I don't classify it at all. You see, I have this private-detective character called Rufe Armlock. He's a sort of tough—"

"Spare me," Evander said, shutting his eyes. "I've heard quite enough about private detectives, Mr. Oswald. The occupation has been an excuse for the worst offenses against good taste that I have ever known. You will pardon me if I am *not* amused."

I admit I was disappointed. Not because Evander didn't like my book; I expected that. But my picture of the author was shattered by meeting him. He looked like a dissipated college professor, and talked like a refugee from a bad English play. I shifted uncomfortably, and began to eye the crowd in search of interesting females.

But Evander wasn't through with me yet.

"Do you know something, Mr. Oswald? Young men like yourself, with their Freudian nightmares translated into violent images of 'private eyes' and 'naked blondes' and assorted cruelties, are primarily responsible for the decline of the detective story."

"Gee, I'm sorry, Mr. Evander—"

"Sorry? If you were truly sorry, Mr. Oswald, you would do the world a favor. You would chop off your hands before they ever touched a typewriter again. Or, if that cure seems too drastic, you would burn every manuscript you write before the world ever sees it."

I still didn't get upset. I told you I was nice.

"Well, Mr. Evander, I don't think I could do that. You see, I write for money."

"Why?"

"To eat, I guess."

"Why?"

I began to get the idea that Mr. Evander wasn't partial to me. I took the hint and wandered off in search of the beforementioned females. Luckily, I found one. Her name was Eileen, and she turned out to be an admirer of mine. It was nice to talk to her, especially since she was a lot prettier than Kirk Evander. After the meeting, we went to her apartment in Greenwich Village. Eileen was an Associate Member of the Mystery Authors, which meant she hadn't sold anything yet. She read me the first chapter of a suspense novel called *Black Night at Bennington*. It was terrible. Unfortunately, I said so, and the evening ended badly.

* * *

It was almost six months before I saw Kirk Evander again, and by that time, my second novel *(A Fistful of Blood)* had become the best-selling paperback on the stands. I went to another MAA meeting, with the vague hope of running into Eileen again. I had already forgotten Evander's acid comments, and even if I hadn't, I was too swelled with my own success to let them worry me. When I saw the little guy, looking as if he had worn the same rumpled suit from the last meeting to this, I greeted him cheerfully.

"How's everything?" I asked. "Got a new book on the fire, Mr. Evander?"

The man standing next to the writer, a snooty-looking guy that worked for Wharton Publishing, the outfit that produced my books and Evander's, coughed and moved away. Evander turned on me and smiled without humor.

"My new book," he said bitingly, "is, indeed, on the fire. As I'm sure you've heard."

I batted my eyes. "Huh?"

"It seems the public doesn't want crime literature any more. It wants filth. It wants garbage! Unfortunately, there are people like you, Mr. Oswald, to provide it in ready supply."

He whirled on his heel and stalked away. Just then, Eileen appeared out of the crowd and pulled me to one side.

"For heavens' sake!" she said, tapping her foot. "Are you still shooting off your mouth, Jeff Oswald?"

"Gosh, it's nice to see you again, Eileen." It *was* nice. She was a remarkably pretty girl, with Oriental eyes and auburn hair.

"I guess you'll never learn," she sighed. "Why must you be so tactless?"

I shifted my feet guiltily. "I'm sorry about that. I wouldn't have told you that about your novel, but you *begged* me for an honest opinion—"

"I don't mean that. I mean Kirk Evander. Didn't you know about his last book?"

"No."

"Well, it was the flop of the year. He considered it his masterpiece, but the reviewers called it a pompous bore. One of these real period pieces. A locked-room murder in the family mansion, with millions of obscure clues."

"Gee, that's too bad. I used to admire that guy."

"He's nothing but an old fool. And maybe something else..." She looked into the crowd thoughtfully. Then she bit her lip, and added: "And how he hates *you.*"

"Hates me?"

"I've heard him carry on about you in other meetings. He thinks you're the sole reason for his failure. He practically has a stroke when your name is mentioned."

"Gosh! I hardly even know the guy."

"That doesn't matter. You're some kind of symbol to him. All the hate that's been building up in him for the last few years—he's directing it at you."

I frowned. I didn't like being hated.

"Ah, the heck with it," I said, trying to be bright. "You and me need a drink."

"You and *I,*" she said primly. "Some writer you are."

So we had a drink. As a matter of fact, we had several. That was my mistake.

Around eleven o'clock, I was carrying seven or eight martinis in my pouch, and my head felt like a sputnik, revolving slowly around the meeting room. I wasn't used to so much alcohol, even if my hero, Rufe Armlock, was. (*He cracked the cap on a bottle of bourbon and tilted the neck into his mouth. He didn't lower it until the brown stuff was below the plimsoll line, but when he put it down, his steely eyes hadn't changed in focus or alertness.*) As a matter of fact, I was pie-eyed, and saying a lot of stupid things. Like telling Kirk Evander just what I thought of him and his "classic" detective novels.

"You're a bore," I said, poking a finger into his chest. "Thash what you are. A bore. And you know what your novels are? Impopable. I mean *improbable.* All those locked-room murders and junk like that. That kind of thing never happens. Never!"

Evander remained calm while I lectured him. But out of my drunken fog, his eyes shone like yellow lanterns.

"Never happens," I said again. "People don't get bumped off that way. Unnerstand, Mister Evander?"

"Of course," he said bowing slightly. "Thank you for the opinion, Mr. Oswald."

"S'all right," I grinned. "Nice to help. You jus' listen to ol' Rufe Armlock. I mean Jeff Oswald. The public does not *believe* that stuff any more. They want *action*. Not that ol' locked-room junk. Unnerstand?"

"Perfectly," Kirk Evander told me.

By this time, Eileen had the good sense to pull me away. She coaxed me out of the meeting hall and took me to her apartment, where I made one slobbering attempt to kiss her. It failed miserably, and she thrust me out the door like a cat. Somehow, I got myself home.

In the morning, an air-raid siren woke me up. After a while, I realized it was only the doorbell. I got up and let my visitor in. It was Aaron Snow, my agent.

"What's the matter with *you?*" he said.

"What time's it?" I groaned.

"Three." Aaron frowned at me, in his fatherly way. He was a year older and fifty years wiser, and he looked like an aging quiz kid. "I've been trying to reach you, but your phone's off the hook. I wanted to report on that Wharton meeting this morning."

"What meeting?"

"I guess you didn't know. Kirk Evander stormed in there this morning, and gave 'em an ultimatum. Either they strike you from their list, or him."

"What?"

"That's the truth. He must have been crazy to do it; his last book sold about eight hundred copies, and I suspect he bought 'em all himself. He should have known they wouldn't drop a hot-rock like you."

"So what happened?"

"They tried to placate him, of course. He was once important to their Mystery Division. And who knows? He might come through with a big book yet. But Evander stood his ground. Either you go—or he does."

"What did Wharton say?"

"What could they say? They simply refused to accept. He stormed out again, promising never to darken their door." Aaron sighed. "Feel sorry for the old guy. He was really a great writer. He'll never get lined up with a first-grade publisher now."

"Gee, that's rough."

"Don't let it worry you. Just concentrate on that next opus of yours. Got a title yet?"

"Yeah, tentatively. *To Kiss A Corpse.* Like it?"

Aaron grimaced. "No. That must mean it's good."

It took me four months to reach the last chapter of that novel. One night, hammering away on my old Remington, the doorbell sounded. I cursed at the interruption, because I had just reached a very crucial moment. *(She swayed toward him, her arms reaching out for the unfinished caress, the shreds of her clothing waving in the breeze from the opened window. But Rufe Armlock wasn't interested; he raised the automatic in his hand and tenderly squeezed the trigger. The bullet ripped into her soft white—)*

"All right, all right!" I shouted, as the ringing persisted.

I flung open the door, and there was Kirk Evander.

For a moment, I was frightened. To tell you the truth, I scare easily. Even the stories I write sort of scare me sometimes, and the realization that my visitor was a man who hated me intensely was disturbing.

But he was smiling.

"Good evening," he said cordially. "I wonder if I could come in, Mr. Oswald?"

"Sure," I gulped.

When he got inside, he took off his shabby homburg and peeled off a pair of gray suede gloves. There was a large hole in the right index finger.

"I hope you'll pardon this intrusion. But I discovered something very interesting in the evening paper, and I thought you'd like to see it."

I blinked at him.

"It relates to our conversation at the MAA meeting,"

Evander said sweetly. "I believe you made certain statements, about the type of crimes I write about. You said they
were—improbable."

"Listen, Mr. Evander, I'm sorry if—"

"No, no," he said quickly, lifting his hand. "I quite understand. But I knew you would be as intrigued as I was—
to read this."

He handed me a newspaper clipping. I took it to the desk
lamp and read:

PUBLISHER'S AIDE
KILLED IN LOCKED
HOTEL ROOM

INEXPLICABLE MURDER
BAFFLES POLICE

March 12, New York. A murder mystery straight
out of a Kirk Evander novel took place last night
at the Hotel Belmartin, where Winston Kale, 46,
publisher's assistant, met his death under mysterious circumstances. Mr. Kale, an employee of
the Wharton Publishing Company, whose spe-
cialty is mystery novels, was shot and killed in
a room securely locked and bolted from the inside.

The unusual nature of the crime was noted by
the police when they were called to the scene by
Zora Brewster, 24, a friend of the deceased. Miss
Brewster claimed that she had left Mr. Kale's
hotel-apartment at one, leaving him in "good
spirits." When she closed the door behind her, she
heard Mr. Kale lock and bolt the door. As she was
waiting outside for the elevator, she heard a shot,
and rushed back to the door. When Mr. Kale
failed to respond, she called the police. Mr. Kale's
body was discovered on the floor, a bullet having
penetrated the back of his head, causing instan-
taneous death. Upon examination of the room,

the police could find no trace of any intruder or weapon. The room was located on the nineteenth floor of the residential hotel, and the windows were locked.

In an interview with Captain William Spencer, Homicide Detail, the police official stated: "The circumstances of Mr. Kale's death are certainly unusual, but we are confident that a logical explanation will be found. We have ruled out suicide completely, due to the direction of the bullet and the lack of any weapon."

Miss Brewster, an actress and singer, is being held as a material witness.

I looked up from the clipping with astonishment evident in my face, because Evander chuckled and said:

"An 'improbable' murder, wouldn't you say, Mr. Oswald?"

"Gosh," I said. "Winston Kale! I saw him only last week—"

"The poor man," Evander clucked. "But if he had to die, what a delicious way to do it. I'm sure the Wharton Publishing Company is pleased by the publicity."

I realized that Wharton wasn't the only one pleased. Kirk Evander's glowing eyes indicated that he was pretty happy himself. The news story was practically an advertisement for his novels. It was a natural promotion gimmick.

"What about this girl?" I said. "Zora Brewster. Maybe she's the one."

"Nonsense. Miss Brewster is an old—er—acquaintance of mine. She's charming and harmless, and her brain compares in size to a pea. She wouldn't have either motive or intellect to commit such a crime."

I decided to be a good sport. I grinned.

"Well, I guess you made your point, Mr. Evander. Guess there *are* improbable crimes. Too bad about old Winston, though."

"Bah. Winston Kale's not worth mourning. He was a sycophant, a yes-man for Douglas Wharton."

I scratched my head and studied the item again.

"But how was it done? You've had experience with this kind of thing, Mr. Evander. In your novels, I mean. How could he get killed in a locked room?"

"That," and Kirk Evander smiled, "is a story I just might reveal. In my next novel, for Gorgon Press. I've just signed a contract with them, for a book to be called *Death of a Publisher*. I imagine this publicity won't harm sales, eh? Good night, Mr. Oswald!"

He picked up his hat and gloves, and left with an air of triumph.

I couldn't get back to work after that visit. I felt as I had when I was a kid, puzzling over a John Dickson Carr or Kirk Evander murder mystery, trying to solve it before the author's revelation on page umptieth. But the fact that this murder was *real*, and that I actually knew the dead man, made it too upsetting for logical thought. It could have been coincidental, but that seemed as improbable as the fact that such a crime had actually taken place.

And then an even more disturbing idea intruded. The mysterious death of Winston Kale had come along as a stroke of luck for Kirk Evander. People would be talking about "locked-room" murders again, and that meant talk about Kirk Evander fiction. It seemed awfully convenient.

Was it maybe *too* convenient?

I gave a shiver, and tried to warm myself over the typewriter.

A few weeks later, I learned that I was right about one thing, and wrong about another. People talked about the locked-room murder, all right, and Gorgon Press announced the new Kirk Evander novel with appropriate fanfare. But the publicity didn't last. The newspapers got awfully quiet about the strange death of Winston Kale, and people started to forget.

Then they were sharply reminded.

Late one morning, I opened the newspaper and saw a front-page bulletin:

ACTRESS KILLED ON STAGE; POLICE BAFFLED BY "IMPOSSIBLE" CRIME

CHIEF WITNESS IN KALE MURDER STABBED DURING PERFORMANCE

April 7, New York. Zora Brewster, attractive songstress in the Broadway production of "Live It Up," was killed last night in circumstances as unusual as the death of Winston Kale on March 11.

Miss Brewster, chief witness to the "locked-room" murder of the publishing-company executive, suddenly collapsed on stage during a musical number and was taken to her dressing room. It was later revealed that she had been stabbed to death by a blow from behind. However, Miss Brewster was the only performer on the stage of the theater at the time...

The article went on for considerable more lineage, and once more the death of Winston Kale came in for examination. Kirk Evander's name was mentioned three times, and his new novel, *Death of a Publisher,* was also cited. It was great publicity, all right.

Too great.

The thought that had troubled me some weeks ago came back. It was all too pat. Evander knew both Kale and Zora Brewster; he might not have liked either one too much. More importantly, they may have been natural victims of some nutty scheme to revive interest in the "classic" detective yarn.

"No," I said aloud. "That's crazy! He wouldn't do such a thing—"

Then I remembered Kirk Evander's eyes, and I began to wonder if he was more than just an embittered author. Maybe he was a mental case, a desperate man.

If anybody could concoct such murders, Evander was the one. He'd spent his whole life thinking about them.

And what if Zora Brewster's death wasn't the last? What if the murders went on, maintaining interest in Kirk Evander's books? All he had to do was keep knocking off people he didn't like, in some inexplicable manner...

People he didn't like?

I swallowed the boulder that had lodged in my throat.

If Evander killed the people he didn't like—who was a better choice than Mrs. Oswald's son, Jeff?

My hand was shaking like a bongo-player's, but I got it steady enough to pick up a phone.

Aaron Snow's voice had a nice quality of gruff reality.

"I think you're nuts," he said, when I babbled out my suspicions. "But if it's going to worry you, why not get in touch with Captain Spencer, the detective on the case? At this point, I think he'd be happy to listen to *any* theory."

"Then you really think I should?"

"Sure. It's about time you met a *real* detective, anyway."

I was too nervous to take offense. I hung up the phone, squared my shoulders, and called police headquarters.

I got even more rattled when I met Captain Bill Spencer. I mean, it was a shock. He was a great big guy, with shoulders almost too wide for my apartment door. He had a strong, rugged face, like chiseled granite. He was practically a double for Rufe Armlock.

"Okay," Spencer frowned, taking a seat. "Let's get down to business, Mr. Oswald. And do me one favor."

"What's that?"

"Stick to the facts. I'm not fond of fiction; particularly your kind."

"You've read my novels?"

"If you want literary criticism, Mr. Oswald, you called the wrong guy. All I'm interested in is murder. Real murder."

"That's what I wanted to talk to you about," I said eagerly. "I've got an idea about these two crimes, and I think it makes sense."

"I'm listening," Captain Spencer said.

He leaned back and lit a cigarette while I talked. I told him everything right from the beginning. I told him about Evander and his hatred for me, and how he bemoaned the decline of the classic detective story. I told him about his fight with Wharton Publishers, and how he knew the girl, Zora Brewster. I told him all I could think of, without putting my theory into a single crisp sentence.

He finally forced me into it.

Spencer said: "Let's get it straight, Mr. Oswald. Are you making an accusation?"

I blinked.

"I guess I am," I said. "I don't have any proof, of course. But I think Kirk Evander killed them both. He had plenty of motive."

"And did you also figure out how?"

"No. But if anybody could, Evander could. His own books prove it."

The captain stood up.

"Well, it's an interesting theory, Mr. Oswald..."

"But you don't believe it?"

"As a matter of fact, I think you may be right. I'll follow it up at once."

I couldn't help looking surprised.

Spencer scowled. "I know what you're thinking. You've read so many novels, you always think the cops never listen to anybody, and go blundering ahead on their own. Well, you're wrong. Some of our best leads come from outside. I happen to believe your theory's a damn good one."

And he went out.

I have to admit I was flabbergasted. I *had* expected Spencer to scoff at my idea; I thought the cops always did. They sure did it in Rufe Armlock novels.

About three days later, I learned that Captain Spencer had acted swiftly.

I was hunched over the typewriter, trying to get Rufe into trouble, when I heard the pounding on the door. It was Kirk Evander, and he was too angry to use the doorbell. He burst into the room like a small tweedy cyclone and said:

"So! I meet my accuser face to face!"

"I don't understand—"

"You don't, eh? Then you deny it? You deny that you accused me of murder? That you were responsible for having me dragged into the dirty hands of the police, like some common hoodlum?"

I didn't know what to say. I would have gladly invented a lie, but I couldn't think of one.

"You thought I wouldn't realize, eh? But I know it was you, Oswald. You couldn't *bear* the fact of my success, could you? So you resort to *this!*"

"Look, Mr. Evander, I'm sorry if—"

"I don't want your apologies!"

He went to the door, but turned before going out.

"All I have to say is this, Mr. Oswald. *Be careful.*"

He laughed, and shut the door.

Well, let me tell you, I was scared. Evander hadn't actually *denied* anything, and his last words sounded like a pure and simple threat.

Even though it was only eight-thirty, I decided that the best place for me was in bed and under the covers.

I couldn't fall asleep until an hour later, and then my dreams weren't the kind I liked to dream.

About ten-fifteen, I thought I heard a sound outside. It might have been a knock on the door, so I padded out of the bedroom and opened the front door. There was nothing there but a breeze, so I went back to my comforter.

A few minutes later, I was in the middle of a dream involving a guillotine. I didn't care for it. I forced myself awake, but when I opened my eyes, I saw that the shreds of the dream were still clinging. There was a shining blade over my head.

"Go 'way," I murmured.

But the blade didn't go away. It started descending. Only now it wasn't a guillotine blade any more; it was a meat chopper, and it seemed interested in the white meat on my neck.

I froze on the bed.

Then the doorbell rang, and just as suddenly, the meat cleaver disappeared out of sight.

I sat up and rubbed my eyes. It *had* been a dream, then. But what a dream.

I opened the door and there was Eileen, tapping her foot.

"Well," she said. "Is that how you usually dress for a night out?"

"Huh?" I looked down at my pajamas.

"It's rather unusual, but you might start a fad. Or did you just forget about our date?"

I slapped my forehead. "Holy cow! I was supposed to meet you at ten. I forgot—"

"I suppose you were keeping a date with dear old Rufe Armlock. Or was it one of those blonde beauties he's always shooting in their soft white—"

"Gosh, I'm sorry, Eileen, it slipped my mind completely. And for good reason, believe me."

I pulled her inside and made her sit down. She was pretty cool towards me, but when I told her about Evander's visit, she got all warm and solicitous.

"You poor thing," she said, patting my cheek. "No wonder you were upset."

I took advantage of her sympathetic attitude for a while, but half an hour later, the telephone's jangle cut off any further ministrations of mercy. I picked it up, and Spencer's rough voice said:

"Oswald? This is Captain Spencer. Thought you might like to know that there's been another murder."

I gasped. "Whose?" I said.

"That's the tough part. I decided tonight that we had enough of him to pull him in for serious questioning, so we dispatched a couple of men to bring him back. That's when we found him."

"Evander?"

"Dead, murdered, just like the others. Only maybe a little worse. Think maybe you ought to come down here."

"All right," I said, trying to stop my trembling. "Where are you?"

"At Evander's apartment, on Central Park South. Better get here before midnight."

"Right," I said.

Eileen insisted on coming down with me, but the police barricade that had been stationed outside Evander's apartment door declined to admit her. She waited outside while I walked in. Captain Spencer was standing by the body, and at first, all I could see was Kirk Evander's slippered feet.

"Just like the last time," Spencer said quietly. "Door was locked from the inside, and so were all the windows. But this is how we found him."

I looked down. Nobody had to tell me that Kirk Evander was dead.

His head was missing, neatly severed from his body.

I didn't get sick or anything. Not me. But when I got outside, *then* did I get sick! Boy!

As you might guess, the news of Evander's murder, the third such mysterious event in a period of less than three months, brought about a journalistic picnic. There wasn't exactly rejoicing in the streets, but in certain circles, like Gorgon Press, there were secret smiles of satisfaction. They knew that Evander's last book would be a best-seller, even before the galleys were made up.

Evander's earthly remains were put in the family vault by the author's only living relation, a brother named Borg Evander. This Borg was quite a character, too, and here's how I came to meet him.

About a week after the murder, my agent, Aaron Snow, showed up at my apartment, looking enthused. Aaron doesn't get enthused very often.

"Great idea," he said, tossing his hat on a chair. "I didn't think Wharton's publicity department had a good idea in them, but this time they came across."

"What are you talking about?"

"Take a look."

He pulled a mimeographed sheet from his pocket. I saw it was a standard news release, with the Wharton Publishing Company masthead. I'd seen them before, but this one made me sit up. The heading read:

MYSTERY AUTHOR VOWS
TO DISCOVER MURDERER
OF KIRK EVANDER

Jeff Oswald, author of *Kill Me Quietly, A Fist-ful of Blood,* and the forthcoming *To Kiss a Corpse* (Wharton Pub. Co.) has vowed to find the killer of his friend, Kirk Evander, the famed mystery novelist. Evander met his death in circumstances as strange as...

I stopped reading, and said:

"This is screwy!"

"No, it isn't. It's a real sweet publicity idea. I know you don't like that 'friendship' bit, but it was necessary."

"That's not what I mean. How can I solve these murders? Even the police don't know where to start. I couldn't possibly—"

"You can make a try, just for appearance's sake. Nobody will blame you if you fail."

"But we're doing all right without phony stunts—"

"We want it to continue, don't we? The public's fickle. Look at the way Kirk Evander's old novels are selling; you couldn't give 'em away six months ago. They could forget about Rufe Armlock in an awful hurry."

"But how do I go about it?"

"Well, you know Captain Spencer pretty well. He can supply you with information. And you can pay a call on Borg Evander, for instance."

"Borg Evander? Who's that?"

"Kirk's brother, who showed up when he was killed. He might know something. Look, I even brought you his address." He dug into his wallet for a scrap of paper. "Dr. Borg Evander, 80 Wiffletree Road, Queens..."

"All right," I said glumly. "If I have to."

"You have to. Especially since I okayed the release this morning."

"You mean the papers will be printing this thing?"

"I hope so."

"But then—what if the murderer sees it? What if he thinks I really *know* something?"

"You're not scared, are you?"

"Who, me? Of course."

The next morning was bright and clear, and the sunshine helped dispel some of the murkiness that surrounded my errand. I went to pay a call on Borg Evander, who lived in a section of town I knew nothing about. After wandering about the streets, I finally found the old wood-frame house at the end of the unpaved street. It was isolated from the rest of the structures on the avenue, and from the moment I walked up to the front door, I knew it was just as well. The place smelled bad.

I rang the doorbell, but heard no sound. Instead, a panel in the door slid open noiselessly, and a light shone in my eyes. I blinked, and swore I saw a lens staring at me. Then the panel slid shut hastily, and a voice said:

"Please state your name and business."

I did, and the door opened. I started to say how-do-you-do to the man behind it, but there wasn't any man. As the door shut behind me, I got the idea that Dr. Borg Evander was one of these gadgeteers.

"Enter the door at the end of the hallway," the voice said.

I obeyed the instruction, but I gasped when I opened the door. There was nothing but air behind it, and a railed platform some four feet square.

"Please step on the platform," the voice told me.

I stepped on. A motor whined, and the platform descended. It took me down about fifteen feet, to the floor of what was obviously a basement laboratory, crowded with scientific paraphernalia. It all looked very imposing and professional, but I couldn't tell if the junk scattered around the place was intended to locate a cure for warts or repair television sets. My host was nowhere in sight.

Then, out of a partitioned area at the end of the basement, out he came. He looked a lot like Kirk Evander, but he was easily five years older. He didn't have Kirk's hot-lamped eyes, either. They were brown and soft.

"I hope you don't mind the elevator," he said gently. "I detest stairs. And my heart—"

"I understand. I—er—gather you're some kind of scientist, Dr. Evander?"

"Ah," was all he said.

"Dr. Evander, I thought maybe you could help me. You see, your brother was a close friend of mine, and I'm interested in uncovering his murderer. I thought if we had a little talk—"

"But I've already spoken to the police," he said, looking bewildered.

"And what did you tell them?"

"Very little, I'm afraid. I hadn't seen Kirk for almost eight years, until he showed up a few months ago. He was always rather distant towards me....Then, when I learned of his death, I came forward to claim his body. That's really all I know."

It was a disappointment, but out of politeness, I chatted a few minutes longer. I was just about ready to leave when he said:

"Would you care to look around? I've been working on several fascinating experiments. The police didn't seem very interested, but you, a writer—"

"Well," I said, looking at my watch.

"It won't take very long. I don't see people very often, Mr. Oswald. I suppose they consider me—odd."

"I wouldn't say that, doctor. But you'll have to admit. That odor—"

"Odor? What odor?"

"Well, frankly, Dr. Evander, there's a smell in this house that's a little hard to take."

"Oh, dear." He put a finger on his mouth. "It's been here so long I've become immune. It's the acaphenimatin compound, probably, a new kind of plant food I'm working on. Or perhaps you're smelling the sulfaborgonium." He lowered his eyes shyly. "A chemical I have named after myself; a scientist's vanity. It has a pungent odor, but only in formulation. I suppose I *could* stop making it, since it doesn't seem to have any practical application."

"Well," I laughed feebly, "it sure stinks, don't it?"

"Yes," he answered vaguely. "Kirk used just that word. Yet he seemed infinitely more interested in the sulfaborgonium than any of my experiemnts."

I perked up at that.

"Kirk was interested? Why?"

"I really don't know. He seemed utterly fascinated by its properties. As a matter of fact, he suggested a splendid use for it, if I could manufacture it in sufficient quantities. But that would be most impractical. The distillation process requires months, and produces only the smallest quantities from an exorbitant amount of raw materials."

"What use did he suggest?"

"Oh, an esthetic one. Kirk was always the esthete of the family. He thought that the unsightly portions of public structures might be painted with the chemical. Bridges and things. In order to make them more attractive."

"I don't think I understand."

"Well, since sulfaborgonium is an anti-pigment and a total barrier of light rays, it would naturally render these ugly portions invisible. However, I don't think—"

"Wait a minute. Would you go around that corner again, doctor?"

"I beg your pardon?"

"Did you use the word *invisible?*"

"Yes, of course. Once transmuted into chemical form, sulfaborgonium becomes a soluble fat, with a consistency of a— well, a facial cream, for instance." He chuckled impetuously. "Yes, Kirk was very amusing about that. He called it Vanishing Cream."

I was staring at the doctor until my eyes were hurting.

"Go on," I said. "Tell me more."

"Well, because of its resistance to pigmentation, and its complete barrierization of light, the chemical renders anything it covers invisible. If I didn't stain it with methyl blue, I wouldn't be able to find it myself." He chuckled again.

My head was swimming, and I wasn't sure if it was the odor or the wild words of Dr. Evander.

"Let me get this straight. If you spread this stuff on something, that something can't be seen?"

"Exactly."

"Anything?"

"Oh, yes."

"Even a human being?"

The doctor looked puzzled.

"I suppose so. But why would anybody want to be invisible?"

"Dr. Evander," I said, licking my lips, "you mean to say you can't think of a single, solitary reason why somebody would want to be invisible? Have you ever heard of H. G. Wells? Have you ever been to the movies? Have you ever—" He wasn't reacting, so I put it more simply. "Criminals, doctor! Just think about what an invisible criminal can accomplish! Or a spy! An army, doctor! Think of how many battles you could win with an invisible army! A plane, a tank, a ship—imagine those invisible! Big things, little things. Good men, bad men! A general or a peeping Tom or a detective..."

"I never thought of it that way," Dr. Evander murmured. "But now that you put it into words..." His face suddenly had more wrinkles than before. "But most of the things you mentioned are terrible things. Evil things—"

"That's right," I said grimly. "Take murder, for example. It would be pretty easy to kill somebody, and not get detected—if you were invisible. In a locked room for instance. All you have to do is walk in and kill somebody, then lock all the doors and windows. When the police finally break in, you walk out. Or on a stage, in front of thousands of witnesses—you could kill someone without the fear of being detected. The perfect crime."

"How awful!"

"I think your brother might have realized these potentials, doctor. I'm not saying he used your chemical to commit the murders which took place. He might have made it available to someone else, however. And that someone may be responsible for all the deaths—including the death of Kirk Evander. And he's free to kill again."

"It can't be true!"

"It must be true, doctor. If this stuff can do what you say—"

Something was making my ankle itch. I reached down and scratched it. My hand touched something furry.

"What the hell," I said.

"Oh," Doctor Borg said, seeing my expression. "That must be Socrates."

He reached down and picked up an armful of nothing. Then he stroked the nothing tenderly.

"What are you doing?" I said.

"It's Socrates, my cat. I rubbed the sulfaborgonium on her last week, as an experiment. To see if the substance was harmful to animals. But she appears to be perfectly all right."

I put my hand out, gingerly.

Socrates was fine. When I pulled my hand away, there were three thin scratches on the skin.

When I got home, I sat down and stared at the typewriter and talked to it like an old friend.

"What would Rufe Armlock do in a case like this?" I said.

The Remington didn't answer, but the thought of Rufe Armlock conjured up another image. Why not go right to Captain Spencer, and tell him the story? It was simple and it was direct, so that's what I did.

"Oh, no," he said. "No, no, no."

"What do you mean, no?"

"I mean no, and that's all I mean. I appreciate your ideas, Mr. Oswald, don't misunderstand. But now you've gotten into fantasy—"

"But what if I could *prove* the story? What if I prove this sulfaborgonium stuff exists?"

"Can you?"

"I wanted to bring you a sample. That's one of the first things I asked Dr. Evander, but he said it was all gone. The last drop went on his cat. But it's my theory that either Kirk Evander or an accomplice swiped some."

"Then you can't really *show* me this sulfawhatever-you-call it? You only have his word for it?"

"But there's the *cat*," I said anxiously. "The cat itself is proof that things can be made invisible. Animals. People!"

"And you seriously think that an invisible man is walking around this minute, bumping off people?"

"I do!"

He screwed up his face and rapped his desk.

"All right. You bring me the cat. Then I'll follow through."

"Right. I'll see Dr. Evander again tomorrow morning, and I'll produce Socrates. Then I'll leave it up to you to find this invisible murderer. I don't envy you the job."

I saw Eileen that evening, and despite the fact that I wanted to keep my discovery quiet, I couldn't help shooting off my mouth. That's a problem of mine.

She listened to me in evident amazement, and then she said something that had us both unnerved.

"But Jeff! If this killer's invisible, then he could be any place. He could be right in this room!"

We both looked around, wide-eyed. Then I took an umbrella from the rack and started to parry it around the room. Eileen did the same, with a rolled-up magazine. It became a kind of crazy game after a while, and we both started to giggle. Pretty soon we were laughing hysterically, poking into the closets and under the chairs and out the window, and we finally collapsed in helpless mirth, hugging each other like a couple of nutty kids. It wasn't the most romantic moment of our lives, but for some reason it seemed right. We got pretty silly and tender for a few minutes, and when we got up off the floor, we were engaged to be married. Funny how a thing like that happens, but that's the way it was with us.

We didn't discuss the invisible murderer much after that. We had too much else to talk about.

In the morning, I took the subway out to Queens and whistled merrily all the way. The world seemed like a pretty nice place, even underground.

But when I rang the front doorbell of Dr. Borg Evander's house, the little panel in the door didn't slide back, and the television lens didn't pop out to examine me. There was no response at all.

I rattled the knob, but the door was locked.

After five minutes of useless pounding, I went around to the other side of the house and tried to find another method of entry. There wasn't any. The back door was bolted, and all the windows were tightly shut.

I didn't have any reason to get panicky. I hadn't told the doctor of my intentions to return. He could have been out. And it was only natural for someone to lock up their house when they left it.

Still, I didn't like it.

There was a luncheon counter at the northwest corner. I went there in the hope of finding a telephone booth; I found one. But the call I placed to the doctor's home wasn't answered. I came out and spoke to the counterman. He said:

"Old Doc Evander? Why, he must be home. Never known the Doc to leave that nutty house of his. Has everything delivered. Regular hermit."

That settled it. I went back to the Evander house and began to pound on the front door. I almost busted my shoulder doing it, but I finally snapped whatever screwy kind of electronic lock held it closed. When it swung open, a bell began clanging a warning throughout the house, but I didn't pay it any attention. I took the elevator platform down to the basement.

Of course, my suspicions had been right. The old man was spread-eagled on the stone floor, and the man who had wanted him dead didn't care about being neat. His head had been struck several times with something blunt and hard, and the result was sickening.

I called the police, and then roamed the house, calling out:

"Here, kitty, kitty, kitty. Here, Socrates. Here kitty, kitty..."

But I knew it was useless. The invisible killer had been thorough, and now every speck of evidence was gone.

I won't say that Captain Spencer completely disbelieved my story. After the murder of Borg Evander, it almost seemed like corroboration. But he was a practical man, too, and he knew that my fantastic explanation for the murders—without tangible evidence—would only produce raised eyebrows and embarrassed coughs if he proposed the theory himself. It was all right for me to suggest the explanation—I was a fiction writer. But he was a detective of homicide, and his stock-in-trade was fact.

So the theory remained private, among Captain Bill Spencer and myself and the girl I wanted to marry.

It might have stayed that way forever, if Douglas Wharton, president of the publishing company, hadn't gone loony.

Now, Douglas Wharton is kind of legendary figure in publishing. As a young man, running a hand-press in the back of a stationery shop, he had established a distinguished reputation for integrity and daring. His company was one of the first to recognize the growing American hunger for mystery stories, and he also published one of the first regular series of science-fiction novels. He established the Wharton Fellowships for new authors in both fields, the first of their kind. He was one of the first truly cooperative publishers in the history of the various author's leagues.

He was in his sixties when I joined the list of the Wharton Publishing Company, but you'll rarely see a better-looking or more vigorous man of forty. He was a tall, slim guy, with movie-actor distinction in his handsome features and graying temples. He looked like a retired British major, but he could talk like a retired U. S. Army First Sergeant.

I liked Douglas Wharton. So I wasn't happy to hear the rumors about him shifting his trolley.

I asked Aaron Snow about it one day.

"Seems to be some truth in it," he said gravely. "The old man's been acting pretty jumpy lately, and saying a lot of queer things. His friends have been trying to get him to take a vacation, but he won't hear of it."

"What's the matter with him?"

Aaron shrugged. "I'm no psychiatrist. But from what I hear, he's seeing things. Things nobody else sees. Hearing them, too. He gets mad as hell when the people around him deny it. Like last week..."

"What happened?"

"The way I get the story, there was a board meeting of the editors. Company policy, stuff like that. The Mystery Book Editor was making a report, when Wharton suddenly starts to curse—and if you've ever heard Doug Wharton curse, you know how fluent he can be. Everybody looks at him, and he accuses the man next to him of tickling his ankle."

"What?"

"That's right," Aaron said sadly. "Raised hell about it. Swore up and down that his ankle was being tickled. The man next to him was Bosley Morse, Senior Editor of the Classical Department. White hair and whiskers, you know the guy, looks like Walt Whitman. Last guy in the world you'd accuse of tickling your ankle. But that's what Wharton claimed."

I whistled.

"Gee, that's tough. Fine man like that."

"Yeah, it's a shame, all right. Of course, he absolutely refuses to get medical attention. Some of his friends tried sneaking a headshrinker in to see him, pretending it was a social call. But Doug was too smart for 'em. Ticked off the doctor immediately, and threw him out of his house."

Maybe you can guess what I was thinking.

"Listen, Aaron," I said. "Can you get me an appointment to see Wharton?"

"What?"

"I'd like to see him. I only met him once, when we were signing the contracts. Maybe you could fix up a lunch date or something."

"What for?"

"I've got an idea. It's a nutty idea, but then most of my ideas are. I'd just like to *see* the man before I do anything about it."

"Well, if that's what you really want. I suppose I can arrange it through the Mystery Editor." He narrowed his eyes shrewdly. "You got something up your sleeve, Jeff?"

"Who, me?" I said innocently.

But when I left Aaron, I knew I did have something up

my sleeve. I had an invisible man, who had killed three people and a cat, and who just might be after a fifth victim—in a slightly different manner.

Aaron went to work quickly to make the arrangements. There was only one snag. Since his "trouble" had started, Douglas Wharton had stopped dining out at lunch time, and confined his noontime meal to a sandwich in the office. However, he didn't mind my joining him.

I kept the appointment promptly at twelve, walking through the impressive oak-rimmed doorway of the presidential office. Wharton was at his desk, looking older and more tired than I remembered him, but his smile was wide and cordial when he greeted me.

"Sit down, Jeff," he invited. "My secretary will bring the lunch in a few minutes. Ordered you a steak sandwich. Okay?"

"Suits me fine," I said.

"How's everything going? You must be working on novel number four now, eh?"

"That's right. It's called *The Noose Hangs High*."

"Well, if it's as successful as the others, we both won't have any cause for complaint. That's quite a character you've got there, that Rufe Armlock."

"Yes, sir. Sometimes I wish he really existed."

He looked up at me sharply. "Why?"

"Oh, I dunno. He just never seems to have any trouble. If there's a case to be solved, he just moves right in and solves it. You always know things'll come out all right in the end."

"Yes," Wharton sighed. "I see what you mean."

The lunch arrived, and we ate in silence for a few minutes. I kept watching Wharton's face, anxious to see if I could detect any signs of the looniness I'd been hearing about. He looked okay to me.

Then it happened.

We were sipping our coffee, and I was giving the president a rough outline of the plot of *The Noose Hangs High* when he seemed to stiffen and look past me towards the closed door. My blood went icy when I saw the change in him.

"What's wrong, Mr. Wharton?"

He continued to stare past me, and his lips were moving soundlessly.

"The knife..." he said hoarsely.

I whirled around, but there was nothing there. When I looked back at the publisher, his hands were covering his eyes.

"Mr. Wharton..."

"I'll be okay, Jeff. I'm sort of—tired."

"Mr. Wharton, you said something about a knife."

"It was nothing."

"Did you *see* a knife?"

"No, no..."

Then suddenly, shockingly, he was laughing, laughing wildly, uncontrollably, dancing and gyrating in the swivel chair.

"Mr. Wharton!" I shouted, standing up.

"Stop it, stop it!" He was shrieking in anguish, even as he laughed, and there were tears running down his cheeks.

"Mr. Wharton, are you all right?"

He stopped as quickly as he had started, and slumped exhausted over the desk blotter. I went to him, and he pointed feebly towards the pitcher of water. I poured him a glass and he drank it quickly, coughing.

"What is it?" I said. "What happened to you?"

He couldn't answer for a moment. Then the door of the office slammed shut violently, and he said:

"I was being tickled. So help me God, I was being tickled. It was horrible..."

It sounded funny. Tickling is a funny word. But I didn't feel funny. Only horrified.

"Has this happened before?"

"Yes, often. I don't know what's the matter with me. Maybe I'm afraid to find out. But first I *see* things...like a knife, floating in midair. Or something else. And then I know it's going to happen, then I know the tickling will start, that awful tickling..."

He broke down and sobbed. Like I said, he was a man in

his sixties, but he sounded like a heartbroken child, sobbing on the impressive desk in front of me.

"This is terrible," I said. "Don't you think you should get help, Mr. Wharton? A doctor?"

He looked up at me, trying to compose himself.

"I'll tell you the truth. I've seen a doctor, my own doctor. He knows of nothing organically wrong. I have a slight heart condition, but nothing major. His only suggestion was that my trouble was mental." His face hardened. "And I know that's not true. I *know* it. No matter what insane symptoms I have, I know that my mind is sound. I'm sure most people wouldn't believe that..."

"I believe it, Mr. Wharton."

"What?"

"I believe it. Because I think I know what's happening to you."

He stared at me, not sure what I meant.

"Mr. Wharton, will you let me tell you a story?" I said. "Not fiction, Mr. Wharton. What I believe is a true story."

He didn't reply, but I took his silence for an affirmative.

I told him the story of Zora Brewster, and the two Evanders. I told him about the missing cat, and the mysterious chemical called sulfaborgonium. I told him my theory about the invisble killer.

"I don't understand," he said, when I was through. "What does that have to do with me?"

"Just this, Mr. Wharton. I think this invisible madman's decided upon *you* as his next victim. Only now he's getting fancy. He must be bored with his old hit-and-run tactics. He wants something more—delicious. That's why he's doing what he's doing. Making you *see* things. Making knives appear out of nowhere. Tickling you. Tickling you to death."

"It's madness," Wharton said hoarsely. "The worst madness I ever heard of."

"There's a captain of Homicide that believes it, too. His name is Bill Spencer, and you can check with him about it if you like."

"But what can we do against such a man? How can we fight him?"

"I don't know yet. It's a terrible power he's got, a power that's hard to stop. He can be anywhere, any time, and we'd never know it. The way he was here a few minutes ago. The way he may *still* be here."

"The door—" Wharton stood up.

"Yes, the door slammed. But he could have stayed on this side, couldn't he? And heard all we said."

"Then he must realize you know about him. He must realize how dangerous you are to him—"

I swallowed, and tried to look placid.

"He must know a lot of things. He hasn't hurt me yet."

"What do you think I should do?"

"I'm not sure. Try and stop him. Carry a gun. The next time he tries his tricks—shoot. Don't be afraid of appearing ridiculous, Mr. Wharton. Grapple with air if you have to, but try and hold on to your man. Meanwhile, I'll talk to Spencer, about this and try to develop some more positive action."

I left the office, without knowing whether Douglas Wharton had been convinced by my strange theory. But at least he was warned.

I was just about to leave the building when Greta, Mr. Wharton's secretary, called to me.

"Oh, Mr. Oswald," she said. "Did you want to pick up your mail, while you're here?"

I nodded. Usually, I average about two dozen fan letters a week, addressed to the publishers. A lot of them are crank letters, mostly from women. Sometimes, I'd get proposals of marriage.

Greta was looking through her files, and her face was puzzled.

"That's funny. I could swear there was nine letters, but I can only find eight. That smelly one is missing—"

"Smelly one?" I grinned. "You mean a perfumed letter?"

"I wouldn't exactly call it perfume," she said. "It arrived last Friday, and we practically had to fumigate the office. It smelled like rotten eggs to me."

"Must be somebody who doesn't like Rufe Armlock," I said. Then I thought it over and exclaimed: "Did you say rotten eggs?"

"Yes. I put it in the bottom drawer of my desk, and forgot all about it. I would have forwarded it to you, but I thought it would be best to deliver it in person. I was afraid I'd get arrested if I sent that awful thing through the mails." She chuckled.

Rotten eggs. Sulphur. The words were stirring a memory in my brain. That was the smell which had pervaded Dr. Borg Evander's house!

"And you say it's missing?"

"Yes. I'll keep looking for it; maybe it went to the mail room by mistake. Do you think it might be something important?"

"Could be," I said. "Could be *very* important. Keep searching for it, huh?"

"I will, Mr. Oswald."

I returned to my apartment, my head aching with the thoughts that were crowding my brain. The letter must have been written by Dr. Evander, and it must have concerned our discussion. It might afford me the proof that I was looking for, the proof that was destroyed by Dr. Evander's murder.

I sat on the sofa, feeling suddenly exhausted. I wanted to forget the whole business, forget about murder and madness and invisible killers and locked rooms. I wanted a little peace and quiet. I wanted to marry Eileen, and head off to some corny honeymoon spot like Niagara Falls, and settle down to the simple life, have a couple of kids, take a trip to Europe now and then. Let somebody else chase around catching insane murderers. I wasn't Rufe Armlock; I was only Jeff Oswald, and I was tired of the whole affair.

Then all Hell broke loose.

First it was Eileen, and her hysterical voice on my telephone sent shivers from one end of my spine to the other. It was some time before I got her to give me a coherent story.

"It's awful, awful," she sobbed. "I can't stand it another minute, Jeff, not another minute..."

"But what's happening, Eileen?"

"It must be *him*. He's been following me, doing awful things. Tearing my clothes, touching me..." She went off into a wave of tearful gasps. "I just can't stand it, Jeff! You've got to help me!"

"I'll be right over!"

I got to Greenwich Village in less than twenty minutes, and found Eileen lying on her bed. She was more than just disheveled. Her dress had been ripped and torn in a dozen places, and her hair was wildly disordered. She was still crying uncontrollably, and I had to hold her in my arms like a child before she could talk sensibly.

"He—he must have followed me home," she said, her voice muffled against my chest. "I suddenly felt this—touch on my leg. I jumped, and then something tore my dress. I started to scream and he stopped. I thought of calling the police, and then I realized what they would think. For a while, nothing happened, and then it started all over again. Out of nowhere, I'd feel this *hand* on me. And then he'd tear at my clothes again—"

"Easy, baby," I said, my heart pounding so hard I thought it would crack inside me.

"Then it stopped again. For almost an hour. I heard the door open and shut, and I thought he was gone. I tried telephoning you at home, but you weren't there. Then I called Aaron Snow, and he told me you were at Wharton. I called there, too. Then it started again—" She began to sob again quietly.

"He's a madman," I said tensely. "No question of that. He's pulling the same kind of stuff on Douglas Wharton. And he must realize that you know about him, too." I grasped her arms. "Listen, Eileen, you've got to get away from here..."

"But where could I go? How can you stop someone like that from finding you?"

"We'll figure something out. But you've got to get out of town before he—God knows *what* he'll do!"

"I—I've got an aunt who lives out in Sauter Beach. I could go there for a few weeks."

"Good idea. Meanwhile, I want to call Bill Spencer and tell him what's been happening. I think we've got to stop playing it so safe. I think we've got to get some official help—even if the whole damn world thinks we're crazy!"

I called Police Headquarters on Eileen's phone, but Captain Spencer was off duty. I talked the desk sergeant into giving me his home telephone number, and dialed it.

From the moment I heard Spencer's voice, I knew that he wasn't alone.

"What is it, Captain?" I said. "Is anything wrong?"

"No," he said tensely. "Nothing's wrong. Everything's just fine. Just remember this, Jeff. If I don't report in tomorrow at the station, and they find the doors locked and bolted—*he'll* still be in the room. That's how they can trap him. Remember that!"

"What are you saying?"

"I think he's with me, right now. He hasn't done anything yet, but I *feel* his presence. But I'm ready for him. One noise, one movement, and I'll have him...."

Even though Spencer's voice was calm, I couldn't help detecting the undercurrent of hysteria. The captain wasn't a guy that scared easily, but there was something unearthly and horrible about an opponent you couldn't see....

"Look," I said, "suppose we get some help? Suppose I call the police—"

"No! I'll take care of this myself. If he wants a fight, I'm—"

He stopped talking.

"Captain!" I said. "Bill!"

There was no answer.

"What is it?" Eileen said.

"Bill, are you okay?"

Eileen must have realized what was happening on the other end of the phone, because she began to sob again, fearfully.

I slammed the receiver down and said:

"I've got to get over there!"

"Jeff, don't leave me—"

"I've got to! That *thing* is in Bill's apartment. I've got to help him!"

I burst out of the house and into the street, and almost went frantic at my failure to hail a taxi. When I finally got one, I sat in the back seat and knew that my attempt would come too late.

I was right, of course. The door of his apartment wasn't locked or bolted; it was flung open. But Bill Spencer was dead, a dagger wound between his wide shoulders.

The next afternoon, I saw Eileen off at LaGuardia Airport. I hated to see her go, but I was glad, too. The plane would take her three hundred miles from New York, and three hundred miles from the invisible lunatic that was tormenting her.

As far as I knew, now there were only two people left in the city that the killer was interested in. Douglas Wharton, and me.

Back in the city, I called Wharton's office and suggested a council of war. He agreed, and I went to his penthouse apartment that evening to talk things over.

"What I can't understand is this," I told the publisher, as we sat in his plushly decorated living room. "This fiend has killed or tormented everybody but me. He hasn't laid a finger on me, or made any attempts against my life. Yet if anybody can do him harm, it's me."

"There was that guillotine stuff you told me about," Wharton said. "How about that?"

"That's true. It must have been the killer that was hovering over my bed. But if he wanted to kill me with that meat chopper, he could have done it. Yet he didn't."

"Obviously, he wants you alive. He must have his reasons."

"But why? The only people I know who *really* care if I'm alive or dead are (1) Me, (2) Eileen, and (3) Aaron Snow. Why should this nut care?"

Wharton chewed his lip thoughtfully.

"Aaron Snow," he repeated. "Wasn't Snow Kirk Evander's agent, at one time?"

"Yes, come to think of it. It was back a few years. They had a violent disagreement over money, and Evander asked for them to cancel the arrangement."

"That was quite a loss for Snow, wasn't it? At that time,

Evander was a hot-selling author. Ten percent of his income was a lot of dough."

"Well, Aaron's doing okay now. Thanks mostly to Rufe Armlock, to tell the truth."

"That's right," Wharton said musingly. "And that in itself would be a good reason to want you alive—"

I stared at him.

"Now, look. You're not suggesting—"

"I'm not suggesting anything."

He got up and mixed us a drink. I watched him, trying to digest the new thought he had planted in my mind. Then I saw him snap his fingers, as if in recollection.

"Just thought of something. Greta gave me a letter for you. Said something about it smelling bad—"

"What?" I shot out of the chair.

Wharton looked surprised at my reaction. "What's wrong? Something important?"

"Maybe very important! Let me see it!"

He put down his drink and went out of the room. When he returned, he was holding a long, rumpled envelope. He put it to his nose and sniffed distastefully.

"I see what she meant," he said. "Damn thing smells like rotten eggs."

I grabbed it from his hands and ripped it open.

There were two scrawled sheets inside. The handwriting was almost indecipherable, but I finally made it out.

> *Dear Mr. Oswald:*
>
> *I have been thinking over what you told me this morning, and have decided to reveal the entire truth. I must admit that the evil potentialities of my chemical had never occurred to me before this. But now that I realize them, I think it is better for you to know the facts.*
>
> *As I told you, I have not seen my brother Kirk for many years, despite the fact that we resided in the same city. A few months ago, he suddenly decided to renew his family ties, and called upon me. I was delighted, of course, since I have always*

admired my talented younger brother.

However, I begin to suspect that his interest in me was only the result of his interest in my work. On several occasions, I have provided Kirk with scientific information which he has utilized in his novels, and some years ago, I informed him of my experiments with sulfaborgonium. It was this particular chemical which held his interest now.

Two weeks ago, Kirk came to me and told me a very sad story. It seemed that there was a great deal of public apathy towards the kind of detective fiction which he wrote, and that apathy was costing him his livelihood. He seemed truly brokenhearted about it, and even though I know nothing of literary matters, I was deeply moved by his plight.

Then he told me that he had an unusual plan, a plan which he believed would restore the lost interest in the classic detective novel. It was actually a hoax, he informed me, an amusing prank which he would play on the public in order to increase interest in his work. As a scientist, of course, I have little interest in practical jokery, but Kirk seemed genuinely convinced that this "joke" would have very practical effect upon his career.

Reluctantly, I agreed to cooperate.

Kirk's plan was this. Quite recently, there had been two highly improbable murders, and he wished to create the semblance of a third—the murder of himself. He was quite delighted with the details of this hoax, for he intended to spread the sulfaborgonium over his head, giving his body the appearance of being decapitated. Then I was to supply him with a chemical means for him to appear truly dead, a method which is used for the performance of heart surgery.

He planned to be discovered this way, and for the world to believe that he had been murdered by some impossible means, just as the victims in his

*novels have been killed. Then I was to claim his
body for burial in the family vault. His "body" of
course, would be perfectly alive and well.*

*We went through the plan as outlined. There
were some difficult moments (the county coroner,
as you probably know, wanted to perform an au-
topsy; fortunately, I was able to stop it in time) but
in general, everything went smoothly. When I
brought Kirk's "body" home, I promptly counter-
acted the heart-stoppage and he was completely
restored to health and vitality. He swore me to
secrecy, and told me that he planned to conceal
himself in another part of the country until the
proper time came to reveal the hoax.*

I have not heard from Kirk since.

*While I cannot believe the terrible idea that
Kirk himself is behind the murders, I now feel that
I must tell you the true circumstances of his dis-
appearance.*

*If there is anything further I can do to help,
please feel free to call upon me.*

Sincerely,

DR. BORG EVANDER

I read the letter with the growing conviction that the answer to our problem was in our hands. I read the letter aloud
to Douglas Wharton, whose face showed a confused mixture
of bewilderment and surprise.

"But what does it mean?" he said. "Is it really Kirk that's
playing these invisible tricks?"

"Of course! Only Kirk would be interested in the death
and torture of these victims. He killed Winston Kale as an
example. He didn't have any great grievance against Kale,
but he didn't like him much, either—especially after Wharton Publishing refused his ultimatum. Then, to keep interest
alive in these puzzle murders, he killed Zora Brewster—the
one person who saw Kale alive before the locked-room murder. Then, he plotted his own "murder," when the police got
on his trail. Now he's killing everyone who knows the story

of the chemical—his own brother, Captain Spencer. In order to complete his insane plan, he has three more to go. You, because he associates his failures with your company. Eileen, because she knows of his existence. And me."

"But why didn't he kill you *first?* You're the one he hates most."

"That's exactly why. Because he hates me so much, he wants me to squirm. He wants me to know that there *are* such things as impossible murders. When he's knocked off everybody in some improbable manner—then he'll be ready to take care of me. But first, he has to demonstrate that I was wrong and he was right."

Wharton folded his arms and shivered.

"All right. So we know it's Kirk Evander. But that doesn't bring us any closer to a solution."

"Sure it does," I said. "Because now that we know it's Kirk, we can act accordingly. We can try and *think* the way Kirk Evander thinks."

"How will that help?"

"I don't know yet," I said miserably. "But we've got to find a way."

That night, I sat and stared at my Remington, and I never thought so hard in my life. It was like trying to work Rufe Armlock out of an escapade, only it was much worse. At least I had control of the characters in a Rufe Armlock novel; if I wanted them to do something, I *made* them do it. If only it was that easy!

My only consolation was that Eileen was presumably out of danger.

Then even that was destroyed. Around ten o'clock, the telephone rang and the long-distance operator told me that there was a call from Sauter Beach. Eileen didn't have to say very much before I realized that her invisible masher was still on the trail. My hands went cold on the phone.

"Maybe I'm wrong," she said, her voice trembling. "But yesterday, on the beach, I thought I saw something glinting in the sun...I looked up and could have sworn I saw a gun, just hanging in the air..."

"Good God," I said, shutting my eyes.

"Jeff, I don't know what to *do*. If he's followed me here..."

"Hang on, sweetie, just hang on. We're working this out. We've learned something we didn't know before. We're going to lick this."

"I don't know what to do! Should I come back to the city? Then you'll all be in danger—"

"Never mind about that. Come back as soon as you can. We've got a plan—"

"What kind of plan?"

"Never mind now. But we won't be so helpless any more."

I hung up, hoping she wouldn't realize that I was bluffing.

But an hour later, slumped over the still typewriter, I *did* have a plan. I got so excited about it that I woke Douglas Wharton out of a sound sleep, not realizing that it was already four in the morning.

The item that appeared in every New York newspaper read something like this:

POSTHUMOUS AWARD TO KIRK EVANDER

BANQUET TO BE HELD IN DEAD MYSTERY NOVELIST'S HONOR

July 2, New York. The Wharton Publishing Company announced today that a new Fellowship was to be added to the company's roster, to be named the Kirk Evander Fellowship. It will provide special awards and scholarships to promising authors of the "classic" detective novel. The official innovation of the Kirk Evander Fellowship will take place at a banquet in honor of the deceased novelist on July 8. Among the speakers will be...

Eileen's brow was ruffled when she studied the item.

"But what good will it do? Honoring that fiend?"

I chuckled. "Think about it, and you'll see. Can you think of anything that would appeal more to an egomaniac like

Evander? How can he resist attending a banquet that's held in his own honor?"

"Then it's a trap?"

"Of course it is. And even if Evander realizes that it's a trap, I don't think he'll be able to resist showing up. He's too convinced of his invincible powers to believe that we could capture him. Besides, the Fellowship idea is genuine. Evander *was* a heck of a good writer, and Wharton does intend to create the award. The speakers will all be real, and the entire event will be authentic. But there'll be some added features..."

"What kind of features?"

"Some preparations. Just in case we have an uninvited guest that night. A special welcome for him."

Eileen's eyes shone.

"Can I come, Jeff?"

"No!"

"Please! After all, he's after me, too. It can't be any more dangerous—"

I scowled like Rufe Armlock and pulled her towards me.

"I said no, baby. And don't give me any argument, or I'll shoot you in your soft, white..."

She didn't argue with me.

It was impressive, no doubt about it. The banquet hall, a ninety-foot chamber in the Hotel Colbert, was splendidly decorated for the occasion, with luxurious drapery and burgundy-red carpets and glittering chandeliers. The speaker's table was raised on a dais, and two long guest tables flanked each other on both sides of the hall. The guests began milling around early in the evening, all of them dress-suited and distinguished looking and seemingly pleased at the prospects of the occasion. The full list of speakers hadn't been announced, but Douglas Wharton was to make the main presentation.

After several rounds of drinks, the time for the formal opening of events arrived.

The guests seated themselves, the doors were closed, and Douglas Wharton rapped a gavel.

"Gentlemen, before we satisfy our appetite, I thought it would be appropriate to have a few words concerning the purpose of this occasion. So it gives me great pleasure to present a young man whose rise to fame is best described in that worn but accurate word 'meteoric.' More important, this young man, perhaps more than anyone present this evening, has good reason to know the qualities of the man we have gathered to honor. Gentlemen, Mr. Jeffrey Oswald."

There was a scattering of applause, and I tugged at the collar of my formal shirt and stepped forward to the speaker's rostrum.

I cleared my throat and said:

"Kirk Evander was and is a great man."

I paused to let that sink in.

"I say was, because at the time of his passing, he had left the world a heritage of some thirty-five mystery novels, the like of which may never be seen again. I say is, because Kirk Evander will remain alive as long as someone, somewhere, thrills to the magic words he put on paper."

There was some more applause.

"Kirk Evander was more than merely a great man. The world has had its share of those. But Kirk Evander was also an *unusual* man. A man of courage and of daring, a man willing to face an unpopular trend and do it battle. Kirk Evander made that battle, and the effort was nothing short of magnificent. It was through him that we owe the present upcurve in the popularity of the classic detective story—and all of us want nothing more than to see that popularity maintained."

Again, they applauded.

"As we all know, Kirk Evander's last novel, *Death of a Publisher,* was released to the reviewers yesterday. I can't think of any more fitting tribute than this review, which will be published in tonight's edition of *The New York Blade.*"

I lifted a sheaf of papers from the table and waved it at the crowd. But I didn't read it. Instead, I placed it carefully in front of me, and went on talking. I talked for another five minutes, and never once took my eyes from the papers.

I was almost ready to sit down, when I saw them move.

"He's here!" I shouted.

Everyone went into action as planned. At the doorway, the two dress-suited men who were standing by reached up and pulled the light switches that plunged the hall into immediate darkness. Throughout the room, I heard the swift movements of the guests as they reached beneath the covered tables and removed the masks that had been placed there in readiness. I found my own beneath the speaker's podium, and slipped it quickly over my face. Somewhere below, a lieutenant of police named Davis was preparing to pull the release on the gas bomb which would spread the thick, deadly stuff in violent clouds throughout the room.

"The door! The door!" I heard Wharton cry, and he leaped from the dais to help form the barrier of bodies that would block the invisible killer from making his escape. By this time, the heavy clouds of gas were filling the room, and I could still smell its sickening-sweet odor through the mask, or imagine that I did.

In the midst of the crowd there was a sudden wave of violent motion, as if Kirk Evander was struggling wildly to make his way to an exit. Hands reached out everywhere to try and pin him down, but he was too clever. At the doorway, Douglas Wharton suddenly cried out and grappled with the air, and then his assailant was gone.

"Don't try and hold him!" I shouted to them. "Let the gas stop him—"

There were frenzied sounds and movements in the darkness, sudden shouts of surprise and fear, unexpected gasps and outbursts. But it was only for the moment; soon there was only stillness.

"The lights!" I said. "Turn on the lights."

They flickered on overhead.

"All right," Douglas Wharton said commandingly. "He's here someplace. Find him."

They backed off against the walls, and started to close in the ring slowly.

From the rear of the hall, Lieutenant Davis of the police department suddenly shouted:

"Here he is!"

I looked. Davis was lifting something from the floor, something that appeared to be a dead weight.

He carried his burden towards one of the banquet tables, pulling aside the cloth to place it down.

Then he threw the cloth over it, and we saw the outline of a small, plump body. The outline of the unconscious body of Kirk Evander.

Davis bent over it.

"We didn't mean for the gas to kill him," he frowned. "But I'm afraid his heart couldn't take it. Evander's dead."

Eileen and I did go to Niagara on our honeymoon. But as far as we were concerned, the Falls could have been invisible, too.

PRIDE

Breathes there a man with soul so dead as not to be proud of his species, his country, his group, his family, himself? That's the very stuff of patriotism, of healthy self-respect. And shouldn't one be proud of one's work, too? Of course. What kind of a man would he be who wouldn't sacrifice everything to maintain that high opinion of that to which he has dedicated his life. And, of course, the final and total sacrifice is that of his very PRIDE.

GALLEY SLAVE

ISAAC ASIMOV

The United States Robot and Mechanical Men, Inc., as defendants in the case, had influence enough to force a closed-doors trial without a jury.

Nor did Northeastern University try hard to prevent it. The trustees knew perfectly well how the public might react to any issue involving misbehavior of a robot, however rarefied that misbehavior might be. They also had a clearly visualized notion of how an anti-robot riot might become an anti-science riot without warning.

The government, as represented in this case by Justice Harlow Shane, was equally anxious for a quiet end to this mess. Both U.S. Robots and the academic world were bad people to antagonize.

Justice Shane said, "Since neither press, public nor jury is present, gentlemen, let us stand on as little ceremony as we can and get to the facts."

He smiled stiffly as he said this, perhaps without much hope that his request would be effective, and hitched at his robe so that he might sit more comfortably. His face was pleasantly rubicund, his chin round and soft, his nose broad and his eyes light in color and wide-set. All in all, it was not a face with much judicial majesty and the judge knew it.

Barnabas H. Goodfellow, Professor of Physics at Northeastern U., was sworn in first, taking the usual vow with an expression that made mincemeat of his name.

After the usual opening-gambit questions, Prosecution shoved his hands deep into his pockets and said, "When was it, Professor, that the matter of the possible employ of Robot EZ-27 was first brought to your attention, and how?"

117

Professor Goodfellow's small and angular face set itself into an uneasy expression, scarcely more benevolent than the one it replaced. He said, "I have had professional contact and some social acquaintance with Dr. Alfred Lanning, Director of Research at U.S. Robots. I was inclined to listen with some tolerance then when I received a rather strange suggestion from him on the 3rd of March of last year—"

"Of 2033?"

"That's right."

"Excuse me for interrupting. Please proceed."

The professor nodded frostily, scowled to fix the facts in his mind, and began to speak.

Professor Goodfellow looked at the robot with a certain uneasiness. It had been carried into the basement supply room in a crate, in accordance with the regulations governing the shipment of robots from place to place on the Earth's surface.

He knew it was coming; it wasn't that he was unprepared. From the moment of Dr. Lanning's first phone call on March 3, he had felt himself giving way to the other's persuasiveness, and now, as an inevitable result, he found himself face to face with a robot.

It looked uncommonly large as it stood within arm's reach.

Alfred Lanning cast a hard glance of his own at the robot, as though making certain it had not been damaged in transit. Then he turned his ferocious eyebrows and his mane of white hair in the professor's direction.

"This is Robot EZ-27, first of its model to be available for public use." He turned to the robot. "This is Professor Goodfellow, Easy."

Easy spoke impassively, but with such suddenness that the professor shied. "Good afternoon, Professor."

Easy stood seven feet tall and had the general proportions of a man—always the prime selling point of U.S. Robots. That and the possession of the basic patents on the positronic brain had given them an actual monopoly on robots and a near-monopoly on computing machines in general.

The two men who had uncrated the robot had left now and

the professor looked from Lanning to the robot and back to Lanning. "It is harmless, I'm sure." He didn't sound sure.

"More harmless than I am," said Lanning. "I could be goaded into striking you. Easy could not be. You know the Three Laws of Robotics, I presume."

"Yes, of course," said Goodfellow.

"They are built into the positronic patterns of the brain and must be observed. The First Law, the prime rule of robotic existence, safeguards the life and well-being of all humans." He paused, rubbed at his cheek, then added, "It's something of which we would like to persuade all Earth if we could."

"It's just that he seems formidable."

"Granted. But whatever he seems, you'll find that he *is* useful."

"I'm not sure in what way. Our conversations were not very helpful in that respect. Still, I agreed to look at the object and I'm doing it."

"We'll do more than look, Professor. Have you brought a book?"

"I have."

"May I see it?"

Professor Goodfellow reached down without actually taking his eyes off the metal-in-human-shape that confronted him. From the briefcase at his feet, he withdrew a book.

Lanning held out his hand for it and looked at the backstrip. *"Physical Chemistry of Electrolytes in Solution.* Fair enough, sir. You selected this yourself, at random. It was no suggestion of mine, this particular text. Am I right?"

"Yes."

Lanning passed the book to Robot EZ-27.

The professor jumped a little. "No! That's a valuable book!"

Lanning raised his eyebrows and they looked like shaggy coconut icing. He said, "Easy has no intention of tearing the book in two as a feat of strength, I assure you. It can handle a book as carefully as you or I. Go ahead, Easy."

"Thank you, sir," said Easy. Then, turning its metal bulk slightly, it added, "With your permission, Professor Goodfellow."

The professor stared, then said, "Yes—yes, of course."

With a slow and steady manipulation of metal fingers, Easy turned the pages of the book, glancing at the left page, then the right; turning the page, glancing left, then right; turning the page and so on for minute after minute.

The sense of its power seemed to dwarf even the large cement-walled room in which they stood and to reduce the two human watchers to something considerably less than life-size.

Goodfellow muttered, "The light isn't very good."

"It will do."

Then, rather more sharply, "But what is he doing?"

"Patience, sir."

The last page was turned eventually. Lanning asked, "Well, Easy?"

The robot said, "It is a most accurate book and there is little to which I can point. On line 22 of page 27, the word 'positive' is spelled p-o-i-s-t-i-v-e. The comma in line 6 of page 32 is superfluous, whereas one should have been used on line 13 of page 54. The plus sign in equation XIV-2 on page 337 should be a minus sign if it is to be consistent with the previous equations—"

"Wait! Wait!" cried the professor. "What is he doing?"

"Doing?" echoed Lanning in sudden irascibility. "Why, man, he has already done it! He has proofread that book."

"Proofread it?"

"Yes. In the short time it took him to turn those pages, he caught every mistake in spelling, grammar and punctuation. He has noted errors in word order and detected inconsistencies. And he will retain the information, letter-perfect, indefinitely."

The professor's mouth was open. He walked rapidly away from Lanning and Easy and as rapidly back. He folded his arms across his chest and stared at them. Finally he said, "You mean this is a proofreading robot?"

Lanning nodded. "Among other things."

"But why do you show it to me?"

"So that you might help me persuade the university to obtain it for use."

"To read proof?"

"Among other things," Lanning repeated patiently.

The professor drew his pinched face together in a kind of sour disbelief. "But this is ridiculous!"

"Why?"

"The university could never afford to buy this half-ton—it must weigh that at least—this half-ton proofreader."

"Proofreading is not all it will do. It will prepare reports from outlines, fill out forms, serve as an accurate memory-file, grade papers—"

"All picayune!"

Lanning said, "Not at all, as I can show you in a moment. But I think we can discuss this more comfortably in your office, if you have no objection."

"No, of course not," began the professor mechanically and took a half-step as though to turn. Then he snapped out, "But the robot—we can't take the robot. Really, Doctor, you'll have to crate it up again."

"Time enough. We can leave Easy here."

"Unattended?"

"Why not? He knows he is to stay. Professor Goodfellow, it is necessary to understand that a robot is far more reliable than a human being."

"I would be responsible for any damage—"

"There will be no damage. I guarantee that. Look, it's after hours. You expect no one here, I imagine, before tomorrow morning. The truck and my two men are outside. U.S. Robots will take any responsibility that may arise. None will. Call it a demonstration of the reliability of the robot."

The professor allowed himself to be led out of the store-room. Nor did he look entirely comfortable in his own office, five stories up.

He dabbed at the line of droplets along the upper half of his forehead with a white handkerchief.

"As you know very well, Dr. Lanning, there are laws against the use of robots on Earth's surface," he pointed out.

"The laws, Professor Goodfellow, are not simple ones. Robots may not be used on public thoroughfares or within public edifices. They may not be used on private grounds or within private structures except under certain restrictions that usually turn out to be prohibitive. The university, however, is a large and privately owned institution that usually receives preferential treatment. If the robot is used only in a specific room for only academic purposes, if certain other restrictions are observed and if the men and women having occasion to enter the room co-operate fully, we may remain within the law."

"But all that trouble just to read proof?"

"The uses would be infinite, Professor. Robotic labor has so far been used only to relieve physical drudgery. Isn't there such a thing as mental drudgery? When a professor capable of the most useful creative thought is forced to spend two weeks painfully checking the spelling of lines of print and I offer you a machine that can do it in thirty minutes, is that picayune?"

"But the price—"

"The price need not bother you. You cannot buy EZ-27. U.S. Robots does not sell its products. But the university can lease EZ-27 for a thousand dollars a year—considerably less than the cost of a single microwave spectograph continuous-recording attachment."

Goodfellow looked stunned. Lanning followed up his advantage by saying, "I only ask that you put it up to whatever group makes the decisions here. I would be glad to speak to them if they want more information."

"Well," Goodfellow said doubtfully, "I can bring it up at next week's Senate meeting. I can't promise that will do any good, though."

"Naturally," said Lanning.

The Defense Attorney was short and stubby and carried himself rather portentously, a stance that had the effect of acentuating his double chin. He stared at Professor Goodfellow, once that witness had been handed over, and said, "You agreed rather readily, did you not?"

The Professor said briskly, "I suppose I was anxious to be rid of Dr. Lanning. I would have agreed to anything."

"With the intention of forgetting about it after he left?"

"Well—"

"Nevertheless, you did present the matter to a meeting of the Executive Board of the University Senate."

"Yes, I did."

"So that you agreed in good faith with Dr. Lanning's suggestions. You weren't just going along with a gag. You actually agreed enthusiastically, did you not?"

"I merely followed ordinary procedures."

"As a matter of fact, you weren't as upset about the robot as you now claim you were. You know the Three Laws of Robotics and you knew them at the time of your interview with Dr. Lanning."

"Well, yes."

"And you were perfectly willing to leave a robot at large and unattended."

"Dr. Lanning assured me—"

"Surely you would never have accepted his assurance if you had had the slightest fear that the robot might be in the least dangerous."

The professor began frigidly, "I had every faith in the word—"

"That is all," said Defense abruptly.

As Professor Goodfellow, more than a bit ruffled, stood down, Justice Shane leaned forward and said, "Since I am not a robotics man myself, I would appreciate knowing precisely what the Three Laws of Robotics are. Would Dr. Lanning quote them for the benefit of the court?"

Dr. Lanning looked startled. He had been virtually bumping heads with the gray-haired woman at his side. He rose to his feet now and the woman looked up, too—expressionlessly.

Dr. Lanning said, "Very well, Your Honor." He paused as though about to launch into an oration and said, with laborious clarity, "First Law: a robot may not injure a human being, or, through inaction, allow a human being to come to harm. Second Law: a robot must obey the orders given it by human beings, except where such orders would conflict with the First Law. Third Law: a robot must protect its own existence as long as such protection does not conflict with the First or Second Laws."

"I see," said the judge, taking rapid notes. "These Laws are built into every robot, are they?"

"Into every one. That will be borne out by any roboticist."

"And into Robot EZ-27 specifically?"

"Yes, Your Honor."

"You will probably be required to repeat those statements under oath."

"I am ready to do so, Your Honor."

He sat down again.

Dr. Susan Calvin, robopsychologist-in-chief for U. S. Robots, who was the gray-haired woman sitting next to Lanning, looked at her titular superior without favor, but then she showed favor to no human being. She said, "Was Goodfellow's testimony accurate, Alfred?"

"Essentially," muttered Lanning. "He wasn't as nervous as all that about the robot and he was anxious enough to talk business with me when he heard the price. But there doesn't seem to be any drastic distortion."

Dr. Calvin said thoughtfully, "It might have been wise to put the price higher than a thousand."

"We were anxious to place Easy."

"I know. Too anxious, perhaps. They'll try to make it look as though we had an ulterior motive."

Lanning looked exasperated. "We did. I admitted that at the University Senate meeting."

"They can make it look as if we had one beyond the one we admitted."

Scott Robertson, son of the founder of U. S. Robots and still owner of a majority of the stock, leaned over from Dr. Calvin's other side and said in a kind of explosive whisper, "Why can't you get Easy to talk so we'll know where we're at?"

"You know he can't talk about it, Mr. Robertson."

"Make him. You're the psychologist, Dr. Calvin. *Make* him."

"If I'm the psychologist, Mr. Robertson," said Susan Calvin

coldly, "let me make the decisions. My robot will not be made to do anything at the price of his well-being."

Robertson frowned and might have answered, but Justice Shane was tapping his gavel in a polite sort of way and they grudgingly fell silent.

Francis J. Hart, head of the Department of English and Dean of Graduate Studies, was on the stand. He was a plump man, meticulously dressed in dark clothing of a conservative cut, and possessing several strands of hair traversing the pink top of his cranium. He sat well back in the witness chair with his hands folded neatly in his lap and displaying, from time to time, a tight-lipped smile.

He said, "My first connection with the matter of the Robot EZ-27 was on the occasion of the session of the University Senate Executive Committee at which the subject was introduced by Professor Goodfellow. Thereafter, on the 10th of April of last year, we held a special meeting on the subject, during which I was in the chair."

"Were minutes kept of the meeting of the Executive Committee? Of the special meeting, that is?"

"Well, no. It was a rather unusual meeting." The dean smiled briefly. "We thought it might remain confidential."

"What transpired at the meeting?"

Dean Hart was not entirely comfortable as chairman of that meeting. Nor did the other members assembled seem completely calm. Only Dr. Lanning appeared at peace with himself. His tall, gaunt figure and the shock of white hair that crowned him reminded Hart of portraits he had seen of Andrew Jackson.

Samples of the robot's work lay scattered along the central regions of the table and the reproduction of a graph drawn by the robot was now in the hands of Professor Minott of Physical Chemistry. The chemist's lips were pursed in obvious approval.

Hart cleared his throat and said, "There seems no doubt that the robot can perform certain routine tasks with adequate competence. I have gone over these, for instance, just before coming in, and there is very little to find fault with."

He picked up a long sheet of printing, some three times as long as the average book page. It was a sheet of galley proof, designed to be corrected by authors before the type was set up in page form. Along both of the wide margins of the galley were proofmarks, neat and superbly legible. Occasionally, a word of print was crossed out and a new word substituted in the margin in characters so fine and regular it might easily have been print itself. Some of the corrections were blue to indicate the original mistake had been the author's, a few in red, where the printer had been wrong.

"Actually," said Lanning, "there is less than very little to find fault with. I should say there is nothing at all to find fault with, Dr. Hart. I'm sure the corrections are perfect, insofar as the original manuscript was. If the manuscript against which this galley was corrected was at fault in a matter of fact rather than of English, the robot is not competent to correct it."

"We accept that. However, the robot corrected word order on occasion and I don't think the rules of English are sufficiently hidebound for us to be sure that in each case the robot's choice was the correct one."

"Easy's positronic brain," said Lanning, showing large teeth as he smiled, "has been molded by the contents of all the standard works on the subject. I'm sure you cannot point to a case where the robot's choice was definitely the incorrect one."

Professor Minott looked up from the graph he still held. "The question in my mind, Dr. Lanning, is why we need a robot at all, with all the difficulties in public relations that would entail. The science of automation has surely reached the point where your company could design a machine, an ordinary computer of a type known and accepted by the public, that would correct galleys."

"I am sure we could," said Lanning stiffly, "but such a machine would require that the galleys be translated into special symbols or, at the least, transcribed on tapes. Any corrections would emerge in symbols. You would need to keep men employed translating words to symbols, symbols to words. Furthermore, such a computer could do no other job.

It couldn't prepare the graph you hold in your hand, for instance."

Minott grunted.

Lanning went on. "The hallmark of the positronic robot is its flexibility. It can do a number of jobs. It is designed like a man so that it can use all the tools and machines that have, after all, been designed to be used by a man. It can talk to you and you can talk to it. You can actually reason with it up to a point. Compared to even a simple robot, an ordinary computer with a nonpositronic brain is only a heavy adding machine."

Goodfellow looked up and said, "If we all talk and reason with the robot, what are the chances of our confusing it? I suppose it doesn't have the capability of absorbing an infinite amount of data."

"No, it hasn't. But it should last five years with ordinary use. It will know when it will require clearing, and the company will do the job without charge."

"The *company* will?"

"Yes. The company reserves the right to service the robot outside the ordinary course of its duties. It is one reason we retain control of our positronic robots and lease rather than sell them. In the pursuit of its ordinary functions, any robot can be directed by any man. Outside its ordinary functions, a robot requires expert handling, and that we can give it. For instance, any of you might clear an EZ robot to an extent by telling it to forget this item or that. But you would be almost certain to phrase the order in such a way as to cause it to forget too much or too little. We would detect such tampering, because we have built-in safeguards. However, since there is no need for clearing the robot in its ordinary work, or for doing other useless things, this raises no problem."

Dean Hart touched his head as though to make sure his carefully cultivated strands lay evenly distributed and said, "You are anxious to have us take the machine. Yet surely it is a losing proposition for U.S. Robots. One thousand a year is a ridiculously low price. Is it that you hope through this to rent other such machines to other universities at a more reasonable price?"

"Certainly that's a fair hope," said Lanning.

"But even so, the number of machines you could rent would be limited. I doubt if you could make it a paying proposition."

Lanning put his elbows on the table and earnestly leaned forward. "Let me put it bluntly, gentlemen. Robots cannot be used on Earth, except in certain special cases, because of prejudice against them on the part of the public. U.S. Robots is a highly successful corporation with our extraterrestrial and space-flight markets alone, to say nothing of our computer subsidiaries. However, we are concerned with more than profits alone. It is our firm belief that the use of robots on Earth itself would mean a better life for all eventually, even if a certain amount of economic dislocation resulted at first.

"The labor unions are naturally against us, but surely we may expect cooperation from the large universities. The robot, Easy, will help you by relieving you of scholastic drudgery—by assuming, if you permit it, the role of galley slave for you. Other universities and research institutions will follow your lead, and if it works out, then perhaps other robots of other types may be placed and the public's objections to them broken down by stages."

Minott murmured, "Today Northeastern University, tomorrow the world."

Angrily, Lanning whispered to Susan Calvin, "I wasn't nearly that eloquent and they weren't nearly that reluctant. At a thousand a year, they were jumping to get Easy. Professor Minott told me he'd never seen as beautiful a job as that graph he was holding and there was no mistake on the galley or anywhere else. Hart admitted it freely."

The severe vertical lines on Dr. Calvin's face did not soften. "You should have demanded more money than they could pay, Alfred, and let them beat you down."

"Maybe," he grumbled.

Prosecution was not quite done with Professor Hart. "After Dr. Lanning left, did you vote on whether to accept Robot EZ-27?"

"Yes, we did."

"With what result?"

"In favor of acceptance, by majority vote."

"What would you say influenced the vote?"

Defense objected immediately.

Prosecution rephrased the question. "What influenced you, personally, in your individual vote? You did vote in favor, I think."

"I voted in favor, yes. I did so largely because I was impressed by Dr. Lanning's feeling that it was our duty as members of the world's intellectual leadership to allow robotics to help Man in the solutions of his problems."

"In other words, Dr. Lanning talked you into it."

"That's his job. He did it very well."

"Your witness."

Defense strode up to the witness chair and surveyed Professor Hart for a long moment. He said, "In reality, you were all pretty eager to have Robot EZ-27 in your employ, weren't you?"

"We thought that if it could do the work, it might be useful."

"*If* it could do the work? I understand you examined the samples of Robot EZ-27's original work with particular care on the day of the meeting which you have just described."

"Yes, I did. Since the machine's work dealt primarily with the handling of the English language, and since that is my field of competence, it seemed logical that I be the one chosen to examine the work."

"Very good. Was there anything on display on the table at the time of the meeting which was less than satisfactory? I have all the material here as exhibits. Can you point to a single unsatisfactory item?"

"Well—"

"It's a simple question. Was there one single solitary unsatisfactory item? You inspected it. Was there?"

The English professor frowned. "There wasn't."

"I also have some samples of work done by Robot EZ-27 during the course of his 14-month employ at Northeastern. Would you examine these and tell me if there is anything wrong with them in even one particular?"

Hart snapped, "When he did make a mistake, it was a beauty."

"Answer my question," thundered Defense, "and only the question I am putting to you! Is there anything wrong with the material?"

Dean Hart looked cautiously at each item. "Well, nothing."

"Barring the matter concerning which we are here engaged, do you know of any mistakes on the part of EZ-27?"

"Barring the matter for which this trial is being held, no."

Defense cleared his throat as though to signal end of paragraph. He said, "Now about the vote concerning whether Robot EZ-27 was to be employed or not. You said there was a majority in favor. What was the actual vote?"

"Thirteen to one, as I remember."

"Thirteen to one! More than just a majority, wouldn't you say?"

"No, sir!" All the pedant in Dean Hart was aroused. "In the English language, the word 'majority' means 'more than half.' Thirteen out of fourteen is a majority, nothing more."

"But an almost unanimous one."

"A majority all the same!"

Defense switched ground. "And who was the lone holdout?"

Dean Hart looked acutely uncomfortable. "Professor Simon Ninheimer."

Defense pretended astonishment. "Professor Ninheimer? The head of the Department of Sociology?"

"Yes, sir."

"The *plaintiff*?"

"Yes, sir."

Defense pursed his lips. "In other words, it turns out that the man bringing the action for payment of $750,000 damages against my client, United States Robot and Mechanical Men, Incorporated, was the one who from the beginning opposed the use of the robot—although everyone else on the Executive Committee of the University Senate was persuaded that it was a good idea."

"He voted against the motion, as was his right."

"You didn't mention in your description of the meeting any remarks made by Professor Ninheimer. Did he make any?"

"I think he spoke."

"You *think?*"

"Well, he *did* speak."

"Against using the robot?"

"Yes."

"Was he violent about it?"

Dean Hart paused. "He was vehement."

Defense grew confidential. "How long have you known Professor Ninheimer, Dean Hart?"

"About twelve years."

"Reasonably well?"

"I should say so, yes."

"Knowing him, then, would you say he was the kind of man who might continue to bear resentment against a robot, all the more so because an adverse vote had—"

Prosecution drowned out the remainder of the question with an indignant and vehement objection of his own. Defense motioned the witness down and Justice Shane called luncheon recess.

Robertson mangled his sandwich. The corporation would not founder for loss of three-quarters of a million, but the loss would do it no particular good. He was conscious, moreover, that there would be a much more costly long-term setback in public relations.

He said sourly, "Why all this business about how Easy got into the university? What do they hope to gain?"

The Attorney for Defense said quietly, "A court action is like a chess game, Mr. Robertson. The winner is usually the one who can see more moves ahead, and my friend at the prosecutor's table is no beginner. They can show damage; that's no problem. Their main effort lies in anticipating our defense. They must be counting on us to try to show that Easy couldn't possibly have committed the offense—because of the Laws of Robotics."

"All right," said Robertson, "that *is* our defense. An absolutely air-tight one."

"To a robotics engineer. Not necessarily to a judge. They're setting themselves up a position from which they can demonstrate that EZ-27 was no ordinary robot. It was the first of its type to be offered to the public. It was an experimental model that needed field testing and the university was the only decent way to provide such testing. That would look plausible in the light of Dr. Lanning's strong efforts to place the robot and the willingness of U.S. Robots to lease it for so little. The prosecution would then argue that the field test proved Easy to have been a failure. Now do you see the purpose of what's been going on?"

"But EZ-27 was a perfectly good model," argued Robertson.

"It was the twenty-seventh in production."

"Which is really a bad point," said Defense somberly. "What was wrong with the first twenty-six? Obviously something. Why shouldn't there be something wrong with the twenty-seventh, too?"

"There was nothing wrong with the first twenty-six except that they weren't complex enough for the task. These were the first positronic brains of the sort to be constructed and it was rather hit-and-miss to begin with. But the Three Laws held in all of them! *No* robot is so imperfect that the Three Laws don't hold."

"Dr. Lanning has explained this to me, Mr. Robertson, and I am willing to take his word for it. The judge, however, may not be. We are expecting a decision from an honest and intelligent man who knows no robotics and thus may be led astray. For instance, if you or Dr. Lanning or Dr. Calvin were to say on the stand that any positronic brains were constructed 'hit-and-miss,' as you just did, Prosecution would tear you apart in cross-examination. Nothing would salvage our case. So that's something to avoid."

Robertson growled, "If only Easy would talk."

Defense shrugged. "A robot is incompetent as a witness, so that would do us no good."

"At least we'd know some of the facts. We'd know how it came to do such a thing."

Susan Calvin fired up. A dullish red touched her cheeks and her voice had a trace of warmth in it. "We *know* how Easy came to do it. It was ordered to! I've explained this to counsel and I'll explain it to you now."

"Ordered by whom?" asked Robertson in honest astonishment. (No one ever told him anything, he thought resentfully. These research people considered *themselves* the owners of U.S. Robots, by God!)

"By the plaintiff," said Dr. Calvin.

"In heaven's name, why?"

"I don't know why yet. Perhaps just that we might be sued, that he might gain some cash." There were blue glints in her eyes as she said that.

"Then why doesn't Easy say so?"

"Isn't that obvious? It's been ordered to keep quiet about the matter."

"Why should that be obvious?" demanded Robertson truculently.

"Well, it's obvious to me. Robot psychology is my profession. If Easy will not answer questions about the matter directly, he will answer questions on the fringe of the matter. By measuring increased hesitation in his answers as the central question is approached, by measuring the area of blankness and the intensity of counter-potentials set up, it is possible to tell with scientific precision that his troubles are the result of an order not to talk, with its strength based on First Law. In other words, he's been told that if he talks, harm will be done a human being. Presumably harm to the unspeakable Professor Ninheimer, the plaintiff, who, to the robot, would seem a human being."

"Well, then," said Robertson, "can't you explain that if he keeps quiet, harm will be done to U.S. Robots?"

"U.S. Robots is not a human being and the First Law of Robotics does not recognize a corporation as a person the way ordinary laws do. Besides, it would be dangerous to try to lift this particular sort of inhibition. The person who laid it on could lift it off least dangerously, because the robot's motivations in that respect are centered on that person. Any other course—" She shook her head and grew almost impassioned. "I won't let the robot be damaged!"

Lanning interrupted with the air of bringing sanity to the problem. "It seems to me that we have only to prove a robot incapable of the act of which Easy is accused. We can do that."

"Exactly," said Defense, in annoyance. "*You* can do that. The only witnesses capable of testifying to Easy's condition and to the nature of Easy's state of mind are employees of U.S. Robots. The judge can't possibly accept their testimony as unprejudiced."

"How can he deny expert testimony?"

"By refusing to be convinced by it. That's his right as the judge. Against the alternative that a man like Professor Ninheimer deliberately set about ruining his own reputation, even for a sizeable sum of money, the judge isn't going to accept the technicalities of your engineers. The judge is a man, after all. If he has to choose between a man doing an impossible thing and a robot doing an impossible thing, he's quite likely to decide in favor of the man."

"A man *can* do an impossible thing," said Lanning, "because we don't know all the complexities of the human mind and we don't know what, in a given human mind, is impossible and what is not. We *do* know what is really impossible to a robot."

"Well, we'll see if we can't convince the judge of that," Defense replied wearily.

"If all you say is so," rumbled Robertson, "I don't see how you can."

"We'll see. It's good to know and be aware of the difficulties involved, but let's not be *too* downhearted. I've tried to look ahead a few moves in the chess game, too." With a stately nod in the direction of the robopsychologist, he added, "*With* the help of the good lady here."

Lanning looked from one to the other and said, "What the devil is this?"

But the bailiff thrust his head into the room and announced somewhat breathlessly that the trial was about to resume.

They took their seats, examining the man who had started all the trouble.

Simon Ninheimer owned a fluffy head of sandy hair, a face that narrowed past a beaked nose toward a pointed chin, and a habit of sometimes hesitating before key words in his conversation that gave him an air of a seeker after an almost unbearable precision. When he said, "The Sun rises in the—uh—east," one was certain he had given due consideration to the possibility that it might at some time rise in the west.

Prosecution said, "Did you oppose employment of Robot EZ-27 by the university?"

"I did, sir."

"Why was that?"

"I did not feel that we understood the—uh—motives of U.S. Robots thoroughly. I mistrusted their anxiety to place the robot with us."

"Did you feel that it was capable of doing the work that it was allegedly designed to do?"

"I know for a fact that it was not."

"Would you state your reasons?"

Simon Ninheimer's book, entitled *Social Tensions Involved in Space-Flight and Their Resolution,* had been eight years in the making. Ninheimer's search for precision was not confined to his habits of speech, and in a subject like sociology, almost inherently imprecise, it left him breathless.

Even with the material in galley proofs, he felt no sense of completion. Rather the reverse, in fact. Staring at the long strips of print, he felt only the itch to tear the lines of type apart and rearrange them differently.

Jim Baker, Instructor and soon to be Assistant Professor of Sociology, found Ninheimer, three days after the first batch of galleys had arrived from the printer, staring at the handful of paper in abstraction. The galleys came in three copies: one for Ninheimer to proofread, one for Baker to proofread independently, and a third, marked "Original," which was to receive the final corrections, a combination of those made by

Ninheimer and by Baker, after a conference at which possible conflicts and disagreements were ironed out. This had been their policy on the several papers on which they had collaborated in the past three years and it worked well.

Baker, young and ingratiatingly soft-voiced, had his own copies of the galleys in his hand. He said eagerly, "I've done the first chapter and they contain some typographical beauts."

"The first chapter always has them," said Ninheimer distantly.

"Do you want to go over it now?"

Ninheimer brought his eyes to grave focus on Baker. "I haven't done anything on the galleys, Jim. I don't think I'll bother."

Baker looked confused. "Not bother?"

Ninheimer pursed his lips. "I've asked about the—uh—workload of the machine. After all, he was originally—uh—promoted as a proofreader. They've set a schedule."

"The *machine?* You mean Easy?"

"I believe that is the foolish name they gave it."

"But, Dr. Ninheimer, I thought you were staying clear of it!"

"I seem to be the only one doing so. Perhaps I ought to take my share of the—uh—advantage."

"Oh. Well, I seem to have wasted time on this first chapter, then," said the younger man ruefully.

"Not wasted. We can compare the machine's result with yours as a check."

"If you want to, but—"

"Yes?"

"I doubt that we'll find anything wrong with Easy's work. It's supposed never to have made a mistake."

"I dare say," said Ninheimer dryly.

The first chapter was brought in again by Baker four days later. This time it was Ninheimer's copy, fresh from the special annex that had been built to house Easy and the equipment it used.

Baker was jubilant. "Dr. Ninheimer, it not only caught everything I caught—it found a dozen errors I missed! The whole thing took it twelve minutes!"

Ninheimer looked over the sheaf, with the neatly printed marks and symbols in the margins. He said, "It is not as complete as you and I would have made it. We should have entered an insert on Suzuki's work on the neurological effects of low gravity."

"You mean his paper in *Sociological Reviews*?"

"Of course."

"Well, you can't expect impossibilities of Easy. It can't read the literature for us."

"I realize that. As a matter of fact, I have prepared the insert. I will see the machine and make certain it knows how to—uh—handle inserts."

"It will know."

"I prefer to make certain."

Ninheimer had to make an appointment to see Easy, and then could get nothing better than fifteen minutes in the late evening.

But the fifteen minutes turned out to be ample. Robot EZ-27 understood the matter of inserts at once.

Ninheimer found himself uncomfortable at close quarters with the robot for the first time. Almost automatically, as though it were human, he found himself asking, "Are you happy with your work?"

"Most happy, Professor Ninheimer," said Easy solemnly, the photocells that were its eyes gleaming their normal deep red.

"You know me?"

"From the fact that you present me with additional material to include in the galleys, it follows that you are the author. The author's name, of course, is at the head of each sheet of galley proof."

"I see. You make—uh—deductions, then. Tell me—" He couldn't resist the question—"What do you think of the book so far?"

Easy said, "I find it very pleasant to work with."

"Pleasant? That is an odd word for a—uh—a mechanism without emotion. I've been told you have no emotion."

"The words of your book go in accordance with my cir-cuits," Easy explained. "They set up little or no counter-potentials. It is in my brain-paths to translate this mechanical fact into a word such as 'pleasant.' The emotional context is fortuitous."

"I see. Why do you find the book pleasant?"

"It deals with human beings, Professor, and not with inorganic materials or mathematical symbols. Your book attempts to understand human beings and to help increase human happiness."

"And this is what you try to do and so my book goes in accordance with your circuits? Is that it?"

"That is it, Professor."

The fifteen minutes were up. Ninheimer left and went to the university library, which was on the point of closing. He kept them open long enough to find an elementary text on robotics. He took it home with him.

Except for occasional insertion of late material, the galleys went to Easy and from him to the publishers with little intervention from Ninheimer at first—and none at all later.

Baker said, a little uneasily, "It almost gives me a feeling of uselessness."

"It should give you a feeling of having time to begin a new project," said Ninheimer, without looking up from the notations he was making in the current issue of *Social Science Abstracts*.

"I'm just not used to it. I keep worrying about the galleys. It's silly, I know."

"It is."

"The other day I got a couple of sheets before Easy sent them off to—"

"What!" Ninheimer looked up, scowling. The copy of *Abstracts* slid shut. "Did you disturb the machine at its work?"

"Only for a minute. Everything was all right. Oh, it changed one word. You referred to something as 'criminal'; it changed the word to 'reckless.' It thought the second adjective fit in better with the context."

Ninheimer grew thoughtful. "What did you think?"

"You know, I agreed with it. I let it stand."

Ninheimer turned in his swivel chair to face his young associate. "See here, I wish you wouldn't do this again. If I am to use the machine, I wish the—uh—full advantage of it. If I am to use it and lose your—uh—services anyway because you supervise it when the whole point is that it requires no supervision, I gain nothing. Do you see?"

"Yes, Dr. Ninheimer," said Baker, subdued.

The advance copies of *Social Tensions* arrived in Dr. Ninheimer's office on the 8th of May. He looked through it briefly, flipping pages and pausing to read a paragraph here and there. Then he put his copies away.

As he explained later, he forgot about it. For eight years, he had worked at it, but now, and for months in the past, other interests had engaged him while Easy had taken the load of the book off his shoulders. He did not even think to donate the usual complimentary copy to the university library. Even Baker, who had thrown himself into work and had steered clear of the department head since receiving his rebuke at their last meeting, received no copy.

On the 16th of June that stage ended. Ninheimer received a phone call and stared at the image in the 'plate with surprise.

"Speidell! Are you in town?"

"No, sir. I'm in Cleveland." Speidell's voice trembled with emotion.

"Then why the call?"

"Because I've just been looking through your new book! Ninheimer, are you *mad*? Have you gone *insane*?"

Ninheimer stiffened. "Is something—uh—wrong?" he asked in alarm.

"Wrong? I refer you to page 562. What in blazes do you mean by interpreting my work as you do? Where in the paper cited do I make the claim that the criminal personality is nonexistent and that it is the *law*-enforcement agencies that are the *true* criminals? Here, let me quote—"

"Wait! Wait!" cried Ninheimer, trying to find the page. "Let me see. Let me see... Good God!"

"Well?"

"Speidell, I don't see how this could have happened. I never wrote this."

"But that's what's printed! And that distortion isn't the

worst. You look at page 690 and imagine what Ipatiev is going to do to you when he sees the hash you've made of his findings! Look, Ninheimer, the book is *riddled* with this sort of thing. I don't know what you were thinking of—but there's nothing to do but get the book off the market. And you'd better be prepared for extensive apologies at the next Association meeting!"

"Speidell, listen to me—"

But Speidell had flashed off with a force that had the 'plate glowing with after-images for fifteen seconds.

It was then that Ninheimer went through the book and began marking off passages with red ink.

He kept his temper remarkably well when he faced Easy again, but his lips were pale. He passed the book to Easy and said, "Will you read the marked passages on pages 562, 631, 664 and 690?"

Easy did so in four glances. "Yes, Professor Ninheimer."

"This is not as I had it in the original galleys."

"No, sir. It is not."

"Did you change it to read as it now does?"

"Yes, sir."

"Why?"

"Sir, the passages as they read in your version were most uncomplimentary to certain groups of human beings. I felt it advisable to change the wording to avoid doing them harm."

"How *dared* you do such a thing?"

"The First Law, Professor, does not let me, through any inaction, allow harm to come to human beings. Certainly, considering your reputation in the world of sociology and the wide circulation your book would receive among scholars, considerable harm would come to a number of the human beings you speak of."

"But do you realize the harm that will come to *me* now?"

"It was necessary to choose the alternative with less harm."

Professor Ninheimer, shaking with fury, staggered away. It was clear to him that U.S. Robots would have to account to him for this.

* * *

There was some excitement at the defendants' table, which increased as Prosecution drove the point home.

"Then Robot EZ-27 informed you that the reason for its action was based on the First Law of Robotics?"

"That is correct, sir."

"That, in effect, it had no choice?"

"Yes, sir."

"It follows then that U.S. Robots designed a robot that would of necessity rewrite books to accord with its own conceptions of what was right. And yet they palmed it off as simple proofreader. Would you say that?"

Defense objected firmly at once, pointing out that the witness was being asked for a decision on a matter in which he had no competence. The judge admonished Prosecution in the usual terms, but there was no doubt that the exchange had sunk home—not least upon the Attorney for the Defense.

Defense asked for a short recess before beginning cross-examination, using a legal technicality for the purpose that got him five minutes.

He leaned over toward Susan Calvin. "Is it possible, Dr. Calvin, that Professor Ninheimer is telling the truth and that Easy was motivated by the First Law?"

Calvin pressed her lips together, then said, "No. It *isn't* possible. The last part of Ninheimer's testimony is deliberate perjury. Easy is not designed to be able to judge matters at the stage of abstraction represented by an advanced textbook on sociology. It would never be able to tell that certain groups of humans would be harmed by a phrase in such a book. Its mind is simply not built for that."

"I suppose, though, that we can't prove this to a layman," said Defense pessimistically.

"No," admitted Calvin. "The proof would be highly complex. Our way out is still what it was. We must prove Ninheimer is lying, and nothing he has said need change our plan of attack."

"Very well, Dr. Calvin," said Defense, "I must accept your word in this. We'll go on as planned."

In the courtroom, the judge's gavel rose and fell and Dr.

Ninheimer took the stand once more. He smiled a little as one who feels his position to be impregnable and rather enjoys the prospect of countering a useless attack.

Defense approached warily and began softly. "Dr. Ninheimer, do you mean to say that you were completely unaware of these alleged changes in your manuscript until such time as Dr. Speidell called you on the 16th of June?"

"That is correct, sir."

"Did you never look at the galleys after Robot EZ-27 had proofread them?"

"At first I did, but it seemed to me a useless task. I relied on the claims of U.S. Robots. The absurd—uh—changes were made only in the last quarter of the book after the robot, I presume, had learned enough about sociology—"

"Never mind your presumptions!" said Defense. "I understood your colleague, Dr. Baker, saw the later galleys on at least one occasion. Do you remember testifying to that effect?"

"Yes, sir. As I said, he told me about seeing one page, and even there, the robot had changed a word."

Again Defense broke in. "Don't you find it strange, sir, that after over a year of implacable hostility to the robot, after having voted against it in the first place and having refused to put it to any use whatever, you suddenly decided to put your book, your *magnum opus,* into its hands?"

"I don't find that strange. I simply decided that I might as well use the machine."

"And you were so confident of Robot EZ-27—all of a sudden—that you didn't even bother to check your galleys?"

"I told you I was—uh—persuaded by U.S. Robots' propaganda."

"So persuaded that when your colleague, Dr. Baker, attempted to check on the robot, you berated him soundly?"

"I didn't berate him. I merely did not wish to have him—uh—waste his time. At least, I thought then it was a waste of time, I did not see the significance of that change in the word at the—"

Defense said with heavy sarcasm, "I have no doubt you were instructed to bring up that point in order that the word change be entered in the record—" He altered his line to forestall objection and said, "The point is that you were extremely angry with Dr. Baker."

"No, sir. Not angry."

"You didn't give him a copy of your book when you received it."

"Simple forgetfulness. I didn't give the library its copy, either." Ninheimer smiled cautiously. "Professors are notoriously absentminded."

Defense said, "Do you find it strange that, after more than a year of perfect work, Robot EZ-27 should go wrong on your book? On a book, that is, which was written by you, who were, of all people, the most implacably hostile to the robot?"

"My book was the only sizable work dealing with mankind that it had to face. The Three Laws of Robotics took hold then."

"Several times, Dr. Ninheimer," said Defense, "you have tried to sound like an expert on robotics. Apparently you suddenly grew interested in robotics and took out books on the subject from the library. You testified to that effect, did you not?"

"One book, sir. That was the result of what seems to me to have been—uh—natural curiosity."

"And it enabled you to explain why the robot should, as you allege, have distorted your book?"

"Yes, sir."

"Very convenient. But are you sure your interest in robotics was not intended to enable you to manipulate the robot for your own purposes?"

Ninheimer flushed. "Certainly not, sir!"

Defense's voice rose. "In fact, are you sure the alleged altered passages were not as you had them in the first place?"

The sociologist half rose. "That's—uh—uh—ridiculous! I have the galleys—"

He had difficulty speaking and Prosecution rose to insert smoothly, "With your permission, Your Honor, I intend to introduce as evidence the set of galleys given by Dr. Ninheimer to Robot EZ-27 and the set of galleys mailed by Robot EZ-27 to the publishers. I will do so now if my esteemed colleague so desires, and will be willing to allow a recess in order that the two sets of galleys may be compared."

Defense waved his hand impatiently. "That is not necessary. My honored opponent can introduce those galleys whenever he chooses. I'm sure they will show whatever discrepancies are claimed by the plaintiff to exist. What I would like to know of the witness, however, is whether he also has in his possession *Dr. Baker's* galleys."

"Dr. Baker's galleys?" Ninheimer frowned. He was not yet quite master of himself.

"Yes, Professor! I mean Dr. Baker's galleys. You testified to the effect that Dr. Baker had received a separate copy of the galleys. I will have the clerk read your testimony if you are suddenly a selective type of amnesiac. Or is it just that professors are, as you say, notoriously absent-minded?"

Ninheimer said, "I remember Dr. Baker's galleys. They weren't necessary once the job was placed in the care of the proofreading machine—"

"So you burned them?"

"*No.* I put them in the waste basket."

"Burned them, dumped them—what's the difference? The point is you got rid of them."

"There's nothing wrong—" began Ninheimer weakly.

"Nothing wrong?" thundered Defense. "Nothing wrong except that there is now no way we can check to see if, on certain crucial galley sheets, you might not have substituted a harmless blank one from Dr. Baker's copy for a sheet in your own copy which you had deliberately mangled in such a way as to force the robot to—"

Prosecution shouted a furious objection. Justice Shane leaned forward, his round face doing its best to assume an expression of anger equivalent to the intensity of the emotion felt by the man.

The judge said, "Do you have any evidence, Counselor, for the extraordinary statement you have just made?"

Defense said quietly, "No direct evidence, Your Honor. But I would like to point out that, viewed properly, the sudden conversion of the plaintiff from anti-roboticism, his sudden interest in robotics, his refusal to check the galleys or to allow anyone else to check them, his careful neglect to allow anyone to see the book immediately after publication, all very clearly point—"

"Counselor," interrupted the judge impatiently, "this is not the place for esoteric deductions. The plaintiff is not on trial. Neither are you prosecuting him. I forbid this line of attack and I can only point out that the desperation that must have induced you to do this cannot help but weaken your case. If you have legitimate questions to ask, Counselor, you may continue with your cross-examination. But I warn you against another such exhibition in this courtroom."

"I have no further questions, Your Honor."

Robertson whispered heatedly as council for the Defense returned to his table, "What good did that do, for God's sake? The judge is dead set against you now."

Defense replied calmly, "But Ninheimer is good and rattled. And we've set him up for tomorrow's move. He'll be ripe."

Susan Calvin nodded gravely.

The rest of Prosecution's case was mild in comparison. Dr. Baker was called and bore out most of Ninheimer's testimony. Drs. Speidell and Ipatiev were called, and they expounded most movingly on their shock and dismay at certain quoted passages in Dr. Ninheimer's book. Both gave their professional opinion that Dr. Ninheimer's professional reputation had been seriously impaired.

The galleys were introduced in evidence, as were copies of the finished book.

Defense cross-examined no more that day. Prosecution rested and the trial was recessed till the next morning.

Defense made his first motion at the beginning of the proceedings on the second day. He requested that Robot EZ-27 be admitted as a spectator to the proceedings.

Prosecution objected at once and Justice Shane called both to the bench.

Prosecution said hotly, "This is obviously illegal. A robot may not be in any edifice used by the general public."

"This courtroom," pointed out Defense, "is closed to all but those having an immediate connection with the case."

"A large machine of *known* erratic behavior would disturb my clients and my witnesses by its very presence! It would make hash out of the proceedings."

The judge seemed inclined to agree. He turned to Defense and said rather unsympathetically, "What are the reasons for your request?"

Defense said, "It will be our contention that Robot EZ-27 could not possibly, by the nature of its construction, have behaved as it has been described as behaving. It will be necessary to present a few demonstrations."

Prosecution said, "I don't see the point, Your Honor. Demonstrations conducted by men employed at U.S. Robots are worth little as evidence when U.S. Robots is the defendant."

"Your Honor," said Defense, "the validity of any evidence is for you to decide, not for the Prosecuting Attorney. At least, that is my understanding."

Justice Shane, his prerogatives encroached upon, said, "Your understanding is correct. Nevertheless, the presence of a robot here does raise important legal questions."

"Surely, Your Honor, nothing that should be allowed to override the requirements of justice. If the robot is not present, we are prevented from presenting our only defense."

The judge considered. "There would be the question of transporting the robot here."

"That is a problem with which U.S. Robots has frequently been faced. We have a truck parked outside the courtroom, constructed according to the laws governing the transportation of robots. Robot EZ-27 is in a packing case inside with two men guarding it. The doors to the truck are properly secured and all other necessary precautions have been taken."

"You seem certain," said Justice Shane, in renewed ill-temper, "that judgment on this point will be in your favor."

"Not at all, Your Honor. If it is not, we simply turn the truck about. I have made no presumptions concerning your decision."

The judge nodded. "The request on the part of the Defense is granted."

The crate was carried in on a large dolly and the two men who handled it opened it. The courtroom was immersed in a dead silence.

Susan Calvin waited as the thick slabs of celluform went down, then held out one hand. "Come, Easy."

The robot looked in her direction and held out its large metal arm. It towered over her by two feet but followed meekly, like a child in the clasp of its mother. Someone giggled nervously and choked it off at a hard glare from Dr. Calvin.

Easy seated itself carefully in a large chair brought by the bailiff, which creaked but held.

Defense said, "When it becomes necessary, Your Honor, we will prove that this is actually Robot EZ-27, the specific robot in the employ of Northeastern University during the period of time with which we are concerned."

"Good," His Honor said. "That will be necessary. I, for one, have no idea how you can tell one robot from another."

"And now," said Defense, "I would like to call my first witness to the stand. Professor Simon Ninheimer, please."

The clerk hesitated, looked at the judge. Justice Shane asked, with visible surprise, "You are calling the *plaintiff* as your witness?"

"Yes, Your Honor."

"I hope that you're aware that as long as he's your witness, you will be allowed none of the latitude you might exercise if you were cross-examining an opposing witness."

Defense said smoothly, "My only purpose in all this is to arrive at the truth. It will not be necessary to do more than ask a few polite questions."

"Well," said the judge dubiously, "you're the one handling the case. Call the witness."

Ninheimer took the stand and was informed that he was still under oath. He looked more nervous than he had the day before, almost apprehensive.

But Defense looked at him benignly.

"Now, Professor Ninheimer, you are suing my clients in the amount of $750,000."

"That is the—uh—sum. Yes."

"That is a great deal of money."

"I have suffered a great deal of harm."

"Surely not that much. The material in question involves only a few passages in a book. Perhaps these were unfortunate passages, but after all, books sometimes appear with curious mistakes in them."

Ninheimer's nostrils flared. "Sir, this book was to have been the climax of my professional career! Instead, it makes me look like an incompetent scholar, a perverter of the views held by my honored friends and associates, and a believer of ridiculous and—uh—outmoded viewpoints. My reputation is irretrievably shattered! I can never hold up my head in any—uh—assemblage of scholars, regardless of the outcome of this trial. I certainly cannot continue in my career, which has been the whole of my life. The very purpose of my life has been—uh—aborted and destroyed."

Defense made no attempt to interrupt the speech, but stared abstractedly at his fingernails as it went on.

He said very soothingly, "But surely, Professor Ninheimer, at your present age, you could not hope to earn more than—let us be generous—$150,000 during the remainder of your life. Yet you are asking the court to award you five times as much."

Ninheimer said, with an even greater burst of emotion, "It is not in my lifetime alone that I am ruined. I do not know for how many generations I shall be pointed at by sociologists as a—uh—a fool or maniac. My real achievements will be buried and ignored. I am ruined not only until the day of my death, but for all time to come, because there will always be people who will not believe that a robot made those insertions—"

It was at this point that Robot EZ-27 rose to his feet. Susan Calvin made no move to stop him. She sat motionless, staring straight ahead. Defense sighed softly.

Easy's melodious voice carried clearly. It said, "I would like to explain to everyone that I did insert certain passages in the galley proofs that seemed directly opposed to what had been there at first—"

Even the Prosecuting Attorney was too startled at the spectacle of a seven-foot robot rising to address the court to be able to demand the stopping of what was obviously a most irregular procedure.

When he could collect his wits, it was too late. For Ninheimer rose in the witness chair, his face working.

He shouted wildly, "Damn you, you were instructed to keep your mouth shut about—"

He ground to a choking halt, and Easy was silent, too.

Prosecution was on his feet now, demanding that a mistrial be declared.

Justice Shane banged his gavel desperately. "Silence! Silence! Certainly there is every reason here to declare a mistrail, except that in the interests of justice I would like to have Professor Ninheimer complete his statement. I distinctly heard him say to the robot that the robot had been instructed to keep its mouth shut about something. There was no mention in your testimony, Professor Ninheimer, as to any instructions to the robot to keep silent about anything!"

Ninheimer stared wordlessly at the judge.

Justice Shane said, "Did you instruct Robot EZ-27 to keep silent about something? And if so, about what?"

"Your Honor—" began Ninheimer hoarsely, and couldn't continue.

The judge's voice grew sharp. "Did you in fact, order the inserts in question to be made in the galleys and then order the robot to keep quiet about your part in this?"

Prosecution objected vigorously, but Ninheimer shouted, "Oh, what's the use? Yes! Yes!" And he ran from the witness stand. He was stopped at the door by the bailiff and sank hopelessly into one of the last rows of seats, head buried in both hands.

Justice Shane said, "It is evident to me that Robot EZ-27 was brought here as a trick. Except for the fact that the trick served to prevent a serious miscarriage of justice, I would certainly hold attorney for the Defense in contempt. It is clear now, beyond any doubt, that the plaintiff has committed what is to me a completely inexplicable fraud since, apparently, he was knowingly ruining his career in the process—"

Judgment, of course, was for the defendant.

Dr. Susan Calvin had herself announced at Dr. Ninheimer's bachelor quarters in University Hall. The young engineer who had driven the car offered to go up with her, but she looked at him scornfully.

"Do you think he'll assault me? Wait down here."

Ninheimer was in no mood to assault anyone. He was packing, wasting no time, anxious to be away before the adverse conclusion of the trail became general knowledge.

He looked at Calvin with a queerly defiant air and said, "Are you coming to warn me of a countersuit? If so, it will get you nothing. I have no money, no job, no future. I can't even meet the costs of the trial."

"If you're looking for sympathy," said Calvin coldly, "don't look for it here. This was your doing. However, there will be no countersuit, neither of you nor of the university. We will even do what we can to keep you from going to prison for perjury. We aren't vindictive."

"Oh, is that why I'm not already in custody for forswearing myself? I had wondered. But then," he added bitterly, "why *should* you be vindictive? You have what you want now."

"Some of what we want, yes," said Calvin. "The university will keep Easy in its employ at a considerably higher rental fee. Furthermore, certain underground publicity concerning the trial will make it possible to place a few more of the EZ models in other institutions without danger of a repetition of this trouble."

"Then why have you come to see me?"

"Because I don't have all of what I want yet. I want to know why you hate robots as you do. Even if you had won the case, your reputation would have been ruined. The money you might have obtained could not have compensated for that. Would the satisfaction of your hatred for robots have done so?"

"Are you interested in *human* minds, Dr. Calvin?" asked Ninheimer, with acid mockery.

"Insofar as their reactions concern the welfare of robots, yes. For that reason, I have learned a little of human psychology."

"Enough of it to be able to trick me!"

"That wasn't hard," said Calvin, without pomposity. "The difficult thing was doing it in such a way as not to damage Easy."

"It is like you to be more concerned for a machine than for a man." He looked at her with savage contempt.

It left her unmoved. "It merely seems so, Professor Ninheimer. It is only by being concerned for robots that one can truly be concerned for twenty-first-century Man. You would understand this if you were a roboticist."

"I have read enough robotics to know I don't *want* to be a roboticist!"

"Pardon me, you have read *a book* on robotics. It has taught you nothing. You learned enough to know that you could order a robot to do many things, even to falsify a book, if you went about it properly. You learned enough to know that you could not order him to forget something entirely without risking detection, but you thought you could order him into simple silence more safely. You were wrong."

"You guessed the truth from his silence?"

"It wasn't guessing. You were an amateur and didn't know enough to cover your tracks completely. My only problem was to prove the matter to the judge and you were kind enough to help us there, in your ignorance of the robotics you claim to despise."

"Is there any purpose in this discussion?" asked Ninheimer wearily.

"For me, yes," said Susan Calvin, "because I want you to understand how completely you have misjudged robots. You silenced Easy by telling him that if he told anyone about your own distortion of the book, you would lose your job. That set up a certain potential within Easy toward silence, one that was strong enough to resist our efforts to break it down. We would have damaged the brain if we had persisted.

"On the witness stand, however, you yourself put up a higher counter-potential. You said that because people would think that you, not a robot, had written the disputed passages in the book, you would lose far more than just your job. You would lose your reputation, your standing, your respect, your reason for living. You would lose the memory of you after death. A new and higher potential was set up by you—and Easy talked."

"Oh, God," said Ninheimer, turning his head away.

Calvin was inexorable. She said, "Do you understand *why* he talked? It was not to accuse you, but to *defend* you! It can be mathematically shown that he was about to assume full blame for your crime, to deny that you had anything to do with it. The First Law required that. He was going to lie—to damage himself—to bring monetary harm to a corporation. All that meant less to him than did the saving of you. If you really understood robots and robotics, you would have let him talk. But you did not understand, as I was sure you wouldn't, as I guaranteed to the defense attorney that you wouldn't. You were certain, in your hatred of robots, that Easy would act as a human being would act and defend itself at your expense. So you flared out at him in panic—and destroyed yourself."

Ninheimer said with feeling, "I hope some day your robots turn on you and kill you!"

"Don't be foolish," said Calvin. "Now I want you to explain why you've done all this."

Ninheimer grinned a distorted, humorless grin. "I am to dissect my mind, am I, for your intellectual curiosity, in return for immunity from a charge of perjury?"

"Put it that way if you like," said Calvin emotionlessly. "But explain."

"So that you can counter future antirobot attempts more efficiently? With greater understanding?"

"I accept that."

"You know," said Ninheimer, "I'll tell you—just to watch it do you no good at all. You can't understand human motivation. You can only understand your damned machines because you're a machine yourself, with skin on."

He was breathing hard and there was no hesitation in his speech, no searching for precision. It was as though he had no further use for precision.

He said, "For two hundred and fifty years, the machine has been replacing Man and destroying the handcraftsman. Pottery is spewed out of molds and presses. Works of art have been replaced by identical gimcracks stamped out on a die. Call it progress, if you wish! The artist is restricted to abstractions, confined to the world of ideas. He must design something in his mind—and then the machine does the rest.

"Do you suppose the potter is content with mental creation? Do you supose the idea is enough? That there is nothing in the feel of the clay itself, in watching the thing grow as hand and mind work *together?* Do you suppose the actual growth doesn't act as a feedback to modify and improve the idea?"

"You are not a potter," said Dr. Calvin.

"I am a creative artist! I design and build articles and books. There is more to it than the mere thinking of words and of putting them in the right order. If that were all, there would be no pleasure in it, no return.

"A book should take shape in the hands of the writer. One must actually see the chapters grow and develop. One must work and rework and watch the changes take place beyond the original concept even. There is taking the galleys in hand and seeing how the sentences look in print and molding them again. There are a hundred contacts between a man and his work at every stage of the game—and the contact itself is pleasurable and repays a man for the work he puts into his creation more than anything else could. *Your robot would take all that away.*"

"So does a typewriter. So does a printing press. Do you propose to return to the hand-illumination of manuscripts?"

"Typewriters and printing presses take away some, but your robot would deprive us of all. Your robot takes over the galleys. Soon it, or other robots, would take over the original writing, the searching of the sources, the checking and cross-checking of passages, perhaps even the deduction of conclusions. What would that leave the scholar? One thing only—

the barren decisions concerning what orders to give the robot next! I want to save the future generations of the world of scholarship from such a final hell. That meant more to me than even my own reputation and so I set out to destroy U.S. Robots by whatever means."

"You were bound to fail," said Susan Calvin.

"I was bound to try," said Simon Ninheimer.

Calvin turned and left. She did her best to feel no pang of sympathy for the broken man.

She did not entirely succeed.

ANGER

It has a use, the rage that shakes us and pours hormones into our blood; that urges us to action and makes us insensible to pity and pain. How would the great deeds of the world get done without the push and shove of that trembling haze of crimson? And what would we not give to undo the hasty things said and done in ANGER.

DIVINE MADNESS

ROGER ZELAZNY

"*...I is this ?hearers wounded-wonder like stand them makes and stars wandering the conjures sorrow of phrase Whose...*"

He blew smoke through the cigarette and it grew longer.

He glanced at the clock and realized that its hands were moving backwards.

The clock told him that it was 10:33, going on 10:32 in the P.M.

Then came the thing like despair, for he knew there was not a thing he could do about it. He was trapped, moving in reverse through the sequence of actions past. Somehow, he had missed the warning.

Usually, there was a prism-effect, a flash of pink static, a drowsiness, then a moment of heightened perception...

He turned the pages, from left to right, his eyes retracing their path back along the lines.

"*?emphasis an such bears grief whose he is What*"

Helpless, there behind his eyes, he watched his body perform.

The cigarette had reached its full length. He clicked on the lighter, which sucked away its glowing point, and then he shook the cigarette back into the pack.

He yawned in reverse: first an exhalation, then an inhalation.

It wasn't real—the doctor had told him. It was grief and epilepsy, meeting to form an unusual syndrome.

He'd already had the seizure. The dialantin wasn't helping. This was a post-traumatic locomotor hallucination, elicited by anxiety, precipitated by the attack.

But he did not believe it, could not believe it—not after

157

twenty minutes had gone by, in the other direction—not after
he had placed the book upon the reading stand, stood, walked
backward across the room to his closet, hung up his robe,
redressed himself in the same shirt and slacks he had worn
all day, backed over to the bar and regurgitated a Martini,
sip by cooling sip, until the glass was filled to the brim and
not a drop spilled.

There was an impending taste of olive, and then everything was changed again.

The second hand was sweeping around his wristwatch in
the proper direction.

The time was 10:07.

He felt free to move as he wished.

He redrank his martini.

Now, if he would be true to the pattern, he would change
into his robe and try to read. Instead, he mixed another drink.

Now the sequence would not occur.

Now the things would not happen as he thought they had
happened, and un-happened.

Now everything was different.

All of which went to prove it had been an hallucination.

Even the notion that it had taken twenty-six minutes each
way was an attempted rationalization.

Nothing had happened.

...Shouldn't be drinking, he decided. It might bring on a
seizure.

He laughed.

Crazy, though, the whole thing...

Remembering, he drank.

In the morning he skipped breakfast, as usual, noted that
it would soon stop being morning, took two aspirins, a luke-
warm shower, a cup of coffee, and a walk.

The park, the fountain, the children with their boats, the
grass, the pond, he hated them; and the morning, and the
sunlight, and the blue moats around the towering clouds.

Hating, he sat there. And remembering.

If he was on the verge of a crackup, he decided, then the

thing he wanted most was to plunge ahead into it, not to totter halfway out, halfway in.

He remembered why.

But it was clear, so clear, the morning, and everything crisp and distinct and burning with the green fires of spring, there in the sign of the Ram, April.

He watched the winds pile up the remains of winter against the far gray fence, and he saw them push the boats across the pond, to come to rest in shallow mud the children tracked.

The fountain jetted its cold umbrella above the green-tinged copper dolphins. The sun ignited it whenever he moved his head. The wind rumpled it.

Clustered on the concrete, birds pecked at part of a candy bar stuck to a red wrapper.

Kites swayed on their tails, nosed downward, rose again, as youngsters tugged at invisible strings. Telephone lines were tangled with wooden frames and torn paper, like broken G clefs and smeared glissandos.

He hated the telephone lines, the kites, the children, the birds.

Most of all, though, he hated himself.

How does a man undo that which has been done? He doesn't. There is no way under the sun. He may suffer, remember, repent, curse, or forget. Nothing else. The past, in this sense, is inevitable.

A woman walked past. He did not look up in time to see her face, but the dusky blonde fall of her hair to her collar and the swell of her sure, sheer-netted legs below the black hem of her coat and above the matching click of her heels heigh-ho, stopped his breath behind his stomach and snared his eyes in the wizard-weft of her walking and her posture and some more, like a rhyme to the last of his thoughts.

He half-rose from the bench when the pink static struck his eyeballs, and the fountain became a volcano spouting rainbows.

The world was frozen and served up to him under glass.

. . . The woman passed back before him and he looked down too soon to see her face.

The hell was beginning once more, he realized, as the backward-flying birds passed before.

He gave himself to it. Let it keep him until he broke, until he was all used up and there was nothing left.

He waited, there on the bench, watching the slithey toves be brillig, as the fountain sucked its waters back within itself, drawing them up in a great arc above the unmoving dolphins, and the boats raced backward across the pond, and the fence divested itself of stray scraps of paper, as the birds replaced the candy bar within the red wrapper, bit by crunchy bit.

His thoughts only were inviolate, his body belonged to the retreating tide.

Eventually, he rose and strolled backwards out of the park.

On the street a boy backed past him, unwhistling snatches of a popular song.

He backed up the stairs to his apartment, his hangover growing worse again, undrank his coffee, unshowered, unswallowed his aspirins, and got into bed, feeling awful.

Let this be it, he decided.

A faintly-remembered nightmare ran in reverse through his mind, giving it an undeserved happy ending.

It was dark when he awakened.

He was very drunk.

He backed over to the bar and began spitting out his drinks, one by one into the same glass he had used the night before, and pouring them from the glass back into the bottles again. Separating the gin and vermouth was no trick at all. The proper liquids leapt into the air as he held the uncorked bottles above the bar.

And he grew less and less drunk as this went on.

Then he stood before an early martini and it was 10:07 in the P.M. There, within the hallucination, he wondered about another hallucination. Would time loop-the-loop, forward and then backward again, through his previous seizure?

No.

It was as though it had not happened, had never been.

He continued on back through the evening, undoing things.

He raised the telephone, said "Good-bye," untold Murray that he would not be coming to work again tomorrow, listened a moment, recradled the phone and looked at it as it rang.

The sun came up in the west and people were backing their cars to work.

He read the weather report and the headlines, folded the evening paper and placed it out in the hall.

It was the longest seizure he had ever had, but he did not really care. He settled himself down within it and watched as the day unwound itself back to morning.

His hangover returned as the day grew smaller, and it was terrible when he got into bed again.

When he awakened the previous evening the drunkenness was high upon him. Two of the bottles he refilled, recorked, resealed. He knew he would take them to the liquor store soon and get his money back.

As he sat there that day, his mouth uncursing and undrinking and his eyes unreading, he knew that new cars were being shipped back to Detroit and disassembled, that corpses were awakening into their death-throes, and that priests the world over were saying black mass, unknowing.

He wanted to chuckle, but he could not tell his mouth to do it.

He unsmoked two and a half packs of cigarettes.

Then came another hangover and he went to bed. Later, the sun set in the east.

Time's winged chariot fled before him as he opened the door and said "Good-bye" to his comforters and they came in and sat down and told him not to grieve overmuch.

And he wept without tears as he realized what was to come.

Despite his madness, he hurt.

...Hurt, as the days rolled backward.

...Backward, inexorably.

...Inexorably, until he knew the time was near at hand.

He gnashed the teeth of his mind.

Great was his grief and his hate and his love.

He was wearing his black suit and undrinking drink after drink, while somewhere the men were scraping the clay back onto the shovels which would be used to undig the grave.

He backed his car to the funeral parlor, parked it, and climbed into the limousine.

They backed all the way to the graveyard.

He stood among his friends and listened to the preacher.

".dust to dust; ashes to Ashes," the man said, which is pretty much the same whichever way you say it.

The casket was taken back to the hearse and returned to the funeral parlor.

He sat through the service and went home and unshaved and unbrushed his teeth and went to bed.

He awakened and dressed again in black and returned to the parlor.

The flowers were all back in place.

Solemn-faced friends unsigned the Sympathy Book and unshook his hand. Then they went inside to sit awhile and stare at the closed casket. Then they left, until he was alone with the funeral director.

Then he was alone with himself.

The tears ran up his cheeks.

His suit and shirt were crisp and unwrinkled again.

He backed home, undressed, uncombed his hair. The day collapsed around him into morning, and he returned to bed to unsleep another night.

The previous evening, when he awakened, he realized where he was headed.

Twice, he exerted all of his will power in an attempt to interrupt the sequence of events. He failed.

He wanted to die. If he had killed himself that day, he would not be headed back toward it now.

There were tears within his mind as he realized the past which lay less than twenty-four hours before him.

The past stalked him that day as he unnegotiated the purchase of the casket, the vault, the accessories.

Then he headed home into the biggest hangover of all and slept until he was awakened to undrink drink after drink and then return to the morgue and come back in time to hang up the telephone on that call, that call which had come to break...

...the silence of his anger with its ringing.

She was dead.

She was lying somewhere in the fragments of her car on Interstate 90 now.

As he paced, unsmoking, he knew she was lying there bleeding.

...Then dying, after that crash at 80 miles an hour.

...Then alive?

Then re-formed, along with the car, and alive again, arisen? Even now backing home at a terrible speed, to re-slam the door on their final argument? To unscream at him and to be unscreamed at?

He cried out within his mind. He wrung the hands of his spirit.

It couldn't stop at this point. No. Not now.

All his grief and his love and his self-hate had brought him back this far, this near to the moment...

It *couldn't* end now.

After a time, he moved to the living room, his legs pacing, his lips cursing, himself waiting.

The door slammed open.

She stared in at him, her mascara smeared, tears upon her cheeks.

"!hell to go Then," he said.

"!going I'm," she said.

She stepped back inside, closed the door.

She hung her coat hurriedly in the hall closet.

".it about feel you way the that's If," he said, shrugging.

"!yourself but anybody about care don't You," she said.

"!child a like behaving You're," he said.

"!sorry you're say least at could You"

Her eyes flashed like emeralds through the pink static, and she was lovely and alive again. In his mind he was dancing.

The change came.

"You could at least say you're sorry!"

"I am," he said, taking her hand in a grip that she could not break. "How much, you'll never know."

"Come here," and she did.

GLUTTONY

Isn't there *something* you don't think you can have enough of? Chocolate creams? Dry martinis? Pâté de foie gras? French-fried potatoes? Roast stuffed duck? Diamond rings? Loni Anderson? A person needs his dreams, and how better to dream than to imagine one's self just *wallowing* in spareribs, sacher torte, emerald necklaces, and jaguars (both coats and cars)—and everything else your little mind can want. Wouldn't that be nice? Are you sure? Or can anything possibly spoil the fun of GLUTTONY?

THE MIDAS PLAGUE

FREDERIK POHL

And so they were married.

The bride and groom made a beautiful couple, she in her twenty-yard frill of immaculate white, he in his formal gray ruffled blouse and pleated pantaloons.

It was a small wedding—the best he could afford. For guests, they had only the immediate family and a few close friends. And when the minister had performed the ceremony, Morey Fry kissed his bride and they drove off to the reception. There were twenty-eight limousines in all (though it is true that twenty of them contained only the caterer's robots) and three flower cars.

"Bless you both," said old man Elon sentimentally. "You've got a fine girl in our Cherry, Morey." He blew his nose on a ragged square of cambric.

The old folks behaved very well, Morey thought. At the reception, surrounded by the enormous stacks of wedding gifts, they drank the champagne and ate a great many of the tiny, delicious canapés. They listened politely to the fifteen-piece orchestra, and Cherry's mother even danced one dance with Morey for sentiment's sake, though it was clear that dancing was far from the usual pattern of her life. They tried as hard as they could to blend into the gathering, but all the same, the two elderly figures in severely simple and probably rented garments were dismayingly conspicuous in the quarter-acre of tapestries and tinkling fountains that was the main ballroom of Morey's country home.

When it was time for the guests to go home and let the newlyweds begin their life together, Cherry's father shook Morey by the hand and Cherry's mother kissed him. But as they drove away in their tiny runabout their faces were full of foreboding.

It was nothing against Morey as a person, of course. But poor people should not marry wealth.

Morey and Cherry loved each other, certainly. That helped. They told each other so, a dozen times an hour, all of the long hours they were together, for all of their first months of their marriage. Morey even took time off to go shopping with his bride, which endeared him to her enormously. They drove their shopping carts through the immense vaulted corridors of the supermarket, Morey checking off the items on the shopping list as Cherry picked out the goods. It was fun.

For a while.

Their first fight started in the supermarket, between Breakfast Foods and Floor Furnishings, just where the new Precious Stones department was being opened.

Morey called off from the list, "Diamond lavaliere, costume rings, earbobs."

Cherry said rebelliously, "Morey, I *have* a lavaliere. Please, dear!"

Morey folded back the pages of the list uncertainly. The lavaliere was on there, all right, and no alternative selection was shown.

"How about a bracelet?" he coaxed. "Look, they have some nice ruby ones there. See how beautifully they go with your hair, darling!" He beckoned a robot clerk, who bustled up and handed Cherry the bracelet tray. "Lovely," Morey exclaimed as Cherry slipped the largest of the lot on her wrist.

"And I don't have to have a lavaliere?" Cherry asked.

"Of course not." He peeked at the tag. "Same number of ration points exactly!" Since Cherry looked only dubious, not convinced, he said briskly, "And now we'd better be getting along to the shoe department. I've got to pick up some dancing pumps."

Cherry made no objection, neither then nor throughout the rest of their shopping tour. At the end, while they were sitting in the supermarket's ground-floor lounge waiting for the robot accountants to tote up their bill and the robot cashiers to stamp their ration books, Morey remembered to have the shipping department save out the bracelet.

"I don't want that sent with the other stuff, darling," he explained. "I want you to wear it right now. Honestly, I don't think I ever saw anything looking so *right* for you."

Cherry looked flustered and pleased. Morey was delighted with himself; it wasn't everybody who knew how to handle these little domestic problems just right!

He stayed self-satisfied all the way home, while Henry, their companion-robot, regaled them with funny stories of the factory in which it had been built and trained. Cherry wasn't used to Henry by a long shot, but it was hard not to like the robot. Jokes and funny stories when you needed amusement, sympathy when you were depressed, a never-failing supply of news and information on any subject you cared to name—Henry was easy enough to take. Cherry even made a special point of asking Henry to keep them company through dinner, and she laughed as thoroughly as Morey himself at its droll anecdotes.

But later, in the conservatory, when Henry had considerately left them alone, the laughter dried up.

Morey didn't notice. He was very conscientiously making the rounds: turning on the tri-D, selecting their after-dinner liqueurs, scanning the evening newspapers.

Cherry cleared her throat self-consciously, and Morey stopped what he was doing. "Dear," she said tentatively, "I'm feeling kind of restless tonight. Could we—I mean do you think we could just sort of stay home and—well, relax?"

Morey looked at her with a touch of concern. She lay back wearily, eyes half closed. "Are you feeling all right?" he asked.

"Perfectly. I just don't want to go out tonight, dear. I don't feel up to it."

He sat down and automatically lit a cigarette. "I see," he said. The tri-D was beginning a comedy show; he got up to turn it off, snapping on the tape-player. Muted strings filled the room.

"We had reservations at the club tonight," he reminded her.

Cherry shifted uncomfortably. "I know."

"And we have the opera tickets that I turned last week's in for. I hate to nag, darling, but we haven't used *any* of our opera tickets."

"We can see them right here on the tri-D," she said in a small voice.

"That has nothing to do with it, sweetheart. I—I didn't want to tell you about it, but Wainwright, down at the office, said something to me yesterday. He told me he would be at the circus last night and as much as said he'd be looking to see if we were there too. Well, we weren't there. Heaven konws what I'll tell him next week."

He waited for Cherry to answer, but she was silent.

He went on reasonably, "So if you *could* see your way clear to going out tonight—"

He stopped, slack-jawed. Cherry was crying, silently and in quantity.

"Darling!" he said inarticulately.

He hurried to her, but she fended him off. He stood helpless over her, watching her cry.

"Dear, what's the matter?" he asked.

She turned her head away.

Morey rocked back on his heels. It wasn't exactly the first time he'd seen Cherry cry—there had been that poignant scene when they Gave Each Other Up, realizing that their backgrounds were too far apart for happiness, before the realization that they *had* to have each other, no matter what....But it was the first time her tears had made him feel guilty.

And he did feel guilty. He stood there staring at her.

Then he turned his back on her and walked over to the bar. He ignored the ready liqueurs and poured two stiff highballs, brought them back to her. He set one down beside her, took a long drink from the other.

In quite a different tone, he said, "Dear, what's the *matter?*"

No answer.

"Come on. What is it?"

She looked up at him and rubbed at her eyes. Almost sullenly, she said, "Sorry."

"I know you're sorry. Look, we love each other. Let's talk this thing out."

She picked up her drink and held it for a moment, before setting it down untasted. "What's the use, Morey?"

"Please. Let's try."

She shrugged.

He went on remorselessly, "You aren't happy, are you? And it's because of—well, all this." His gesture took in the richly furnished conservatory, the thick-piled carpet, the host of machines and contrivances for their comfort and entertainment that waited for their touch. By implication it took in twenty-six rooms, five cars, nine robots. Morey said, with an effort, "It isn't what you're used to, is it?"

"I can't help it," Cherry said. "Morey, you know I've tried. But back home—"

"Dammit," he flared, "*this* is your home. You don't live with your father any more in that five-room cottage; you don't spend your evenings hoeing the garden or playing cards for matchsticks. You live here, with me, your husband! You knew what you were getting into. We talked all this out long before we were married—"

The words stopped, because words were useless. Cherry was crying again, but not silently.

Through her tears, she wailed: "Darling, I've tried. You don't *know* how I've tried! I've worn all those silly clothes and I've played all those silly games and I've gone out with you as much as I *possibly* could and—I've eaten all that terrible food until I'm actually getting fa-fa-fat! I thought I could stand it. But I just can't go on like this; I'm not used to it. I—I love you, Morey, but I'm going crazy, living like this. I can't help it, Morey—*I'm tired of being poor!*"

Eventually the tears dried up, and the quarrel healed, and the lovers kissed and made up. But Morey lay awake that night, listening to his wife's gentle breathing from the suite next to his own, staring into the darkness as tragically as any pauper before him had ever done.

Blessed are the poor, for they shall inherit the earth.

Blessed Morey, heir to more worldly goods than he could possibly consume.

Morey Fry, steeped in grinding poverty, had never gone hungry a day in his life, never lacked for anything his heart could desire in the way of food, or clothing, or a place to sleep. In Morey's world, no one lacked for these things; no one could.

Malthus was right—for a civilization without machines, automatic factories, hydroponics and food synthesis, nuclear breeder plants, ocean mining for metals and minerals...

And a vastly increasing supply of labor...

And architecture that rose high in the air and dug deep in the ground and floated far out on the water on piers and pontoons...architecture that could be poured one day and lived in the next...

And robots.

Above all, robots...robots to burrow and haul and smelt and fabricate, to build and farm and weave and sew.

What the land lacked in wealth, the sea was made to yield, and the laboratory invented the rest...and the factories became a pipeline of plenty, churning out enough to feed and clothe and house a dozen worlds.

Limitless discovery, infinite power in the atom, tireless labor of humanity and robots, mechanization that drove jungle and swamp and ice off the Earth, and put up office buildings and manufacturing centers and rocket ports in their place...

The pipeline of production spewed out riches that no king in the time of Malthus could have known.

But a pipeline has two ends. The invention and power and labor pouring in at one end must somehow be drained out at the other...

Lucky Morey, blessed economic-consuming unit, drowning in the pipeline's flood, striving manfully to eat and drink and wear and wear out his share of the ceaseless tide of wealth.

Morey felt far from blessed, for the blessings of the poor are always best appreciated from afar.

* * *

Quotas worried his sleep until he awoke at eight o'clock the next morning, red-eyed and haggard, but inwardly resolved. He had reached a decision. He was starting a new life.

There was trouble in the morning mail. Under the letterhead of the National Ration Board, it said:

"We regret to advise you that the following items returned by you in connection with your August quotas as used and no longer serviceable have been inspected and found insufficiently worn." The list followed—a long one, Morey saw to his sick disappointment. "Credit is hereby disallowed for these and you are therefore given an additional consuming quota for the current month in the amount of four-hundred and thirty-five points, at least three-hundred and fifty points of which must be in the textile and home-furnishing categories."

Morey dashed the letter to the floor. The valet picked it up emotionlessly, creased it and set it on his desk.

It wasn't fair! All right, maybe the bathing trunks and beach umbrellas hadn't been *really* used very much—though how the devil, he asked himself bitterly, did you go about using up swimming gear when you didn't have time for such leisurely pursuits as swimming? But certainly the hiking slacks were used! He'd worn them for three whole days and part of a fourth; what did they expect him to do, go around in *rags*?

Morey looked belligerently at the coffee and toast that the valet-robot had brought in with the mail, and then steeled his resolve. Unfair or not, he had to play the game according to the rules. It was for Cherry, more than for himself, and the way to begin a new way of life was to begin it.

Morey was going to consume for two.

He told the valet-robot, "Take that stuff back. I want cream and sugar with the coffee—*lots* of cream and sugar. And besides the toast, scrambled eggs, fried potatoes, orange juice—no, make it half a grapefruit. *And* orange juice, come to think of it."

"Right away, sir," said the valet. "You won't be having breakfast at nine then, will you, sir?"

"I certainly will," said Morey virtuously. "Double portions!" As the robot was closing the door, he called after it, "Butter and marmalade with the toast!"

He went to the bath; he had a full schedule and no time to waste. In the shower, he carefully sprayed himself with lather three times. When he had rinsed the soap off, he went through the whole assortment of taps in order: three lotions, plain talcum, scented talcum and thirty seconds of ultra-violet. Then he lathered and rinsed again, and dried himself with a towel instead of using the hot-air drying jet. Most of the miscellaneous scents went down the drain with the rinse water, but if the Ration Board accused him of waste, he could claim he was experimenting. The effect, as a matter of fact, wasn't bad at all.

He stepped out, full of exuberance. Cherry was awake, staring in dismay at the tray the valet had brought. "Good morning, dear," she said faintly. "Ugh."

Morey kissed her and patted her hand. "Well!" he said, looking at the tray with a big, hollow smile. "Food!"

"Isn't that a *lot* for just the two of us?"

"Two of us?" repeated Morey masterfully. "Nonsense, my dear, I'm going to eat it all by myself!"

"Oh, Morey!" gasped Cherry, and the adoring look she gave him was enough to pay for a dozen such meals.

Which, he thought as he finished his morning exercises with the sparring-robot and sat down to his *real* breakfast, it just about had to be, day in and day out, for a long, long time.

Still, Morey had made up his mind. As he worked his way through the kippered herring, tea and crumpets, he ran over his plans with Henry. He swallowed a mouthful and said, "I want you to line up some appointments for me right away. Three hours a week in an exercise gym—pick one with lots of reducing equipment, Henry. I think I'm going to need it. And fittings for some new clothes—I've had these for weeks. And, let's see, doctor, dentist—say, Henry, don't I have a psychiatrist's date coming up?"

"Indeed you do, sir!" it said warmly. "This morning, in fact. I've already instructed the chauffeur and notified your office."

"Fine! Well, get started on the other things, Henry."

"Yes, sir," said Henry, and assumed the curious absent look of a robot talking on its TBR circuits—the "Talk Between Robots" radio—as it arranged the appointments for its master.

Morey finished his breakfast in silence, pleased with his own virtue, at peace with the world. It wasn't so hard to be a proper, industrious consumer if you *worked* at it, he reflected. It was only the malcontents, the ne'er-do-wells and the incompetents who simply could not adjust to the world around them. Well, he thought with distant pity, someone had to suffer; you couldn't break eggs without making an omelet. And his proper duty was not to be some sort of wild-eyed crank, challenging the social order and beating his breast about injustice, but to take care of his wife and his home.

It was too bad he couldn't really get right down to work on consuming today. But this was his one day a week to hold a *job*—four of the other six days were devoted to solid consuming—and besides, he had a group therapy session scheduled as well. His analysis, Morey told himself, would certainly take a sharp turn for the better, now that he had faced up to his problems.

Morey was immersed in a glow of self-righteousness as he kissed Cherry good-by (she had finally got up, all in a confusion of delight at the new regime) and walked out the door to his car. He hardly noticed the little man in enormous floppy hat and garishly ruffled trousers who was standing almost hidden in the shrubs.

"Hey, Mac." The man's voice was almost a whisper.

"Huh? Oh—what is it?"

The man looked around furtively. "Listen, friend," he said rapidly, "You look like an intelligent man who could use a little help. Times are tough; you help me, I'll help you. Want to make a deal on ration stamps? Six for one. One of yours for six of mine, the best deal you'll get anywhere in town.

Naturally, my stamps aren't exactly the real McCoy, but they'll pass, friend, they'll pass—"

Morey blinked at him. "No!" he said violently, and pushed the man aside. Now it's racketeers, he thought bitterly. Slums and endless sordid preoccupation with rations weren't enough to inflict on Cherry; now the neighborhood was becoming a hangout for people on the shady side of the law. It was not, of course, the first time he had ever been approached by a counterfeit-ration-stamp hoodlum, but never at his own front door!

Morey thought briefly, as he climbed into his car, of calling the police. But certainly the man would be gone before they could get there; and after all, he had handled it pretty well as it was.

Of course, it would be nice to get six stamps for one.

But very far from nice if he got caught.

"Good morning, Mr. Fry," tinkled the robot receptionist. "Won't you go right in?" With a steel-tipped finger, it pointed to the door marked GROUP THERAPY.

Someday, Morey vowed to himself as he nodded and complied, he would be in a position to afford a private analyst of his own. Group therapy helped relieve the infinite stresses of modern living, and without it he might find himself as badly off as the hysterical mobs in the ration riots, or as dangerously anti-social as the counterfeiters. But it lacked the personal touch. It was, he thought, too public a performance of what should be a private affair, like trying to live a happy married life with an interfering, ever-present crowd of robots in the house—

Morey brought himself up in panic. How had *that* thought crept in? He was shaken visibly as he entered the room and greeted the group to which he was assigned.

There were eleven of them: four Freudians, two Reichians, two Jungians, a Gestalter, a shock therapist and the elderly and rather quiet Sullivanite. Even the members of the majority groups had their own individual differences in technique and creed, but despite four years with this particular group of analysts, Morey hadn't quite been able to keep them separate in his mind. Their names, though, he knew well enough.

"Morning, Doctors," he said. "What is it today?"

"Morning," said Semmelweiss morosely. "Today you come into the room for the first time looking as if something is really bothering you, and yet the schedule calls for psychodrama. Dr. Fairless," he appealed, "can't we change the schedule a little bit? Fry here is obviously under a strain; *that's* the time to start digging and see what he can find. We can do your psychodrama next time, can't we?"

Fairless shook his gracefully bald old head. "Sorry, Doctor. If it were up to me, of course—but you know the rules."

"Rules, rules," jeered Semmelweiss. "Ah, what's the use? Here's a patient in an acute anxiety state if I ever saw one—and believe me, I saw plenty—and we ignore it because the *rules* say ignore it. Is that professional? Is that how to cure a patient?"

Little Blaine said frostily, "If I may say so, Dr. Semmelweiss, there have been a great many cures made without the necessity of departing from the rules. I myself, in fact—"

"You yourself!" mimicked Semmelweiss. "You yourself never handled a patient alone in your life. When you going to get out of a group, Blaine?"

Blaine said furiously, "Dr. Fairless, I don't think I have to stand for this sort of personal attack. Just because Semmelweiss has seniority and a couple of private patients one day a week, he thinks—"

"Gentlemen," said Fairless mildly. "Please, let's get on with the work. Mr. Fry has come to us for help, not to listen to us losing our tempers."

"Sorry," said Semmelweiss curtly. "All the same, I appeal from the arbitrary and mechanistic ruling of the chair."

Fairless inclined his head. "All in favor of the ruling of the chair? Nine, I count. That leaves only you opposed, Dr. Semmelweiss. We'll proceed with the psychodrama, if the recorder will read us the notes and comments of the last session."

The recorder, a pudgy, low-ranking youngster named Sprogue, flipped back the pages of his notebook and read in a chanting voice, "Session of twenty-fourth May, subject, Morey Fry; in attendance, Doctors Fairless, Bileck, Semmelweiss, Carrado, Weber—"

Fairless interrupted kindly, "Just the last page, if you please, Dr. Sprogue."

"Um—oh, yes. After a ten-minute recess for additional Rorschachs and an electro-encephalogram, the group convened and conducted rapid-fire word association. Results were tabulated and compared with standard deviation patterns, and it was determined that subject's major traumas derived from, respectively—"

Morey found his attention waning. Therapy was *good;* everybody knew that, but every once in a while he found it a little dull. If it weren't for therapy, though, there was no telling what might happen. Certainly, Morey told himself, he had been helped considerably—at least he hadn't set fire to his house and shrieked at the fire-robots, like Newell down the block when his eldest daughter divorced her husband and came back to live with him, bringing her ration quota along, of course. Morey hadn't even been *tempted* to do anything as outrageously, frighteningly immoral as *destroy* things or *waste* them—well, he admitted to himself honestly, perhaps a little tempted, once in a great while. But never anything important enough to worry about; he was sound, perfectly sound.

He looked up, startled. All the doctors were staring at him. "Mr. Fry," Fairless repeated, "will you take your place?"

"Certainly," Morey said hastily. "Uh—where?"

Semmelweiss guffawed. *"Told* you. Never mind, Morey; you didn't miss much. We're going to run through one of the big scenes in your life, the one you told us about last time. Remember? You were fourteen years old, you said. Christmas time. Your mother had made you a promise."

Morey swallowed. "I remember," he said unhappily. "Well, all right. Where do I stand?"

"Right here," said Fairless. "You're you; Carrado is your mother; I'm your father. Will the doctors not participating mind moving back? Fine. Now, Morey, here we are on Christmas morning. Merry Christmas, Morey!"

"Merry Christmas," Morey said half-heartedly. "Uh—Father dear, where's my—uh—my puppy that Mother promised me?"

"Puppy!" said Fairless heartily. "Your mother and I have something much better than a puppy for you. Just take a look under the tree there—it's a *robot!* Yes, Morey, your very own robot—a full-size thirty-eight-tube fully automatic companion robot for you! Go ahead, Morey, go right up and speak to it. Its name is Henry. Go on, boy."

Morey felt a sudden, incomprehensible tingle inside the bridge of his nose. He said shakily, "But I—I didn't *want* a robot."

"Of course you want a robot," Carrado interrupted. "Go on, child, play with your nice robot."

Morey said violently, "I *hate* robots!" He looked around him at the doctors, at the gray-paneled consulting room. He added defiantly, "You hear me, all of you? I *still* hate robots!"

There was a second's pause; then the questions began.

It was half an hour before the receptionist came in and announced that time was up.

In that half hour, Morey had got over his trembling and lost his wild, momentary passion, but he had remembered what for thirteen years he had forgotten.

He hated robots.

The surprising thing was not that young Morey had hated robots. It was that the Robot Riots, the ultimate violent outbreak of flesh against metal, the battle to the death between mankind and its machine heirs...never happened. A little boy hated robots, but the man he became worked with them hand in hand.

And yet, always and always before, the new worker, the competitor for the job, was at once and inevitably outside the law. The waves swelled in—the Irish, the Negroes, the Jews, the Italians. They were squeezed into their ghettoes, where they encysted, seethed and struck out, until the burgeoning generations became indistinguishable.

For the robots, that genetic relief was not in sight. And still the conflict never came. The feedback circuits aimed the anti-aircraft guns and, reshaped and newly planned, found a place in a new sort of machine—together with a miraculous trail of cams and levers, and indestructible and potent power source and a hundred thousand parts and subassemblies.

And the first robot clanked off the bench.

Its mission was its own destruction; but from the scavenged wreck of its pilot body, a hundred better robots drew their inspiration. And the hundred went to work, and hundreds more, until there were millions upon untold millions.

And still the riots never happened.

For the robots came bearing a gift and the name of it was "Plenty."

And by the time the gift had shown its own unguessed ills, the time for a Robot Riot was past. Plenty is a habit-forming drug. You do not cut the dosage down. You kick it if you can; you stop the dose entirely. But the convulsions that follow may wreck the body once and for all.

The addict craves the grainy white powder; he doesn't hate it, or the runner who sells it to him. And if Morey as a little boy could hate the robot that had deprived him of his pup, Morey the man was perfectly aware that the robots were his servants and his friends.

But the little Morey inside the man—*he* had never been convinced.

Morey ordinarily looked forward to his work. The one day a week at which he *did* anything was a wonderful change from the dreary consume, consume, consume grind. He entered the bright-lit drafting room of the Bradmoor Amusements Company with a feeling of uplift.

But as he was changing from street garb to his drafting smock, Howland from Procurement came over with a knowing look. "Wainwright's been looking for you," Howland whispered. "Better get right in there."

Morey nervously thanked him and got. Wainwright's office was the size of a phone booth and as bare as Antarctic ice. Every time Morey saw it, he felt his insides churn with envy. Think of a desk with nothing on it but work surface—

no calendar-clock, no twelve-color pen rack, no dictating machines!

He squeezed himself in and sat down while Wainwright finished a phone call. He mentally reviewed the possible reasons why Wainwright would want to talk to him in person instead of over the phone, or by dropping a word to him as he passed through the drafting room.

Very few of them were good.

Wainwright put down the phone and Morey straightened up. "You sent for me?" he asked.

Wainwright in a chubby world was aristocratically lean. As General Superintendent of the Design & Development Section of the Bradmoor Amusements Company, he ranked high in the upper section of the well-to-do. He rasped, "I certainly did. Fry, just what the hell do you think you're up to now?"

"I don't know what you m-mean, Mr. Wainwright," Morey stammered, crossing off the list of possible reasons for the interview all of the good ones.

Wainwright snorted. "I guess you don't. Not because you weren't told, but because you don't want to know. Think back a whole week. What did I have you on the carpet for then?"

Morey said sickly, "My ration book. Look, Mr. Wainwright, I know I'm running a little bit behind, but—"

"But nothing! How do you think it looks to the Committee, Fry? They got a complaint from the Ration Board about you. Naturally they passed it on to me. And naturally I'm going to pass it right along to you. The question is, what are you going to do about it? Good God, man, look at these figures— textiles, fifty-one per cent; food, sixty-seven per cent; amusements and entertainment, *thirty* per cent! You haven't come up to your ration in anything for months!"

Morey stared at the card miserably. "We—that is, my wife and I—just had a long talk about that last night, Mr. Wainwright. And, believe me, we're going to do better. We're going to buckle right down and get to work and—uh—do better," he finished weakly.

Wainwright nodded, and for the first time there was a

note of sympathy in his voice. "Your wife. Judge Elon's daughter, isn't she? Good family. I've met the Judge many times." Then, gruffly: "Well, nevertheless, Fry, I'm warning you. I don't care how you straighten this out, but *don't let the Committee mention this to me again.*"

"No, sir."

"All right. Finished with the schematics on the new K-50?"

Morey brightened. "Just about, sir! I'm putting the first section on tape today. I'm very pleased with it, Mr. Wainwright, honestly I am. I've got more than eighteen thousand moving parts in it now, and that's without—"

"Good. Good." Wainwright glanced down at his desk. "Get back to it. And straighten out this other thing. You can do it, Fry. Consuming is everybody's duty. Just keep that in mind."

Howland followed Morey out of the drafting room, down to the spotless shops. "Bad time?" he inquired solicitously. Morey grunted. It was none of Howland's business.

Howland looked over his shoulder as he was setting up the programing panel. Morey studied the matrices silently, then got busy reading the summary tapes, checking them back against the schematics, setting up the instructions on the programing board. Howland kept quiet as Morey completed the setup and ran off a test tape. It checked perfectly; Morey stepped back to light a cigarette in celebration before pushing the *start* button.

Howland said, "Go on, run it. I can't go until you put it in the works."

Morey grinned and pushed the button. The board lighted up; within it, a tiny metronomic beep began to pulse. That was all. At the other end of the quarter-mile shed, Morey knew, the automatic sorters and conveyers were fingering through the copper reels and steel ingots, measuring hoppers of plastic powder and colors, setting up an intricate weaving path for the thousands of individual components that would make up Bradmoor's new K-50 Spin-a-Game. But from where they stood, in the elaborately muraled programing room, nothing showed. Bradmoor was an ultra-modernized plant;

in the manufacturing end, even robots had been dispensed with in favor of machines that guided themselves.

Morey glanced at his watch and logged in the starting time while Howland quickly counterchecked Morey's raw-material flow program.

"Checks out," Howland said solemnly, slapping him on the back. "Calls for a celebration. Anyway, it's your first design, isn't it?"

"Yes. First all by myself, at any rate."

Howland was already fishing in his private locker for the bottle he kept against emergency needs. He poured with a flourish. "To Morey Fry," he said, "our most favorite designer, in whom we are much pleased."

Morey drank. It went down easily enough. Morey had conscientiously used his liquor rations for years, but he had never gone beyond the minimum, so that although liquor was no new experience to him, the single drink immediately warmed him. It warmed his mouth, his throat, the hollows of his chest; and it settled down with a warm glow inside him. Howland, exerting himself to be nice, complimented Morey fatuously on the design and poured another drink. Morey didn't utter any protest at all.

Howland drained his glass. "You may wonder," he said formally, "why I am so pleased with you, Morey Fry. I will tell you why this is."

Morey grinned. "Please do."

Howland nodded. "I will. It's because I am pleased with the world, Morey. My wife left me last night."

Morey was as shocked as only a recent bridegroom can be by the news of a crumbling marriage. "That's too ba— I mean, is that a fact?"

"Yes, she left my beds and board and five robots, and I'm happy to see her go." He poured another drink for both of them. "Women. Can't live with them and can't live without them. First you sigh and pant and chase after 'em—you like poetry?" he demanded suddenly.

Morey said cautiously, "Some poetry."

Howland quoted: "'How long, my love, shall I behold this wall between our gardens—yours the rose, and mine the swooning lily' Like it? I wrote it for Jocelyn—that's my wife—when we were first going together?"

"It's beautiful," said Morey.

"She wouldn't talk to me for two days." Howland drained his drink. "Lots of spirit, that girl. Anyway, I hunted her like a tiger. And then I caught her. *Wow!*"

Morey took a deep drink from his own glass. "What do you mean, *wow?*" he asked.

"*Wow.*" Howland pointed his finger at Morey. "*Wow*, that's what I mean. We got married and I took her home to the dive I was living in, and *wow* we had a kid, and *wow* I got in a little trouble with the Ration Board—nothing serious, of course, but there was a mixup—and *wow* fights.

"Everything was a fight," he explained. "She'd start with a little nagging, and naturally I'd say something or other back, and *bang* we were off. Budget, budget, budget; I hope to die if I ever hear the word 'budget' again. Morey, you're a married man; you know what it's like. Tell me the truth, weren't you just about ready to blow your top the first time you caught your wife cheating on the budget?"

"Cheating on the budget?" Morey was startled. "Cheating how?"

"Oh, lots of ways. Making your portions bigger than hers. Sneaking extra shirts for you on her clothing ration. You know."

"Damn it, I do *not* know!" cried Morey. "Cherry wouldn't do anything like that!"

Howland looked at him opaquely for a long second. "Of course not," he said at last. "Let's have another drink."

Ruffled, Morey held out his glass. Cherry wasn't the type of girl to *cheat*. Of course she wasn't. A fine, loving girl like her—a pretty girl, of a good family; she wouldn't know how to begin.

Howland was saying, in a sort of chant, "No more budget. No more fights. No more, 'Daddy never treated me like this.' No more nagging. No more extra rations for household allowance. No more—Morey, what do you say we go out and have a few drinks? I know a place where—"

"Sorry, Howland," Morey said. "I've got to get back to the office, you know."

Howland guffawed. He held out his wristwatch. As Morey, a little unsteadily, bent over it, it tinkled out the hour. It was a matter of minutes before the office closed for the day.

"Oh," said Morey. "I didn't realize—Well, anyway, Howland, thanks, but I can't. My wife will be expecting me."

"She certainly will," Howland sniggered. "Won't catch *her* eating up your rations and hers tonight."

Morey said tightly, "Howland!"

"Oh, sorry, sorry." Howland waved an arm. "Don't mean to say anything against *your* wife, of course. Guess maybe Jocelyn soured me on women. But honest, Morey, you'd like this place. Name of Uncle Piggotty's, down in the Old Town. Crazy bunch hangs out there. You'd like them. Couple nights last week they had—I mean, you understand, Morey, I don't go there as often as all that, but I just happened to drop in and—"

Morey interrupted firmly. "Thank you, Howland. Must go home. Wife expects it. Decent of you to offer. Good night. Be seeing you."

He walked out, turned at the door to bow politely, and in turning back cracked the side of his face against the door jamb. A sort of pleasant numbness had taken possession of his entire skin surface, though, and it wasn't until he perceived Henry chattering at him sympathetically that he noticed a trickle of blood running down the side of his face.

"Mere flesh wound," he said with dignity. "Nothing to cause you *least* conshter—consternation, Henry. Now kindly shut your ugly face. Want to think."

And he slept in the car all the way home.

It was worse than a hangover. The name is "holdover." You've had some drinks; you've started to sober up by catching a little sleep. Then you are required to be awake and to function. The consequent state has the worst features of hangover and intoxication; your head thumps and your mouth tastes like the floor of a bear pit, but you are nowhere near sober.

There is one cure. Morey said thickly, "Let's have a cocktail, dear."

Cherry was delighted to share a cocktail with him before dinner. Cherry, Morey thought lovingly, was a wonderful, wonderful, wonderful—

He found his head nodding in time to his thoughts, and the motion made him wince.

Cherry flew to his side and touched his temple. "Is it bothering you, darling?" she asked solicitously. "Where you ran into the door, I mean?"

Morey looked at her sharply, but her expression was open and adoring. He said bravely, "Just a little. Nothing to it, really."

The butler brought the cocktails and retired. Cherry lifted her glass. Morey raised his, caught a whiff of the liquor, and nearly dropped it. He bit down hard on his churning insides and forced himself to swallow.

He was surprised but grateful: It stayed down. In a moment, the curious phenomenon of warmth began to repeat itself. He swallowed the rest of the drink and held out his glass for a refill. He even tried a smile. Oddly enough, his face didn't fall off.

One more drink did it. Morey felt happy and relaxed, but by no means drunk. They went in to dinner in fine spirits. They chatted cheerfully with each other and Henry, and Morey found time to feel sentimentally sorry for poor Howland, who couldn't make a go of his marriage, when marriage was obviously such an easy relationship, so beneficial to both sides, so warm and relaxing—

Startled, he said, "What?"

Cherry repeated, "It's the cleverest scheme I ever heard of. Such a funny little man, dear. All kind of *nervous*, if you know what I mean. He kept looking at the door as if he was expecting someone, but of course that was silly. None of his friends would have come to *our* house to see him."

Morey said tensely, "Cherry, *please!* What was that you said about ration stamps?"

"But I told you, darling! it was just after you left this morning. This funny little man came to the door; the butler said he wouldn't give his name. Anyway, I talked to him. I thought he might be a neighbor, and I certainly would *never* be rude to any neighbor who might come to call, even if the neighborhood was—"

"The ration stamps!" Morey begged. "Did I hear you say he was peddling phony ration stamps?"

Cherry said uncertainly, "Well, I suppose that in a *way* they're phony. The way he explained it, they weren't the regular official kind. But it was four for one, dear—four of his stamps for one of ours. So I just took out our household book and steamed off a couple of weeks' stamps and—"

"How many?" Morey bellowed.

Cherry blinked. "About—about two weeks' quota," she said faintly. "Was that wrong, dear?"

Morey closed his eyes dizzily. "A couple of weeks' stamps," he repeated. "Four for one—you didn't even get the regular rate."

Cherry wailed, "How was I supposed to know? I never had anything like this when I was *home!* We didn't have food riots and slums and all these horrible robots and filthy little revolting men coming to the door!"

Morey stared at her woodenly. She was crying again, but it made no impression on the case-hardened armor that was suddenly thrown around his heart.

Henry made a tentative sound that, in a human, would have been a preparatory cough, but Morey froze him with a white-eyed look.

Morey said in a dreary monotone that barely penetrated the sound of Cherry's tears, "Let me tell you just what it was you did. Assuming, at best, that these stamps you got are at least average good counterfeits, and not so bad that the best thing to do with them is throw them away before we get caught with them in our possession, you have approximately a two-month supply of funny stamps. In case you didn't know it, those ration books are not merely ornamental. They have to be turned in every month to prove that we have completed our consuming quota for the month.

"When they are turned in, they are spot-checked. Every book is at least glanced at. A big chunk of them are gone over very carefully by the inspectors, and a certain percentage are tested by ultra-violet, infra-red, X-ray, radioisotopes, bleaches, fumes, paper chromatography and every other damned test known to Man." His voice was rising to an uneven crescendo. "*If* we are lucky enough to get away with using any of these stamps at all, we daren't—we simply *dare* not—use more than one or two counterfeits to every dozen or more real stamps.

"That means, Cherry, that what you bought is not a two-month supply, but maybe a two-*year* supply—and since, as you no doubt have never noticed, the things have expiration dates on them, there is probably no chance in the world that we can ever hope to use more than half of them." He was bellowing by the time he pushed back his chair and towered over her. "Moreover," he went on, "right *now*, right as of this *minute*, we have to make up the stamps you gave away, which means that at the very best we are going to be on double rations for two weeks or so.

"And that says nothing about the one feature of this whole grisly mess that you seem to have thought of least—namely that counterfeit stamps are against the *law!* I'm poor, Cherry; I live in a slum, and I know it; I've got a long way to go before I'm as rich or respected or powerful as your father, about whom I am beginning to get considerably tired of hearing. But poor as I may be, I can tell you *this* for sure: Up until now, at any rate, I have been *honest.*"

Cherry's tears had stopped entirely and she was bowed white-faced and dry-eyed by the time Morey had finished. He had spent himself; there was no violence left in him.

He stared dismally at Cherry for a moment, then turned wordlessly and stamped out of the house.

Marriage! he thought as he left.

He walked for hours, blind to where he was going.

What brought him back to awareness was a sensation he had not felt in a dozen years. It was not, Morey abruptly realized, the dying traces of his hangover that made his stomach feel so queer. He was hungry—actually hungry.

He looked about him. He was in the Old Town, miles from

home, jostled by crowds of lower-class people. The block he was on was as atrocious a slum as Morey had ever seen— Chinese pagodas stood next to rococo imitations of the chapels around Versailles; gingerbread marred every façade; no building was without its brilliant signs and flarelights.

He saw a blindingly overdecorated eating establishment called Billie's Budget Busy Bee and crossed the street toward it, dodging through the unending streams of traffic. It was a miserable excuse for a restaurant, but Morey was in no mood to care. He found a seat under a potted palm, as far from the tinkling fountains and robot string ensemble as he could manage, and ordered recklessly, paying no attention to the ration prices. As the waiter was gliding noiselessly away, Morey had a sickening realization: He'd come out without his ration book. He groaned out loud; it was too late to leave without causing a disturbance. But then, he thought rebelliously, what difference did one more unrationed meal make anyhow?

Food made him feel a little better. He finished the last of his *profiterole au chocolate,* not even leaving on the plate the uneaten one-third that tradition permitted, and paid his check. The robot cashier reached automatically for his ration book. Morey had a moment of grandeur as he said simply, "No ration stamps."

Robot cashiers are not equipped to display surprise, but this one tried. The man behind Morey in line audibly caught his breath, and less audibly mumbled something about *slummers.* Morey took it as a compliment and strode outside feeling almost in good humor.

Good enough to go home to Cherry? Morey thought seriously of it for a second; but he wasn't going to pretend he was wrong and certainly Cherry wasn't going to be willing to admit that *she* was at fault.

Besides, Morey told himself grimly, she was undoubtedly asleep. That was an annoying thing about Cherry at best: She never had any trouble getting to sleep. Didn't even use her quota of sleeping tablets, though Morey had spoken to her about it more than once. Of course, he reminded himself, he had been so polite and tactful about it, as befits a newlywed, that very likely she hadn't even understood that it was a complaint. Well, *that* would stop!

Man's man Morey Fry, wearing no collar ruff but his own, strode determinedly down the streets of the Old Town.

"Hey, Joe, want a good time?"

Morey took one unbelieving look. "You again!" he roared.

The little man stared at him in genuine surprise. Then a faint glimmer of recognition crossed his face. "Oh, yeah," he said. "This morning, huh?" He clucked commiseratingly. "Too bad you wouldn't deal with me. Your wife was a lot smarter. Of course, you got me a little sore, Jack, so naturally I had to raise the price a little bit."

"You skunk, you cheated my poor wife blind! You and I are going to the local station house and talk this over."

The little man pursed his lips. "We are, huh?"

Morey nodded vigorously. "Damn right! And let me tell you—" He stopped in the middle of a threat as a large hand cupped around his shoulder.

The equally large man who owned the hand said, in a mild and cultured voice, "Is this gentleman disturbing you, Sam?"

"Not so far," the little man conceded. "He might want to, though, so don't go away."

Morey wrenched his shoulder away. "Don't think you can strongarm me. I'm taking you to the police."

Sam shook his head unbelievingly. "You mean you're going to call the law in on this?"

"I certainly am!"

Sam sighed regretfully. "What do you think of that, Walter? Treating his wife like that. Such a nice lady, too."

What are you talking about?" Morey demanded, stung on a peculiarly sensitive spot.

"I'm talking about your wife," Sam explained. "Of course, I'm not married myself. But it seems to me that if I was, I wouldn't call the police when my wife was engaged in some kind of criminal activity or other. No, sir, I'd try to settle it myself. Tell you what," he advised, "why don't you talk this over with her? Make her see the error of—"

"Wait a minute," Morey interrupted. "You mean you'd involve my wife in this thing?"

The man spread his hands helplessly. "It's not me that would involve her, Buster," he said. "She already involved her own self. It takes two to make a crime, you know. I sell, maybe; I won't deny it. But after all, I can't sell unless somebody buys, can I?"

Morey stared at him glumly. He glanced in quick speculation at the large-sized Walter; but Walter was just as big as he'd remembered, so that took care of that. Violence was out; the police were out; that left no really attractive way of capitalizing on the good luck of running into the man again.

Sam said, "Well, I'm glad to see that's off your mind. Now, returning to my original question, Mac, how would you like a good time? You look like a smart fellow to me; you look like you'd be kind of interested in a place I happen to know of down the block."

Morey said bitterly, "So you're a dive-steerer too. A real talented man."

"I admit it," Sam agreed. "Stamp business is slow at night, in my experience. People have their minds more on a good time. And, believe me, a good time is what I can show 'em. Take this place I'm talking about, Uncle Piggotty's is the name of it, it's what I would call an unusual kind of place. Wouldn't you say so, Walter?"

"Oh, I agree with you entirely," Walter rumbled.

But Morey was hardly listening. He said, "Uncle Piggotty's, you say?"

"That's right," said Sam.

Morey frowned for a moment, digesting an idea. Uncle Piggotty's sounded like the place Howland had been talking about back at the plant; it might be interesting, at that.

While he was making up his mind, Sam slipped an arm through his on one side and Walter amiably wrapped a big hand around the other. Morey found himself walking.

"You'll like it," Sam promised comfortably. "No hard feelings about this morning, sport? Of course not. Once you get a look at Piggotty's, you'll get over your mad, anyhow. It's something special. I swear, on what they pay me for bringing in customers, I wouldn't do it unless I *believed* in it."

"Dance, Jack?" the hostess yelled over the noise at the bar. She stepped back, lifted her flounced skirts to ankle height and executed a tricky nine-step.

"My name is Morey," Morey yelled back. "And I don't want to dance, thanks."

The hostess shrugged, frowned meaningfully at Sam and danced away.

Sam flagged the bartender. "First round's on us," he explained to Morey. "Then we won't bother you any more. Unless you want us to, of course. Like the place?" Morey hesitated, but Sam didn't wait. "Fine place," he yelled, and picked up the drink the bartender left him. "See you around."

He and the big man were gone. Morey stared after them uncertainly, then gave it up. He was here, anyhow; might as well at least have a drink. He ordered and looked around.

Uncle Piggotty's was a third-rate dive disguised to look, in parts of it at least, like one of the exclusive upper-class country clubs. The bar, for instance, was treated to resemble the clean lines of nailed wood; but underneath the surface treatment, Morey could detect the intricate laminations of plyplastic. What at first glance appeared to be burlap hangings were in actuality elaborately textured synthetics. And all through the bar the motif was carried out.

A floor show of sorts was going on, but nobody seemed to be paying much attention to it. Morey, straining briefly to hear the master of ceremonies, gathered that the wit was on a more than mildly vulgar level. There was a dispirited string of chorus beauties in long ruffled pantaloons and diaphanous tops; one of them, Morey was almost sure, was the hostess who had talked to him just a few moments before.

Next to him a man was declaiming to a middle-aged woman:

> *"Smote I the monstrous rock, yahoo!*
> *Smote I the turgid tube, Bully Boy!*
> *Smote I the cankered hill—*

Why, Morey!" he interrupted himself. "What are you doing here?"

He turned farther around and Morey recognized him. "Hello, Howland," he said. "I—uh—I happened to be free tonight, so I thought—"

Howland sniggered. "Well, guess your wife is more liberal than mine was. Order a drink, boy."

"Thanks, I've got one," said Morey.

The woman, with a tigerish look at Morey, said, "Don't stop, Everett. That was one of your most beautiful things."

"Oh, Morey's heard my poetry," Howland said. "Morey, I'd like you to meet a very lovely and talented young lady, Tanaquil Bigelow. Morey works in the office with me, Tan."

"Obviously," said Tanaquil Bigelow in a frozen voice, and Morey hastily withdrew the hand he had begun to put out.

The conversation stuck there, impaled, the woman cold, Howland relaxed and abstracted, Morey wondering if, after all, this had been such a good idea. He caught the eye-cell of the robot bartender and ordered a round of drinks for the three of them, politely putting them on Howland's ration book. By the time the drinks had come and Morey had just got around to deciding that it wasn't a very good idea, the woman had all of a sudden become thawed.

She said abruptly, "You look like the kind of man who thinks, Morey, and I like to talk to that kind of man. Frankly, Morey, I just don't have any patience at all with the stupid, stodgy men who just work in their offices all day and eat all their dinners every night, and gad about and consume like mad and where does it all get them anyhow? That's right; I can see you understand. Just one crazy rush of consume, consume from the day you're born *plop* to the day you're buried *pop!* And who's to blame if not the robots?"

Faintly, a tinge of worry began to appear on the surface of Howland's relaxed chin. "Tan," he chided, "Morey may not be very interested in politics."

Politics, Morey thought; well, at least that was a clue.

He'd had the dizzying feeling, while the woman was talking, that he himself was the ball in the games machine he had designed for the shop earlier that day. Following the woman's conversation might, at that, give his next design some valuable pointers in swoops, curves, and obstacles.

He said, with more than half truth, "No, please go on, Miss Bigelow. I'm very much interested."

She smiled; then abruptly her face changed to a frightening scowl. Morey flinched, but evidently the scowl wasn't meant for him. "Robots!" she hissed. "Supposed to work for us, aren't they? Hah! We're their slaves, slaves for every moment of every miserable day of our lives. Slaves! Wouldn't you like to join us and be free, Morey?"

Morey took cover in his drink. He made an expressive gesture with his free hand—expressive of exactly what, he didn't truly know, for he was lost. But it seemed to satisfy the woman.

She said accusingly, "Did you know that more than three-quarters of the people in this country have had a nervous breakdown in the past five years and four months? That more than half of them are under the constant care of psychiatrists for psychosis—not just plain ordinary neurosis like my husband's got and Howland here has got and you've got, but psychosis. Like I've got. Did you know that? Did you know that forty percent of the population are essentially manic depressive, thirty-one percent are schizoid, thirty-eight percent have an assortment of other unfixed psychogenic disturbances, and twenty-four—"

"Hold it a minute, Tan," Howland interrupted critically. "You've got too many percents there. Start over again."

"Oh, the hell with it," the woman said moodily. "I wish my husband were here. He expresses it so much better than I do." She swallowed her drink. "Since you've wriggled off the hook," she said nastily to Morey, "how about setting up another round—on my ration book this time?"

Morey did; it was the simplest thing to do in his confusion. When that was gone, they had another on Howland's book.

As near as he could figure out, the woman, her husband and quite possibly Howland as well belonged to some kind of anti-robot group. Morey had heard of such things; they had a quasi-legal status, neither approved nor prohibited, but he had never come into contact with them before. Remembering the hatred he had so painfully relived at the psychodrama session, he thought anxiously that perhaps he belonged with them. But, question them though he might, he couldn't seem to get the principles of the organization firmly in mind.

The woman finally gave up trying to explain it, and went off to find her husband while Morey and Howland had another drink and listened to two drunks squabble over who bought the next round. They were at the Alphonse-Gaston stage of inebriation; they would regret it in the morning; for each was bending over backward to permit the other to pay the ration points. Morey wondered uneasily about his own points; Howland was certainly getting credit for a lot of Morey's drinking tonight. Served him right for forgetting his book, of course.

When the woman came back, it was with the large man Morey had encountered in the company of Sam, the counterfeiter, steerer and general man about Old Town.

"A remarkably small world, isn't it?" boomed Walter Bigelow, only slightly crushing Morey's hand in his. "Well, sir, my wife has told me how interested you are in the basic philosophical drives behind our movement, and I should like to discuss them further with you. To begin with, sir, have you considered the principle of Twoness?"

Morey said, "Why—"

"Very good," said Bigelow courteously. He cleared his throat and declaimed:

> *Han-headed Cathay saw it first,*
> *Bright as brightest solar burst;*
> *Whipped it into boy and girl,*
> *The blinding spiral-sliced swirl:*
> *Yang*
> *And Yin.*

* * *

He shrugged deprecatingly. "Just the first stanza," he said. "I don't know if you got much out of it."

"Well, no," Morey admitted.

"Second stanza," Bigelow said firmly:

> *Hegel saw it, saw it clear;*
> *Jackal Marx drew near, drew near;*
> *O'er his shoulder saw it plain,*
> *Turned it upside down again:*
> *Yang*
> *And Yin.*

There was an expectant pause. Morey said, "I—uh—"

"Wraps it all up, doesn't it?" Bigelow's wife demanded. "Oh, if only others could see it as clearly as you do! The robot peril *and* the robot savior. Starvation *and* surfeit. Always twoness, always!"

Bigelow patted Morey's shoulder. "The next stanza makes it even clearer," he said. "It's really very clever—I shouldn't say it, of course, but it's Howland's as much as it's mine. He helped me with the verses." Morey darted a glance at Howland, but Howland was carefully looking away. "Third stanza," said Bigelow. "This is a hard one, because it's long, so pay attention."

> *Justice, tip your sightless scales;*
> *One pan rises, one pan falls.*

"Howland," he interrupted himself, "are you *sure* about that rhyme? I always trip over it. Well, anyway:

> *Add to A and B grows less;*
> *A's B's partner, nonetheless.*
> *Next, the Twoness that there be*
> *In even electricity.*
> *Chart the current as it's found:*
> *Sine the hot lead; line the ground.*
> *The wild sine dances, soars, and falls,*
> *But only to figures the zero calls.*

Sine wave, scales, all things that be
Share a reciprocity.
Male and female, light and dark:
Name the numbers of Noah's Ark!
Yang
And Yin!

"Dearest!" shrieked Bigelow's wife. "You've never done it better!" There was a spatter of applause, and Morey realized for the first time that half the bar had stopped its noisy revel to listen to them. Bigelow was evidently quite a well-known figure here.

Morey said weakly, "I've never heard anything like it."

He turned hesitantly to Howland, who promptly said, "Drink! What we all need right now is a drink."

They had a drink on Bigelow's book.

Morey got Howland aside and asked him, "Look, level with me. Are these people nuts?"

Howland showed pique. "No. Certainly not."

"Does that poem mean anything? Does this whole business of twoness mean anything?"

Howland shrugged. "If it means something to them, it means something. They're philosophers, Morey. They see deep into things. You don't know what a privilege it is for me to be allowed to associate with them."

They had another drink. On Howland's book, of course.

Morey eased Walter Bigelow over to a quiet spot. He said, "Leaving twoness out of it for the moment, what's this about the robots?"

Bigelow looked at him round-eyed. "Didn't you understand the poem?"

"Of course I did. But diagram it for me in simple terms so I can tell my wife."

Bigelow beamed. "It's about the dichotomy of robots," he explained. "Like the little salt mill that the boy wished for: it ground out salt and ground out salt and ground out salt. He had to have salt, but not *that* much salt. Whitehead explains it clearly—"

They had another drink on Bigelow's book.

Morey wavered over Tanaquil Bigelow. He said fuzzily, "Listen. Mrs. Walter Tanaquil Strongarm Bigelow. Listen."

She grinned smugly at him. "Brown hair," she said dreamily.

Morey shook his head vigorously. "Never mind hair," he ordered. "Never mind poem. Listen. In *pre-cise* and el-e-*men*-ta-ry terms, explain to me what is wrong with the world today."

"Not enough brown hair," she said promptly.

"Never mind hair!"

"All right," she said agreeably. "Too many robots. Too many robots make too much of everything."

"Ha! Got it!" Morey exclaimed triumphantly. "Get rid of robots!"

"Oh, no. No! No! No. We wouldn't eat. Everything is mechanized. Can't get rid of them, can't slow down production—slowing down is dying, stopping is quicker dying. Principle of twoness is the concept that clarifies all these—"

"No!" Morey said violently. "What should we *do?*"

"Do? I'll tell you what we should do, if that's what you want. I can tell you."

"Then tell me."

"What we should do is"—Tanaquil hiccupped with a look of refined consternation—"have another drink."

They had another drink. He gallantly let her pay, of course. She ungallantly argued with the bartender about the ration points due her.

Though not a two-fisted drinker, Morey tried. He really worked at it.

He paid the price, too. For some little time before his limbs stopped moving, his mind stopped functioning. Blackout. Almost a blackout, at any rate, for all he retained of the late evening was a kaleidoscope of people and places and things. Howland was there, drunk as a skunk, disgracefully drunk, Morey remembered thinking as he stared up at Howland from the floor. The Bigelows were there. His wife, Cherry, solicitous and amused, was there. And oddly enough, Henry was there.

It was very, very hard to reconstruct. Morey devoted a whole morning's hangover to the effort. It was *important* to reconstruct it, for some reason. But Morey couldn't even remember what the reason was; and finally he dismissed it, guessing that he had either solved the secret of twoness or whether Tanaquil Bigelow's remarkable figure was natural.

He did, however, know that the next morning he had waked in his own bed, with no recollection of getting there. No recollection of anything much, at least not of anything that fit into the proper chronological order or seemed to mesh with anything else, after the dozenth drink, when he and Howland, arms around each other's shoulders, composed a new verse on twoness and, plagiarizing an old marching tune, howled it across the boisterous barroom:

> *A twoness on the scene much later*
> *Rest in your refrigerator.*
> *Heat your house and insulate it.*
> *Next your food: Refrigerate it.*
> *Frost will damp your Freon coils,*
> *So flux in nichrome till it boils.*
> *See the picture? Heat in cold*
> *In heat in cold, the story's told!*
> *Giant-writ the sacred scrawl:*
> *Oh, the twoness of it all!*
> *Yang*
> *And Yin!*

It had, at any rate, seemed to mean something at the time.

If alcohol opened Morey's eyes to the fact that there *was* a twoness, perhaps alcohol was what he needed. For there was.

Call it a dichotomy, if the word seems more couth. A kind of two-pronged struggle, the struggle of two unwearying runners in an immortal race. There is the refrigerator inside the house. The cold air, the bubble of heated air that is in the house, the bubble of cooled air that is the refrigerator, the momentary bubble of heated air that defrosts it. Call the heat Yang, if you will. Call the cold Yin. Yang overtakes Yin. Then Yin passes Yang. Then Yang passes Yin. Then—

Give them other names. Call Yin a mouth; call Yang a hand.

If the hand rests, the mouth will starve. If the mouth stops, the hand will die. The hand, Yang, moves faster.

Yin may not lag behind.

Then call Yang a robot.

And remember that a pipeline has two ends.

Like any once-in-a-lifetime lush, Morey braced himself for the consequences—and found startledly that there were none.

Cherry was a surprise to him. "You were so funny," she giggled. "And, honestly, so *romantic*."

He shakily swallowed his breakfast coffee.

The office staff roared and slapped him on the back. "Howland tells us you're living high, boy!" they bellowed more or less in the same words. "Hey, listen to what Morey did—went on the town for the night of a lifetime *and didn't even bring his ration book along to cash in!*"

They thought it was a wonderful joke.

But, then, everything was going well. Cherry, it seemed, had reformed out of recognition. True, she still hated to go out in the evening and Morey never saw her forcing herself to gorge on unwanted food or play undesired games. But, moping into the pantry one afternoon, he found to his incredulous delight that they were well ahead of their ration quotas. In some items, in fact, they were *out*—a month's supply and more was gone ahead of schedule!

Nor was it the counterfeit stamps, for he had found them tucked behind a bain-marie and quietly burned them. He cast about for ways of complimenting her, but caution prevailed. She was sensitive on the subject; leave it be.

And virtue had its reward.

Wainwright called him in, all smiles. "Morey, great news! We've appreciated your work here, and we've been able to show it in some more tangible way than compliments. I didn't want to say anything till it was definite, but—your status has been reviewed by Classification and the Ration Board. You're out of class Four Minor, Morey!"

Morey said tremulously, hardly daring to hope, "I'm a full Class Four?"

"Class Five, Morey. *Class Five!* When we do something, we do it right. We asked for a special waiver and got it—you've skipped a whole class." He added honestly, "Not that it was just our backing that did it, of course. Your own recent splendid record of consumption helped a lot. I told you you could do it!"

Morey had to sit down. He missed the rest of what Wainwright had to say, but it couldn't have mattered. He escaped from the office, sidestepped the knot of fellow employees waiting to congratulate him, and got to a phone.

Cherry was as ecstatic and inarticulate as he. "Oh, darling!" was all she could say.

"And I couldn't have done it without you," he babbled, "Wainwright as much as said so himself. Said if it wasn't for the way we—well, *you* have been keeping up with the rations, it never would have got by the Board. I've been meaning to say something to you about that, dear, but I just haven't known how. But I do appreciate it. I—Hello?" There was a curious silence at the other end of the phone. "Hello?" he repeated worriedly.

Cherry's voice was intense and low. "Morey Fry, I think you're mean. I wish you hadn't spoiled the good news." And she hung up.

Morey stared slack-jawed at the phone.

Howland appeared behind him, chuckling. "Women," he said. "Never try to figure them. Anyway, congratulations, Morey."

"Thanks," Morey mumbled.

Howland coughed and said, "Uh—by the way, Morey, now that you're one of the big shots, so to speak, you won't—uh—feel obliged to—well, say anything to Wainwright, for instance, about anything I may have said while we—"

"Excuse me," Morey said, unhearing, and pushed past him. He thought wildly of calling Cherry back, of racing home to see just what he'd said that was wrong. Not that there was much doubt, of course. He'd touched her on her sore point.

Anyhow, his wristwatch was chiming a reminder of the fact that his psychiatric appointment for the week was coming up.

Morey sighed. The day gives and the day takes away. Blessed is the day that gives only good things.

If any.

The session went badly. Many of the sessions had been going badly, Morey decided; there had been more and more whispering in knots of doctors from which he was excluded, poking and probing in the dark instead of the precise psychic surgery he was used to. Something was wrong, he thought.

Something was. Semmelweiss confirmed it when he adjourned the group session. After the other doctors had left, he sat Morey down for a private talk. On his own time too—he didn't ask for his usual ration fee. That told Morey how important the problem was.

"Morey," said Semmelweiss, "you're holding back."

"I don't mean to, Doctor," Morey said earnestly.

"Who knows what you 'mean' to do? Part of you 'means' to. We've dug pretty deep, and we've found some important things. Now there's something I can't put my finger on. Exploring the mind, Morey, is like sending scouts through cannibal territory. You can't see the cannibals—until it's too late. But if you send a scout through the jungle and he doesn't show up on the other side, it's a fair assumption that something obstructed his way. In that case, we would label the obstruction 'cannibals.' In the case of the human mind, we label the obstruction a 'trauma.' What the trauma is, or what its effects on behavior will be, we have to find out, once we know that it's there."

Morey nodded. All of this was familiar; he couldn't see what Semmelweiss was driving at.

Semmelweiss sighed. "The trouble with healing traumas and penetrating psychic blocks and releasing inhibitions—the trouble with everything we psychiatrists do, in fact, is that we can't afford to do it too well. An inhibited man is under a strain. We try to relieve the strain. But if we succeed completely, leaving him with no inhibitions at all, we have an outlaw, Morey. Inhibitions are often socially necessary. Suppose, for instance, that an average man were not inhibited against blatant waste. It could happen, you know. Suppose that instead of consuming his ration quota in an orderly and responsible way, he did such things as set fire to his house and everything in it or dumped his food allotment in the river.

"When only a few individuals are doing it, we treat the individuals. But if it were done on a mass scale, Morey, it would be the end of society as we know it. Think of the whole collection of anti-social actions that you see in every paper. Man beats wife; wife turns into a harpy; junior smashes up windows; husband starts a black-market stamp racket. And every one of them traces to a basic weakness in the mind's defenses against the most important single anti-social phenomenon—failure to consume."

Morey flared, "That's not fair, Doctor! That was weeks ago! We've certainly been on the ball lately. I was just commended by the Board, in fact—"

The doctor said mildly, "Why so violent, Morey? I only made a general remark."

"It's just natural to resent being accused."

The doctor shrugged. "First, foremost, and above all, we do *not* accuse patients of things. We try to help you find things out." He lit his end-of-session cigarette. "Think about it, please. I'll see you next week."

Cherry was composed and unapproachable. She kissed him remotely when he came in. She said, "I called Mother and told her the good news. She and Dad promised to come over here to celebrate."

"Yeah," said Morey. "Darling, what did I say wrong on the phone?"

"They'll be here about six."

"Sure. But what did I say? Was it about the rations? If you're sensitive, I swear I'll never mention them again."

"I *am* sensitive, Morey."

He said despairingly, "I'm sorry. I just—"

He had a better idea. He kissed her.

Cherry was passive at first, but not for long. When he had finished kissing her, she pushed him away and actually giggled. "Let me get dressed for dinner."

"Certainly. Anyhow, I was just—"

She laid a finger on his lips.

He let her escape, and feeling much less tense, drifted into the library. The afternoon papers were waiting for him. Virtuously, he sat down and began going through them in order. Midway through the *World-Telegram-Sun-Post-and-News,* he rang for Henry.

Morey had read clear through to the drama section of the *Times-Herald-Tribune-Mirror* before the robot appeared. "Good evening," it said politely.

"What took you so long?" Morey demanded. "Where are all the robots?"

Robots do not stammer, but there was a distinct pause before Henry said, "Belowstairs, sir. Did you want them for something?"

"Well, no. I just haven't seen them around. Get me a drink."

It hesitated. "Scotch, sir?"

"Before dinner? Get me a manhattan."

"We're all out of vermouth, sir."

"All out? Would you mind telling me how?"

"It's all used up, sir."

"Now that's just ridiculous," Morey snapped. "We have never run out of liquor in our whole lives, and you know it. Good heavens, we just got our allotment in the other day, and I certainly—"

He checked himself. There was a sudden flicker of horror in his eyes as he stared at Henry.

"You certainly what, sir?" the robot prompted.

Morey swallowed. "Henry, did I—did I do something I shouldn't have?"

"I'm sure I wouldn't know, sir. It isn't up to me to say what you should and shouldn't do."

"Of course not," Morey agreed grayly.

He sat rigid, staring hopelessly into space, remembering. What he remembered was no pleasure to him at all.

"Henry," he said. "Come along, we're going belowstairs. Right now!"

It had been Tanaquil Bigelow's remark about the robots. *Too many robots—make too much of everything.*

That had implanted the idea; it germinated in Morey's home. More than a little drunk, less than ordinarily inhibited, he had found the problem clear and the answer obvious.

He stared around him in dismal worry. His own robots, following his own orders, given weeks before...

Henry said, "It's just what you *told* us to do, sir."

Morey groaned. He was watching a scene of unparalleled activity, and it sent shivers up and down his spine.

There was the butler-robot, hard at work, his copper face expressionless. Dressed in Morey's own sports knickers and golfing shoes, the robot solemnly hit a ball against the wall, picked it up, and teed it, hit it again, over and again, with Morey's own clubs. Until the ball wore ragged and was replaced; and the shafts of the clubs leaned out of true; and the close-stitched seams in the clothing began to stretch and abrade.

"My God!" said Morey hollowly.

There were the maid-robots, exquisitely dressed in Cherry's best, walking up and down in the delicate, slim shoes, sitting and rising and bending and turning. The cook-robots and the serving-robots were preparing dionysian meals.

Morey swallowed. "You—you've been doing this right along," he said to Henry. "That's why the quotas have been filled."

"Oh, yes, sir. Just as you told us."

Morey had to sit down. One of the serving-robots politely scurried over with a chair, brought from upstairs for their new chores.

Waste.

Morey tasted the word between his lips.

Waste.

You never wasted things. You *used* them. If necessary,

you drove yourself to the edge of breakdown to use them; you made every breath a burden and every hour a torment to use them, until through diligent consuming and/or occupational merit, you were promoted to the next higher class, and were allowed to consume less frantically. But you didn't wantonly destroy or throw out. You *consumed.*

Morey thought fearfully: When the Board finds out about this...

Still, he reminded himself, the Board hadn't found out. It might take some time before they did, for humans, after all, never entered robot quarters. There was no law against it, not even a sacrosanct custom. But there was no reason to. When breaks occurred, which was infrequently, maintenance robots or repair squads came in and put them back in order. Usually the humans involved didn't even know it had happened, because the robots used their own TBR radio circuits and the process was next thing to automatic.

Morey said reprovingly, "Henry, you should have told—well, I mean reminded me about this."

"But, sir!" Henry protested. "'Don't tell a living soul,' you said. You made it a direct order."

"Umph. Well, keep it that way. I—uh—I have to go back upstairs. Better get the rest of the robots started on dinner."

Morey left, not comfortably.

The dinner to celebrate Morey's promotion was difficult. Morey liked Cherry's parents. Old Elon, after the premarriage inquisition that father must inevitably give to daughter's suitor, had buckled right down to the job of adjustment. The old folks were good about not interfering, good about keeping their superior social status to themselves, good about helping out on the budget—at least once a week, they could be relied on to come over for a hearty meal, and Mrs. Elon had more than once remade some of Cherry's new dresses to fit herself, even to the extent of wearing all the high-point ornamentation.

And they had been wonderful about the wedding gifts, when Morey and their daughter got married. The most any member of Morey's family had been willing to take was a silver set or a few crystal table pieces. The Elons had come through with a dazzling promise to accept a car, a bird-bath for their garden and a complete set of living-room furniture! Of course, they could afford it—they had to consume so little that it wasn't much strain for them even to take gifts of that magnitude. But without their help, Morey knew, the first few months of matrimony would have been even tougher consuming than they were.

But on this particular night it was hard for Morey to like anyone. He responded with monosyllables; he barely grunted when Elon proposed a toast to his promotion and his brilliant future. He was preoccupied.

Rightly so. Morey, in his deepest, bravest searching, could find no clue in his memory as to just what the punishment might be for what he had done. But he had a sick certainty that trouble lay ahead.

Morey went over his problem so many times that an anesthesia set in. By the time dinner was ended and he and his father-in-law were in the den with their brandy, he was more or less functioning again.

Elon, for the first time since Morey had known him, offered him one of *his* cigars. "You're Grade Five—can afford to smoke somebody else's now, hey?"

"Yeah," Morey said glumly.

There was a moment of silence. Then Elon, as punctilious as any companion-robot, coughed and tried again. "Remember being peaked till I hit Grade Five," he reminisced meaningfully. "Consuming keeps a man on the go, all right. Things piled up at the law office, couldn't be taken care of while ration points piled up, too. And consuming comes first, of course—that's a citizen's prime duty. Mother and I had our share of grief over that, but a couple that wants to make a go of marriage and citizenship just pitches in and does the job, hey?"

Morey repressed a shudder and managed to nod.

"Best thing about upgrading," Elon went on, as if he had elicited a satisfactory answer, "don't have to spend so much time consuming, give more attention to work. Greatest luxury in the world, work. Wish I had as much stamina as you young fellows. Five days a week in court are about all I can manage. Hit six for a while; relaxed first time in my life, but my doctor made me cut down. Said we can't overdo pleasures. You'll be working two days a week now, hey?"

Morey produced another nod.

Elon drew deeply on his cigar, his eyes bright as they watched Morey. He was visibly puzzled, and Morey, even in his half-daze, could recognize the exact moment at which Elon drew the wrong inference. "Ah, everything okay with you and Cherry?" he asked diplomatically.

"Fine!" Morey exclaimed. "Couldn't be better!"

"Good, Good." Elon changed the subject with almost an audible wrench. "Speaking of court, had an interesting case the other day. Young fellow—year or two younger than you, I guess—came in with a Section Ninety-seven on him. Know what that is? Breaking and entering!"

"Breaking and entering," Morey repeated wonderingly, interested in spite of himself. "Breaking and entering what?"

"Houses. Old term; law's full of them. Originally applied to stealing things. Still does, I discovered."

"You mean he *stole* something?" Morey asked in bewilderment.

"Exactly! He *stole*. Strangest thing I ever came across. Talked it over with one of his bunch of lawyers later; new one on him, too. Seems this kid had a girl friend, nice kid but a little, you know, plump. She got interested in art."

"There's nothing wrong with that," Morey said.

"Nothing wrong with her, either. She didn't do anything. She didn't like him too much, though. Wouldn't marry him. Kid got to thinking about how he could get her to change her mind and—well, you know that big Mondrian in the Museum?"

"I've never been there," Morey said, somewhat embarrassed.

"Um. Ought to try it some day, boy. Anyway, comes closing time at the Museum the other day, this kid sneaks in. He steals the painting. That's right—*steals* it. Takes it to give to the girl."

Morey shook his head blankly. "I never heard of anything like that in my life."

"Not many have. Girl wouldn't take it, by the way. Got scared when he brought it to her. She must've tipped off the police, I guess. Somebody did. Took 'em three hours to find it, even when they knew it was hanging on a wall. Pretty poor kid. Forty-two room house."

"And there was a *law* against it?" Morey asked. "I mean it's like making a law against breathing."

"Certainly was. Old law, of course. Kid got set back two grades. Would have been more but, my God, he was only a Grade Three as it was."

"Yeah," said Morey, wetting his lips. "Say, Dad—"

"Um?"

Morey cleared his throat. "Uh—I wonder—I mean, what's the penalty, for instance, for things like—well, misusing rations or anything like that?"

Elon's eyebrows went high. "Misusing rations?"

"Say you had a liquor ration, it might be, and instead of drinking it, you—well, flushed it down the drain or something..."

His voice trailed off. Elon was frowning. He said, "Funny thing, seems I'm not as broadminded as I thought I was. For some reason, I don't find that amusing."

"Sorry," Morey croaked.

And he certainly was.

It might be dishonest, but it was doing him a lot of good, for days went by and no one seemed to have penetrated his secret. Cherry was happy. Wainwright found occasion after occasion to pat Morey's back. The wages of sin were turning out to be prosperity and happiness.

There was a bad moment when Morey came home to find Cherry in the middle of supervising a team of packing robots; the new house, suitable to his higher grade, was ready, and they were expected to move in the next day. But Cherry hadn't been belowstairs, and Morey had his household robots clean up the evidences of what they had been doing before the packers got that far.

The new house was, by Morey's standards, pure luxury.

It was only fifteen rooms. Morey had shrewdly retained one more robot than was required for a Class Five, and had been allowed a compensating deduction in the size of his house.

The robot quarters were less secluded than in the old house, though, and that was a disadvantage. More than once Cherry had snuggled up to him in the delightful intimacy of their one bed in their single bedroom and said, with faint curiosity, "I wish they'd stop that noise." And Morey had promised to speak to Henry about it in the morning. But there was nothing he could say to Henry, of course, unless he ordered Henry to stop the tireless consuming through each of the day's twenty-four hours that kept them always ahead, but never quite far enough ahead, of the inexorable weekly increment of ration quotas.

But, though Cherry might once in a while have a moment's curiosity about what the robots were doing, she was not likely to be able to guess at the facts. Her upbringing was, for once, on Morey's side—she knew so little of the grind, grind, grind of consuming that was the lot of the lower classes that she scarcely noticed that there was less of it.

Morey almost, sometimes, relaxed.

He thought of many ingenious chores for robots, and the robots politely and emotionlessly obeyed.

Morey was a success.

It wasn't all gravy. There was a nervous moment for Morey when the quarterly survey report came in the mail. As the day for the Ration Board to check over the degree of wear on the turned-in discards came due, Morey began to sweat. The clothing and furniture and household goods the robots had consumed for him were very nearly in shreds. It had to look plausible, that was the big thing—no normal person would wear a hole completely through the knee of a pair of pants, as Henry had done with his dress suit before Morey stopped him. Would the Board question it?

Worse, was there something about the *way* the robots consumed the stuff that would give the whole show away? Some special wear point in the robot anatomy, for instance, that would rub a hole where no human's body could, or stretch a seam that should normally be under no strain at all?"

It was worrisome. But the worry was needless. When the report of survey came, Morey let out a long-held breath. *Not a single item disallowed!*

Morey was a success—and so was his scheme!

To the successful man come the rewards of success. Morey arrived home one evening after a hard day's work at the office and was alarmed to find another car parked in his drive. It was a tiny two-seater, the sort affected by top officials and the very well-to-do.

Right then and there Morey learned the first half of the embezzler's lesson: Anything different is dangerous. He came uneasily into his own house, fearful that some high officer of the Ration Board had come to ask questions.

But Cherry was glowing. "Mr. Porfirio is a newspaper feature writer and he wants to write you up for their 'Consumers of Distinction' page! Morey, I *couldn't* be more proud!"

"Thanks," said Morey glumly. "Hello."

Mr. Porfirio shook Morey's hand warmly. "I'm not exactly from a newspaper," he corrected. "Trans-video Press is what it is, actually. We're a news wire service; we supply forty-seven hundred papers with news and feature material. Every one of them," he added complacently, "on the required consumption list of Grades One through Six inclusive. We have a Sunday supplement self-help feature on consuming problems and we like to—well, give credit where credit is due. You've established an enviable record, Mr. Fry. We'd like to tell our readers about it."

"Um," said Morey. "Let's go in the drawing room."

"Oh, no!" Cherry said firmly. "I want to hear this. He's so modest, Mr. Porfirio, you'd really never know what kind of a man he is just to listen to him talk. Why, my goodness, I'm his wife and I swear *I* don't know how he does all the consuming he does. He simply—"

"Have a drink Mr. Porfirio," Morey said, against all etiquette. "Rye? Scotch? Bourbon? Gin-and-tonic? Brandy alexander? Dry manha—I mean what would you like?" He became conscious that he was babbling like a fool.

"Anything," said the newsman. "Rye is fine. Now, Mr. Fry, I notice you've fixed up your place very attractively here and your wife says that your country home is just as nice. As soon as I came in, I said to myself, 'Beautiful home. Hardly a stick of furniture that isn't absolutely necessary. Might be a Grade Six or Seven.' And Mrs. Fry says the other place is even barer."

"She does, does she?" Morey challenged sharply. "Well, let me tell you, Mr. Porfirio, that every last scrap of my furniture allowance is accounted for! I don't know what you're getting at, but—"

"Oh, I certainly didn't mean to imply anything like *that!* I just want to get some information from you that I can pass on to our readers. You know, to sort of help them do as well as yourself. How *do* you do it?"

Morey swallowed. "We—uh—well, we just keep after it. Hard work, that's all."

Porfirio nodded admiringly. "Hard work," he repeated, and fished a triple-folded sheet of paper out of his pocket to make notes on. "Would you say," he went on, "that anyone could do well as you simply by devoting himself to it—setting a regular schedule, for example, and keeping to it very strictly?"

"Oh, yes," said Morey.

"In other words, it's only a matter of doing what you have to do every day?"

"That's it exactly. I handle the budget in my house—more experience than my wife, you see—but no reason a woman can't do it."

"Budgeting," Porfirio recorded approvingly. "That's our policy, too."

The interview was not the terror it had seemed, not even when Porfirio tactfully called attention to Cherry's slim waistline ("So many housewives, Mrs. Fry, find it difficult to keep from being—well, a little plump.") and Morey had to invent endless hours on the exercise machines, while Cherry looked faintly perplexed, but did not interrupt.

From the interview, however, Morey learned the second half of the embezzler's lesson. After Porfirio had gone, he leaped in and spoke more than a little firmly to Cherry. "That business of exercise, dear. We really have to start doing it. I don't know if you've noticed it, but you *are* beginning to get just a trifle heavier and we don't want that to happen, do we?"

In the following grim and unnecessary sessions on the mechanical horses, Morey had plenty of time to reflect on the lesson. Stolen treasures are less sweet than one would like, when one dare not enjoy them in the open.

But some of Morey's treasures were fairly earned.

The new Bradmoor K-50 Spin-a-Game, for instance, was his very own. His job was design and creation, and he was a fortunate man in that his efforts were permitted to be expended along the line of greatest social utility—namely, to increase consumption.

The Spin-a-Game was a well-nigh perfect machine for the purpose. "Brilliant," said Wainwright, beaming, when the pilot machine had been put through its first tests. "Guess they don't call me the Talent-picker for nothing. I knew you could do it, boy!"

Even Howland was lavish in his praise. He sat munching on a plate of petits-fours (he was still only a Grade Three) while the tests were going on, and when they were over, he said enthusiastically, "It's a beauty, Morey. That series-corrupter—sensational! Never saw a prettier piece of machinery."

Morey flushed gratefully.

Wainwright left, exuding praise, and Morey patted his pilot model affectionately and admired its polychrome gleam. The looks of the machine, as Wainwright had lectured many a time, were as important as its function: "You have to make them *want* to play it, boy! They won't play it if they don't *see* it!" And consequently the whole K series was distinguished by flashing rainbows of light, provocative strains of music, haunting scents that drifted into the nostrils of the passerby with compelling effect.

Morey had drawn heavily on all the old masterpieces of

design—the one-arm bandit, the pinball machine, the juke box. You put your ration book in the hopper. You spun the wheels until you selected the game you wanted to play against the machine. You punched buttons or spun dials or, in any of 325 different ways, you pitted your human skill against the magnetic-taped skills of the machine.

And you lost. You had a chance to win, but the inexorable statistics of the machine's setting made sure that if you played long enough, you had to lose.

That is to say, if you risked a ten-point ration stamp— showing, perhaps, that you had consumed three six-course meals—your statistic return was eight points. You might hit the jackpot and get a thousand points back, and thus be exempt from a whole freezerful of steaks and joints and pre-pared vegetables; but it seldom happened. Most likely you lost and got nothing.

Got nothing, that is, in the way of your hazarded ration stamps. But the beauty of the machine, which was Morey's main contribution, was that, win or lose, you *always* found a pellet of vitamin-drenched, sugar-coated antibiotic hor-mone gum in the hopper. You played your game, won or lost your stake, popped your hormone gum into your mouth and played another. By the time that game was ended, the gum was used up, the coating dissolved; you discarded it and started another.

"That's what the man from the NRB liked," Howland told Morey confidentially. "He took a set of schematics back with him; they might install it on *all* new machines. Oh, you're the fair-haired boy, all right!"

It was the first Morey had heard about a man from the National Ration Board. It was good news. He excused himself and hurried to phone Cherry the story of his latest successes. He reached her at her mother's, where she was spending the evening, and she was properly impressed and affectionate. He came back to Howland in a glowing humor.

"Drink?" said Howland diffidently.

"Sure," said Morey. He could afford, he thought, to drink as much of Howland's liquor as he liked; poor guy, sunk in the consuming quicksands of Class Three. Only fair for somebody a little more successful to give him a hand once in a while.

And when Howland, learning that Cherry had left Morey a bachelor for the evening, proposed Uncle Piggotty's again, Morey hardly hesitated at all.

The Bigelows were delighted to see him. Morey wondered briefly if they *had* a home; certainly they didn't seem to spend much time in it.

It turned out they did, because when Morey indicated virtuously that he'd only stopped in at Piggotty's for a single drink before dinner, and Howland revealed that he was free for the evening, they captured Morey and bore him off to their house.

Tanaquil Bigelow was haughtily apologetic. "I don't suppose this is the kind of place Mr. Fry is used to," she observed to her husband, right across Morey, who was standing between them. "Still, we call it home."

Morey made an appropriately polite remark. Actually, the place nearly turned his stomach. It was an enormous glaringly new mansion, bigger even than Morey's former house, stuffed to bursting with bulging sofas and pianos and massive mahogany chairs and tri-D sets and bedrooms and drawing rooms and breakfast rooms and nurseries.

The nurseries were a shock to Morey; it had never occurred to him that the Bigelows had children. But they did, and though the children were only five and eight, they were still up, under the care of a brace of robot nursemaids, doggedly playing with their overstuffed animals and miniature trains.

"You don't know what a comfort Tony and Dick are," Tanaquil Bigelow told Morey. "They consume *so* much more than their rations. Walter says that every family ought to have at least two or three children to, you know, help out. Walter's so intelligent about these things, it's a pleasure to hear him talk. Have you heard his poem, Morey? The one he calls *The Twoness of—*"

Morey hastily admitted that he had. He reconciled himself to a glum evening. The Bigelows had been eccentric but fun back at Uncle Piggotty's. On their own ground, they seemed just as eccentric, but painfully dull.

They had a round of cocktails, and another, and then the Bigelows no longer seemed so dull. Dinner was ghastly, of course; Morey was nouveau-riche enough to be a snob about his relatively Spartan table. But he minded his manners and sampled, with grim concentration, each successive course of chunky protein and rich marinades. With the help of the endless succession of table wines and liqueurs, dinner ended without destroying his evening or his strained digestive system.

And afterward, they were a pleasant company in the Bigelow's ornate drawing room. Tanaquil Bigelow, in consultation with the children, checked over their ration books and came up with the announcement that they would have a brief recital by a pair of robot dancers, followed by string music by a robot quartet. Morey prepared himself for the worst, but found before the dancers were through that he was enjoying himself. Strange lesson for Morey: When you didn't *have* to watch them, the robot entertainers were fun!

"Good night, dears," Tanaquil Bigelow said firmly to the children when the dancers were done. The boys rebelled, naturally, but they went. It was only a matter of minutes, though, before one of them was back, clutching at Morey's sleeve with a pudgy hand.

Morey looked at the boy uneasily, having little experience with children. He said, "Uh—what is it, Tony?"

"Dick, you mean," the boy said. "Gimme your autograph." He poked an engraved pad and a vulgarly jeweled pencil at Morey.

Morey dazedly signed and the child ran off, Morey staring after him. Tanaquil Bigelow laughed and explained, "He saw your name in Porfirio's column. Dick *loves* Porfirio, reads him every day. He's such an intelligent kid, really. He'd always have his nose in a book if I didn't keep after him to play with his trains and watch tri-D."

"That was quite a nice write-up," Walter Bigelow commented—a little enviously, Morey thought. "Bet you make Consumer of the Year. I wish," he sighed, "that we could get a little ahead on the quotas the way you did. But it just never seems to work out. We eat and play and consume like crazy, and somehow at the end of the month we're always a little behind in something—everything keeps piling up—and then the Board sends us a warning, and they call me down and, first thing you know, I've got a couple of hundred added penalty points and we're worse off than before."

"Never you mind," Tanaquil replied staunchly. "Consuming isn't everything in life. You have your work."

Bigelow nodded judiciously and offered Morey another drink. Another drink, however, was not what Morey needed. He was sitting in a rosy glow, less of alcohol than of sheer contentment with the world.

He said suddenly, "Listen."

Bigelow looked up from his own drink. "Eh?"

"If I tell you something that's a *secret*, will you keep it that way?"

Bigelow rumbled, "Why, I guess so, Morey."

But his wife cut in sharply, "Certainly we will, Morey. Of course! What is it?" There was a gleam in her eye, Morey noticed. It puzzled him, but he decided to ignore it.

He said, "About that write-up. I—I'm not such a hotshot consumer, really, you know. In fact—" All of a sudden, everyone's eyes seemed to be on him. For a tortured moment, Morey wondered if he was doing the right thing. A secret that two people know is compromised, and a secret known to three people is no secret. Still—

"It's like this," he said firmly. "You remember what we were talking about at Uncle Piggotty's that night? Well, when I went home I went down to the robot quarters, and I—"

He went on from there.

Tanaquil Bigelow said triumphantly, "I *knew* it!"

Walter Bigelow gave his wife a mild, reproving look. He declared soberly. "You've done a big thing, Morey. A mighty big thing. God willing, you've pronounced the death sentence on our society as we know it. Future generations will revere the name of Morey Fry." He solemnly shook Morey's hand.

Morey said dazedly, "I *what?*"

Walter nodded. It was a valedictory. He turned to his wife. "Tanaquil, we'll have to call an emergency meeting."

"Of course, Walter," she said devotedly.

"And Morey will have to be there. Yes, you'll have to, Morey; no excuses. We want the Brotherhood to meet you. Right, Howland?"

Howland coughed uneasily. He nodded noncommittally and took another drink.

Morey demanded desperately, "What are you talking about? Howland, you tell me!"

Howland fiddled with his drink. "Well," he said, "it's like Tan was telling you that night. A few of us, well, politically mature persons have formed a little group. We—"

"*Little* group!" Tanaquil Bigelow said scornfully. "Howland, sometimes I wonder if you really catch the spirit of the thing at all! It's everybody, Morey, everybody in the world. Why, there are eighteen of us right here in Old Town! There are *scores more* all over the world! I knew you were up to something like this, Morey. I told Walter so the morning after we met you. I said, 'Walter mark my words, that man Morey is up to something.' But I must say," she admitted worshipfully, "I didn't know it would have the *scope* of what you're proposing now! Imagine— a whole world of consumers, rising as one man, shouting the name of Morey Fry, fighting the Ration Board with the Board's own weapon—the robots. What poetic justice!"

Bigelow nodded enthusiastically. "Call Uncle Piggotty's, dear," he ordered. "See if you can round up a quorum right now! Meanwhile, Morey and I are going belowstairs. Let's go, Morey—let's get the new world started!"

Morey sat there open-mouthed. He closed it with a snap. "Bigelow," he whispered, "do you mean to say that you're going to spread this idea around through some kind of subversive organization?"

"Subversive?" Bigelow repeated stiffly. "My dear man, *all* creative minds are subversive, whether they operate singly or in such a group as the Brotherhood of Freemen. I scarcely like—"

"Never mind what you like," Morey insisted. "You're going

to call a meeting of this Brotherhood and you want *me* to tell them what I just told you. Is that right?"

"Well—yes."

Morey got up. "I wish I could say it's been nice, but it hasn't. Good night!"

And he stormed out before they could stop him.

Out on the street, though, his resolution deserted him. He hailed a robot cab and ordered the driver to take him on the traditional time-killing ride through the park while he made up his mind.

The fact that he had left, of course, was not going to keep Bigelow from going through with his announced intention. Morey remembered, now, fragments of conversation from Bigelow and his wife at Uncle Piggotty's, and cursed himself. They had, it was perfectly true, said and hinted enough about politics and purposes to put him on his guard. All that nonsense about twoness had diverted him from what should have been perfectly clear: They were subversives indeed.

He glanced at his watch. Late, but not too late; Cherry would still be at her parents' home.

He leaned forward and gave the driver their address. It was like beginning the first of a hundred-shot series of injections: you know it's going to cure you, but it hurts just the same.

Morey said manfully: "And that's it, sir. I know I've been a fool. I'm willing to take the consequences."

Old Elon rubbed his jaw thoughtfully. "Um," he said.

Cherry and her mother had long passed the point where they could say anything at all; they were seated side by side on a couch across the room, listening with expressions of strain and incredulity.

Elon said abruptly, "Excuse me. Phone call to make." He left the room to make a brief call and returned. He said over his shoulder to his wife, "Coffee. We'll need it. Got a problem here."

Morey said, "Do you think—I mean what should I do?"

Elon shrugged, then, surprisingly, grinned. "What can you do?" he demanded cheerfully. "Done plenty already, I'd say.

Drink some coffee. Call I made," he explained, "was to Jim, my law clerk. He'll be here in a minute. Get some dope from Jim, then we'll know better."

Cherry came over to Morey and sat beside him. All she said was, "Don't worry," but to Morey it conveyed all the meaning in the world. He returned the pressure of her hand with a feeling of deepest relief. Hell, he said to himself, why *should* I worry? Worst they can do to me is drop me a couple of grades, and what's so bad about that?

He grimaced involuntarily. He had remembered his own early struggles as a Class One and what *was* so bad about that.

The law clerk arrived, a smallish robot with a battered stainless-steel hide and dull coppery features. Elon took the robot aside for a terse conversation before he came back to Morey.

"As I thought," he said in satisfaction. "No precedent. No laws prohibiting. Therefore no crime."

"Thank heaven!" Morey said in ecstatic relief.

Elon shook his head. "They'll probably give you a reconditioning and you can't expect to keep your Grade Five. Probably call it anti-social behavior. Is, isn't it?"

Dashed, Morey said, "Oh." He frowned briefly, then looked up. "All right, Dad, if I've got it coming to me, I'll take my medicine."

"Way to talk," Elon said approvingly. "Now go home. Get a good night's sleep. First thing in the morning, go to the Ration Board. Tell 'em the whole story, beginning to end. They'll be easy on you." Elon hesitated. "Well, fairly easy," he amended. "I hope."

The condemned man ate a hearty breakfast.

He had to. That morning, as Morey awoke, he had the sick certainty that he was going to be consuming triple rations for a long, long time to come.

He kissed Cherry good-by and took the long ride to the Ration Board in silence. He even left Henry behind.

At the Board, he stammered at a series of receptionist

robots and was finally brought into the presence of a mildly supercilious young man named Hachette.

"My name," he started, "is Morey Fry. I—I've come to—talk over something I've been doing with—"

"Certainly, Mr. Fry," said Hachette. "I'll take you in to Mr. Newman right away."

"Don't you want to know what I did?" demanded Morey.

Hachette smiled. "What makes you think we don't know?" he said, and left.

That was Surprise Number One.

Newman explained it. He grinned at Morey and ruefully shook his head. "All the time we get this," he complained. "People just don't take the trouble to learn anything about the world around them. Son," he demanded, "what do you think a robot is?"

Morey said, "Huh?"

"I mean how do you think it operates? Do you think it's just a kind of a man with a tin skin and wire nerves?"

"Why, no. It's a machine, of course. It isn't *human*."

Newman beamed. "Fine!" he said. "It's a machine. It hasn't got flesh or blood or intestines—or a brain. Oh—" he held up a hand—"robots are *smart* enough. I don't mean that. But an electronic thinking machine, Mr. Fry, takes about as much space as the house you're living in. It has to. Robots don't carry brains around with them; brains are too heavy and much too bulky."

"Then how do they think?"

"With their brains, of course."

"But you just said—"

"I said they didn't *carry* them. Each robot is in constant radio communication with the Master Control on its TBR circuit—the 'Talk Between Robots' radio. Master Control gives the answer; the robot acts."

"I see," said Morey. "Well, that's very interesting but—"

"But you still don't see," said Newman. "Figure it out. If the robot gets information from Master Control, do you see that Master Control in return necessarily gets information from the robot?"

"Oh," said Morey. Then, louder, "Oh! You mean that all my robots have been—" The words wouldn't come.

Newman nodded in satisfaction. "Every bit of information of that sort comes to us as a matter of course. Why, Mr. Fry, if you hadn't come in today, we would have been sending for you within a very short time."

That was the second surprise. Morey bore up under it bravely. After all, it changed nothing, he reminded himself.

He said, "Well, be that as it may, sir, here I am. I came in of my own free will. I've been using my robots to consume my ration quotas—"

"Indeed you have," said Newman.

"—and I'm willing to sign a statement to that effect any time you like. I don't know what the penalty is, but I'll take it. I'm guilty; I admit my guilt."

Newman's eyes were wide. "Guilty?" he repeated. "Penalty?"

Morey was startled. "Why, yes," he said. "I'm not denying anything."

"Penalties," repeated Newman musingly. Then he began to laugh. He laughed, Morey thought, to considerable excess; Morey saw nothing he could laugh at, himself, in the situation. But the situation, Morey was forced to admit, was rapidly getting completely incomprehensible.

"Sorry," said Newman at last, wiping his eyes, "but I couldn't help it. Penalties! Well, Mr. Fry, let me set your mind at rest. I wouldn't worry about the penalties if I were you. As soon as the reports began coming through on what you had done with your robots, we naturally assigned a special team to keep observing you, and we forwarded a report to the national headquarters. We made certain—ah—recommendations in it and—well, to make a long story short, the answers came back yesterday.

"Mr. Fry, the National Ration Board is delighted to know of your contribution toward improving our distribution problem. Pending a further study, a tentative program has been adopted for setting up consuming-robot units all over the country based on your scheme. Penalties? Mr. Fry, you're a *hero!*"

* * *

A hero has responsibilities. Morey's were quickly made clear to him. He was allowed time for a brief reassuring visit to Cherry, a triumphal tour of his old office, and then he was rushed off to Washington to be quizzed. He found the National Ration Board in a frenzy of work.

"The most important job we've ever done," one of the high officers told him. "I wouldn't be surprised if it's the last one we ever have! Yes, sir, we're trying to put ourselves out of business for good and we don't want a single thing to go wrong."

"Anything I can do to help—" Morey began diffidently.

"You've done fine, Mr. Fry. Gave us just the push we've been needing. It was there all the time for us to see, but we were too close to the forest to see the trees, if you get what I mean. Look, I'm not much on rhetoric and this is the biggest step mankind has taken in centuries and I can't put it into words. Let me show you what we've been doing."

He and a delegation of other officials of the Ration Board and men whose names Morey had repeatedly seen in the newspapers took Morey on an inspection tour of the entire plant.

"It's a closed cycle, you see," he was told, as they looked over a chamber of industriously plodding consumer-robots working off a shipment of shoes. "Nothing is permanently lost. If you want a car, you get one of the newest and best. If not, your car gets driven by a robot until it's ready to be turned in and a new one gets built for next year. We don't lose the metals—they can be salvaged. All we lose is a little power and labor. And the Sun and the atom give us all the power we need, and the robots give us more labor than we can use. Same thing applies, of course, to all products."

"But what's in it for the robots?" Morey asked.

"I beg your pardon?" one of the biggest men in the country said uncomprehendingly.

Morey had a difficult moment. His analysis had conditioned him against waste and this decidedly was sheer destruction of goods, no matter how scientific the jargon might be.

"If the consumer is just using up things for the sake of using them up," he said doggedly, realizing the danger he was inviting, "we could use wear-and-tear machines instead of robots. After all, why waste *them?*"

They looked at each other worriedly.

"But that's what *you* were doing," one pointed out with a faint note of threat.

"Oh, no!" Morey quickly objected. "I built in satisfaction circuits—my training in design, you know. Adjustable circuits, of course."

"Satisfaction circuits?" he was asked. "Adjustable?"

"Well, sure. If the robot gets no satisfaction out of using up things—"

"Don't talk nonsense," growled the Ration Board official. "Robots aren't human. How do you make them feel satisfaction? And adjustable satisfaction at that!"

Morey explained. It was a highly technical explanation, involving the use of great sheets of paper and elaborate diagrams. But there were trained men in the group and they became even more excited than before.

"Beautiful!" one cried in scientific rapture. "Why, it takes care of every possible moral, legal and psychological argument!"

"What does?" the Ration Board official demanded. "How?"

"You tell him, Mr. Fry."

Morey tried and couldn't. But he could *show* how his principle operated. The Ration Board lab was turned over to him, complete with more assistants than he knew how to give orders to, and they built satisfaction circuits for a squad of robots working in a hat factory.

Then Morey gave his demonstration. The robots manufactured hats of all sorts. He adjusted the circuits at the end of the day and the robots began trying on the hats, squabbling over them, each coming away triumphantly with a huge and diverse selection. Their metallic features were incapable of showing pride or pleasure, but both were evident in the way they wore their hats, their fierce possessiveness...and their faster, neater, more intensive, more *dedicated* work to produce a still greater quantity of hats...which they also were allowed to own.

"You see?" an engineer exclaimed delightedly. "They can be adjusted to *want* hats, to wear them lovingly, to wear the hats to pieces. And not just for the sake of wearing them out—the hats are an incentive for them!"

"But how can we go on producing just hats and more hats?" the Ration Board man asked puzzledly. "Civilization does not live by hats alone."

"That," said Morey modestly, "is the beauty of it. Look."

He set the adjustment of the satisfaction circuit as porter-robots brought in skids of gloves. The hat-manufacturing robots fought over the gloves with the same mechanical passion as they had for hats.

"And that can apply to anything we—or the robots—produce," Morey added. "Everything from pins to yachts. But the point is that they get satisfaction from possession, and the craving can be regulated according to the glut in various industries, and the robots show their appreciation by working harder." He hesitated. "That's what I did for my servant-robots. It's a feedback, you see. Satisfaction leads to more work—and *better* work—and that means more goods, which they can be made to want, which means incentive to work, and so on, all around."

"Closed cycle," whispered the Ration Board man in awe. "A *real* closed cycle this time!"

And so the inexorable laws of supply and demand were irrevocably repealed. No longer was mankind hampered by inadequate supply or drowned by overproduction. What mankind needed was there. What the race did not require passed into the insatiable—and adjustable—robot maw. Nothing was wasted.

For a pipeline has two ends.

Morey was thanked, complimented, rewarded, given a ticker-tape parade through the city, and put on a plane back home. By that time, the Ration Board had liquidated itself.

* * *

Cherry met him at the airport. They jabbered excitedly at each other all the way to the house.

In their own living room, they finished the kiss they had greeted each other with. At last Cherry broke away, laughing.

Morey said, "Did I tell you I'm through with Bradmoor? From now on I work for the Board as civilian consultant. *And,*" he added impressively, "starting right away, I'm a Class Eight!"

"My!" gasped Cherry, so worshipfully that Morey felt a twinge of conscience.

He said honestly, "Of course, if what they were saying in Washington is so, the classes aren't going to mean much pretty soon. Still, it's quite an honor."

"It certainly is," Cherry said staunchly. "Why, Dad's only a Class Eight himself and he's been a judge for I don't know *how* many years."

Morey pursed his lips. "We can't all be fortunate," he said generously. "Of course, the classes still will count for *something*—that is, a Class One will have so much to consume in a year; a Class Two will have a little less; and so on. But each person in each class will have robot help, you see, to do the actual consuming. The way it's going to be, special facsimile robots will—"

Cherry flagged him down. "I know, dear. Each family gets a robot duplicate of every person in the family."

"Oh," said Morey, slightly annoyed. "How did you know?"

"Ours came yesterday," she explained. "The man from the Board said we were the first in the area—because it was your idea, of course. They haven't even been activated yet. I've still got them in the Green Room. Want to see them?"

"Sure," said Morey buoyantly. He dashed ahead of Cherry to inspect the results of his own brainstorm. There they were, standing statue-still against the wall, waiting to be energized to begin their endless tasks.

"Yours is real pretty," Morey said gallantly. "But—say, is that thing supposed to look like me?" He inspected the chromium face of the man-robot disapprovingly.

"Only roughly, the man said." Cherry was right behind him. "Notice anything else?"

Morey leaned closer, inspecting the features of the facsimile robot at a close range. "Well, no," he said. "It's got a kind of a squint that I don't like, but—Oh, you mean *that!*" He bent over to examine a smaller robot, half hidden between the other pair. It was less than two feet high, big-headed, pudgy-limbed, thick-bellied. In fact, Morey thought wonderingly, it looked almost like—

"My God!" Morey spun around, staring wide eyed at his wife. "You mean—"

"I mean," said Cherry, blushing slightly.

Morey reached out to grab her in his arms.

"Darling!" he cried. "Why didn't you *tell* me?"

GLUTTONY

And what could be more appropriate than two stories to represent GLUTTONY, especially when we can present Fred Pohl's lesser known but equally good companion to "The Midas Plague."

Incidentally, this marks the first time these two stories have ever appeared in one volume, and we are to be forgiven if we exhibit a large degree of PRIDE in arranging this for your enjoyment!

THE MAN WHO ATE THE WORLD

FREDERIK POHL

He had a name, but at home he was called "Sonny," and he was almost always at home. He hated it. Other boys his age went to school. Sonny would have done anything to go to school, but his family was, to put it mildly, not well off. It wasn't Sonny's fault that his father was spectacularly unsuccessful. But it meant—no school for Sonny, no boys of his own age for Sonny to play with. All childhoods are tragic (as all adults forget), but Sonny's was misery all the way through.

The worst time was at night, when the baby sister was asleep and the parents were grimly eating and reading and dancing and drinking, until they were ready to drop. And of all bad nights, the night before his twelfth birthday was perhaps Sonny's worst. He was old enough to know what a birthday party was like. It would be cake and candy, shows and games; it would be presents, presents, presents. It would be a terrible, endless day.

He switched off the color-D television and the recorded tapes of sea chanteys and, with an appearance of absent-mindedness, walked toward the door of his playroom.

Davey Crockett got up from beside the model rocket field and said, "Hold on thar, Sonny. Mought take a stroll with you." Davey's face was serene and strong as a Tennessee crag; it swung its long huntin' rifle under one arm and put its other arm around Sonny's shoulders. "Where you reckon we ought to head?"

Sonny shook Davey Crockett's arm off. "Get lost," he said petulantly. "Who wants you around?"

Long John Silver came out of the closet, hobbling on its wooden leg, crouched over its knobby cane. "Ah, young master," it said reproachfully, "you shouldn't ought to talk to old Davey like that! He's a good friend to you, Davey is. Many's the weary day Davey and me has been a-keepin' of your company. I asks you this, young master: Is it fair and square that you should be a-tellin' him to get lost? Is it fair, young master? Is it square?"

Sonny looked at the floor stubbornly and didn't answer. My gosh, what was the use of answering dummies like them? He stood rebelliously silent and still until he just felt like saying something. And then he said: "You go in the closet, both of you. I don't want to play with you. I'm going to play with my trains."

Long John said unctuously, "Now there's a good idea, that is! You just be a-havin' of a good time with your trains, and old Davey and me'll—"

"Go ahead!" shouted Sonny. He stood stamping his foot until they were out of sight.

His fire truck was in the middle of the floor; he kicked at it, but it rolled quickly out of reach and slid into its little garage under the tanks of tropical fish. He scuffed over to the model-railroad layout and glared at it. As he approached, the Twentieth Century Limited came roaring out of a tunnel, sparks flying from its stack. It crossed a bridge, whistled at a grade crossing, steamed into the Union Station. The roof of the station glowed and suddenly became transparent, and through it Sonny saw the bustling crowds of redcaps and travelers—

"I don't want that," he said. "Casey, crack up old Number Ninety-Nine again."

Obediently the layout quivered and revolved a half-turn. Old Casey Jones, one and an eighth inches tall, leaned out of the cab of the S.P. locomotive and waved good-by to Sonny. The locomotive whistled shrilly twice and started to pick up speed—

It was a good crackup. Little old Casey's body, thrown

completely free, developed real blisters from the steam and bled real blood. But Sonny turned his back on it. He had liked that crackup for a long time—longer than he liked almost any other toy he owned. But he was tired of it.

He looked around the room.

Tarzan of the Apes, leaning against a foot-thick tree trunk, one hand on a vine, lifted its head and looked at him. But Tarzan, Sonny calculated craftily, was clear across the room. The others were in the closet—

Sonny ran out and slammed the door. He saw Tarzan start to come after him, but even before Sonny was out of the room Tarzan slumped and stood stock-still.

It wasn't fair, Sonny thought angrily. It wasn't fair! They wouldn't even *chase* him, so that at least he could have some kind of chance to get away by himself. They'd just talk to each other on their little radios, and in a minute one of the tutors, or one of the maids, or whatever else happened to be handy, would vector in on him. And that would be that.

But for the moment he was free.

He slowed down and walked down the Great Hall toward his baby sister's room. The fountains began to splash as he entered the hall; the mosaics on the wall began to tinkle music and sparkle with moving colors.

"Now, chile, whut you up to!"

He turned around, but he knew it was Mammy coming toward him. It was slapping toward him on big, flat feet, its pink-palmed hands lifted to its shoulders. The face under the red bandanna was frowning, the gold tooth sparkling as it scolded: "Chile, you is got us'n's so worried we's fit to *die*! How you 'speck us to take good keer of you ef'n you run off lak that? Now you jes come on back to your nice room with Mammy an' we'll see if there ain't some real nice program on the teevee."

Sonny stopped and waited for it, but he wouldn't give it the satisfaction of looking at it. Slap-slap the big feet waddled cumbersomely toward him; but he didn't have any illusions. Waddle, big feet, three hundred pounds and all, Mammy could catch him in twenty yards with a ten-yard start. Any of them could.

He said in his best icily indignant voice, "I was just going in to look at my baby sister."

Pause. "You was?" The plump black face looked suspicious.

"Yes, I was. Doris is my very own sister, and I love her very much."

Pause—long pause. "Dat's nice," said Mammy, but its voice was still doubtful. "I 'speck I better come 'long with you. You wouldn't want to wake your lil baby sister up. Ef I come I'll he'p you keep real quiet."

Sonny shook free of it—they were always putting their hands on you! "I don't *want* you to come with me, Mammy!"

"Aw now, honey! Mammy ain't gwine bother nothin', you knows that."

Sonny turned his back on it and marched grimly toward his sister's room. If only they would leave him *alone!* But they never did. It was always that way, always one darn old robot—yes, *robot,* he thought, savagely tasting the naughty word. Always one darn *robot* after another. Why couldn't Daddy be like other daddies, so they could live in a decent little house and get rid of these darn *robots*—so he could go to a real school and be in a class with other boys, instead of being taught at home by Miss Brooks and Mr. Chips and all those other *robots?*

They spoiled everything. And they would spoil what he wanted to do now. But he was going to do it all the same, because there was something in Doris's room that he wanted very much.

It was probably the only tangible thing he wanted in the world.

As they passed the imitation tumbled rocks of the Bear Cave, Mama Bear poked its head out and growled: "Hello, Sonny. Don't you think you ought to be in bed? It's nice and warm in our bear bed, Sonny."

He didn't even look at it. Time was when he had liked that sort of thing too, but he wasn't a four-year-old like Doris any more. All the same, there was one thing a four-year-old had—

He stopped at the door of her room. "Doris?" he whispered.

Mammy scolded: "Now, chile, you knows that lil baby is asleep! How come you tryin' to wake her up?"

"I won't wake her up." The farthest thing from Sonny's mind was to wake his sister up. He tiptoed into the room and stood beside the little girl's bed. Lucky kid! he thought enviously. Being four, she was allowed to have a tiny little room and a tiny bed—where Sonny had to wallow around in a forty-foot bedchamber and a bed eight feet long.

He looked down at his sister. Behind him Mammy clucked approvingly. "Dat's nice when chilluns loves each other lak you an' that lil baby," it whispered.

Doris was sound asleep, clutching her teddy-bear. It wriggled slightly and opened an eye to look at Sonny, but it didn't say anything.

Sonny took a deep breath, leaned forward and gently slipped the teddy-bear out of the bed.

It scrambled pathetically, trying to get free. Behind him Mammy whispered urgently: "Sonny! Now you let dat ole teddy-bear alone, you heah me?"

Sonny whispered, "I'm not hurting anything. Leave me alone, will you?"

"Sonny!"

He clutched the little furry robot desperately around its middle. The stubby arms pawed at him, the furred feet scratched against his arms. It growled a tiny doll-bear growl, and whined, and suddenly his hands were wet with its real salt tears.

"Sonny! Come on now, honey, you know that's Doris's teddy. Aw, chile!"

He said, "It's mine!" It wasn't his. He knew it wasn't his. His was long gone, taken away from him when he was six because it was *old,* and because he had been six and six-year-olds had to have bigger, more elaborate companion-robots. It wasn't even the same color as his—it was brown, where his had been black and white. But it was cuddly and gently warm; and he had heard it whispering little make-believe bedtime stories to Doris. And he wanted it, very much.

Footsteps in the hall outside. A low-pitched pleading voice

from the door: "Sonny, you must not interfere with your sister's toys. One has obligations."

He stood forlornly, holding the teddy-bear. "Go away, Mr. Chips!"

"Really, Sonny! This isn't proper behavior. Please return the toy."

He cried: "I won't!"

Mammy, dark face pleading in the shadowed room, leaned toward him and tried to take it away from him. "Aw, honey, now you knows dat's not—"

"Leave me alone!" he shouted. There was a gasp and a little cry from the bed, and Doris sat up and began to weep.

Well, they had their way. The little girl's bedroom was suddenly filled with robots—and not only robots, for in a moment the butler robot appeared, its face stern and sorrowful, leading Sonny's actual flesh-and-blood mother and father. Sonny made a terrible scene. He cried, and he swore at them childishly for being the unsuccessful clods they were; and they nearly wept too, because they were aware that their lack of standing was bad for the children.

But he couldn't keep the teddy.

They got it away from him and marched him back to his room, where his father lectured him while his mother stayed behind to watch Mammy comfort the little girl. His father said: "Sonny, you're a big boy now. We aren't as well off as other people, but you have to help us. Don't you know that, Sonny? We all have to do our part. Your mother and I'll be up till midnight now, consuming, because you've interrupted us with this scene. Can't you at least *try* to consume something bigger than a teddy-bear? It's all right for Doris because she's so little, but a big boy like you—"

"I hate you!" cried Sonny, and he turned his face to the wall.

They punished him, naturally. The first punishment was that they gave him an extra birthday party the week following.

The second punishment was even worse.

II

Later—much, much later, nearly a score of years—a man named Roger Garrick in a place named Fisherman's Island walked into his hotel room.

The light didn't go on.

The bellhop apologized. "We're sorry, sir. We'll have it attended to, if possible."

"If possible?" Garrick's eyebrows went up. The bellhop made putting in a new light tube sound like a major industrial operation. "All right." He waved the bellhop out of the room. It bowed and closed the door.

Garrick looked around him, frowning. One light tube more or less didn't make an awful lot of difference; there was still the light from the sconces at the walls, from the reading lamps at the chairs and chaise longue and from the photomural on the long side of the room—to say nothing of the fact that it was broad, hot daylight outside and light poured through the windows. All the same, it was a new sensation to be in a room where the central lighting wasn't on. He didn't like it. It was—creepy.

A rap on the door. A girl was standing there, young, attractive, rather small. But a woman grown, it was apparent. "Mr. Garrick? Mr. Roosenburg is expecting you on the sun deck."

"All right." He rummaged around in the pile of luggage, looking for his briefcase. It wasn't even sorted out! The bellhop had merely dumped the lot and left.

The girl said, "Is that what you're looking for?" He looked where she was pointing; it was his briefcase, behind another bag. "You'll get used to that around here. Nothing in the right place, nothing working right. We've all got used to it."

We. He looked at her sharply, but she was no robot; there was life, not the glow of electronic tubes, in her eyes. "Pretty bad, is it?"

She shrugged. "Let's go see Mr. Roosenburg. I'm Kathryn Pender, by the way. I'm his statistician."

He followed her out into the hall. "Statistician?"

She turned and smiled—a tight, grim smile of annoyance. "That's right. Surprised?"

Garrick said slowly, "Well, it's more a robot job. Of course, I'm not familiar with the practice in this sector..."

"You will be," she said shortly. "No, we aren't taking the elevator, Mr. Roosenburg's in a hurry to see you."

"But—"

She turned and glared at him. "Don't you understand? Day before yesterday I took the elevator, and I was hung up between floors for an hour and a half. Something was going on at North Guardian, and it took all the power in the lines. Would it happen again today? I don't know. But, believe me, an hour and a half is a long time to be hanging in an elevator." She turned and led him to the fire stairs. Over her shoulder she said: "Get it straight once and for all, Mr. Garrick. You're in a disaster area here... Anyway, it's only ten more flights."

Ten flights.

Nobody climbed ten flights of stairs any more! Garrick was huffing and puffing before they were halfway, but the girl kept on ahead, light as a gazelle. Her skirt cut midway between hip and knees, and Garrick had plenty of opportunity to observe that her legs were attractively tanned. Even so, he couldn't help looking around him. It was a robot's-eye view of the hotel that he was getting; this was the bare wire armature that held up the confectionery suites and halls where the humans went. Garrick knew, as everyone absent-mindedly knew, that there were places like this behind the scenes everywhere. Belowstairs the robots worked; behind scenes, they moved about their errands and did their jobs. But nobody *went* there. It was funny about the backs of this girl's knees; they were paler than the rest of the leg—

Garrick wrenched his mind back to his surroundings. Take the guard rail along the steps, for instance. It was wire-thin, frail-looking. No doubt it could bear any weight it was required to, but why couldn't it look that way? The answer, obviously, was that robots did not have humanity's built-in concepts of how strong a rail should look before they could believe it really was strong. If a robot should be in any doubt—and how improbable, that a robot should be in doubt—it would perhaps reach out a sculptured hand and test it. Once. And then it would remember, and never doubt again; and it wouldn't be continually edging toward the wall, away from the spider-strand between him and the vertical drop—

He conscientiously took the middle of the steps all the rest of the way up.

Of course that merely meant a different distraction, when he really wanted to do some thinking. But it was a pleasurable distraction. And by the time they reached the top he had solved the problem; the pale spots at the back of Miss Pender's knees meant she had got her suntan the hard way—walking in the sun, perhaps working in the sun, so that the bending knees kept the sun from the patches at the back; not, as anyone else would acquire a tan, by lying beneath a normal, healthful sunlamp held by a robot masseur.

He wheezed: "You don't mean we're all the way up?"

"All the way up," she agreed, and looked at him closely. "Here, lean on me if you want to."

"No, thanks!" He staggered over to the door, which opened naturally enough as he approached it, and stepped out into the flood of sunlight on the roof, to meet Mr. Roosenburg.

Garrick wasn't a medical doctor, but he remembered enough of his basic pre-specialization to know there was something in that fizzy golden drink. It tasted perfectly splendid—just cold enough, just fizzy enough, not quite too sweet. And after two sips of it he was buoyant with strength and well-being.

He put the glass down and said: "Thank you for whatever it was. Now let's talk."

"Gladly, gladly!" boomed Mr. Roosenburg. "Kathryn, the files!"

Garrick looked after her, shaking his head. Not only was she a statistician, which was robot work, she was also a file clerk—and that was barely even robot work, it was the kind of thing handled by a semisentient punch-card sorter in a decently run sector.

Roosenburg said sharply: "Shocks you, doesn't it? But that's why you're here." He was a slim, fair little man, and he wore a golden beard cropped square.

Garrick took another sip of the fizzy drink. It was good stuff; it didn't intoxicate, but it cheered. He said, "I'm glad to know why I'm here."

The golden beard quivered. "Area Control sent you down and didn't tell you this was a disaster area?"

Garrick put down the glass. "I'm a psychist. Area Control said you needed a psychist. From what I've seen, it's a supply problem, but—"

"Here are the files," said Kathryn Pender, and stood watching him.

Roosenburg took the spools of tape from her and dropped them in his lap. He said tangentially, "How old are you, Roger?"

Garrick was annoyed. "I'm a qualified psychist! I happen to be assigned to Area Control and—"

"How old are you?"

Garrick scowled. "Twenty-four."

Roosenburg nodded. "Um. Rather young," he observed. "Maybe you don't remember how things used to be."

Garrick said dangerously, "All the information I need is on that tape. I don't need any lectures from you."

Roosenburg pursed his lips and got up. "Come here a minute, will you?"

He moved over to the rail of the sun deck and pointed. "See those things down there?"

Garrick looked. Twenty stories down, the village straggled off toward the sea in a tangle of pastel oblongs and towers. Over the bay the hills of the mainland were faintly visible through the mist; and riding the bay, the flat white floats of the solar receptors.

"It's a power plant. That what you mean?"

Roosenburg boomed, "A power plant. All the power the world can ever use, out of this one and all the others, all over the world." He peered out at the bobbing floats, soaking up energy from the sun. "And people used to try to wreck them," he said.

Garrick said stiffly: "I may only be twenty-four years old, Mr. Roosenburg, but I have completed school."

"Oh, yes. Oh, of course you have, Roger. But maybe schooling isn't the same thing as living through a time like that. I grew up in the Era of Plenty, when the law was: *Consume*. My parents were poor, and I still remember the misery of my childhood. Eat and consume, wear and use. I never had a moment's peace, Roger! For the very poor it was a treadmill; we had to consume so much that we could never catch up, and the farther we fell behind, the more the Ration Board forced on us—"

Roger Garrick said: "That's ancient history, Mr. Roosenburg. Morey Fry liberated us from all that."

The girl said softly: "Not all of us."

The man with the golden beard nodded. "Not all of us. As you should know, Roger, being a psychist."

Garrick sat up straight, and Roosenburg went on: "Fry showed us that the robots could help at both ends—by making, by consuming. But it came a little late for some of us. The patterns of childhood—they linger on."

Kathryn Pender leaned toward Garrick. "What he's trying to say, Mr. Garrick—we've got a compulsive consumer on our hands."

III

North Guardian Island—nine miles away. It wasn't as much as a mile wide, and not much more than that in length. But it had its city and its bathing beaches, its parks and theaters. It was possibly the most densely populated island in the world...for the number of its inhabitants.

The President of the Council convened their afternoon meeting in a large and lavish room. There were nineteen councilmen around a lustrous mahogany table. Over the President's shoulder the others could see the situation map of North Guardian and the areas surrounding. North Guardian glowed blue, cool, impregnable. The sea was misty green;

the mainland, Fisherman's Island, South Guardian and the rest of the little archipelago were a hot and hostile red.

Little flickering fingers of red attacked the blue. Flick, and a ruddy flame wiped out a corner of a beach; flick, and a red spark appeared in the middle of the city, to grow and blossom, and then to die. Each little red whipflick was a point where, momentarily, the defenses of the island were down; but always and always, the cool blue brightened around the red, and drowned it.

The President was tall, stooped, old. It wore glasses, though robot eyes saw well enough without. It said, in a voice that throbbed with power and pride: "The first item of the order of business will be a report of the Defense Secretary."

The Defense Secretary rose to its feet, hooked a thumb in its vest and cleared its throat. "Mr. President—"

"Excuse me, sir." A whisper from the sweet-faced young blonde taking down the minutes of the meeting. "Mr. Trumie has just left Bowling Green, heading north."

The whole council turned to glance at the situation map, where Bowling Green had just flared red.

The President nodded stiffly, like the crown of an old redwood nodding. "You may proceed, Mr. Secretary," it said after a moment.

"Our invasion fleet," began the Secretary, in its high, clear voice, "is ready for sailing on the first suitable tide. Certain units have been—ah—inactivated, at the—ah—instigation of Mr. Trumie, but on the whole repairs have been completed and the units will be serviceable within the next few hours." Its lean, attractive face turned solemn. "I am afraid, however, that the Air Command has sustained certain, ah, increments of attrition—due, I should emphasize, to chances involved in certain calculated risks—"

"Question, question!" It was the Commissioner of Public Safety, small, dark, fire-eyed, angry.

"Mr. Commissioner?" the President began, but it was interrupted again by the soft whisper of the recording stenographer, listening intently to the earphones that brought news from outside.

"Mr. President," it whispered, "Mr. Trumie has passed the

Navy Yard." The robots turned to look at the situation map. Bowling Green, though it smoldered in spots, had mostly gone back to blue. But the jagged oblong of the Yard flared red and bright. There was a faint electronic hum in the air, almost a sigh.

The robots turned back to face each other. "Mr. President! I demand the Defense Secretary explain the loss of the *Graf Zeppelin* and the 456th Bomb Group!"

The Defense Secretary nodded to the Commissioner of Public Safety. "Mr. Trumie threw them away," it said sorrowfully.

Once again, that sighing electronic drone from the assembled robots.

The Council fussed and fiddled with its papers, while the situation map on the wall flared and dwindled, flared and dwindled. The Defense Secretary cleared its throat again. "Mr. President, there is no question that the—ah—absence of an effective air component will seriously hamper, not to say endanger, our prospects of a suitable landing. Nevertheless—and I say this, Mr. President, in full knowledge of the conclusions that may—indeed, should!—be drawn from such a statement—nevertheless, Mr. President, I say that our forward elements will successfully complete an assault landing—"

"Mr. President!" The breathless whisper of the blonde stenographer again. "Mr. President, Mr. Trumie is in the building!"

On the situation map behind it, the Pentagon—the building they were in—flared scarlet.

The Attorney General, nearest the door, leaped to its feet. "Mr. President, I hear him!"

And they could all hear now. Far off, down the long corridors, a crash. A faint explosion, and another crash; and a raging, querulous, high-pitched voice. A nearer crash, and a sustained, smashing, banging sound, coming toward them.

The oak-paneled doors flew open, splintering.

A tall, dark male figure in gray leather jacket, rocket-gun holsters swinging at its hips, stepped through the splintered

doors and stood surveying the Council. Its hands hung just
below the butts of the rocket guns.

It drawled: "Mistuh Anderson Trumie!"

It stepped aside. Another male figure—shorter, darker,
hobbling with the aid of a stainless-steel cane that concealed
a ray-pencil, wearing the same gray leather jacket and the
same rocket-gun holsters—entered, stood for a moment, and
took a position on the other side of the door.

Between them, Mr. Anderson Trumie shambled ponder-
ously into the Council Chamber to call on his Council.

Sonny Trumie, come of age.

He wasn't much more than five feet tall; but his weight
was close to four hundred pounds. He stood there in the door,
leaning against the splintered oak, quivering jowls obliter-
ating his neck, his eyes nearly swallowed in the fat that
swamped his skull, his thick legs trembling as they tried to
support him.

"You're all under arrest!" he shrilled. "Traitors! Traitors!"

He panted ferociously, staring at them. They waited with
bowed heads. Beyond the ring of councilmen, the situation
map slowly blotted out the patches of red, as the repair-robots
worked feverishly to fix what Sonny Trumie had destroyed.

"Mr. Crockett!" he cried shrilly. "Slay me these traitors!"

Wheep-wheep, and the guns whistled out of their holsters
into the tall bodyguard's hands. *Rata-tat-tat,* and two by two,
the nineteen councilmen leaped, clutched at air and fell, as
the rocket pellets pierced them through.

"That one too!" cried Mr. Trumie, pointing at the sweet-
faced blonde. *Bang.* The sweet young face convulsed and
froze; it fell, slumping across its little table. On the wall the
situation map flared red again, but only faintly—for what
were twenty robots?

Sonny gestured curtly to his other bodyguard. It leaped
forward, tucking the stainless-steel cane under one arm, putting the other around the larded shoulders of Sonny Trumie.
"Ah, now, young master," it crooned. "You just get ahold o'
Long John's arm now—"

"Get them fixed," Sonny ordered abruptly. He pushed the

President of the Council out of its chair and, with the robot's help, sank into it himself. "Get them fixed *right*, you hear? I've had enough traitors. I want them to do what I tell them!"

"Sartin sure, young marster. Long John'll—"

"Do it *now*! And you, Davey! I want my lunch."

"Reckoned you would, Mistuh Trumie. It's right hyar." The Crockett-robot kicked the fallen councilmen out of the way as a procession of waiters filed in from the corridor.

He ate.

He ate until eating was pain, and then he sat there sobbing, his arms braced against the tabletop, until he could eat no more. The Crockett-robot said worriedly: "Mistuh Trumie, moughtn't you hold back a little? Old Doc Aeschylus, he don't keer much to have you eatin' too much, you know."

"I hate Doc!" Trumie said bitterly. He pushed the plates off the table. They fell with a rattle and a clatter, and they went spinning away as he heaved himself up and lurched alone over to the window. "I hate Doc!" he brayed again, sobbing, staring through tears out the window at his kingdom with its hurrying throngs and marching troops and roaring waterfront. The tallow shoulders tried to shake with pain. He felt as though hot cinderblocks were being thrust up into his body cavities, the ragged edges cutting, the hot weight crushing. "Take me back," he sobbed to the robots. "Take me away from these traitors. Take me to my Private Place!"

IV

"So you see," said Roosenburg, "He's dangerous."

Garrick looked out over the water, toward North Guardian. "I'd better look at his tapes," he said. The girl swiftly picked up the reels and began to thread them into the projector. Dangerous. This Trumie was dangerous, all right, Garrick conceded. Dangerous to the balanced, stable world; for it only took one Trumie to topple its stability. It had taken thousands and thousands of years for society to learn its delicate tightrope walk. It was a matter for a psychist, all right. . . .

And Garrick was uncomfortably aware that he was only twenty-four.

"Here you are," said the girl.

"Look them over," said Roosenburg. "Then, after you've studied the tapes on Trumie, we've got something else. One of his robots. But you'll need the tapes first."

"Let's go," said Garrick.

The girl flicked a switch, and the life of Anderson Trumie appeared before them, in color, in three dimensions—in miniature.

Robots have eyes; and where the robots go, the eyes of Robot Central go with them. And the robots go everywhere. From the stored files of Robot Central came the spool of tape that was the life story of Sonny Trumie.

The tapes played into the globe-shaped viewer, ten inches high, a crystal ball that looked back into the past. First, from the recording eyes of the robots in Sonny Trumie's nursery. The lonely little boy, twenty years before, lost in the enormous nursery.

"Disgusting!" breathed Kathryn Pender, wrinkling her nose. "How could people live like that?"

Garrick said, "Please, let me watch this. It's important." In the gleaming globe the little boy-figure kicked at his toys, threw himself across his huge bed, sobbed. Garrick squinted, frowned, reached out, tried to make contact.... It was hard. The tapes showed the objective facts, all right; but for a psychist it was the subjective reality behind the facts that mattered. Kicking at his toys. Yes, but why? Because he was tired of them—and why was he tired? Because he feared them? *Kicking at his toys.* Because—because they were the *wrong* toys? *Kicking—hate them! Don't want them! Want—*

A bluish flare in the viewing globe. Garrick blinked and jumped; and that was the end of that section.

The colors flowed, and suddenly jelled into bright life. Anderson Trumie, a young man. Garrick recognized the scene after a moment—it was right there on Fisherman's Island, some pleasure spot overlooking the water. A bar, and at the end of it was Anderson Trumie, pimply and twenty, staring omberly into an empty glass. The view was through the eyes of the robot bartender.

Anderson Trumie was weeping.

Once again, there was the objective fact—but the fact behind the fact, what was it? Trumie had been drinking, drinking. Why? *Drinking, drinking.* With a sudden sense of shock, Garrick saw what the drink was—the golden, fizzy liquor. Not intoxicating. Not habit-forming! Trumie had become no drunk, it was something else that kept him *drinking, drinking, must drink, must keep on drinking, or else—*

And again the bluish flare.

There was more; there was Trumie feverishly collecting objects of art, there was Trumie decorating a palace; there was Trumie on a world tour, and Trumie returned to Fisherman's Island.

And then there was no more.

"That," said Roosenburg, "is the file. Of course, if you want the raw, unedited tapes, we can try to get them from Robot Central, but—"

"No." The way things were, it was best to stay away from Robot Central; there might be more breakdowns, and there wasn't much time. Besides, something was beginning to suggest itself.

"Run the first one again," said Garrick. "I think maybe there's something there..."

Garrick made out a quick requisition slip and handed it to Kathryn Pender, who looked at it, raised her eyebrows, shrugged and went off to have it filled.

By the time she came back, Roosenburg had escorted Garrick to the room where the captured Trumie robot lay enchained. "He's cut off from Robot Central," Roosenburg was saying. "I suppose you figured that out. Imagine! Not only has he built a whole city for himself—but even his own robot control!"

Garrick looked at the robot. It was a fisherman, or so Roosenburg had said. It was small, dark, black-haired, and possibly the hair would have been curly, if the sea water hadn't plastered the curls to the scalp. It was still damp from

the tussle that had landed it in the water, and eventually ir
Roosenburg's hands.

Roosenburg was already at work. Garrick tried to think
of it as a machine, but it wasn't easy. The thing looked very
nearly human—except for the crystal and copper that showed
where the back of its head had been removed.

"It's as bad as a brain operation," said Roosenburg, work
ing rapidly without looking up. "I've got to short out the
input leads without disturbing the electronic balance..."

Snip, snip. A curl of copper fell free, to be grabbed by
Roosenburg's tweezers. The fisherman's arms and legs kicked
sharply like a galvanized frog's.

Kathryn Pender said: "They found him this morning, cast
ing nets into the bay and singing 'O Sole Mio.' He's from
North Guardian, all right."

Abruptly the lights flickered and turned yellow, ther
slowly returned to normal brightness. Roger Garrick got up
and walked over to the window. North Guardian was a haze
of light in the sky, across the water.

Click, snap. The fisherman-robot began to sing:

> *Tutte le serre, dopo quel fanal,*
> *Dietro la caserma, ti staró ed—*

Click. Roosenburg muttered under his breath and probed
further. Kathryn Pender joined Garrick at the window. "Now
you see," she said.

Garrick shrugged. "You can't blame him."

"*I* blame him!" she said hotly. "I've lived here all my life
Fisherman's Island used to be a tourist spot—why, it was
lovely here. And look at it now. The elevators don't work
The lights don't work. Practically all of our robots are gone
Spare parts, construction material, everything—it's all gone
to North Guardian! There isn't a day that passes, Garrick
when half a dozen bargeloads of stuff don't go north, because
he requisitioned them. Blame him? I'd like to kill him!"

Snap. Sputter*snap.* The fisherman lifted its head and car
oled:

Forse dommani, piangerai,
E dopo tu, sorriderai—

Snap. Roosenburg's probe uncovered a flat black disc. "Kathryn, look this up, will you?" He read the serial number from the disc, and then put down the probe. He stood flexing his fingers, staring irritably at the motionless figure.

Garrick joined him. Roosenburg jerked his head at the fisherman. "That's robot work, trying to tinker with their insides. Trumie has his own control center, you see. What I have to do is recontrol this one from the substation on the mainland, but keep its receptor circuits open to North Guardian on the symbol level. You understand what I'm talking about? It'll think from North Guardian, but act from the mainland."

"Sure," said Garrick, far from sure.

"And it's damned close work. There isn't much room inside one of those things..." He stared at the figure and picked up the probe again.

Kathryn Pender came back with a punchcard in her hand. "It was one of ours, all right. Used to be a busboy in the cafeteria at the beach club." She scowled. "That Trumie!"

"You can't blame him," Garrick said reasonably. "He's only trying to be good."

She looked at him queerly. "He's only—" she began; but Roosenburg interrupted with an exultant cry.

"Got it! All right, you. Sit up and start telling us what Trumie's up to now!"

The fisherman figure said obligingly, "Sure, boss. Whatcha wanna know?"

What they wanted to know they asked; and what they asked it told them, volunteering nothing, concealing nothing.

There was Anderson Trumie, king of his island, the compulsive consumer.

It was like an echo of the bad old days of the Age of Plenty, when the world was smothering under the endless, pounding flow of goods from the robot factories and the desperate race between consumption and production strained the human fabric. But Trumie's orders came not from society, but from within. *Consume!* commanded something inside him, and *Use!* it cried, and *Devour!* it ordered. And Trumie obeyed, heroically.

They listened to what the fisherman-robot had to say; and the picture was dark. Armies had sprung up on North Guardian, navies floated in its waters. Anderson Trumie stalked among his creations like a blubbery god, wrecking and ruling. Garrick could see the pattern in what the fisherman had to say. In Trumie's mind, he was Hitler, Hoover, and Genghis Khan; he was dictator, building a war machine; he was supreme engineer, constructing a mighty state. He was warrior.

"He was playing tin soldiers," said Roger Garrick, and Roosenburg and the girl nodded.

"The trouble is," boomed Roosenburg, "he has stopped playing. Invasion fleets, Garrick! He isn't content with North Guardian any more, he wants the rest of the country too!"

"You can't blame him," said Roger Garrick for the third time, and stood up.

"The question is," he said, "what do we do about it?"

"That's what you're here for," Kathryn told him.

"All right. We can forget," said Roger Garrick, "about the soldiers—*qua* soldiers, that is. I promise you they won't hurt anyone. Robots can't."

"I understand that," Kathryn snapped.

"The problem is what to do about Trumie's drain on the world's resources." He pursed his lips. "According to my directive from Area Control, the first plan was to let him alone—after all, there is still plenty of everything for anyone. Why not let Trumie enjoy himself? But that didn't work out too well."

"You're so right," said Kathryn Pender.

"No, no—not on your local level," Garrick explained quickly. "After all—what are a few thousand robots, a few hundred million dollars worth of equipment? We could resupply this area in a week."

"And in a week," boomed Roosenburg, "Trumie would have us cleaned out again!"

Garrick nodded. "That's the trouble," he admitted. "He doesn't seem to have a stopping point. Yet—we can't *refuse* his orders. Speaking as a psychist, that would set a very bad precedent. It would put ideas in the minds of a lot of persons—minds that, in some cases, might not be reliably stable in the absence of a stable, certain source of everything they need, on request. If we say 'no' to Trumie, we open the door on some mighty dark corners of the human mind. Covetousness. Greed. Pride of possession—"

"So what are you going to do?" cried Kathryn Pender.

Garrick said resentfully. "The only thing there is *to* do. I'm going to look over Trumie's folder again. And then I'm going to North Guardian Island."

V

Roger Garrick was all too aware of the fact that he was only twenty-four.

It didn't make a great deal of difference. The oldest and wisest psychist in Area Control's wide sphere might have been doubtful of success in as thorny a job as the one ahead.

They started out at daybreak. Vapor was rising from the sea about them, and the little battery motor of their launch whined softly beneath the keelson. Garrick sat patting the little box that contained their invasion equipment, while the girl steered. The workshops of Fisherman's Island had been all night making some of the things in that box—not because they were so difficult to make, but because it had been a bad night. Big things were going on at North Guardian; twice the power had been out entirely for nearly an hour, as the demand on the lines from North Guardian took all the power the system could deliver.

The sun was well up as they came within hailing distance of the Navy Yard.

Robots were hard at work; the Yard was bustling with activity. An overhead traveling crane, eight feet tall, laboriously lowered a prefabricated fighting top onto an eleven-foot aircraft carrier. A motor torpedo boat—full-sized, this one was, not to scale—rocked at anchor just before the bow of their launch. Kathryn steered around it, ignoring the hail from the robot lieutenant-j.g. at its rail.

She glanced at Garrick over her shoulder, her face taut. "It's—it's all mixed up."

Garrick nodded. The battleships were model-sized, the small boats full scale. In the city beyond the Yard, the pinnacle of the Empire State Building barely cleared the Pentagon, next door. A soaring suspension bridge leaped out from the shore a quarter of a mile away, and stopped short a thousand yards out, over empty water.

It was easy enough to understand—even for a psychist just out of school, on his first real assignment. Trumie was trying to run a world singlehanded, and where there were gaps in his conception of what his world should be, the results showed. "Get me battleships!" he ordered his robot supply clerks; and they found the only battleships there were in the world to copy, the child-sized toy-scaled play battleships that still delighted kids. "Get me an Air Force!" And a thousand model bombers were hastily put together. "Build me a bridge!" But perhaps he had forgot to say to where.

"Come on, Garrick!"

He shook his head and focused on the world around him. Kathryn Pender was standing on a gray steel stage, the mooring line from their launch secured to what looked like a coast-defense cannon—but only about four feet long. Garrick picked up his little box and leaped up to the stage beside her. She turned to look at the city. . . .

"Hold on a second." He was opening the box, taking out two little cardboard placards. He turned her by the shoulder and, with pins from the box, attached one of the cards to her back. "Now me," he said, turning his back to her.

She read the placard dubiously:

I

AM A

SPY!

"Garrick," she began, "you're sure you know what you're doing—"

"Put it on!" She shrugged and pinned it to the folds of his jacket.

Side by side, they entered the citadel of the enemy.

According to the fisherman-robot, Trumie lived in a gingerbread castle south of the Pentagon. Most of the robots got no chance to enter it. The city outside the castle was Trumie's kingdom, and he roamed about it, overseeing, changing, destroying, rebuilding. But inside the castle was his Private Place; the only robots that had both an inside- and outside-the-castle existence were his two bodyguards.

"That," said Garrick, "must be the Private Place."

It was a gingerbread castle, all right. The "gingerbread" was stonework, gargoyles and columns; there was a moat and a drawbridge, and there were robot guards with crooked little rifles, wearing scarlet tunics and fur shakos three feet tall. The drawbridge was up and the guards at stiff attention.

"Let's reconnoiter," said Garrick. He was unpleasantly conscious of the fact that every robot they passed—and they had passed thousands—had turned to look at the signs on their backs. Yet—it was right, wasn't it? There was no hope of avoiding observation in any event. The only hope was to fit somehow into the pattern—and spies would certainly be a part of the pattern. Wouldn't they?

Garrick turned his back on doubts and led the way around the gingerbread palace.

The only entrance was the drawbridge.

They stopped out of sight of the ramrod-stiff guards. Garrick said: "We'll go in. As soon as we get inside, you put on your costume." He handed her the box. "You know what to do. All you have to do is keep him quiet for a while and let me talk to him."

The girl said doubtfully, "Garrick. Is this going to work?"

Garrick exploded: "How the devil do I know? I had Trumie's dossier to work with. I know everything that happened

to him when he was a kid—when this trouble started. But
to reach him, to talk to the boy inside the man—that takes
a long time, Kathryn. And we don't have a long time. So..."

He took her elbow and marched her toward the guards.
"So you know what to do," he said.

"I hope so," breathed Kathryn Pender, looking very small
and very young.

They marched down the wide white pavement, past the
motionless guards...

Something was coming toward them. Kathryn held back.
"Come on!" Garrick muttered.

"No, look!" she whispered. "Is that—is that Trumie?"

He looked.

It was Trumie, larger than life. It was Anderson Trumie,
the entire human population of the most-congested-island-
for-its-population in the world. On one side of him was a tall,
dark figure, on the other side a squat dark figure, helping
him along. They looked at his face and it was horror, drowned
in fat. The bloated cheeks shook damply, wet with tears. The
eyes looked out with fright on the world he had made.

Trumie and his bodyguards rolled up to them and past.
And then Anderson Trumie stopped.

He turned the blubbery head, and read the sign on the
back of the girl. *I am a spy.* Panting heavily, clutching the
shoulder of the Crockett-robot, he stared wildly at her.

Garrick cleared his throat. This far his plan had gone, and
then there was a gap. There had to be a gap. Trumie's history,
in the folder that Roosenburg had supplied, had told him
what to do with Trumie; and Garrick's own ingenuity had
told him how to reach the man. But a link was missing. Here
was the subject, and here was the psychist who could cure
him; and it was up to Garrick to start the cure.

Trumie cried, in a staccato bleat: "You! What are you?
Where do you belong?"

He was talking to the girl. Beside him the Crockett-robot
murmured, "Rackin she's a spy, Mistuh Trumie. See thet sign
a-hangin' on her back?"

"Spy? Spy?" The quivering lips pouted. "Curse you, are
you Mata Hari? What are you doing out here? It's changed

ts face," Trumie complained to the Crockett-robot. "It doesn't belong here. It's supposed to be in the harem. Go on, Crockett, get it back!"

"Wait!" cried Garrick, but the Crockett-robot was ahead of him. It took Kathryn Pender by the arm.

"Come along thar," it said soothingly, and urged her across the drawbridge. She glanced back at Garrick, and for a moment it looked as though she were going to speak. Then she shook her head, as though she were giving an order.

"Kathryn!" cried Garrick. "Trumie, wait a minute. That isn't Mata Hari!"

No one was listening. Kathryn Pender disappeared into the Private Place. Trumie, leaning heavily on the hobbling Silver-robot, followed.

Garrick, coming back to life, leaped after them...

The scarlet-coated guards jumped before him, their shakos bobbing, their crooked little rifles crossed to bar his way.

He cried, "One side! Out of my way, you! I'm a human, don't you understand? You've got to let me pass!"

They didn't even look at him; trying to get by them was like trying to walk through a wall of moving, thrusting steel. He shoved, and they pushed him back; he tried to dodge, and they were before him. It was hopeless.

And then it was hopeless indeed, because behind them, he saw, the drawbridge had gone up.

VI

Sonny Trumie collapsed into a chair like a mound of blubber falling to the deck of a whaler.

Though he made no signal, the procession of serving robots started at once. In minced the maître d', bowing and waving its graceful hands; in marched the sommelier, clanking its necklace of keys, bearing its wines in their buckets of ice. In came the lovely waitress-robots and the sturdy steward-robots, with the platters and tureens, the plates and bowls and cups. They spread a meal—a dozen meals—before him, and he began to eat. He ate as a penned pig eats, gobbling until

it chokes, forcing the food down because there is nothing to
do *but* eat. He ate, with a sighing accompaniment of moans
and gasps, and some of the food was salted with the tears of
pain he wept into it, and some of the wine was spilled by his
shaking hand. But he ate. Not for the first time that day, and
not for the tenth.

Sonny Trumie wept as he ate. He no longer even knew he
was weeping. There was the gaping void inside him that he
had to fill, had to fill; there was the gaping world about him
that he had to people and build and furnish—and *use*. He
moaned to himself. Four hundred pounds of meat and lard,
and he had to lug it from end to end of his island, every hour
of every day, never resting, never at peace! There should
have been a place somewhere, there should have been a time,
when he could rest. When he could sleep without dreaming,
sleep without waking after a scant few hours with the goad-
ing drive to eat and to use, to use and to eat...And it was
all so *wrong*! The robots didn't understand. They didn't try
to understand, they didn't think for themselves. Let him take
his eyes from any one of them for a single day, and everything
went *wrong*. It was necessary to keep after them, from end
to end of the island, checking and overseeing and ordering—
yes, and destroying to rebuild, over and over!

He moaned again, and pushed the plate away.

He rested, with his tallow forehead flat against the table,
waiting, while inside him the pain ripped and ripped, and
finally became bearable again. And slowly he pushed himself
up again, and rested for a moment, and pulled a fresh plate
toward him, and began again to eat...

After a while he stopped. Not because he didn't want to
go on, but because he couldn't.

He was bone-tired, but something was bothering him—
one more detail to check, one more thing that was *wrong*.
The houri at the drawbridge. It shouldn't have been out of
the Private Place. It should have been in the harem, of course.
Not that it mattered, except to Sonny Trumie's sense of what
was right. Time was when the houris of the harem had their
uses, but that time was long and long ago; now they were
property, to be fussed over and made to be *right*, to be replaced

if they were worn, destroyed if they were *wrong*. But only property, as all of North Guardian was property—as all of the world would be his property, if only he could manage it.

But property shouldn't be *wrong*.

He signaled to the Crockett-robot and, leaning on it, walked down the long terrazzo hall toward the harem. He tried to remember what the houri had looked like. It had worn a sheer red blouse and a brief red skirt, he was nearly sure, but the face.... It had had a face, of course. But Sonny had lost the habit of faces. This one had been somehow different, but he couldn't remember just why. Still—the blouse and skirt, they were red, he was nearly sure. And it had been carrying something in a box. And that was odd, too.

He waddled a little faster, for now he was sure it was *wrong*.

"That's the harem, Mistuh Trumie," said the robot at his side. It disengaged itself gently, leaped forward and held the door to the harem for him.

"Wait for me," Sonny commanded, and waddled forward into the harem halls. Once he had so arranged the harem that he needed no help inside it; the halls were railed, at a height where it was easy for a pudgy hand to grasp the rail; the distances were short, the rooms close together. He paused and called over his shoulder, "Stay where you can hear me." It had occurred to him that if the houri-robot was *wrong* he would need Crockett's guns to make it right.

A chorus of female voices sprang into song as he entered the main patio. They were a bevy of beauties, clustered around a fountain, diaphanously dressed, languorously glancing at Sonny Trumie as he waddled inside. "Shut up!" he commanded. "Go back to your rooms." They bowed their heads and, one by one, slipped into the cubicles.

No sign of the red blouse and the red skirt. He began the rounds of the cubicles, panting, peering into them. "Hello, Sonny," whispered Theda Bara, lithe on a leopard rug, and he passed on. "I love you!" cried Nell Gwynn, and, "Come to me!" commanded Cleopatra, but he passed them by. He passed Dubarry and Marilyn Monroe, he passed Moll Flan-

ders and he passed Troy's Helen. No sign of the houri in
red...

And then he saw signs. He didn't see the houri, but he
saw the signs of the houri's presence; the red blouse and the
red skirt, lying limp and empty on the floor.

Sonny gasped, "You! Where are you? Come out here where
I can see you!"

Nobody answered Sonny. "Come out!" he bawled.

And then he stopped. A door opened and someone came
out; not a houri, not female; a figure without sex but loaded
with love, a teddy-bear figure, as tall as pudgy Sonny Trumie
himself, waddling as he waddled, its stubbed arms stretched
out to him.

Sonny could hardly believe his eyes. Its color was a little
darker than Teddy. It was a good deal taller than Teddy. But
unquestionably, undoubtedly, in everything that mattered
it was—"Teddy," whispered Sonny Trumie, and let the furry
arms go around his four hundred pounds.

Twenty years disappeared. "They wouldn't let me have
you," Sonny told the teddy; and it said, in a voice musical
and warm:

"It's all right, Sonny. You can have me now, Sonny. You
can have everything, Sonny."

"They took you away," he whispered, remembering. They
took the teddy-bear away; he had never forgotten. They took
it away, and they were wild. Mother was wild, and father
was furious; they raged at the little boy and scolded him, and
threatened him. Didn't he know they were *poor*, and did he
want to ruin them all, and what was wrong with him anyway,
that he wanted his little sister's silly stuffed robots when he
was big enough to use nearly grown-up goods.

The night had been a terror, with the frowning, sad robots
ringed around and the little girl crying; and what had made
it terror was not the scolding—he'd had scoldings—but the
worry, the fear and almost the panic in his parents' voices.
For what he did, he came to understand, was no longer a
childish sin; it was a *big* sin, a failure to consume his
quota—

And it had to be punished. The first punishment was the

extra birthday party; the second was—shame. Sonny Trumie, not quite twelve, was made to feel shame and humiliation. Shame is only a little thing, but it makes the one who owns it little too. Shame. The robots were reset to scorn him. He woke to mockery, and went to bed with contempt. Even his little sister lisped the catalogue of his failures. You aren't trying, Sonny, and You don't care, Sonny, and You're a terrible disappointment to us, Sonny. And finally all the things were true; because Sonny at twelve was what his elders made him.

And they made him... "neurotic" is the term; a pretty-sounding word that means ugly things like fear and worry and endless self-reproach...

"Don't worry," whispered the teddy. "Don't worry, Sonny. You can have me. You can have what you want. You don't have to have anything else..."

VII

Garrick raged through the halls of the Private Place like a tiger upon a kid. "Kathryn!" he cried. "Kathryn Pender!" Finally he had found a way in, unguarded, forgotten. But it had taken time. And he was worried. "Kathryn!" The robots peeped out at him, worriedly, and sometimes they got in his way and he bowled them aside. They didn't fight back, naturally—what robot would hurt a human? But sometimes they spoke to him, pleading, for it was not according to the wishes of Mr. Trumie that anyone but him rage destroying through North Guardian Island. He passed them by. "Kathryn!" he called. "Kathryn!"

It wasn't that Trumie was dangerous.

He told himself fiercely: Trumie was *not* dangerous. Trumie was laid bare in his folder, the one that Roosenburg had supplied. He couldn't be blamed, and he meant no harm. He was once a bad little boy who was trying to be good by consuming, consuming; and he wore himself into neurosis doing it; and then they changed the rules on him. End of the ration; end of forced consumption, as the robots took over for mankind at the other end of the cornucopia. It wasn't necessary to struggle to consume, so the rules were changed....

And maybe Mr. Trumie knew that the rules had been changed; but Sonny didn't. It was Sonny, the bad little boy trying to be good, who had made North Guardian Island....

And it was Sonny who owned the Private Place, and all it held—including Kathryn Pender.

Garrick called hoarsely, "Kathryn! If you hear me, *answer me!*"

It had seemed so simple. The fulcrum on which the weight of Trumie's neurosis might move was a teddy-bear; give him a teddy-bear—or, perhaps, a teddy-bear suit, made by night in the factories of Fisherman's Island, with a girl named Kathryn Pender inside—and let him hear, from a source he could trust, the welcome news that it was no longer necessary to struggle, that compulsive consumption could have an end. Permissive analysis would clear it up; but only if Trumie would listen.

"Kathryn!" roared Roger Garrick, racing through a room of mirrors and carved statues. Because, just in case Trumie didn't listen, just in case the folder was wrong and the teddy wasn't the key—

Why, then, the teddy to Trumie was only a robot. And Trumie destroyed them by the score.

"Kathryn!" cried Roger Garrick, trotting through the silent palace; and at last he heard what might have been an answer. At least it was a voice—a girl's voice, at that. He was before a passage that led to a room with a fountain and silent female robots, standing and watching him. The voice came from a small room. He ran to the door.

It was the right door.

There was Trumie, four hundred pounds of lard, lying on a marble bench with a foam-rubber cushion, the jowled head in the small lap of—

Teddy. Or Kathryn Pender in the teddy-bear suit, the stick-like legs pointed straight out, the stick-like arms clumsily patting him. She was talking to him, gently and reassuringly. She was telling him what he needed to know—that he had eaten *enough*, that he had used *enough*, that he had consumed enough to win the respect of all, and an end to consuming.

Garrick himself could not have done better.

It was a sight from Mother Goose, the child being soothed by his toy. But it was not a sight that fit in well with its surroundings, for the seraglio was upholstered in mauve and pink, and wicked paintings hung about.

Sonny Trumie rolled the pendulous head and looked squarely at Garrick. The worry was gone from the fearful little eyes.

Garrick stepped back.

No need for him just at this moment. Let Trumie relax for a while, as he had not been able to relax for a score of years. Then the psychist could pick up where the girl had been unable to proceed; but in the meantime, Trumie was finally at rest.

The teddy looked up at Garrick, and in its bright blue eyes, the eyes that belonged to the girl named Kathryn, he saw a queer tincture of triumph and compassion.

Garrick nodded and left, and went out to the robots of North Guardian and started them clearing away.

Sonny Trumie nestled his swine's head in the lap of the teddy-bear. It was talking to him so nicely, so nicely. It was droning away, "Don't worry, Sonny. Don't worry. Everything's all right. Everything's all right." Why, it was almost as though it were real.

It had been, he calculated with the part of his mind that was razor-sharp and never relaxed, it had been nearly two hours since he had eaten. Two hours! And he felt as though he could go another hour at least, maybe two. Maybe—maybe even not eat at all again that day. Maybe even learn to live on three meals. Perhaps two. Perhaps—

He wriggled—as well as four hundred greasy pounds can wriggle—and pressed against the soft warm fur of the teddy-bear. It was so soothing! "You don't have to eat so much, Sonny. You don't have to drink so much. No one will mind. Your father won't mind, Sonny. Your mother won't mind..."

It was very comfortable to hear the teddy-bear telling him those things. It made him drowsy. So deliciously drowsy! It wasn't like going to sleep, as Sonny Trumie had known going to sleep for a dozen or more years, the bitterly fought surrender to the anesthetic weariness. It was just drowsy...

And he did want to go to sleep.

And finally he slept. All of him slept. Not just the four hundred pounds of blubber and the little pig eyes, but even the razor-sharp mind-Trumie that lived in the sad, obedient hulk; it slept; and it had never slept before.

AVARICE

"Millions for defense, but not one cent for tribute."
There's a bold, heroic, military statement which we
can all admire, hats off, hearts pounding. What,
count pennies, when principle is at stake?—And yet,
on the other hand, there is also the bold, heroic,
military statement: "There is no substitute for vic-
tory." Well, then what if heroics lose and a little
computational compromise wins? In that case—
"Count the profits and the wars will take care of
themselves," says AVARICE.

MARGIN OF PROFIT

POUL ANDERSON

It was an anachronism to have a human receptionist in this hall of lucent plastic, among the machines that winked and talked between jade columns soaring up into vaulted dimness—but a remarkably pleasant one when she was as long-legged and red-headed a stun-blast as the girl behind the desk. Captain Torres drew to a crisp halt, and a gauntleted hand went to his gilt helmet. Traveling down sumptuous curves, his eye was jarred by the small needler at her waist.

"Good day, sir," she smiled. "One moment, please, I'll see if Freeman van Rijn is ready for you." She switched on the intercom and a three-megavolt oath bounced out. "No, he's still conferring on the vid. Won't you be seated?"

Before she turned it off, Torres caught a few words: "...By damn, he'll give us the exclusive franchise or do without our business. Who do these little emperors think they are? All right, so he has a million soldiers under arms. You can tell him to take those soldiers, with field artillery and hobnailed boots, by damn, and—" *Click.*

Torres wrapped his cape about the deep-blue tunic and sat down, laying one polished boot across the other knee of his white culottes. He felt out of his depth, simultaneously overdressed and naked. The regalia of a Lodgemaster in the Federated Brotherhood of Spacemen was stiff with gold braid, medals, and jewelry, far removed from the gray coverall he wore on deck or the loungers of planet leave. Worse, the guards in the tower entrance, a kilometer below, had not only checked his credentials and retinal patterns, but had unloaded his sidearm.

Blast Nicholas van Rijn and the whole Polesotechnic

League! Good saints, drop him on Pluto without his underwear!

Of course, a merchant prince did have to be wary of assassins—and most of them went to great lengths to avoid formal duels, though Van Rijn himself was supposed to be murderously fast with a handgun. Nevertheless, arming your receptionist was not a high-born thing to do—

Torres wondered, rather wistfully, if she was one of the old devil's mistresses. Perhaps not; but with the trouble between the Company—no, the whole League—and the Brotherhood, she'd have no time for him, being doubtless bound by a contract of personal fealty. His gaze went to the League emblem on the wall, a golden sunburst afire with opals, surrounding an ancient-style rocketship of the Caravel model, and the motto: *All the traffic will bear.* That could be taken two ways, he reflected sourly. Beneath it was the trademark of Van Rijn's own outfit, the Solar Spice & Liquors Company.

The girl turned on the intercom again and heard the vidophone being switched off; there followed a steady rumble of obscenities. "Go on in now, sir," she said, and into the speaker: "Captain Rafael Torres, representing the Brotherhood."

The spaceman straightened himself and went through the inner door. His lean dark face clamped into careful lines. It would be a new experience, meeting his ultimate boss; for ten years, as captain of a ship and lodgemaster of the union local, he had not called anyone "sir."

The office was big, with an entire side transparent, overlooking a precipitous vista of Batavia's towers, green landscape, hot with tropical gardens, and the molten glitter of the Java Sea. The other walls were lined with the biggest referobot Torres had ever seen, with shelves of extraterrestrial curios, and—astonishingly—a thousand or more old-type folio books, exquisitely bound in tooled leather and looking well-worn. The room and the desk were littered, close to maximum entropy, and the ventilators could not quite dismiss a tobacco haze. The most noticeable object on the desk was a small image of St. Dismas, carved from sandroot in the

Martian style. The precise and perfect patron for Nicholas van Rijn, thought Torres.

He clicked his heels and bowed till the helmet plume swept his nose. "Lodgemaster-Captain Torres speaking for the Brotherhood, sir."

Van Rijn grunted. He was a huge man, two meters high, and the triple chin and swag belly did not make him appear soft. Rings glittered on the hairy hands and bracelets on the thick wrists, under snuff-soiled lace. Small gray eyes, set close to the great hook nose under a sloping forehead, blinked at the spaceman. He went back to filling his churchwarden, and said nothing until he had a good head of steam up.

"So, by damn," he muttered then. "You speak for the whole louse-bound union, I hope." The long handlebar mustaches and goatee waggled over a gorgeously embroidered waistcoat. Beneath it was only a sarong, columnar legs, and bare splay feet.

Torres checked his temper. "Yes, sir. For all the locals in the Solar Federation, and every other lodge within ten light-years. We understood that you would represent the League."

"Only tentatively. I will convey your demands to my colleagues, such of them as I can drag out of their offices and harems. Sit."

Torres did not give the chair an opportunity to mold itself to him; he sat on the edge and said harshly: "It's simple enough, sir. You already know our decision. We aren't calling a real strike...yet. We just refuse to take any more ships through the Kossaluth of Borthu till the menace there has been stopped. If you insist that we do so, we will strike."

"By damn, you cut your own throats," replied Van Rijn with surprising mildness. "Not alone the loss of pay and commissions. No, but if Antares is not kept steady supplied, she loses taste maybe for cinnamon and London dry gin. Not to speak of products offered by other companies. Like if Jo-Boy Technical Services bring in no more indentured scientists, Antares builds her own academies. Hell and lawyers! In a few years, no more market at Antares and all fifteen planets. You lose, I lose, we all lose."

"The answer is simple enough, sir. We just detour around

the Kossaluth. I know that'll take us through more hazardous regions, we'll have more wrecks, but the brothers don't mind that risk."

"What?" Somehow, Van Rijn managed a basso scream. "Pest and cannon balls! Double the length of the voyage! Double the fuel bills, salaries, ship and cargo losses...halve the deliveries per year! We are ruined! Better we give up Antares at once!"

It was already an expensive route, Torres knew; whether or not the companies could actually afford the extra cost, he didn't know, for by the standard treaty which Sol had also signed, the League's books were its own secret. He waited out the dramatics, then said patiently:

"The Borthudian press gangs have been operating for two years now, sir. We've tried to fight them, and can't. We didn't make this decision overnight; if it had been up to the brothers at large, we'd have voted right at the start not to go through that hellhole. But the Lodgemasters held back, hoping something could be worked out. Apparently it can't."

"See here," growled Van Rijn. "I don't like this losing of men and ships any better than you. Worse, maybe. A million credits a year or more it costs this company alone. But we can afford it. Only fifteen percent of our ships are captured. We would lose more, detouring through the Gamma Mist or the Stonefields. Crewfolk should be men, not jellyfish."

"Easy enough for you to say!" snapped Torres. "We'll face meteors and dust clouds, rogue planets and hostile natives, warped space and hard radiation...but I've *seen* one of those pressed men. That's what decided me. I'm not going to risk it happening to me, and neither is anyone else."

"Ah, so?" Van Rijn leaned over the desk. "By damn, you tell me."

"Met him on *Arkan III,* autonomous planet on the fringe of the Kossaluth, where we put in to deliver some tea. One of their ships was in, too, and you can bet your brain we went around in armed parties and were ready to shoot anyone who even looked like a crimp. I saw him, this man they'd kidnaped, going on some errand, spoke to him, we even tried to snatch him back so we could bring him to Earth for deconditioning— He fought us and got away. God! He wasn't human any more, not inside. And still you could tell he wanted out, he wanted to break the conditioning, and he couldn't, *and he couldn't go crazy either—*"

Torres grew aware that Van Rijn was thrusting a full goblet into his hand. "Here, you drink this." It burned all the way down. "I have seen conditioned men. I was a rough-and-tumbler myself in younger days." The merchant went back behind his desk and rekindled his pipe. "It is a fiendish thing to do, *ja.*"

"If you want to outfit a punitive expedition, sir," said Torres savagely, "I guarantee you can get full crews."

"No." The curled, shoulder-length black locks swished greasily as Van Rijn shook his head. "The League does not have many capital ships. It is unprofitable. The cost of a war with Borthu would wipe out ten years' gains. And then we will have trouble with the milksop governments of a hundred planets. No."

"Isn't there some kind of pressure you can put on the Kossalu himself?"

"Hah! You think maybe we have not tried? Economic sanctions do not work; they are not interested in trade outside their own empire. Threats they laugh at. They know that they have more navy than we will ever build. Assassins never get close to the big potatoes." Van Rijn cursed for two straight minutes without repeating himself. "And there they sit, fat and greedy-gut, across the route to Antares and all stars beyond! It is not to be stood!"

He had been prowling the floor; now he whirled about with surprising speed for so large and clumsy a man. "This strike of yours brings it to a head. And speaking of heads, it is getting time for a tall cold beer. I shall have to confer with my fellows. Tell your men there will be steps taken if it is financially possible. Now get out!"

It is a truism that the structure of a society is basically determined by its technology. Not in an absolute sense— there may be totally different cultures using identical tools— but the tools settle the possibilities: you can't have interstellar trade without spaceships. A race limited to one planet, possessing a high knowledge of mechanics but with all its basic machines of commerce and war requiring a large capital investment, will inevitably tend toward collectivism under one name or another. Free enterprise needs elbow room.

Automation made manufacturing cheap, and the cost of energy nose-dived when the proton converter was invented. Gravity control and the hyperdrive opened a galaxy to exploitation. They also provided a safety valve: A citizen who found his government oppressive could usually emigrate elsewhere, which strengthened the libertarian planets; their influence in turn loosened the bonds of the older world.

Interstellar distances being what they are, and intelligent races all having their own ideas of culture, there was no union of planetary systems. Neither was there much war: too destructive, with small chance for either side to escape ruin, and there was little to fight about. A race doesn't get to be intelligent without an undue share of built-in ruthlessness, so all was not sweetness and brotherhood—but the balance of power remained fairly stable. And there was a brisk demand for trade goods. Not only did colonies want the luxuries of home, and the home planets want colonial produce, but the old worlds had much to swap.

Under such conditions, an exuberant capitalism was bound to strike root. It was also bound to find mutual interest, to form alliances and settle spheres of influence. The powerful companies joined together to squeeze out competitors, jack up prices, and generally make the best of a good thing. Governments were limited to a few planetary systems at most; they could do little to control their cosmopolitan merchants. One by one, through bribery, coercion, or sheer despair, they gave up the struggle.

Selfishness is a potent force. Governments, officially dedicated to altruism, remained divided; the Polesotechnic League became a super-government, sprawling from Canopus to Polaris, drawing its membership from a thousand species. It was a horizontal society, cutting across all political and cultural boundaries. It set its own policies, made its own treaties, established its own bases, fought its own minor wars—and, in the course of milking the Milky Way, did more to spread a truly universal civilization and enforce a lasting *Pax* than all the diplomats in the galaxy.

But it had its own troubles.

One of Nicholas Van Rijn's mansions lay on the peak of Kilimanjaro, up among the undying snows. It was an easy spot to defend, and a favorite for conferences.

His gravcar slanted down through a night of needle-sharp stars, toward the high turrets and glowing lanterns. Looking through the roof, he picked out the cold sprawl of Scorpio. Antares flashed a red promise, and he shook his fist at the suns between. "So! Monkey business with Van Rijn, by damn. The whole Sagittarius clusters waiting to be opened, and you in the way. This will cost you money, my friends, gut and kipper me if it don't."

He thought back to days when he had ridden a bucketing ruin of a ship through the great hollow spaces, bargaining under green skies, and in poisonous winds for jewels Earth had never seen before, and a moment's wistfulness tugged at him. A long time now since he had been any farther than the Moon... poor old fat man, chained to one miserable planet and unable to turn an honest credit. The Antares route was more important than he dared admit; if he lost it, he lost his chance at the Sagittarian developments to corporations with offices on the other side of the Kossaluth. In today's pitiless competition, you either went on expanding or you went under. And he had made too many enemies, they were waiting for the day of his weakness.

The car landed itself, and the guards jumped out to flank him. He wheezed the thin chill air into sooty lungs, drew his cloak of phosphorescent onthar skin tightly about him, and scrunched across frosty paving to the house. There was a new maid at the door, pretty little baggage... Venusian-French, was she? He tossed his plumed hat at her as the butler said the Freemen were already here. He sat down and told the chair, "Conference Room" and went along corridors darkly paneled in the wood of a hundred planets.

There were four colleagues around the table when he entered. Kraaknach of the Martian Transport Company was glowing his yellow eyes at a Frans Hals on the wall. Firmage of North American Engineering puffed an impatient cigar. Mjambo, who owned Jo-Boy Technical Services—which supplied indentured labor to colonial planets—was talking into his wristphone. Gornas-Kiew happened to be on Earth and was authorized to speak for the Centaurians; he sat quietly waiting, hunched into his shell, only the delicate antennae moving.

Van Rijn plumped himself into the armchair at the head of the table. Waiters appeared with trays of drinks, smokes, and snacks. He took a large bite from a ham sandwich and looked inquiringly at the others.

Kraaknach's owl-face turned to him. "Well, Freeman host, I understand we are met on account of this Borthudian *brokna*. Did the spacemen make their ultimatum?"

"*Ja.*" Van Rijn picked up a cigar and rolled it between his fingers. "It grows serious. They will not take ships through the Kossaluth, except to get revenge, while this shanghai business goes on."

"So why not blast the Borthudian home planet?" asked Mjambo.

"Death and damnation!" Van Rijn tugged at his goatee. "I had a little computation run off today. Assuming we lost no ships—and Borthu has good defenses—but allowing for salaries, risk bonus, fuel, ammunition, maintenance, depreciation, estimated loss due to lack of protection elsewhere, lawsuits by governments afraid the Kossaluth may strike back, bribes, and loss of profits to be had if the cost were invested peaceably—the bill for that little operation would come to about thirty trillion credits. In a nutshell, we cannot afford it. Simmons, a bowl of Brazils!"

"You will pardon my ignorance, good sirs," clicked Gornas-Kiew's artificial vocalizer. "My main interests lie elsewhere, and I have been only marginally aware of this trouble. *Why* are the Borthudians impressing our men?"

Van Rijn cracked a nut between his teeth and reached for a glass of brandy. "The gruntbrains have not enough of their own," he replied shortly.

"Perhaps I can make it clear," said Kraaknach. Like most Martians of the Sirruch Horde, he had a mind orderly to the point of boredom. He ran a clawlike hand through his gray feathers and lit a rinn-tube. "Borthu is a backward planet...terrestroid to eight points, with humanoid natives. They were in the early stage of nuclear energy when explorers visited them seventy-eight years ago, and their reaction to the presence of a superior culture was paranoid. They soon learned how to make modern engines of all types, and then set out to conquer themselves an empire. They now hold a volume of space about forty light-years across, though they only occupy a few Soltype systems within it. They want nothing to do with the outside universe, and are quite able to supply all their needs within their own boundaries—with the one exception of efficient spacemen."

"Hm-m-m," said Firmage. "Their commoners might see things differently, if we could get a few trading ships in there. I've already suggested we use subversive agents—get the Kossalu and his whole bloody government overthrown from within."

"Of course, of course," said Van Rijn. "But that takes more time than we have got, unless we want Spica and Canopus to sew up the Sagittarius frontier while we are stopped dead here."

"To continue," said Kraaknach, "the Borthudians can produce as many spaceships as they want, which is a great many since their economy is expanding. In fact, its structure—capitalism not unlike ours—requires constant expansion if the whole society is not to collapse. But they cannot produce trained crews fast enough. Pride, and a not unjustified fear of our gradually taking them over, will not let them send students to us any more, or hire from us, and they have only one understaffed academy of their own."

"I know," said Mjambo. "It'd be a hell of a good market for indentures if we could change their minds for them."

"Accordingly, they have in the past two years taken to waylaying our ships—in defiance of us and of all interstellar law. They capture the men, hypnocondition them, and assign them to their own merchant fleet. It takes two years to train a spaceman; we are losing an important asset in this alone."

"Can't we improve our evasive action?" wondered Firmage. "Interstellar space is so big. Why can't we avoid their patrols altogether?"

"Eighty-five percent of our ships do precisely that," Van Rijn told him. "But the hyperdrive vibrations can be detected a light-year away if you have sensitive instruments—pseudogravitational pulses of infinite velocity. Then they close in, using naval vessels, which are faster and more maneuverable than merchantmen. It will not be possible to cut our losses much by evasion tactics. Satan and small pox! You think maybe I have not considered it?"

"Well, then, how about convoying our ships through?"

"At what cost? I have been with the figures. It would mean operating the Antares run at a loss—quite apart from all the extra naval units we would have to build."

"Then how about our arming our merchantmen?"

"Bah! A frigate-class ship needs twenty men for all the guns and instruments. A merchant ship needs only four. Consider the salaries paid to spacemen. And sixteen extra men on every ship would mean cutting down all our operations elsewhere, for lack of crews. Same pestiferous result: we cannot afford it, we would lose money in big fat gobs. What is worse, the Kossalu knows we would. He needs only wait, holding back his fig-plucking patrols, till we were too broke to continue. Then he would be able to start conquering systems like Antares."

Firmage tapped the inlaid table with a restless finger. "Bribery, assassination, war, political and economic pressure, all seem to be ruled out," he said. "The meeting is now open to suggestions."

There was a silence, under the radiant ceiling.

Gornas-Kiew broke it: "Just how is this shanghaiing done? It is impossible to exchange shots while in hyperdrive."

"Well, good sir, statistically impossible," amended Kraaknach. "The shells have to be hypered themselves, of course, or they would revert to sublight velocity and be left behind as soon as they emerged from the drive field. Furthermore, to make a hit, they would have to be precisely in phase with the target. A good pilot can phase in on another ship, but the operation is too complex, it involves too many factors, for any artificial brain of useful size."

"I tell you how," snarled Van Rijn. "The pest-bedamned Borthudian ships detect the vibration-wake from afar. They compute the target course and intercept. Coming close, they phase in and slap on a tractor beam. Then they haul themselves up alongside, burn through the hull or the air lock, and board."

"Why, the answer looks simple enough," said Mjambo. "Equip our boats with pressor beams. Keep the enemy ships at arm's length."

"You forget, esteemed colleague, that beams of either positive or negative sign are powered from the engines," said Kraaknach. "And a naval ship has larger engines than a merchantman."

"Well, then, why not arm our crews? Give 'em heavy blasters and let 'em blow the boarding parties to hell."

"The illegitimate-offspring-of-interspecies-crosses Borthudians have just such weapons already," snorted Van Rijn. "Sulfur and acid! Do you think that four men can stand off twenty?"

"Mm-m-m...yes, I see your point," agreed Firmage. "But look here, we can't do anything about this without laying out *some* cash. I'm not sure offhand what our margin of profit is—"

"On the average, for all our combined Antarean voyages, about thirty percent on each voyage," said Van Rijn promptly.

Mjambo started. "How the devil do you get the figures for *my* company?"

Van Rijn grinned and drew on his cigar.

"That gives us a margin to use," said Gornas-Kiew. "We can invest in fighting equipment to such an extent that our profit is less—though I agree that there must still be a final result in the black—for the duration of the emergency."

"*Ja,*" said Van Rijn, "only I have just told you we have not the men available to handle such fighting equipment."

"It'd be worth it," said Mjambo viciously. "I'd take a fair-sized loss just to teach them a lesson."

"No, no." Van Rijn lifted a hand which, after forty years of offices, was still the broad muscular paw of a working spaceman. "Revenge and destruction are un-Christian thoughts. Also, they will not pay very well, since it is hard to sell anything to a corpse. The problem is to find some means within our resources which will make it *unprofitable* for Borthu to raid us. Not being stupid heads, they will then stop raiding and we can maybe later do business."

"You're a cold-blooded one," said Firmage.

Van Rijn drooped his eyes and covered a shiver by pouring himself another glass. He had suddenly had an idea.

He let the others argue for a fruitless hour, then said: "Freemen, this gets us nowhere, *nie?* Perhaps we are not stimulated enough to think clear."

"What would you suggest?" asked Mjambo wearily.

"Oh...an agreement. A pool, or prize, or reward for whoever solves this problem. For example, ten percent of all the others' Antarean profits for the next ten years."

"Hoy there!" cried Firmage. "If I know you, you robber, you've just come up with the answer."

"Oh, no, no, no. By good St. Dismas I swear it. I have some beginning thoughts, maybe, but I am only a poor rough old space walloper without the fine education all your Freemen had. I could so easy be wrong."

"What is your idea?"

"Best I not say just yet, until it is more clear in my thick head. But please to note, he who tries solving this problem takes on all the risk, and it may well be some small expense. Also, without his solution nobody has any more profits. Does not a little return on his investment sound fair and proper?"

There was more argument. Van Rijn smiled with infinite benevolence.

He was satisfied with an agreement in principle, sworn to by mercantile honor, the details to be computed later.

Beaming, he clapped his hands. "Freemen, we have

worked hard tonight and soon comes much harder work. By damn, I think we deserve a little celebration. Simmons, prepare an orgy."

Captain Torres was shocked. "Are you seriously asking us to risk that?"

Van Rijn stared out through the office wall. "In all secrecy," he answered. "I must have a crew I can trust."

"But—"

"We will not be stingy with the bonuses."

Torres shook his head. "Sir, I'm afraid it's impossible. The Brotherhood has voted absolute refusal of any trips into the Kossaluth except punitive expeditions—which this one is not. Under the constitution, we can't change that policy without another vote, which would have to be a public matter."

"It can be publicly voted on after we see if it works," urged Van Rijn. "The first trip will have to be secret."

"Then the first trip will have to do without a crew."

"Rot and pestilence!" Van Rijn's fist crashed down on the desk and he surged to his feet. "What sort of cowards do I deal with? In my day we were men! We would have sailed through Hell's open gates if you paid us enough!"

Torres sucked hard on his cigarette. "I'm stuck with the rules, sir," he declared. "Only a Lodgemaster can...well, all right, let me say it!" His temper flared up. "You're asking us to take an untried ship into enemy sky and cruise around till we're attacked. If we succeed, we win a few measly kilocredits of bonus. If we lose, we're condemned to a lifetime of purgatory, locked up in our own skulls and unable to will anything but obedience and *knowing* how our brains have been chained. Win, lose, or draw for us, you sit back here plump and safe and rake in the money. *No.*"

Van Rijn sat quiet for a while. This was something he had not foreseen.

His eyes wandered forth again, to the narrow sea. There was a yacht out there, a lovely thing of white sails and gleaming brass. Really, he ought to spend more time on his own ketch—money wasn't as important as all that. It was not such a bad world, this Earth, even for a lonely old fat man, it was full of blossoms and good wine, clean winds and beautiful women and fine books. In his forebrain, he knew how much his memories of earlier-days were colored by nostalgia—space is big and cruel, not meant for humankind. Let's face it, here on Earth we belong.

He turned around. "You say a Lodgemaster can legally come on such a trip without telling anyone," he remarked quietly. "You think you can raise two more like yourself, hah?"

"I told you, we won't! And you're only making it worse. Asking an officer to serve as a common crewhand is grounds for a duel."

"Even if I myself am the skipper?"

The *Mercury* did not, outwardly, look different after the engineers were finished with her. And the cargo was the same as usual: cinnamon, ginger, pepper, cloves, tea, whiskey, gin. If he was going to Antares, Van Rijn did not intend to waste the voyage. Only wines were omitted from the list, for he doubted if they could stand a trip as rough as this one was likely to be.

The alteration was internal, extra hull bracing and a new and monstrously powerful engine. The actuarial computers gave the cost of such an outfitting—averaged over many ships and voyages—as equal to three times the total profit from all the vessel's Antarean journeys during her estimated lifetime. Van Rijn had winced, but ordered his shipyards to work.

It was, in all truth, a very slim margin he had, and he had gambled more on it than he could afford. But if the Kossalu of Borthu had statistical experts of his own—always assuming, of course, that the idea worked in the first place—

Well, if it didn't, Nicholas van Rijn would die in battle or be executed as useless; or end his days as a brain-churned slave on a filthy Borthudian freighter; or be held for a ruinous ransom. The alternatives all looked equally bad.

He installed himself, the dark-haired and multiply curved Dorothea McIntyre, and a good supply of brandy, tobacco, and ripe cheese, in the captain's cabin. One might as well be comfortable. Torres was his mate, Captains Petrovich and Seichi his engineers. The *Mercury* listed from Quito Spaceport without fanfare, hung unpretentiously in orbit till clearance was given, and accelerated on gravity beams away from the sun. At the required half-billion kilometers' distance, she went on hyperdrive and outpaced light.

Van Rijn sat back on the bridge and stuffed his churchwarden. "Now is a month's voyage to Antares," he said piously. "Good St. Dismas watch over us."

"I'll stick by St. Nicholas," murmured Torres. "Even if you do bear the same name."

Van Rijn looked hurt. "Do you not respect my integrity?"

Torres grinned. "I admire your courage—nobody can say you lack guts—and you may very well be able to pull this off. Set a pirate to catch a pirate."

"You younger generations have a loud mouth and no courtesy." The merchant lit his pipe and blew reeking clouds. "In my day we said 'sir' to the captain even when we mutinied."

"I'm worrying about one thing," said Torres. "I realize that the enemy probably doesn't know about the strike yet, and so they won't be suspicious of us—and I realize that by passing within one light-year of Borthu itself we're certain to be attacked—but suppose half a dozen of them jump us at once?"

"On the basis of what we know about their patrol patterns, the estimated probability of more than one ship finding us is only ten percent, plus or minus three." Van Rijn heaved his bulk onto his feet. One good thing about spacefaring, you could set the artificial gravity low and feel almost young again. "What you do not know so well yet, my young friend, is that there are very few certainties in life. Always we must go on probabilities. The secret of success is to arrange things so the odds favor you—then in the long run you are sure to come out ahead. It is your watch now, and I recommend to you a book on statistical theory to pass the time. As for me, I will be in conference with Freelady McIntyre and a liter of brandy."

"I wish I could arrange my own captain's chores the way you do," said Torres mournfully.

Van Rijn waved an expansive hand. "Why not, my boy, why not? So long as you make money and no trouble for the Company, the Company does not interfere with your private life. The trouble with you younger generations is you lack initiative. When you are a poor old feeble fat man like me you will look back and regret so many lost opportunities."

Even in low-gee, the deck vibrated under his tread as he left.

Here there was darkness and cold and a blazing glory of suns. The viewscreens held the spilling silver of the Milky Way, the ruby spark of Antares among distorted constellations, the curling edge of a nebula limned by the blue glare of a dwarf star. Brightest among the suns was Borthu's, yellow as minted gold.

The ship drove on through night, pulsing in and out of four-dimensional reality and filled with waiting.

Dorothea sat on a wardroom couch, posing long legs and high prow with a care so practiced as to be unconscious. She could not get her eyes from the screen.

"It's beautiful," she said in a small voice. "And horrible."

Nicholas van Rijn sprawled beside her, his majestic nose aimed at the ceiling. "What is so bad, my little sinusoid?"

"Them ... lying out there to pounce on us and— Why did I come? Why did I let you talk me into it?"

"I believe there was mention of a tygron coat and Santorian flamedrop earrings."

"But suppose they catch us?" Her fingers fell cold on his wrist. "What will happen to me?"

"I told you I have set up a ransom fund for you. I also warned you maybe they would not bother to collect, and maybe we get broken to bits in this fight and all die. Satan's horns and the devil who gave them to him! Be still, will you?"

The intraship speaker burped and Torres' voice said: "Wake of highpowered ship detected, approaching from direction of Borthu."

"All hands to posts!" roared Van Rijn.

Dorothea screamed. He picked her up under one arm, carried her down the hall—collecting a few scratches and bruises en route—tossed her into his cabin, and locked the door. Puffing, he arrived on the bridge. The visual intercom showed Petrovich and Seichi, radiation-armored, the engines gigantic behind them. Their faces were drawn tight and glistening with sweat. Torres was gnawing his lip, fingers shaking as he tuned in the hypervid.

"All right," said Van Rijn, "this is the thing we have come for. I hope you each remember what you have to do, because if not we will soon be very dead." He dropped into the main control chair and buckled on the harness. His fingers tickled the keys, feeling the sensitive response of the ship. So far they had been using only normal power, the great converter had been almost idling; it was good to know how many wild horses he could call up.

The hypervid chimed. Torres pressed the *Accept* button and the screen came to life.

It was a Borthudian officer who looked out at them. Skin-tight garments were dead black on the cat-lithe frame. The face was almost human, but hairless and tinged with blue; yellow eyes smoldered under the narrow forehead. Behind him could be seen the bridge, a crouching gunnery officer, and the usual six-armed basalt idol.

"Terran ship ahoy!" He ripped out crisp, fluent Anglic, only subtly accented by a larynx and palate of different shape. "This is Captain Rentharik of the Kossalu's frigate *Gantok*. By the law, most sacred, of the Kossaluth of Borthu, you are guilty of trespass on the dominions of His Frightfulness. Stand by to be boarded."

"By double-damn, you out-from-under-wet-logs-crawling poppycock!" Van Rijn flushed turkey red. "Not bad enough you pirate my men and ships, with all their good expensive cargoes, but you have the copperbound nerve to call it legal!"

Rentharik fingered the ceremonial dagger hung about his neck. "Old man, the writ of the Kossalu runs through this entire volume of space. You can save yourself punishment—nerve-pulsing, to be exact—by surrendering peacefully and submitting to judgment."

"By treaty, open space is free to ships of all planets," said

Van Rijn. "And it is understood by all *civilized* races that treaties override any local law."

Rentharik smiled bleakly. "Force is the basis of law, Captain."

"*Ja,* it is, and now you make the mistake of using force on Van Rijn! I shall have a surprise for your strutting little slime mold of a king."

Rentharik turned to a recorder tube and spoke into it. "I have just made a note to have you assigned to the Ilyan run after conditioning. We have never found any way to prevent seepage of the Ilyan air into the crewman's helmets; and it holds chlorine."

Van Rijn's face lit up. "That is a horrible waste of trained personnel, captain. Now it so happens that on Earth we can make absolutely impervious air systems, and I would gladly act as middleman if you wish to purchase them—at a small fee, of course."

"There has been enough discussion," said Rentharik. "You will now be grappled and boarded. There is a fixed scale of punishments for captured men, depending on the extent of their resistance."

The screen blanked.

Torres licked sandy lips. Tuning the nearest viewscreen, he got the phase of the Borthudian frigate. She was a black shark-form, longer and slimmer than the dumpy merchantman, of only half the tonnage but with armor and gun turrets etched against remote star-clouds. She came riding in along a curve that would have been impossible without gravitic acceleration compensators, matching velocities in practiced grace, until she loomed huge a bare kilometer away.

The intercom broke into a scream. Van Rijn swore as he saw Dorothea having hysterics in the cabin. He cut her out of the circuit and thought with anguish that she would probably smash all the bottles—and Antares still eleven days off!

There was a small, pulsing jar. The *Gantok* was in phase and the gravity-fingers of a tractor beam had reached across to lay hold of the *Mercury*.

"Torres," said Van Rijn. "You stand by, boy, and take over if anything happens to me. I may want your help anyway, if it gets too rough. Petrovich, Seichi, you got to maintain our beams and hold 'em tight, no matter what the enemy does. O.K.? We go!"

The *Gantok* was pulling herself in, hulls almost touching now. Petrovich kicked in the full power of his converter. Arcs blazed blue with million-volt discharges, the engine bawled, and ozone was spat forth sharp and smelling of thunder.

A pressor beam lashed out, an invisible hammerblow of repulsion, five times the strength of the enemy tractor. Van Rijn heard the *Mercury's* ribs groan with the stress. The *Gantok* shot away, turning end over end. Ten kilometers removed, she was lost to vision among the stars.

"Ha, ha!" bellowed Van Rijn. "We spill all their apples, eh? By damn! Now we show them some fun!"

The Borthudian hove back into sight. She clamped on again, full strength attraction. Despite the pressor, the *Mercury* was yanked toward her with a brutal surge of acceleration. Seichi cursed and threw in all the pressor power he had.

For a moment Van Rijn thought his ship would burst open. He saw the deckplates buckle under his feet and heard steel shear. Fifty million tons of force were not to be handled lightly. The *Gantok* was batted away as if by a troll's fist.

"Not so far! Not so far, you dumbhead! Let me control the beams." Van Rijn's hands danced over the pilot board. "We want to keep him for a souvenir!"

He used a spurt of drive to overhaul the *Gantok*. His right hand steered the *Mercury* while his left wielded the tractor and the pressor, seeking a balance. The engine thunder rolled and boomed in his skull. The acceleration compensator could not handle all the fury now loosed, and straps creaked as his weight was hurled against them. Torres, Petrovich, and Seichi were forgotten, part of the machinery, implementing the commands his fingers gave.

Now thoroughly scared, the Borthudian opened her drive to get away. Van Rijn equalized positive and negative forces, in effect welding himself to her hull by a three-kilometer bar. Grinning, he threw his superpowered engine into reverse. The *Gantok* strained to a halt and went backwards with him.

Lightning cracked and crashed over his engineers' heads. The hull shuddered as the enemy fought to break free. Her own drive was added to the frantic repulsion of her pressors, and the gap widened. Van Rijn stepped down his own pressors. When she was slammed to a dead stop, the blow echoed back at him.

"Ha, like a fish we play him! Good St. Peter the Fisherman, help us not let him get away!"

It was a bleak and savage battle, nine and a half trillion empty kilometers from anyone's home, with no one to watch but the stars. Rentharik was a good pilot, and a desperate one. He had less power and less mass than the *Mercury*, but he knew how to use them, lunging, bucking, wheeling about in an attempt to ram. Live flesh could only take so much, thought Van Rijn while the thunders clattered around him. The question was, who would have to give up first?

Something snapped, loud and tortured, and he felt a rush of stinging electrified air. Petrovich cried it for him: "Burst plate—Section Four. I'll throw a patch on, but someone's got to weld it back or we'll break in two."

Van Rijn signaled curtly to Torres. "Can you play our fish? I think he is getting tired. Where are the bedamned spacesuits?"

He reeled from his chair and across the pitching deck. The *Gantok* was making full-powered leaps, trying to stress the *Mercury* into ruin. By varying their own velocity and beamforce, the humans could nullify most of the effect, but it took skill and nerve. God, but it took nerve! Van Rijn felt his clothes drenched on his body.

He found the lockers and climbed awkwardly into his specially built suit. Hadn't worn armor in a long time—forgotten how it stank. Where was that beblistered torch, anyhow? When he got out on the hull, surrounded by the glaze of all the universe, fear was cold within him.

One of those shocks that rolled and yawed the ship underfoot could break the gravitic hold of his boots. Pitched out beyond the hyperdrive field and reverting to normal state, he would be forever lost in a microsecond as the craft flashed by at translight speeds. It would be a long fall through eternity.

Electric fire crawled over the hull. He saw the flash of the *Gantok's* guns—she was firing wildly, on the one-in-a-billion chance that some shell would happen to be in phase with the *Mercury*. Good—let her use up her ammunition. Even so, it was a heart-bumping eerie thing when a nuclear missile passed through Van Rijn's own body. No, by damn, through the space where they coexisted with different frequencies—must be precise—now here is that fit-for-damnation hull plate. Clamp on the jack, bend it back toward shape. Ah, heave ho, even with hydraulics it takes a strong man to do this, maybe some muscle remains under all that goose grease. Slap down your glare filter, weld the plate, handle a flame and remember the brave old days when you went hell-roaring halfway across this arm of the galaxy. Whoops, that lunge nearly tossed him off into God's great icebox!

He finished his job, reflected that there would have to be still heavier bracing on the next ship of this model, and crept back to the air lock, trying to ignore the ache which was his body. As he entered, the rolling and plunging and racketing stopped. For a moment he thought he had been stricken deaf.

Then Torres' face swam into the intercom, wet and haggard, and said hoarsely: "They've quit. I don't think they expect their own boat can take any more of this—"

Van Rijn straightened his bruised back and whooped. "Excellent! Wonderful! But pull us up alongside quick, you lardhead, before—"

There was the twisting sensation of reversion to normal state, and the hyperdrive noise spun into silence. Van Rijn lost his footing as the *Mercury* sprang forward and banged against the enemy.

It had been an obvious tactic for Rentharik to use: Switching off his interstellar drive, in the hope that the Terran ship would remain hyper and flash so far away he could never be found again. The answer was equally simple—a detector coupled to an automatic cutoff, so that the *Mercury* would instantly do likewise. And now the League shop was immediately alongside the *Gantok*, snuggled beneath the very guns the frigate could no longer bring to bear and held by a tractor force she could not break.

Van Rijn struggled back to his feet and removed his helmet. The intercom blushed at his language.

"Captain!" Petrovich yelped the realization. *"They're going to board us!"*

"Name of Judas!" Van Rijn's breastplate clashed on the deck. "Must I do all your thinking for you? What use is our pressor if not to swat off unwelcome guests?" He threw back his head and bellowed with laughter. "Let them try, let them try! Our drive field envelops theirs, so it does not matter whether they use their engines or not—and we are stronger, *nie?* We can drag them with us even if they fight it. All my life I have been a deep-sea fisherman. And now, full speed ahead to Antares with this little minnow that thought it was a shark!"

A hypervid call to Antares as soon as they were in range brought a League carrier out to meet them. Van Rijn turned the *Gantok* over to her and let Torres pilot the battered *Mercury* in. Himself, he wanted only to sleep.

Not that the Borthudians had tried any further stunts, after their boarding party was so cold-bloodedly shoved into deep space. Rentharik was sensible enough to know when he was beaten, and had passively let his ship be hauled away. But the strain of waiting for any possible resistance had been considerable.

Torres had wanted to communicate with the prisoned crew, but Van Rijn would not allow it. "No, no, my boy, we demoralize them more by refusing the light of our eyes. I want the good Captain Rentharik's fingernails chewed down to the elbow when I see him."

That was, in the governor's mansion, in Redsun City. Van Rijn had appropriated it for his own use, complete with wine cellar and concubines. Between banquets he had found time to check on local prices and raise the tag on pepper a millicredit per gram. The colonists would grumble, but they could afford it; if it weren't for him, their meals would be drab affairs, so didn't he deserve an honest profit?

After three days of this, he decided it was time to see Rentharik. He lounged on the governor's throne, pipe in one hand.

Rentharik advanced across the parquet floor, gaunt and bitter under the guns of two League gentlemen. He halted before the throne.

"Ah, so there you are!" Van Rijn beamed and waved the bottle. "I trust you have had the pleasant stay? Redsun City jails are much recommended, I am told."

"My government will take measures," spat the Borthudian. "You will not escape the consequences of this piracy."

"Your maggoty little kinglet will do nothing of the sort," declared Van Rijn. "If the civilized planets did not dare fight when he was playing buccaneer, he will not when it is the other way around. He will accept the facts and learn to love them."

"What do you plan to do with us?"

"Well, now, it may be we can collect a little ransom for you, perhaps, eh? If not, the local iron mines are always short of labor. But out of the great goodness of my heart, I let you choose one man who may go home freely and report what has happened. After that we negotiate."

Rentharik narrowed his lids. "See here, I know how your filthy trading system works. You won't do anything that doesn't pay you. And to equip a vessel like yours—one able to capture a warship—costs more than the vessel could ever hope to earn."

"Quite so. It costs just about three times as much."

"So...we'll ruin the Antares route for you! Don't think we'll give up our patrols in our own sovereign territory. We can outlast you, if you want a struggle of attrition."

"Ah!" Van Rijn waggled his pipestem. "That is what you cannot do, my friend. You can reduce our profit considerably, but you cannot eliminate it; therefore, we can continue the route indefinitely under present conditions. You see, each voyage nets a thirty per cent profit."

"And it costs three hundred per cent of your profit to outfit a ship—"

"Indeed. But we are only so equipping every *fourth* ship. That means we operate on a smaller margin, yes, but a little arithmetic should show you we can still scrape by in the black ink."

"Every fourth—!" Rentharik shook his head, frankly puzzled. "But what will you gain? Out of every four encounters, we will win three."

"Just so. And by those three victories, you will capture twelve slaves. The fourth time, we rope in twenty Borthudian spacemen. Naturally, you will never know beforehand which ship is going to be the one that can fight back. You will either have to give up your press gangs or see them whittled away." Van Rijn rubbed his horny palms together. "So you see, by damn, always I operate on the statistics, and always I load the statistics. My friend, you have had it edgewise."

Rentharik crouched where he stood and blazed at his captor: "I learned, here, that your union will not travel through the Kossaluth. Do you think reducing the number of impressed men by one fourth will change their minds?"

Van Rijn grinned. "If I know my spacemen—why, of course. Because if you do continue to raid us, you will soon reduce yourselves to so few crews as to be helpless. Then you will *have* to deal with us, and our terms will include freeing all of the slaves, deconditioning, and good fat indemnities. Any man worth his salt can stand a couple years' service, even on your moldly rustbuckets, if he knows he will then be freed and paid enough to retire on."

He cleared his throat, buttered his tone, and went on: "So is it not wise that you make terms at once? We will be very lenient if you do. You will have to release and indemnify all your present captives, and stop raiding, but you can send students to our academies at not much more than the usual fees. We will want a few minor trade concessions as well, of course—"

"And in a hundred years you'll own us!" It was a snarl.

"If you do not agree, by damn, in three years we will own you. The choice is yours. You must have a continuously expanding supply of spacemen or your economy collapses. You can either let us train them in civilized fashion, and give us a wedge by which we ruin you in three generations, or you can impress them and be ruined inside this decade. Pick your man; we will let him report to your king-pig. And never forget that I, Nicholas van Rijn of the Polesotechnic League, do nothing without very good reason. Even the name of my ship could have warned you."

"The name—?" whispered Rentharik.

"Mercury," explained Van Rijn, "was the god of commerce, gambling—and thieves."

COVETOUSNESS

We're not supposed to want things that don't belong to us. We shouldn't covet our neighbor's possessions and yet, come on, folks—how can business proceed if we don't covet each other's customers and commissions and positions. And as long as we establish that princple as sound business practice, how about hankering for our neighbors' arms and kidneys and hearts? Now there's COVETOUSNESS.

THE HOOK, THE EYE AND THE WHIP

MICHAEL G. CONEY

Often in the spring evenings I would stroll down to the Skipper's Marina in Dollar Bay and watch the bonded S.P. men working on their bosses' boats. I would chat with them as they scraped, painted and varnished, and try to discover what made them tick. In general they were a cheerful lot and it was rarely that a man would openly admit that he was dissatisfied, or that he wished he had never elected to be bonded. Indeed, it was not always obvious that an S.P. man *was* bonded—for the rough work in the boat yards he wore coveralls with the letters S.P. front and back, just as did any other State Prisoner.

Perhaps the most interesting of these characters was Charles, Doug Marshall's man. I would see him at work even on weekends, scraping and filling, preparing the boat for the coming season while the Freemen and their chattering wives wandered about the slipway and the wharves, grotesque marine pets flopping at their heels. These weekends had become social events, each Freeman trying to outdo his fellow in hearty commendation of his own sleek boat, while the wives vied over such niceties as minipile cookers and autoflush heads. They would stand beside their boats, these Freemen would, patting them and stroking them like racehorse owners, meanwhile barking instructions at their bonded men.

Even Carioca Jones appeared on occasion—once she came wearing the slitheskin dress I had made for her the previous autumn and the emotion-sensitive skin turned a faint pink as our eyes met and we both thought of Joanna. Her young, smooth hands rose to her vulture's throat almost of their own accord, while her hard black eyes wrinkled in a smile.

"I must say I'm surprised to see *you* here, Joe, knowing your views," she greeted me.

"I like to look at the boats."

"Yes, but all these—*people,* darling. Aren't they simply *terrible?*"

"No worse than anyone else, I guess," I said coldly, wishing she would move on.

Carioca Jones was ostensibly a reformed character since the incident last year that had caused the entire Peninsula to ostracize her socially—a bitter blow for the ex-3-V star. Predictably for a woman of her drive and personality, she had thrown herself into a round of social do-gooding by way of atonement and was expected to become the next president of the Foes of Bondage Association, which had been making its presence felt around the Peninsula recently.

Unfortunately, anyone meeting her for the first time always commented on what beautiful hands she had for her age—and somewhere in the squalid workshops of the State Prison an S.P. girl named Joanna was now stitching coveralls with steel fingers.

One Friday afternoon in May I left the slithe farm in the capable hands of Dave Froehlich, my bonded man, and walked down to the Marina. By now the boats were in good shape—most of the paintwork having been completed—and the S.P. men were working on decks and below, polishing brass, overhauling engines. About twenty hydrofoils stood in line on their insect legs, looking virile and rakish.

Alone among the S.P. men, Charles was working on the outside hull of his boss's boat, lubricating the heavy rollers of the Eye. I walked over and greeted him. He looked up from his work.

"Hi, Joe," he said. That was one of the things I liked about him. He was able to treat me as an equal and whenever I talked with him I forgot that he was a State Prisoner and I a Freeman.

Unlike my foreman, Dave, who will address me as "Mr. Sagar" no matter how often I tell him to use my Christian name. Dave is a good man, but he will go on hating me until his time is served. Nothing personal about it—I just happen to be a Freeman.

"When are you going to get her in the water?" I asked Charles.

"About three weeks' time, I reckon." He stood, wiped his hands on his coveralls and gripped the huge steel loop of the Eye in both hands. He pulled, extending it on well-greased runners until it projected some eight feet from the hull of the boat, a giant polished metal D. He grinned at me and tapped it with a small hammer—it rang like a bell.

Rumor had it that an Eye fractured in use down south somewhere last summer, although the accident was hushed up. A sling-glider must have complete confidence in his equipment. Satisfied, Charles gave the Eye a seemingly gentle push. Four hundred and twenty pounds of glittering steel-titanium alloy rolled smoothly back into the hull of the boat, the flat upright of the D—the outermost part of the Eye—fitting so snugly with the contours of the hull that the joining could hardly be seen.

Charles turned his attention to the Whip, which lay on the slipway beside the boat and stretched to a small mooring buoy out in the water—a total distance of some eighty yards. This year everyone had bought new Ultrafiber-X Whips— they lay rigid across the surface in parallel green lines.

"What do you think about, Charles?" I asked curiously. "When Doug's up in his glider and the Hook hits the Eye— what thoughts occur to you?"

He grinned, kneading grease into the attachment where the Whip joined the pilot's harness. "There's no time to think. I'm too busy pinning down the Whip, rolling out the Eye, trying to control the boat at the same time—while I listen to some damfool observer panicking in the stern."

I smiled, too. I had crewed for Doug Marshall as observer and had panicked when I thought the sling-glider had gotten out of control.

"But there's one thing I never think about," continued

Charles. "You want me to say I worry about Doug's getting hurt, don't you?"

"It must occur to you."

"It doesn't. You'd have to be a glider pilot yourself to understand. I used to be a pilot a few years back. It's a new sport—we've got a lot to learn—but it's a great sport. Joe—there's nothing like the thrill of being up there in that little glider that's hardly bigger than yourself—at two hundred and fifty miles per hour."

Charles stood over six feet, blond and weatherbeaten—he looked the sling-glider type, though hardly the State Prisoner type. Doug Marshall had told me about that once. Charles had been sentenced for rape, of all things, after some incident on board his boat. I personally thought the whole thing sounded unlikely and obviously the judge had had his doubts, too—Charles only got four years.

He had applied for bonding—which carries an automatic one-third sentence remission—after he had served the six months compulsory. Doug Marshall had known him slightly in the past and had agreed to take him on. Charles was now bound by the terms of the one-sided contract to serve his master faithfully and well to the utmost of his ability, until the death of either party or completion of his sentence—whichever came sooner.

The sling-glider pilot is entirely in his steersman's hands.

I looked at Charles. Surely he must think *something* while Doug was in the air in that flimsy glider.

For example—he might think of Doug's dying. If that happened, Charles' contract would be up and with it his sentence—he would be a free man. A Freeman.

For example—he had to think of Doug's possibly being seriously injured. In which case Charles would, as ever, be required to serve Doug to the utmost.

Which might mean the donation of an organ.

Charles worked on impassively, talking technicalities as he checked and greased Doug Marshall's harness.

* * *

It is difficult to define an air of suppressed excitement. It can be observed most easily, perhaps, in the way people will suddenly address comparative strangers, asking their views on whatever is causing the furor. Such an air was in evidence at the Skipper's Marina during those last few weeks before the start of the sling-gliding season. Freemen talked of competitions and Freewomen spoke of the clothes they would wear at the President's Opening Scratch Trophy—while at their feet, brought into unaccustomed proximity, land sharks fought German shepherds, pet octopi devoured micropekes.

The sloping landscape of the long slipway was busy every day and crowded on weekends when the owners arrived to assist or berate their S.P. men, according to personality. Huge boats towered everywhere. Men scuttled underneath with paintbrushes and power tools, putting on finishing touches.

I frequently dropped by on Sunday afternoons to assist Marshall. For a few hours I breathed sawdust and cellulose as we cleaned up the boat's interior—then we drank beer with him and Charles in the dim cabin as slow nightfall came. Sometimes other boat owners would climb the ladder, hammer on the cabin roof and shout a greeting, then squeeze into the small cabin to share our beer and prolong the party past midnight.

On the last Sunday before the season began Carioca Jones came again to the marina, spectacularly dressed, land shark lopping at her heels. The brute was growing fast—by now he was over six feet long. Doug Marshall was bent double and sweating as he adjusted the shear-pin on one of the props, when the land shark undulated over to lie beside him and watch him coldly, stinking like a fishmarket. The implanted oxygenator caused its gills to pulsate unpleasantly. Doug caught sight of the fish suddenly, straightened, and cracked his head on the keel.

He had not liked Carioca Jones since the Joanna episode and now he exploded. "Get that bastard away from me before I put this drill through its skull!" He brandished his whirring power tool like a rapier.

Carioca hurried over and laid a hand on her pet's collar. She was wearing slitheskin gloves—products of my small

factory—and I noticed they had turned mauve in sympathy
with her temper. "Wilberforce is quite harmless." She spoke
coolly enough. "There's no call to lose your temper with him
Mr. Marshall. He wasn't doing anything wrong."

"Wrong." Doug was massaging his scalp. "The swine
nearly fractured my skull for me."

"Come now, Mr. Marshall. A big brave sling pilot shouldn't
be frightened of a mere land shark, should he now?"

Doug recovered slightly, swallowed hard and spoke care
fully. "Miss Jones, that fish is a menace. He's been allowed
to grow too big. Look at those teeth. He could have your leg
off without batting an eyelid. You ought to have him put
down."

"Put down?" Carioca's gloves were purple and trembling
Doug met her stare levelly. She looked elsewhere for a scape
goat and, as I was edging out of the scene, Charles descended
the ladder from the cockpit and glanced at the protagonists
with interest. He was wearing his State Prison coveralls
Carioca's gaze lit on the letters S.P. and her eyes flashed
"Oh, so you have a slave here doing your work for you."

The abrupt change of subject foxed Doug. "What the hell's
that got to do with it?" he asked, baffled. "Anyway, Charles
is my bonded man."

"Oh, a bonded man, is he? I might have guessed. No won
der you love sling-gliding. Who wouldn't, with a spare-parts
man standing by?"

Doug's eyes widened. He looked at Charles, who seemed
to have been struck speechless. I couldn't think of much to
say myself—arrant bad taste has that effect on me. Fortu
nately help was at hand in the unlikely guise of the club
secretary, who happened to be passing. He stepped in quickly

"Miss Jones, did I hear you rightly?"

"Who are you, you strange little man?"

Bryce Alcester, secretary of the Peninsula Sling-gliding
Club, flushed. "I think I heard you use an expression we don'
like around here, Miss Jones. Was I right? Did you use such
an expression?" He was a small man with a face like a beaver
but he had reserves of determination.

"Of course you don't like the expression, because it's true

How else can men like you summon the nerve to go up in those nasty little gliders?"

"I must ask you to leave the premises, madam. I must also remind you that you are not a member."

"And I must tell you that the Foes of Bondage will picket the President's Trophy next week. You haven't heard the last of this, not by a long way."

Reluctantly, with Alcester's hand on her arm, she began to move away. Her eye caught mine. "Really, Joe, I can't think why you associate with such cowards."

After seeing her off the premises Alcester hurried back to us. There was a tear in the leg of his pants where the land shark had taken a snap at him. "I'm terribly sorry, gentlemen." He looked at Charles, swallowed and said awkwardly, "And—uh—I would like to apologize to you, Charles, on behalf of the club."

Charles smiled blandly. "I've been called names before."

Later that evening as we drank beer in the cabin I asked Charles, "What does it really feel like to be called—what Carioca called you?" I must have had several drinks by then.

Charles grinned. "Always trying to pump me, aren't you, Joe? I often wonder if you're a revolutionary on the quiet, gathering information."

"Maybe, but I'm not a Foe of Bondage."

"But Carioca Jones is right, you know," he said surprisingly. "I am a spare-parts man. I've wagered my body against a shorter sentence. I went into it with my eyes open and so far I've been lucky. I've still got all my limbs and other items. And I don't mind Doug's sling-gliding, because I've done it myself and I know the thrill of it. Now that's where Carioca Jones is wrong. I know that we would glide whether or not—uh—spare parts were available. Miss Jones doesn't know that. She can't. She's a woman."

I addressed Doug, pushing it a bit further. "Doug, suppose you smashed yourself up and you needed, say, a leg. Would you use Charles? Or would you spend the rest of your life limbless, watching Charles walk about whole?"

"The beer has brought honesty," said Doug quietly. "And

I can say in honesty that I don't know. And it's one thing about myself I never want to know."

II

In the last days before the first race I had become totally infected with the sling-gliding fever. Up to then I had had no intention of competing despite Doug Marshall's hints about the difficulty he was having in finding a competent observer. I spent most afternoons and every evening on the slipway, helping with the feverish last-minute preparations. Sling-gliding has this in common with any sport where complex equipment is used: No matter how careful the preparations, no matter how long ago such preparations started, there is always a panic at the finish. The Skipper's Marina had put its truck at the disposal of the club and the vehicle was in constant use, commuting between Louise and the marina with suddenly remembered necessities.

Carioca Jones did not appear, although there were rumors from time to time of the form the picketing was going to take. Some said that the Foes of Bondage had hired a boat and intended to upset the racing by zigzagging across the course on the pretext that the sea was free to all. Then, a couple of days before the first race, they were seen with their banners and placards boarding a plane for Lake William in the far north. It seemed that some idiots were going to walk the glacial coast as far as Wall Bay, a distance of several hundred miles. There were three bonded men and a doctor in the party of ten—it was reported that the doctor was taking a full set of surgical instruments along in case someone suffered severe frostbite. Not only that, but there were backup parties hovertrucking supplies to remote rendezvous where the terrain was too broken and the weather too severe to allow aircraft to get in. The personnel for this hazardous task had been hired from the State Prison.

On the Thursday, under pressure from Doug, Charles and several beers, I agreed to join Doug's crew as observer. That evening I stayed late at the marina. I had—later—a hazy recollection of a party developing in the cramped space of somebody's cabin—but first I awoke with a powerful headache and a desire to be sick, to find that I was lying on the floor in unfamiliar surroundings. I crawled to my feet, got as far as the door, and poked my head out into the chill night air.

After a few deep breaths I felt better. I glanced around the cabin and saw a sleeping girl, partly clothed, on one of the berths. Her mouth was hanging open and she was a mess—lipstick all over her face, hair matted. Crumpled around her throat was a slitheskin neckerchief, its dull brown hue testifying the extent to which she was drained of emotion. I hoped it wasn't I who had drained her and thought briefly of Charles and his rape case—and of how easy it is to transgress the law these days.

I shut the cabin door quietly behind me and stood in the cockpit of the beached hydrofoil, allowing the night breezes to cool my head. I felt sweaty and stale. It occurred to me that technically I was trespassing by being in the Skipper's Marina after the club was closed and without having a sleep-in permit. Since the shortage of State Prisoners—which hit the country last autumn—there has been a tightening up in various facets of the law and I'm not sure that trespass isn't one of them. I stepped over the cockpit coaming, found the ladder, and climbed quietly down to the slipway.

The next thing I did was to trip over the Whip of the unknown boat and fall flat and noisily on my face. Whips are of incredible lightness and rigidity, particularly this season's improved models. The end of this particular Whip must have been balanced on a box—anyway, it followed me to the ground with a ringing clatter that set up a sympathetic resonance throughout its entire eighty-yard length, causing it to protest with a wail that must have come close to awakening the very fossils under the sedimentary mud of which the Peninsula is composed.

As I lay there trying not to vomit, a scurrying, rustling noise came nearby and the hair at the nape of my neck prickled. The brute who made that noise could have been anything—Carioca Jones' appalling land shark was quite innocuous compared with some of the bizarre pets I had seen that spring. It was becoming unsafe to leave one's car or house at night, since many of the creatures, unsuited to human company, had escaped and were roaming the flat countryside, fighting one another and attacking man on sight.

I lay still and waited. The sounds continued: an uneven series of footsteps—or some sort of steps—an occasional clatter of a can of paint or similar slipway debris being knocked over and a vocal gasping noise I tried to tell myself was human. Encouragingly, the sounds began retreating and soon they faded away. I heard the distant whine of a hovercar starting up—then that too receded and all was quiet again.

Obviously there had been a trespasser among the boats. In the morning someone would find his paintwork scored or his rudder pintles loosened. That sort of thing annoys me— I just can't see the sense in it. I wished I'd had the courage to tackle the intruder.

Twenty minutes later I was driving through my farm gates. I got out of the car and listened. Everything seemed to be in order; the reptiles were uttering that bubbling sound that characterizes the contented slithe. Relieved, I made for the house. Recently I've been having trouble again with otters getting into the pens and carrying off the slithes and I had mentioned to Dave the necessity for strengthening our defenses. Increasingly there are dangerous predators at large on the Peninsula.

The following morning Dave and I made a tour of inspection. The little reptiles were in good shape, trotting about with a faintly red tone to their skins, the shade that denotes happiness and, presumably, health. As we threw the fodder over the chicken wire the slithes scurried forward, turning pink with pleasure and feeding voraciously. Dave gave one of his rare grins. Then, noticing me testing the strength of the chicken wire with my feet, his manner assumed its accustomed seriousness.

"I heard a rumor yesterday," he said. "Someone saw a garden barracuda loose over Long Beach way. This guy was walking along the nature trail at the back of the lagoon there and the bastard came for him straight out of the bushes, all snapping teeth—you know what they're like. It's getting serious. There are things running wild all over the place."

"I was thinking about that last night. Perhaps you'd get one of the men to double the wire. It's a good thing the brutes can't live long."

He glanced at me. "You haven't heard about the new oxygenator they've been implanting recently? It doesn't have to be renewed. They say it stimulates the gills into a modified operation. They do a bit of surgery on the beast as well, and then the fish or whatever is totally adapted to living on land for the rest of its life."

"I don't like the sound of that," I said. The possibilities this development opened up were somewhat alarming. At this moment a car drove up and saved me further anxiety on the subject.

"Hi, Joe darling." Carioca Jones.

"I thought you were up in the snow somewhere," I said tactlessly.

"Joe, it was the most idiotic hoax! Someone sent me a transcript of a Newspocket report up at Lake William and it sounded like the most heartrending thing. Dozens of poor S.P. men are supposedly being used as nothing better than pack animals. And there were some bonded men with the actual party, going across the glaciers—you know what frostbite is—and they had a surgeon with them as well. My dear, the report was positively sinister. I mean, you know and I know that I've learned my lesson and we both think these transplants are abominable. Barbaric."

"Yes," I said carefully, not looking at her hands.

"And when we got there with all our banners and placards nothing was happening! We marched down the street singing and everyone looked at us as though we were mad. And it was so cold—you've no idea! So we booked into the nearest hotel and I went to the local Newspocket agency—and do you know, they'd never even heard of the Great Arctic Trek, as it was supposed to be called."

"You must have been very disappointed."

She shot me a glance of birdlike suspicion but apparently my expression satisfied her. "Quite—and it was dreadfully embarrassing. We hadn't really allowed for the cold there. Some of my girls were frostbitten quite badly. They were very upset and four of them resigned from the Foes for good."

I nearly asked her just how badly those four had been hurt and whether, if surgery had been necessary, they had contacted the nearest State Prison. As Foes of Bondage, it was hardly likely they would have bonded S.P. girls. So if fingers were needed they would have to take their chances with the Ambulatory Organ Pool—a euphemism for long-term prisoners first on the list of compulsory donors. I nearly asked her, but I didn't.

Instead I asked, "Are men allowed to join the Foes?"

"Of course," she said firmly. "Why ever not?"

"I just wondered. The members all seem to be women."

"Oh, but that's the way it works out, my dear. You see, it's men who go in for these dangerous sports—it's men who get smashed up and need transplants—so naturally men will support the status quo."

"Pardon me, Carioca, but that's garbage. Only a fraction of the male population can afford to sling-glide or tramp through the Arctic."

"You men all stick together—that's the trouble. Look at you, Joe. You admit you're against legalized slavery, yet you've got your own bonded man and you're friendly with lice like Marshall who risk someone else's neck for fun. You wouldn't join the Foes of Bondage if I begged you to, so I won't bother."

Just for the record, at this point I gave Carioca something from the depths of my soul, if I have one. "Dave Froehlich is a good man whom I rescued from that stinking prison— and I get no thanks from Dave. I'm friendly with Marshall because I enjoy his personality and to hell with his views— even if his views were unsound, which I doubt, I won't join the Foes because I'd be the only man there and people would look on me as a crank, added to which I don't agree with the Foes' methods. Regardless of whether or not the members are women, they are exactly the *type* of person I don't like. Your members get a vicarious personal satisfaction from the annoyance they cause others. Their methods are wrong, in that they think it right to counter problems with problems."

Carioca Jones' mouth had fallen agape. When I finished she hitched it up, thought a bit, then said, "You take the whole thing too seriously, Joe. The Foes are a club, that's all. A woman's club, if you will. This talk is nonsense. When we demonstrate we just think what fun it is to be doing it together. If it helps you any, Joe, I don't think the members consider the objects of the Association as deeply as you seem to do."

"Then we need a new Association. Damn it, Carioca, they shout obscenities at people."

"Well, isn't it fun to have the chance to shout obscenities at people without fear of any comeback?"

I nearly lost my temper—and a good customer. "I've never felt any desire to shout obscenities at people. That's the mentality of a teen-age vandal."

She took my arm suddenly. "Oh, come on, Joe. Let's not quarrel. I came to do business with you. You and I are on the same side, basically. It's people like your friend Marshall I don't like. It was he who faked the Newspocket transcript, of course."

"Oh, come off it, Carioca."

"No, I mean it. It's typical of his sense of humor. And I can tell you, it's not so funny up at William Lake for a person of my age, Joe."

It was the first time I'd ever heard her mention her age. I changed the subject hastily. "You said you came to do business."

"Of course—you must be busy." Her manner had become stiff. "I'd like to buy four dozen slitheskin wristlets, please."

"Four dozen?"

"They're for the Foes of Bondage. We shall wear them at the demonstration tomorrow and they will show the solidarity of our feelings."

I had a mental image of four dozen Foes with fists upraised but with wristlets unfortunately showing colors of rainbow diversity. "Do you think it's wise?" I ventured.

"Look, Joe Sagar, do you want the business or don't you?"

Resignedly I took her into the showroom. While she was selecting the wristlets she persisted in asking about Charles, his crime, his sentence. She seemed to be trying to work up a feeling of pity for the man.

III

Although the President's Trophy is the first event of the season and tends to be looked on as a mere hors d'oeuvre to the main course of races later in the summer, it is nevertheless an event worth winning. The psychological boost to the visitor will frequently start a winning vein in subsequent weeks that can be worth a good deal of prize money. And more than any other sport, sling-gliding depends on confidence. Confidence in one's glider, one's Whip, one's boat, one's observer and steersman—all of which comes with practice, but which is proved and improved by winning.

Traditionally, the main body of spectators gathers along the ancient stone seawall that was one of the few human artifacts on the Peninsula to escape total destruction by the tidal waves of the Western Seaboard Slide. Here gather the curious, the casual, the enthusiasts—and the Foes of Bondage. Out across the bay, a half-mile distant, the gaunt pillar of the Fulcrum rises from the calm water.

The Foes had already picketed the entrance to the marina, screaming their epithets at the hovercars as they arrived with pilots, crews, and maintenance men. On stepping from my own vehicle I had been surprised when a woman I hardly knew thrust herself before me and referred to my slithe farm as a "plantation." This was the latest dirty word unearthed by the Foes and apparently referred to some early phase of man's relationship with his fellows. When I replied, rather weakly, that I didn't plant anything at the farm—if the growing of crops was what she objected to—she merely uttered a jeering noise and called me a "boss man."

Then Carioca Jones appeared. "My God, Joe," she shrilled. "Do you mean to tell me you're actually taking part in this pantomime?"

Fortunately the press of the crowd had taken her away from me at this point, so I was spared the embarrassment of conversation.

The President's Trophy is a distance/placement event and not strictly a race, because the time factor does not enter the judges' calculations—although the very fact of the high speeds attained during sling-gliding tend to cause the general public to refer to any event as a race. In this particular event the glider flies to a point out in the Strait, drops a marker and returns, the pilot endeavoring to land at a point as close as possible to the seawall. A buoy, just offshore from the spectators, indicates the optimum. It is this finish close to the crowd—allied to the fact of its being the first event of the season—that gives the race its enormous popularity.

By the time the boats were cruising about, testing their engines, the Foes of Bondage had positioned themselves at a point near the northern end of the sea wall, close to the marina. From time to time their president, an elderly woman—and, I supposed, the woman Carioca Jones hoped to supplant—whipped them into a frenzy with a few well-turned phrases. She had an imposing, almost puritanical presence that lent weight to her oracular delivery. From my position at the end of the slipway I couldn't hear her words, but judging from the cheers of her supporters it was all good stuff. From time to time the Foes' fists would curve forward and upward in a fair and feminine imitation of a right uppercut—symbol of the Association—but the wristlets remained neutral brown. You can't fool slitheskin. Maybe the colors would come later, when the racing started.

In the distance a hydrofoil was racing toward the Fulcrum. The crowd was still. Behind the boat a tiny glider rose into the sky. It was too far away for us to see the Whip as the boat snapped around the Fulcrum, but we could judge the fearsome acceleration as the little dart was flung low above the water at a speed around two hundred and fifty miles per hour. For an instant we lost it against the trees of the dark island opposite, then it slipped into view above the strait. There was a murmur as those with binoculars saw the marker buoy drop away as the glider turned to make its approach.

The distance of this buoy from the Fulcrum was taken into account in the final placings, encouraging pilots to go for speed and distance instead of merely stalling slowly in for an accurate landing.

Archer was gliding and he had squeezed a little too much distance from his speed. He was coming in fast and low after a wide turn and it was apparent he would not make the finishing buoy. Skimming the sea so close I'll swear he raised ripples on the calm surface, he used his last breath of flying speed in a shallow climb, then stalled and dropped into the water about two hundred yards away. The spectators clapped politely as he struggled clear of his harness and trod water waiting to be picked up. The Foes of Bondage were silent, watching. Their wristlets remained neutral to a woman—neither showing the purple of engaged distaste nor the pink of pleasure. I assumed they had done their homework and discovered that Archer had no bonded S.P. man.

I caught sight of Carioca Jones at the instant she glanced at me—and suddenly I knew that the Foes' rancor was being reserved for our boat and Doug Marshall in particular.

Marshall was gliding, Charles was steering and I was observing, sitting in the stern and watching for trouble, Charles' attention naturally being concentrated on the Fulcrum ahead. I stole a quick glance over my shoulder and saw the black post rising solitary out of the flat sea about half a mile ahead. I looked back and Marshall was waving.

"Right!" I shouted to Charles.

He gunned the motor. The Whip took the strain and rose dripping from the water with hardly a sag in its rigid length. A feather of foam appeared at Marshall's skis as he began to move, rising upright with the glider attached to his back like a bright vampire.

The boat rose on its foils and the last of the roiling wake fled abruptly astern to be replaced by twin hissing threads of spray. Marshall began to experience lift and kicked off the skis, raising his hands to grip the controls in the nose of the glider. He drew up his legs, jackknifing and thrusting them back into the slender fuselage. He was flying, the Whip attached to his chest harness with snap-fastening. He sailed easily behind us at about fifty miles per hour, lying face down within the belly of the tiny dart-shaped glider. I suppressed a shudder—the takeoff always affects me like that, ever since Patterson's mistake last season. Patterson had grasped the controls clumsily—so we assumed afterward. Anyway, his glider had plunged down suddenly, the Whip had smashed through the nose, jamming. Then the angle of the Whip to the glider had taken it down through the water, deeper, deeper...I think the most terrifying thing was watching the Whip shortening, shortening despite the deceleration of the boat, as the glider and Patterson dove uncontrollably into the black pressure of the deeps. He must have descended over fifty feet in about eight seconds.

A sight not easily forgotten.

But Marshall was safely aloft and veering out toward our starboard beam, ready to take advantage of the initial effect of the Fulcrum post. He had banked and I could see him grinning at us, grinning with exhilaration, a six-foot man in a ten-foot glider.

At moments like this the oddest notions come to the front of one's racing stream of thoughts. Suddenly I was thinking of Thursday night on the slipway and of the fact that Doug Marshall seemed to be a target of the Foes of Bondage, who had returned from William Lake earlier than expected.

Charles hit the water brake for just the instant necessary to swing Doug directly abeam and, at precisely the right moment, leaned across to the Whip bracket...

And slipped the pin easily into its housing, locking the Whip at right angles to the boat. He eased the throttle away and we leaped forward again, the glider riveted to a parallel course eighty yards from our port beam and matching our speed of about ninety miles per hour. I exhaled a gasp of relief, which was lost in the scream of the turbines. Just for a moment the thought of sabotage had crossed my mind.

"Coming up!" shouted Charles.

I glanced around quickly and saw the Fulcrum post racing nearer, the giant Hook jutting out black and solid toward us.

In June of last year, I think it was, Bennett had misjudged the clearance and run into the Hook...

Charles thumbed a button and the Eye slid out from the reinforced portside of the hull. The craft listed as the huge steel loop extended and I made the conventional sign to Marshall—the O of finger and thumb. He dipped in acknowledgment.

"Brace yourself!" shouted the bonded man. He leaned into the padded pillar to the right of the wheel. I huddled into the seat, cushioning my head in my hands.

The Hook engaged the Eye.

I probably screamed a little as the G's hit me—I'm told I usually do. The Hook engaged the Eye—and snatched the hydrofoil, by now traveling at around a hundred and twenty miles per hour, into a thirty-yard radius turn.

Around about this time I never know what's happening— I just cower there and wait for it to finish. I've seen it from a distance, of course, and it looks quite simple. The pilot has taken his glider to a station off the starboard of the boat, so that when the Hook engages the Eye, the boat veers sharply away. Despite its rigidity, the Whip bends. The glider begins to accelerate as the centrifugal force allied to the incredible strength of the Whip takes effect.

I've seen boats circle the Fulcrum post on the swiveling Hook so fast that the Whip spirals like a watchspring, the glider lagging behind at first but accelerating, accelerating until the Whip finally snaps straight and flings the glider outward at speeds of up to three hundred miles per hour. A glider ten feet long with a wingspan of perhaps seven feet, made of stressed permaplast...

There is a certain margin for error. If the observer senses that the glider is not in the correct position, that the pilot is not quite ready, he can tell the steersman to abort at any distance up to forty yards from the Fulcrum and the boat will veer right, slowing, while the pilot detaches the Whip from his harness, closes in and, stalling, drops into the water alongside. This is the textbook procedure, although I've seen teams take a wide, wide circle and approach the Hook again without dropping the glider.

As the G's forced my head into the backrest of the seat I again sensed something was wrong. I opened my eyes, saw the dizzy blur of water racing past, the gaunt blackness of the Fulcrum post partly obscuring the view. Then, climbing rapidly against the sky, the glider. The Whip spiraled back from Marshall, beyond my field of vision. I could see him fumbling one-handed with the release mechanism.

The glider lagged back, dropped out of view as the Whip curled. Marshall's snap-fastening had jammed. He could not break clear of the Whip. Shortly all that coiled energy would be spent in smashing him into the sea—or whirling him and his glider into broken pieces vertically overhead...

Once, and once only, I saw a man make a perfect landing on the surface with the Whip still attached to his jammed fastening—yet that man died, too. Farrel. We watched from the shore as the Eye hit the Hook and the boat snapped into its turn at exceptionally high speed—the occasion was the finals of the National Distance Championships. The Whip coiled into a venomous high-tensile spring which reminds the overly imaginative of a striking cobra. Farrel had gone into his slow climb and was accelerating as the boat slowed at the post and the Whip began to straighten. Farrel's wife was watching through binoculars and I heard her gasp suddenly—a sudden gasp that was almost a scream. I remember the expression on the face of Farrel's bonded man—who was standing next to Mrs. Farrel—as he snatched the glasses from her and clamped them to his eyes. Mrs. Farrel turned to me. Her face was twisted and she was only able to utter one word—but it was probably the only word applicable to the situation.

"Why?" she asked.

And the boat had slowly descended from its hydrofoils and was wallowing around the Fulcrum, while the Whip spent its venom in hurling Farrel into a speed of three hundred miles per hour. He had stopped trying to fight the release mechanism now and was concentrating on his attitude, maintaining level flight as the Whip straightened and began to slow.

At this point the other spectators had realized something was wrong. Sometimes a foolhardy pilot will delay release until the very last instant of acceleration, taking chances on the control problems that arise with a dying Whip. But Farrel had gone past even that point. There was a slow murmur of communal horror.

There were also a few anticipatory chuckles from S.P. men standing near. Except for Farrel's man, of course—he stood like a statue, binoculars jammed against his face.

The Whip slowed—although we couldn't tell from where we stood, the Whip must have been slowing—but still Farrel retained control, retained his horizontal attitude. He was rapidly losing lift due to the dragging effect of the Whip at his chest, but he avoided overcorrecting and plunging into the sea, and he avoided the disastrous stall that would have started an end-over-end spin and a breakup of the glider. He was giving a masterly exhibition.

And it was all pointless, of course. There were murmurs of appreciation from around us and I think some people really thought Farrel was going to get away with it. But they didn't know sling-gliding the way the rest of us did. You *never* escaped from a jammed fastening.

Farrel was decelerating visibly now, edging closer to the water, extricating his legs from the slender fuselage and dangling them, soles upturned, like a swan coming into land.

An S.P. man chuckled, watching the Whip.

There was a communal sigh as Farrel touched the water and his speed fell to zero. He flipped the nose of the glider up in a last-minute stall. I think, even then, he felt he could avoid the inevitable if he could get the drag of the glider's surface area against the water in addition to his own weight.

He didn't make it. He was probably up to his waist in water when the Whip reacted. The deceleration had coiled it backward, building up a reverse tension, which now exploded in snatching Farrel from the water and dragging him backward, end over end in the scattering remnants of his glider, spinning along the surface in a curved, frantic plume of spray...

The Whip waved to and fro a few times, gradually losing

momentum, until at last it lay quiet and twitching on the surface and the boat was able to cast loose from the Hook and pick up Farrel. His neck was broken—his back and legs were broken. Hardly a bone in his body had escaped fracture—hardly an organ was not ruptured.

It might have been possible to do something about all that. But Farrel was dead, too.

It had taken just a few seconds. I remember the look on the face of the bonded man when they brought the body ashore. Absolved of all his obligations, his past crime, whatever it was, atoned for—released from his bond by the death of his principal, he was now a free man. He turned silently away from the drenched and broken thing they had laid on the seawall and he walked off, saying nothing.

Then Farrel, now Marshall. Pressed hard against the latex headrest, I watched helplessly as the Whip straightened, preparatory to coiling in the reverse direction, while Marshall stayed high in the sky, transfixed by the tip. I rolled my head against the force that held it and saw Charles fighting his way clear of the G-post. His eyes were wide and dead as they met mine—I knew he was going to try something desperate, but his motives were anybody's guess. He edged clear of the post and centrifugal force snatched him instantly from my view.

All this happened so quickly that I had every excuse for doing nothing—in any case, there was no way I could have gotten clear of the seat. Then the boat was slowing. The landscape ceased its crazy spin. The Fulcrum post became a solid object of iron and rust and rivets. As is the way of boats built for speed, ours stopped quickly. I stood up, my head reeling.

Marshall was clear, gliding landward, trailing the Whip behind him, the broken end hanging a short distance above the surface. I satisfied myself that he was descending quickly enough to avoid a stall—the Whip in total length is no aid to a smooth landing—and turned my attention to Charles. He was floundering in the water some twenty feet off the port bow. I grabbed the wheel, revved the engine and slipped it into reverse, backed clear of the Hook, retracted the Eye, and motored toward him. I got my hands under his armpits and dragged him aboard. He was a big man, strong and heavy, but he was unable to help himself or me.

"Where's Doug?" he asked faintly.

"Almost down. He'll be okay." I glanced at the rig that fastened the Whip to the boat. The steel tubing was bent— the Whip itself had snapped off short where Charles' flying body had smashed into the swivel joint.

It was one of those occasions where the last thing you want to do is to consider the implications. I pillowed Charles' head on a life jacket and spun the wheel, heading for shore. Marshall was traveling parallel to the sea wall now, diving to maintain speed and at the same time lose height before the trailing end of the Whip began to drag in the water and the abrupt deceleration began. Gauging the point of impact, I drove the boat on at full throttle.

Less than a minute later I was pulling Marshall from the water and extricating him from his harness, aided by men from a milling cluster of small boats. I pulled in against the sea wall and we carried Charles to the shore, laying him on the grass while someone ran to call the ambulopter.

Almost instantly, it seemed, the Foes of Bondage were standing over us in force, and I shuddered involuntarily because I'll swear there was something akin to predatory satisfaction in their eyes as they looked at the broken figure of Charles, his soaked life jacket oozing crimson. But he was alive.

Two women were to the fore—the president of the Foes, and Carioca Jones. Carioca was the first to speak. She indicated Marshall, who was bending over Charles lifting a bottle to the injured man's lips.

"That's the man I told you about, Evadne," the ex-3-V star said in a voice sufficiently loud for all to hear. "He's the prankster who tried to get us all out of the way so that we couldn't spoil his fun. Well, you big brave man," she addressed Doug, "how do you feel now? Your man saved you— and we all know why. And now, look at him, poor thing."

There was a murmur of agreement from the Foes, and I

believe someone tried to start up a chant, but some remnants of decency prevailed. Not to be outdone by Carioca, the elderly Evadne said her piece.

"It is a terrible comment on our society when a man will, quite deliberately, risk his life to save another."

Fortunately there was a diversion at this juncture. A man stepped forward and touched Doug on the shoulder. He was carrying the harness that had been cut away from the glider. He indicated the snap release.

"Look, like you said, Doug. Someone's been fooling with this. The release pin's been bent. You can see the marks of pliers."

The crowd had gathered itself without conscious volition into two distinct factions around the bleeding man on the seawall. To the landward side were the Foes of Bondage, an unyielding bloc of womanhood, upright and militant. Along the edge of the embankment, backs to the sea, were the pilots, their crews and supporters, who up to now had been quietly on the defensive.

The mechanic's words changed this. Doug left Charles and stood, flushing. An angry muttering spread through the ranks of the pilots. The Foes backed off guiltily.

"I can assure you all—" began the president, hands fluttering, wristlet yellowing.

Carioca took one glance at her fading leader and knew her opportunity had come. She stepped forward boldly.

"It's quite obviously a frame-up. And clever, too. Done by one of your own pilots with the object of discrediting the Foes and, incidentally, getting a competitor out of the way. Your treasurer himself told me he heard someone prowling about the slipway on Thursday night." Her black eyes blazed at the elderly man, forcing a nervous nodding agreement. "So there you are. Only club members are familiar with the slipway and the gear you use. And only a slave-owner would think this way, knowing that a bonded man would risk injury himself rather than allow harm to come to his master."

She bent forward over Charles. "You poor man," she said. "And you only had a year or so to go." Her voice hardened.

"Couldn't you have taken the chance that the bastard would kill himself? You'd have been free, then."

She moved back a little, a theatrical gesture to direct the attention to Charles and insure that we all heard his reply—so confident was Carioca Jones. Faintly, but growing louder, we could hear the hissing whine of the ambulopter. The Foes of Bondage wore righteous expressions as they contemplated their prize specimen, their *raison d'etre,* while he lay bleeding on the sea wall.

Charles managed a smile.

"I've been a Freeman since Thursday, Miss Jones."

It was fairly typical of Carioca Jones to have forgotten the factor of Charles' one-third remission in her enthusiasm for the witch hunt. The uproar that followed Charles' revelation lasted in various ways for several months and was discussed whenever sling-gliders met that summer. The arguments waxed furious but it was all rather pointless because, in fact, there were not many bonded men involved in sling-gliding. Many a pilot had the same fear as Doug Marshall—if he were injured so seriously that he needed a transplant, what would he do? Better by far to be able to draw on the anonymity of the Ambulatory Organ Pool, which is not available to Freemen with their own bonded men. Nobody *wants* to take a limb from a person with whom he may be associated for years.

Charles made a good recovery although it was feared at first that he had suffered irreparable damage to both kidneys. Luckily the original diagnosis proved false.

In the strange, sometimes primitive atmosphere of the Peninsula, issues are seldom clear-cut, and solutions or explanations almost never at hand. We never discovered just who had sabotaged Doug's equipment. Conversely, the Foes of Bondage failed to unmask the perpetrators of the Lake William hoax. There is a simple, neat possibility—but one we consider highly improbable. Things just don't work out that way around here.

Carioca Jones weathered the setback, of course. After the elderly Evadne resigned following the Charles incident, she put her own name forward and was duly elected president f the Foes of Bondage. After a decent interval for things to uiet down she began to push herself and the Association orward as forcefully as ever.

People don't change on the Peninsula. Their fortunes may luctuate but their characters are inflexibly formed by the ime they arrive here.

**From planet Earth
you will be able to
communicate with other worlds—
Just read—**

SCIENCE FICTION

THE GODS THEMSELVES by Isaac Asimov	23756	$1.9!
BLACK HOLES edited by Jerry Pournelle	23962	$2.2!
THE NAKED SUN by Isaac Asimov	24243	$1.9.
BALLROOM OF THE SKIES by John D. MacDonald	14143	$1.7!
DAUGHTER OF IS by Michael Davidson	04285	$1.7!
EARTH ABIDES by George Stewart	23252	$1.9!
THE JARGOON PARD by Andre Norton	23615	$1.9!
STAR RANGERS by Andre Norton	24076	$1.9!
THE THIRD BODY by Sam Dann	04458	$1.7!

Buy them at your local bookstore or use this handy coupon for ordering.

COLUMBIA BOOK SERVICE (a CBS Publications Co.)
32275 Mally Road, P.O. Box FB, Madison Heights, MI 48071

Please send me the books I have checked above. Orders for less than
5 books must include 75¢ for the first book and 25¢ for each additional book to cover postage and handling. Orders for 5 books or
more postage is FREE. Send check or money order only.

Cost $_____   Name _____

Sales tax*_____   Address _____

Postage_____   City _____

Total $_____   State _____ Zip _____

*The government requires us to collect sales tax in all states except
AK, DE, MT, NH and OR.*

This offer expires 1 July 81   8079

CLASSIC BESTSELLERS
from FAWCETT BOOKS

BERIA y James A. Michener	23804	$3.50
THE ICE AGE y Margaret Drabble	04300	$2.25
ALL QUIET ON THE WESTERN FRONT y Erich Maria Remarque	23808	$2.50
TO KILL A MOCKINGBIRD y Harper Lee	08376	$2.50
HOW BOAT y Edna Ferber	23191	$1.95
THEM y Joyce Carol Oates	23944	$2.50
THE SLAVE y Isaac Bashevis Singer	24188	$2.50
THE FLOUNDER y Gunter Grass	24180	$2.95
THE CHOSEN y Chaim Potok	24200	$2.25
NORTHWEST PASSAGE y Kenneth Roberts	02719	$2.50
RABBIT RUN y John Updike	24031	$2.25

Buy them at your local bookstore or use this handy coupon for ordering.

COLUMBIA BOOK SERVICE (a CBS Publications Co.)
32275 Mally Road, P.O. Box FB, Madison Heights, MI 48071

Please send me the books I have checked above. Orders for less than 5 books must include 75¢ for the first book and 25¢ for each additional book to cover postage and handling. Orders for 5 books or more postage is FREE. Send check or money order only.

Cost $_____   Name _____

Sales tax*_____   Address _____

Postage_____   City _____

Total $_____   State _____ Zip _____

* *The government requires us to collect sales tax in all states except AK, DE, MT, NH and OR.*

This offer expires 1 July 81

8078

NEW FROM FAWCETT CREST

AUNT ERMA'S COPE BOOK by *Erma Bombeck*	24334	$2.7
WHISKEY MAN by *Howell Raines*	24335	$2.5(
SEX—IF I DIDN'T LAUGH, I'D CRY by *Jess Lair*, Ph.D.	24336	$2.5(
LIFETIMES: TRUE ACCOUNTS OF REINCARNATION by *Frederick Lenz*, Ph.D.	24337	$2.25
DINAH FAIRE by *Virginia Coffman*	24324	$2.5(
THE RED STAIRCASE by *Gwendoline Butler*	24338	$2.50
THE MARCHINGTON INHERITANCE by *Isabelle Holland*	24339	$2.25
HUON OF THE HORN by *Andre Norton*	24340	$1.95

Buy them at your local bookstore or use this handy coupon for ordering.

COLUMBIA BOOK SERVICE (a CBS Publications Co.)
32275 Mally Road, P.O. Box FB, Madison Heights. MI 48071

Please send me the books I have checked above. Orders for less than
5 books must include 75¢ for the first book and 25¢ for each additional book to cover postage and handling. Orders for 5 books or
more postage is FREE. Send check or money order only.

Cost $_____   Name _____

Sales tax*_____   Address _____

Postage_____   City _____

Total $_____   State _____ Zip _____

The government requires us to collect sales tax in all states except
AK, DE, MT, NH and OR.

This offer expires 1 June 81

8074